JACOB'S OATH

ALSO BY MARTIN FLETCHER

The List

Walking Israel

Breaking News

JACOB'S OATH

a Novel

Martin Fletcher

Thomas Dunne Books
St. Martin's Press ❧ New York

This is a work of fiction. All of the characters, organizations, and events portrayed in this novel are either products of the author's imagination or are used fictitiously.

THOMAS DUNNE BOOKS.

An imprint of St. Martin's Press.

www.thomasdunnebooks.com

www.stmartins.com

Library of Congress Cataloging-in-Publication Data

Fletcher, Martin, 1947–
    Jacob's oath : a novel / Martin Fletcher.
        pages cm
    ISBN 978-1-250-02761-0 (hardcover)
    ISBN 978-1-250-02760-3 (e-book)
    1. Holocaust survivors—Fiction.   2. Brothers and sisters—Fiction.
    3. Revenge—Fiction.   4. Jewish families—Fiction.   I. Title.
    PS3606.L486J33 2013
    813'.6—dc23   2013020532

St. Martin's Press books may be purchased for educational, business, or promotional use. For information on bulk purchases, please contact Macmillan Corporate and Premium Sales Department at 1-800-221-7945, extension 5442, or write specialmarkets@macmillan.com.

First Edition: October 2013

10   9   8   7   6   5   4   3   2   1

For Hagar of course, forever

ACKNOWLEDGMENTS

Thanks, Cheryl Gould. Chatting over a bottle of wine, you said, "I wonder why some German Holocaust survivors chose to live in Germany?" And I said, "What a great question. That's my next book." And here it is.

I was cheered along, as always, by my great friend and insightful first reader, Robbie Anna Hare, whose early comments, along with those of my editor, Marcia Markland; my agents, Carol Mann and Eliza Dreier; and my wife, Hagar, helped shape the telling of this story.

I had the great fortune to spend a week browsing through the library of the University of Heidelberg, and was also greatly helped in my research by the Jüdische Kultusgemeinde there.

One slim volume was particularly useful: *Heidelberg zur Stunde Null* (*Heidelberg: Hour Zero*), by Werner Pieper, a collection of photos, documents, and eyewitness reports of life in Heidelberg at war's end.

And I'd like to thank Monika Jäger and her father, Hans, for their generous help in Heidelberg with local logistics, and for sharing their memories.

Also the ever-helpful Gail Shirazi at the Library of Congress in Washington, the German historian Dr. Thomas Rahe, and Dr. Robert Rozett, head of the library at Yad Vashem in Jerusalem.

For the history of the secretive Jewish assassins I drew heavily on published accounts, especially excellent books by Morris Beckman, Rich Cohen, Michael Elkins, Joseph Harmatz, and, in particular, Howard Blum's *The Brigade*. Blum quotes one of the Avengers, Israel Carmi, as always killing with these words on his lips: "In the name of the Jewish people, I sentence you to death."

Jonathan Freedland of London's *The Guardian,* who writes thrillers under the name of Sam Bourne, also wrote fascinating reports on the deeds of the Jewish death squads.

And if you want to know more about the horrors faced by women in Berlin at war's end, read *A Woman in Berlin,* a diary by Anonymous.

The New Yorker's reporting from Germany in 1944, 1945, and 1946 was another great resource, especially the editions of July 23 and August 4, 1945, on bartering and the black market.

All this was for the geographical, historical, political, and military context of my story.

For the tale itself, there were no specific sources. European Jews absorb their heritage with their mother's milk, and when it came time to write, the story poured out.

"Everyone goes home. One day. Where else would you go when the war ends? When the camps shut down. You'll come home. And I'll find you."

PART ONE

ONE

In the Human Laundry at Camp 2 they barely knew they were naked, man or woman. Laid out like corpses on shiny metal tables, washed, shaved, and disinfected by German nurses, their hips and shoulders jutted out like knives.

Murky water sloshed to the floor and drained away in the central gutter that ran between the stalls of the stable.

Nurses in white coats and white kerchiefs, shrouded in steam, ethereal, scrubbed in silence, one hand resting on an arm or a leg or a head. Helpless inmates squirmed as soap burned their sores and scabs.

Jacob's sunken eyes were screwed tight. He didn't want to open them. He didn't want to see these Nazis with their pursed lips, their frowns and busy hands. Who are you to help, now that you lost? It's a bit late, you bastards.

Gently, the nurse gestured that he turn over. She smiled and cupped his shoulder and pushed lightly with her hand. He was less bony than her others that morning. He opened his eyes and winced, scalded in the sudden heat. Through a haze of burning tears he saw her big chest, big hips, blond hair pulled back into a bun, sweat pouring from her puckered brow. Flushed cheeks. Her name must be Brunhilde, he thought, and remembered: Warrior Woman, from the old Norse. How perfect. How ironic. The cow.

His penis flopped as he turned. He lay on it. He hadn't thought about it in months and now he did. It pressed against him in the warm dampness. Whoa, he thought. It's still there.

And then he stiffened.

He raised his head, his neck muscles flexed. He looked at the back of the naked man a few tables away who had rolled onto his side, placed one leg on the floor, and stood up. Jacob had glimpsed the side of his face. He was standing now, the nurse was handing him a towel. He took it, wiped his face, pulled it across his shoulders, quickly rubbed his body, and turned again to walk away.

The nurse put her hand on Jacob's head, saying, "Relax, relax." She pushed him down so that she could scrub his neck but he pushed back. "Sorry, did I hurt you?" the nurse asked. Now his whole back arched and he stretched to see better.

The man looked different. He didn't fit in. Not as skinny. Not skinny at all. Lean, yes. Broad. Tall. As he turned and Jacob readied to see his face, a British doctor stopped to talk to a nurse, blocking Jacob's view. The man raised his arm to rub his hair with the towel; his bare arm seemed to emerge from the doctor's white sleeve.

Jacob strained his eyes, not shut this time, but to peer through the damp mist of the Laundry. The man's left armpit was black with wisps and curls, but there it was. Even at three meters, in this bad light, Jacob saw it.

A blue stain. He couldn't see what it said but he could see that it was there. A tattoo? His SS blood group?

Yes. It was him. It must be. Those ears, those stiff round ears sticking out like a rat. A shiver shook Jacob, his neck hairs stood. He opened his mouth to shout but nothing came out. His body stiffened and he tried again, but he only shuddered.

Alarmed, the nurse pushed him down, harder this time. "Relax," she said, "please relax, there is nothing to worry about, I just need to spray the DDT, you will come out of here nice and clean. No more itching."

Now Jacob bellowed, at least he wanted to, but all that came out were high-pitched gasps, one after another, as if he were panting, choking.

The man was walking toward the door, rubbing his hair. Most inmates had to be carried on stretchers, others hobbled in pain or took it step by breathless step. He was striding. It flashed through Jacob's mind: He could be whistling. The marching song, the Horst Wessel song: "Die Fahne hoch, die Reihen fest geschlossen . . ."

Jacob's eyes darkened, a flash of memory. Maxie. His brother, his baby brother. Murdered.

Jacob screamed with his little might: "Stop!"

"You stop it now," the nurse said, and she called for help. Two nurses rushed to her side, the doctor too, they pushed Jacob to the table while the nurse pressed the plunger and a spray of DDT powder made him cough and his eyes water.

"That's better. That'll kill the lice. You'll feel better, no more scratching."

"Stop, you bastard," he yelled. "Stop!"

"Hey, be quiet," the doctor said. "That's no way to talk. She's only trying to help."

"It's all right, I don't mind, after all they've been through," the nurse said in German, stroking Jacob's head, trying to calm him. "You'll feel better very soon. No typhus."

"Stop," Jacob yelled, straining against them. "Hans, you rat!"

At the door the lean man turned. He took in the struggle on the table, the naked stringy Jew yelling, his little head straining forward like a tortoise, the nurses and doctor pushing him down. He saw into Jacob's crazed eyes. Smirked, spat, and left.

TWO

Bergen-Belsen,
April 28, 1945

Black smoke billowed upward in a cloud that blocked the sun. Flashes of light filtered through, to be blocked again as another one-second burst of fire whooshed into the wooden hut. Flames swept through the open door while columns of smoke escaped through the windows. They curled upward like black puffs from a dragon. The late-spring breeze stank of burning fuel. The only sound was of crackling wood, until someone shouted in English, "Good riddance!"

Another burst of flame, the hut exploded into a fireball, and the converted machine gun on the British tank swung slowly toward Square 9, Block 2.

An unfamiliar curling of the lips began to stretch Jacob's mouth, he felt his cheek muscles respond, his eyes seemed to narrow as he waited for his prison to go up in flames. His face crinkled, just a bit. Jacob thought, So I still know how to smile. It was hard to grasp: It's really over.

"So what do you think?" Benno Lazansky said at Jacob's

shoulder, behind the barbed wire fence that ringed Camp 1 of
Bergen-Belsen.

"I don't."

"How long were you there?" Benno asked.

"Drei verdammte Jahren."

Benno snorted. "Three years."

"Yes. Three damn years." The tight smile vanished. Jacob's
jaw muscles twitched. He'd made it. Who else had survived?
Anyone?

The Churchill Crocodile spat out another four gallons of
fuel, propelled by a burst of liquid nitrogen, and for one second a jet of flame shot from the tank-mounted flamethrower
into the next hut.

"It stank in there," Jacob said. "You could throw up just from
the smell."

A fifth burst from the flamethrower was sucked into the
structure. There was a moment of calm, as if the hut had swallowed the flame, as if it resisted, followed by a loud crack, and
the hut exploded in a ball of fire and heat that made them
flinch from fifty meters.

"So are you really off, then?" Benno said, blinking away the
embers in the air.

"Oh, yes," Jacob said, turning away. "I just needed to see
this. Be sure it's really over. Those lice are frying now."

"What about getting some kind of permit to get through
the lines? You don't have anything. What will you do, walk? If
you wait a few days I can get you something. A piece of paper.
Anything. It'll help." Jacob was striding now, Benno at his
side.

"How? Anyway, I already told you, I won't be the only one.
Everyone's walking, there isn't any other way, and nobody's
got papers. And I must get home to Heidelberg quickly, or it'll
be too late."

"Home?" Benno pulled his elbow, forced him to a halt. "Don't be stupid. What home? There's no one left, you know that. You got lucky in the Star Camp, that's all." He pointed into Jacob's face, grazed his nose. "We need you. Come with me. In a week or two we'll be organized, the boys from the Jewish Brigade are working it out." Benno paused as two British soldiers strolled by, heading toward the camp gate. He looked after them as they passed, and turned back to Jacob.

"I'm in contact with their special units. Secret ones. We'll get to Palestine, they want us there. Here, it's over. Home! You must be joking. You think anyone wants you in Germany? There's nothing for us here."

Jacob pulled his arm away. He looked over his shoulder. The flamethrower had moved on to the next hut as the others erupted in a ball of fire. When one wall collapsed inward, sparks jumped. An officer was hosing down the trees nearby to prevent the fire from spreading. A crowd of British soldiers and nurses were cheering and laughing, celebrating. And why not? Their war was over. While Allied forces fought through Germany, mopping up the last Nazi resistance, their only battle now was against typhus and typhoid.

Inmates—Jews, Gypsies, politicals—huddled at the barbed wire in silence, staring into the inferno. Jacob thought: What's on their minds? Those stinking, fetid, typhus-diseased bunks we shared, two or three in each, head to toe, in the freezing, leaky huts, where we clung to life and fought over scraps of food, those of us who didn't give up and die. Still. It had been home. All we had. A broken brush. A matchbox with a cube of sugar. Two cubes and you were rich. A filthy rag for a pillow. And now, all going up in smoke. Well, better than going up in smoke yourself.

Or was it? Jacob shivered. He put his hand on Benno's shoulder. He'd only known him a few days. Benno had been transferred to Bergen-Belsen a week before liberation with a small group of prisoners who seemed in good health. The Germans had caught them in the south only a month earlier. They were Zionists. Benno had made that pretty clear: He was recruiting for Palestine.

"There is something for me," Jacob said. "Listen, thanks for your concern but I'm going home. Now. Or it'll be too late. There's someone I must find."

"Don't you get it? There's no one left. After what you've been through in the camp, torture, murders, you want to stay in Germany? How could you? After what they've done to us? How could anyone want to stay in this hellhole?"

Jacob took his hand from Benno's shoulder and stared into his eyes. "You don't get it. There is someone. I know it. And I promised. Afterwards? Who knows where I'll end up? But first, I'm going home. I swore an oath."

THREE

Berlin,
April 29, 1945

Sarah sensed it first in her bare feet, the faintest quivering of the ground. She looked up and cocked her head, her right hand rising to pull her shirt tight at the throat. Her left hand held a squashed tin bucket. She had been about to leave her shelter to see if the water pump on Dorfstrasse was working. It had been dry for two days.

The tremor grew and her body trembled with it. That's strange, she thought, observing her own body. Is it the ground moving? Is it the cold?

Fear?

It sounded like a cat's purr.

It became louder. The cracked window-frame rattled and cement flakes shook loose and fluttered to the floor. Larger bits dislodged and fell with a thud. The rumble became a growl and then a continuous roar and the basement walls shook so much Sarah cowered in a corner in case more of the ceiling crashed down on her. Her shelter was already a pile of rubble from the bombs. She had built four low walls from loose bricks and smashed wooden rafters and for two weeks had slept and hidden in the dusty space between them. A sheet of tin on top kept in some warmth.

The mirror fell to the floor, shattering into a dozen shards.

Sarah flinched as it fell and thought, Seven years bad luck. But: How much worse can it get?

She looked at the trembling door-frame and knew it could get much worse, quickly. She understood now what it was.

It was the rumble of tanks and armored cars. The Germans pulling out or the Russians moving in. Either way, thousands of marching men. She knew, If they're German, they'll kill me, if they're Russian, they'll rape me. She had to stay hidden. She was safe underground. But for how long?

Sarah looked down at the empty bucket and her tongue flickered across her dry lips. Not a drop of water had passed them for two days.

By afternoon it was clear. She could hear loud voices with those strangled long vowels and hissing sounds, the shouted orders, the revving of engines, the dragging of equipment outside, and from upstairs, barely, the hushed voices and fearful tiptoeing of Herr and Frau Eberhardt.

Sarah thought, I should feel happy. The Russians are here, which means the war must be over, or will be soon. And she did feel a kind of relief that washed through her body and made her blood feel heavy. It weighed her down. So tired! Now what? Still she did not emerge from her hiding place.

Sarah lay behind her low wall of debris, dusty, thirsty, exhausted, too scared to move, every nerve on edge. Looking at the door, listening to the street, she was thinking of Hoppi, and the little one, who she had never had the joy of knowing. How hard it had been. And all she had done to survive. That had led her here, to now. Sarah closed her eyes and flopped against the wall, legs straight out, her head to one side, arms hanging to the floor. I'll get up in a moment, she thought. Go outside and ask for water. Hope they don't rape me. Maybe it's safer in a crowd after all, they won't touch me there. It's more dangerous here, if someone finds me alone. Yes, it's safer outside.

Sarah made to move, but couldn't. A few moments more, she thought, close your eyes, think of Hoppi. Her lips moved with her thoughts. She was used to talking to herself.

Their first year or two on the run hadn't been too bad, thanks to their friends. Gunther. Sasha. Elinora. The old lady who they hadn't even known, who had just offered, what was her name, with white hair? Can't remember. Peter and his wife. The ones who listened to the BBC on the wireless. They'd all risked their lives to help her and Hoppi, given them shelter.

In the early days they could even take off the yellow star, walk across town, go to a café. It was strange, it didn't weigh anything, that little bit of yellow cloth, but they both felt lighter without it. They didn't have ration cards, so their hosts shared their food and helped them find ways to earn money. They had risked their lives for two terrified Jews. There were enough good Germans, in the beginning at least. They went from safe house to safe house, leaving each before Nazi neighbors could become suspicious; a week here, if they were lucky a month there. Not that it was easy. Creeping in their apartments like mice, using the toilet only when their friends did, never running water from the tap, always terrified of the nosy concierge, of a rap on the door at four in the morning. Still. A little smile of thanks played on Sarah's lips. She licked them with her dry tongue. She'd have to get up in a minute though, find some water.

"U-boats." Submarines. That's what we are, she was thinking, as she lay in the dust, there were thousands of us. Once.

Jews, submerged. Living underground, out of sight. Others, too: Gypsies, Communists. So-called enemies of the Reich, a subterranean subculture, hunted by the Gestapo, with no papers, no homes, where one false step, one miscalculation, one nasty neighbor, meant torture and death. It was worst in the winter, it was so cold. By day they rode the subway, the S-bahn or U-bahn, changing all the time so that inspectors wouldn't notice them and ask for their ID cards, which had J for Jew stamped on them. By night they slept in the station toilets, locking the door, and had to wake early to leave before the cleaners came. In the summer it wasn't so bad. They could sleep under bushes in the woods or the parks.

Hoppi, remember in the Tierpark? Jews weren't allowed but we sat on a bench without our yellow stars. And then we walked along the flower bed and your shoelace was untied and you kept treading on it and tripping up but you didn't dare stop and bend down to tie it up in case people looked at us. And then, remember the new rule that the warden had to take the names of everybody in the bomb shelters, that was in Holzstrasse, with Peter and his wife, remember?

So during the air raids we had to stay in the apartment, and we prayed. Oh, and remember that time we made love during the raid. Oh, it was so beautiful. As if it were our last time. We were mad. But what else was there to do? We could have been dead at any moment. And I know that was the time. As you finished, oh how you shouted in my ear, I said quiet! they'll hear us. And you said, Don't worry, there are too many bombs. We were on the floor, under the bed, I said to you, right then and there, We just made a baby.

Our baby. Tears rolled down Sarah's cheeks. Oh, our baby. So long ago, so very long ago. Hoppi, we were so young then, you and I.

I was twenty-three and I loved you so.

Sarah talked to Hoppi every day. Could he hear? Who was she to say no?

She heard footsteps above. The lighter ones of Frau Eberhardt, who was the only neighbor to ever ask how she was; the heavier, more plodding steps of her older, frail husband. They aren't so scared anymore, she thought. They've stopped tiptoeing. With so much of the ceiling missing, Sarah could make out their tiniest movement. She hoped they wouldn't fall through the floor. Sarah wondered: Did they hang white flags? The Russians are right outside. Will they come in? They'll have to. They'll check the buildings for fighters, for guns.

But she was too tired to move. She had survived. But what for? What's left? Who's left?

It had been Hoppi's idea. Right after the transport of . . . when? November? Was it 1941? It had been cold and raining; when they still had their papers and lived in their apartment on Flemsburgergasse. She'd been sewing uniforms at the tailor's. The Gestapo and police had knocked on all the doors to give notice to the Jews: "You and your family are to report at eight a.m. Thursday to the Grunewald train station to go on labor assignment to the east."

Permitted to take one small bag of clothes and ten marks.

Hoppi was so smart. They hid in the basement and as soon as the transport was over they came out of hiding and walked to the lake, the Grosser Wannsee, left a neat pile of clothes with a suicide note, and called the police, pretending to be shocked walkers out for a stroll. The police opened a file at the Kriminalpolizei, who hated the Gestapo, and sure enough, no questions, no search, the police simply wrote a report that two corpses had been found and buried. Josef Farber, Jewish male, aged 27, of Haspelgasse 12. Sarah Kaufman, Jewish female, aged 22, of Schlosstrasse 97. File opened and closed: Deceased. Suicide. The Gestapo stopped looking for them, and that's when they became submarines.

But it didn't last long. Oh, Hoppi. Why did you go out that day? Wilhelm, yes that was who, Wilhelm Gruber. He saw it, he was hiding in a doorway. He told me. You ran, you fought, they beat you, and that was it. Once they have you, nobody gets away.

Three years. Alone. It was almost a blessing to lose the baby. To be honest. What would I have done with a baby? Scurry through the streets at night with my yellow star and a bundle of tiny arms and legs? We'd both be dead. Sarah's tears had stopped, and her body stiffened. And what life would he have had? Or was it a she? What life?

For years she had choked at the thought, wept as she still felt the kick of her baby, as one feels a lost limb.

Eyes closed, almost asleep now, Sarah went back to that place, the worst of all, when she wanted to die, when her baby had dropped, alone in the cemetery, where she had been living, she was doubled up in pain and anguish, unable to cry or make a sound because of the curfew for Jews. There was blood and pain and mess and above all, pure terror. Terror at what was happening to her body, terror that someone would pass by, terror at what would happen if she was caught.

Sarah froze. Each nerve screamed. She heard the scrape of material brushing against the door-frame, the crunch of a heavy foot settling on plaster, crackling as if treading on paper, followed by another. Even the air moved. Or was that her imagination?

Someone is coming.

Someone is here.

Sarah tried to dissolve into the ground. Could he hear the thud in her chest? Her wall, maybe a meter high, separated her from the door of the basement room. She heard another crunch, lighter, like biting into a cookie, as a man shifted the weight of his feet. Her hair stood on end.

One strange word, softly spoken, an inquiring kind of sound, came from the doorway. Russian.

A soldier. She must not surprise him. He may be scared too. He may shoot. Sarah forced out a little sound, a weak baby sound, a whimper of fear, high-pitched, as nonthreatening as possible. There was an answering word in Russian, and another, louder, it pierced the little room, and Sarah whimpered a little more. Slowly she raised a hand so that he could see it, her little hand, and she whimpered again. She raised her head, bit by bit, and looked at the door.

All she could see was dim light glinting on metal, long and sharp. A bayonet poked into the room. Behind it, a barrel and then a hand as the soldier leaned forward, followed now by his nose and his hair and his face. His cap perched to the side, covering curly blond hair, he was just a boy. She whimpered again, and now the soldier was standing above her as she sat up by the wall of debris.

She looked at him and their eyes met. He stared at her, his mouth opening. He glanced around, taking in the room. It wasn't really a room, just some kind of abandoned storage space with a partially collapsed ceiling. It was tiny and dim, barely lit by daylight through a small grill at street level. His gaze settled on Sarah.

What did he see? A young woman with gray smudges of dirt on her face, and arms covered in dust like camouflage. From beneath a faded kerchief, her brown hair fell in knotted curls, with white plaster flakes clinging to them, as if trying to age her, to conceal her beauty. Wearing a ripped heavy wool dress, a man's brown shirt, and a torn, stained jacket. Hands pulling her shirt closed at the neck, her eyes wide with fear.

He saw it all but all he noticed was a young woman with bare legs.

He looked around, keeping his gun on Sarah as he turned.

And they were alone.

Sarah pointed to her mouth, touched her lower lip with her right index finger. With her baby voice, her cowering voice, her nonthreatening voice, she said, "Wasser? Bitte. Haben Sie 'was zum trinken? Ich hab' ein solcher Durst. Bitte. Wasser?"

He lowered his rifle. Looked around again as if he couldn't believe his luck. He smiled shyly. She almost smiled back. He can't be more than sixteen. "Please. Water?"

Now she heard heavy steps, confident steps. More crunching of plaster and another soldier elbowed by the first. He had a flashlight that he shone in Sarah's face. His eyes lingered on her, looked her up and down. Sarah pointed to her lips and licked them. The second soldier gave an order and the younger one left.

The older man lashed out with a black leather boot. The wall of debris, Sarah's shelter, collapsed in a cloud of dust and white plaster. He jerked his weapon. In Russian: Stand up. Against the wall.

Now with a true whimper, Sarah, still holding her shirt closed with both hands, scrambled to her feet and obeyed, without understanding the words. The soldier slowly raised his gun and pointed it at her and kept it pointing at her stomach. Again, his eyes wandered across her body. He said something to her. It seemed that he was sneering. Sarah didn't answer, her shoulders sank, she cradled her belly with her hands. Tears welled in her eyes. She felt naked.

The soldier was a big older man, with graying hair and large hands, like a farmer. He stood with legs apart, relaxed, staring at her. He put a finger under a dirty field dressing over his left ear and scratched, keeping his eyes on her body.

The young soldier returned, holding out a bottle and an olive-green water canteen. He handed them to the older soldier, who said something. The boy looked at Sarah, shrugged as if there were nothing he could do, turned and left.

The soldier unscrewed the bottle and with a smile that showed broken yellow teeth handed it to Sarah. "Danke schöen, danke schöen," she said as she lifted the bottle to her lips. The soldier acknowledged her thanks by showing his teeth again and with an upward jerk gestured with his rifle: drink.

Sarah breathed out and took a deep swallow. It took a moment before she gasped and spat and shouted in surprise and disgust. The soldier threw his head back and roared with laughter till his body shook. "Vodka, vodka," he said. His eyes sparkled, his stupid face was creased in a broad grin as he gestured as if to say, Funny, yes?

He handed Sarah the olive-green canteen. She raised it and let a drop fall into her mouth. She tasted it, licked her lips, took a bit more, and then gulped down half the contents. She poured a little water onto her hand and wiped her eyes. Dirt smudged her forehead more, she looked as if she hadn't washed in a week, which was true. She breathed in and out, a long draw of satisfaction, and drank another long swallow.

"Danke schöen," she said, passing the canteen back to the soldier, who remained, legs apart, gun up, contemplating Sarah.

Now what? she thought, looking down.

He said something in Russian, laughed, and gave the canteen back to Sarah with a gesture: Drink, it's yours.

He turned and left.

Sarah sank against the wall. She put the canteen to her lips, sipped and sipped again. No point in hiding anymore, she thought, I must get out of here. He'll be back. But where to go? The Russians are everywhere. And if not them, the Germans. Oh, where are the Americans? That's what everybody had hoped. That the Americans or the British would get here first. That's where I must go, she thought. To the Americans.

But I'm so tired, she thought, surrendering herself to the weight of her head, her arms, her back, which pulled her down. Hoppi. Her eyes closed as she laid herself flat on the floor and a drowsy cloud descended. "Hoppe Hoppe Reiter, Wenn er fällt da schreit er . . ." The nursery rhyme. Parents put their children on their knees and jiggled them up and down and said: "Hoppe Hoppe Reiter"—Hup Hup Rider—and the rhyme ended with a loud "Macht der Reiter Plumps"—the rider goes plumps—and the parents opened their legs and the baby fell through them with a happy shriek. Every German knew the rhyme.

Sleep was taking her. A smile played on her lips as she remembered how Hoppi loved to hold her. With Sarah on his knees, her legs straddling him, he deep, deep inside her, hugging each other so they could hardly breathe, kissing for as long as it took, as they moved and slid and cupped each other's bottom, it was so warm and loving and beautiful. Oh, Hoppi. He would jiggle her up and down and look into her eyes and with a wicked smile, just before he came, he would say, he was always such a joker, he would shout, "Hoppe Hoppe Reiter!" That made her the rider. So that made him Hoppi.

And now he's gone. Or is he? Could he have survived, somehow? Escaped? No, they killed everyone, don't fool yourself. It's been three years. Still, we promised each other. If ever we were separated, we would go home, find each other there. On the bench at the bottom of the steps by the river. We promised.

Home. Sweet Heidelberg. Sweet Hoppi. Sweet dreams.

Sprawled on the floor, with a sheen of perspiration on her

face like a translucent death mask, drool escaping from the corner of her open mouth, Sarah slipped into a deep sleep.

The rumble now was Sarah snoring.

Fields of flowers glow in the early sun, a haze of pink and yellow, and rustle in the gentle breeze like a sea of glinting sun-washed waves. Lush low green hills with meadows of golden wheat rise and fall like the sea breaking on a yellow sandy beach. It is harvest time and boys and girls in Lederhosen are working hand in hand and humming and singing, and the sound of youth and joy is a low murmur across the bountiful land gifting hay and sunflowers and trees laden with heavy fruit. Shafts of light through the dense branches make the white almond and apple blossoms that smell so sweet and dainty and fragrant explode in luminescence. It is a farm, a farm of love. There, over there. See? The tall boy with long brown hair flopping over his eyes, laughing so gayly. Is that Hoppi leaning down, picking the red flower, putting it to his nose, breathing deeply, smiling and handing it to a baby, who laughs and tries to eat it? A baby? Lying on the ground, cooing, waving its little fists? Now the picture is fading, receding, like a street drawing in chalk washed away in the rain, storm, hail. Now the delicate fragrance is changing, it is stained with a different aroma, edgy, sickly, becoming bitter. Are the almond blossoms already rotting? Is the wheat old and dry? Is the sun going down? It is dark, and chilly. The smell. It is sharp, yet suffocating. What is it?

Sarah's eyes fluttered as she moaned and drifted out of her dream and sniffed. Beer. Alcohol. She opened her eyes and could barely see in the gloom. She heard breathing. Not her own.

Sarah looked up.

His few teeth glinted in the dim light. He smiled and said

something. A whiff of alcoholic stink, like rotting potatoes, made her snap her head aside and gasp.

"Viktor," he said, stabbing his finger into his chest. "Viktor." He said something else and stuck out a bottle. "Wasser?"

He gave her his canteen. Bleary and giddy, she sat up and took a tiny sip as if tasting a fine wine, and when she was sure it was water all but drained it.

Feeling pressure on her bladder, she rose to her feet. Viktor stood with her. He didn't have his rifle with the bayonet. He had his bottle with a pistol. He pulled the gun from its holster, pressed it sharply into the back of Sarah's head, behind her right ear, prodded her to the door and into the corridor. With his free hand he pointed to the doorway leading to the yard.

Sarah was pale, trembling and nauseated. But she had to pee. Unable to communicate beyond simple gestures, humiliated, she went behind a wooden crate in the yard. She gathered her dress about her, squatted, pulled down her knickers, and felt release and heard the flow and sensed the warmth as her urine flowed into the earth around her.

The soldier faced the door with his pistol raised, as if protecting his spoils. He looked like an ogre guarding its cave. As she finished she looked up. His body half faced her but his head was to the other side. As she pulled up her knickers and began to stand her heart raced. She was thinking, This is my chance, it's now or never. She prepared to spring, to run. But the yard was sealed on all sides, it was an inner courtyard at the back of the building with rows of earth once used to grow vegetables and flowers. These had been pulled out by the roots long ago, replaced by grass and weeds, which would soon also go into a pot of soup. Now she was standing. Maybe I can push him aside and run, she thought. But where to? The street is full of Russian soldiers. They've put up a roadblock. And he's so big and strong.

Sarah felt small and weak. Which she was, in body. In mind, she had been through so much. And now this. All the talk of the women at the water pump, at the clothes line— Sarah couldn't join them at the shops with their ration cards because she didn't have one—was of what would happen if the Russians came. There were no real German men to protect them; all the males were very young or very old. The soldiers had long since fled and the Young Guards were either killed or captured.

The street was peopled by the sick, the helpless, and the women. And it was controlled by drunk Russian peasants in uniform, who had been at the front for years.

So what did you expect?

There is no point fighting or screaming, Sarah said to herself. Nobody will help. It will only make it worse. With a resigned sneer she adjusted her dress and walked past him, back into the gloomy room.

He followed her. She sat on the floor against the wall, drew up her knees, and wrapped her arms around them, chin down, looking at her feet. Her hair fell over her face and she closed her eyes. It was a pose of utter dejection.

He crouched and arranged some bricks into a flat shape, as if to sit. He put his hand inside his bulky jacket. Sarah heard the rustle and looked up. Oh, no, she thought. A knife? A rope? A gag? What will this disgusting man do? She felt the bitter tang of bile.

He took out two candles and a match. Now there was light and flickering shadows and a smoky smell. She felt herself detaching, ephemeral, observing this shadowy space. Her soul rose to see the outline of a stranger with this Russian brute. Candles? Is he wooing her? Is he mad?

All was quiet. The neighbors were hiding in their homes. Outside, the Russians must have been resting or guarding or whatever they did. Probably this little scene was being played out all across Berlin. She thought: To the victors go the spoils.

Still on his haunches, from inside his jacket the soldier Viktor pulled out a little bundle and spread it across the stack of bricks that Sarah now realized was a table. The bundle was a towel, and he spread it to reveal a loaf of fresh-smelling bread, a jar of herring, and a large chunk of white cheese. From a side pocket he took a bottle of vodka and set it next to the loaf. From another pocket, a sausage and a red apple. She hadn't seen so much food for years. I'm being wined and dined, she thought. Does he think I'm his girlfriend?

She caught a whiff of stale sweat as Viktor took off his jacket and laid it across some bricks. He arranged other bricks into a low stool. He perched on it, took out a deadly-looking knife with a squat serrated edge, and cut a slice of bread, cut more slices of cheese and sausage, which he laid on the bread and offered to Sarah. Her stomach juices churned, her mouth watered as she stared at the offering.

"Here, enjoy it," Viktor said in Russian.

"No, thank you," Sarah said in German, shaking her head. They communicated by hand movements. He offered it again, waving it, he teased her by holding it under her nose. She was dying to eat it. "Eat, bitch," he said in Russian. "Eat, get strong, and then I'll have you." He laughed at her. Holding out the sandwich, with his other hand he took a long swig from the bottle.

Sarah pulled her head away. On the wall she saw the shadow of her head jerk back.

"You need strength," he said, and pushed the sandwich against Sarah's mouth, brushing her lips. Again, she pulled back. "So you're not hungry?" he asked, and put half the sandwich into his own mouth, pushing a few stray bits in with his fingers. As he munched he smiled at her, teasing her again, opening his mouth to show the half-chewed food. He nodded his head, smacked his lips, licked them, rubbed his stomach. He took another long swig of vodka and burped. He took his time cutting some more cheese and sausage. The sausage he ate by itself, the cheese he smeared with his knife over a slice of bread, which he raised to his mouth. He looked at Sarah, looked down at his supplies, mimed surprise as if he had just discovered the jar of herrings, and unscrewed the top. He speared one, crimson and dripping and sweet-smelling, sniffed it, licked it, put it in his mouth, and took a bite of bread and cheese. Sarah, still leaning back against the wall, felt she could faint with hunger. Her mouth was open and she breathed quickly. She stopped her tongue from licking her lips. She looked away.

But it was too much. When Viktor held out another slice of bread with everything on it, succulent herring, aromatic cheese, and spicy sausage, she fell on it, bit into it, chewing like a crazy woman. She had never tasted anything so good. She had been living on scraps rejected by the neighbors, their leftovers. She drank some water and tried to eat some more; but she couldn't, her stomach must have shrunk. She lay back, sated, hands on her belly, closed her eyes, and sighed.

Until terror rose within her and she opened them.

Viktor was standing, his thick fingers unbuttoning his trousers. His shadow flickered up the wall and across the ceiling. He looked a monster. He slid out his leather belt with its metal buckle, let it hang from one hand, and snapped it like a gunshot. With his other hand he drank from the bottle. He flicked the belt again and pointed at Sarah. Up, he said, with the bottle at his lips.

Off, he gestured, pointing at her shirt. Off, pointing at her dress. Off, he panted, pointing at her knickers.

He pointed at her knickers again.

Off, he said.

Off, you bitch.

Off!

Sarah couldn't, her strength deserted her. She sank to her knees, covering her bare breasts with her crossed arms. She cried, she begged, tears ran into her mouth. She screamed and screamed again as the leather bit into her bare back. She looked up to beg for mercy and she saw him drinking from the bottle. As the belt came down again she stopped it with her arm. It curled around her wrist and its speed burned her and the buckle caught her in the eye, which went black and starry. With a yelp she stood up and fell against him and bit his hand as hard as she could and scratched his face.

He roared. And then he roared again, this time in laughter. Another swig, and he hurled the bottle against the wall and it smashed to pieces. The motion made him stumble. He grabbed Sarah by the hair and pulled her around so hard she felt her scalp would be pulled from her head. He twisted her arm until she felt it wrenching from her shoulder. With one tug he tore her knickers from her body. I'm going to die here, her head screamed, I don't want to die, don't let me die. She sobbed and whispered, "Don't hurt me."

Sarah sank to the ground. Her jerking limbs were all around her, spreadeagled across the bricks and debris. She had lost control of her body. The soldier kicked her in the stomach and then kicked away the mess to clear a space.

Her sobbing and shaking ended when an icy hand gripped Sarah from inside and clutched her heart. It froze her senses. She felt nothing, saw nothing, heard nothing. It was all happening without her. She wanted to live. She would do anything to live.

FOUR

Near Bergen-Belsen,
April 30, 1945

Jacob stretched in a field of white blossoms at the foot of a giant birch tree on the Lüneburg Heath. His head rested on moss that softened the tangle of knotted roots. A stray nightingale, its ocher tail glinting in the sun, trilled as it perched on a branch over purple lavender. He inhaled the fragrant herbs, sweet and full, and gazed through shimmering leaves at puffs of clouds drifting in from the east across the sharp blue sky.

And felt free as a bird.

I'll take my clothes off and lie in the clear water, he thought. Surely there's a babbling brook nearby, it's so perfect here. I'll lie on the pebbles and let the water run over me. I'll dip my head and shake my hair like a happy dog. I'll sit in the water and wash my sorry body.

He shivered. How often had he gazed at the sky and dreamed of this? They all had. The Nazis had taken everything in the camp, especially their lives. But two things they couldn't take: their dreams and the sky. He closed his eyes and there, urging themselves across his inner vision, was all he could remember of the faces of Willi, Mordka, Mendel, Zelman, Abela, as much as he could remember of them, and Maxie, poor little Maxie.

He stroked the earth that held their bones.

Shading his eyes from the sun, following a little bird that was swooping and plunging after its mate, seeing them come to rest side by side on a branch, Jacob became aware of a dull ache in his head. He closed his eyes and saw Maxie again, clear as a photo, with a slowly spreading smile. Jacob smiled back. It was baby Maxie, not dying Maxie. Little Maxie shrugged his shoulders and his face became old and lined. Jacob's smile became a frown as Maxie raised the palms of his hands, as if to say, My brother, I'd like to be there with you, under the tree . . . but, well . . . you know how it is . . .

Hans Seeler. They knew him as Hans the Rat, the lanky camp guard with the rat's ears whose daily sport was to torment Maxie until finally he beat him to death.

Just the thought made Jacob retch, but nothing had passed his lips in twenty-four hours. A croaking sound spilled out, as if a hand twisted his belly from inside.

Jacob sat up suddenly, looked around, and as he began to stand felt the ground sway and rise and fall. He was disoriented, he felt nauseated and lowered himself onto his back. Seconds passed until he remembered where he was.

When the ground steadied, Jacob pushed himself to his knees again, and rose with care. He breathed deeply and took in the sharp, clear air of the heath, the sweet aroma of the heather.

I need food, he thought, and water. Urgently.

He returned to the lane that he had been following. He knew refugees had passed this way, because in his hunger he had wanted to pick the flowers at the side of the road and eat them, but for kilometers there were no flowers, just torn stems.

He headed south to Celle and Hanover. At first he walked in the woods to avoid British soldiers, who seemed to be everywhere. Other people he'd met on the way had told him why. Only fifty kilometers from Bergen-Belsen, the northern German army had surrendered to the British field marshal, Bernard Montgomery. Some German units might still be hiding on the heath and might still be hostile. That's all I need, he thought, survive the camp and get shot when I'm free. So he'd returned to take his chances on the road, heading for the rail station in Hanover, where he had heard the trains may be running. He didn't have any papers so, like thousands of others, when he saw a British army roadblock he left the road, and walked around it.

An hour on, cresting a low hill, he saw that at the bottom of a long decline the lane met the main road again, about half a mile away. A mass of people spilled into the field, and as he got closer Jacob saw why. Yet another British roadblock. With no more strength for another detour he decided to walk straight through it. What could they do, shoot him?

Still, Benno was right, Jacob thought. He should have waited and got some kind of travel document. He didn't have any identification papers. And he was German. He could have been an SS general as far as the Tommies were concerned. That's what Benno had said, he'd warned him, that the SS were trying to hide among the population, and without papers he'd always be suspicious.

But Jacob had been too eager, in too much of a hurry to get back to Heidelberg. How long had it been since he left home, since he went to Berlin? Seven years? And he was looking for someone. It couldn't wait.

His head pounded, his throat was parched. He had to eat and drink.

Jacob joined the lines of people waiting to go through.

Most were Germans but he heard Russian and French and any number of languages he didn't recognize. All of Europe was on the move. Jacob shuffled forward until his turn came.

"Papers, mate. Papieren," the soldier said. He didn't seem too interested. Jacob patted his pockets and looked concerned, but didn't have the strength to pretend further. He shrugged. "I don't have any. Sorry. No papers."

"Stand over there," the soldier said. He pointed at a Land Rover where a young officer was drinking from a canteen. "Next."

Jacob stood by the lieutenant and looked at him with as much friendliness as he could muster.

"What's your story?" the officer said. "What do you want?"

"A drink?" Jacob said in English. "Please, sir." He couldn't take his eyes off the officer's canteen.

"You speak English?" the officer said.

"Yes, sir."

"How come?"

"My mother was English. From Manchester."

"Really? I'm from Sheffield. Where is she?"

"She died when I was eight. Made me interested in learning the language, though."

"You thirsty, you said?"

"A bit. Yes."

The officer leaned into the car and took out another canteen. "We just filled up this morning. Take a swig."

Jacob sighed and put it to his mouth. He drained half of it and handed it back with another long sigh.

"Hungry?" the officer said.

Jacob sniffed. "Actually, a little, yes."

The officer stretched back again and pulled out half a loaf of bread and a sausage. With a smile of thanks Jacob took a big bite of the sausage and chewed, until he felt beads of sweat on his forehead. He wiped them with the back of his hand and leaned for support against the side of the jeep. His hand with the sausage fell to his side as he closed his eyes and waited for the nausea to pass.

"What is it?" the officer asked. "You okay?"

Jacob nodded, took in a deep breath.

"What do you feel?" the officer asked.

"Sick, headache. I've had it for a couple of days. Dizzy sometimes."

The officer looked concerned. "Where you from?"

Jacob began to say Bergen-Belsen but some instinct honed in the camp stopped him. "Bremen."

"Near the coast," the officer said. "Up near Hamburg?"

"Yes."

"Because we're on the lookout for typhus. There's concentration camps near here with typhus. It's hard to stop it from spreading. Those are some of the symptoms. There's also typhoid."

Jacob tried a smile. "Oh, no. Just a cold, maybe. Hunger . . ."

"Well, you better stay here while I find our medic, make sure. Don't want you wandering around if you're sick. If you're okay we could use you, you know, if you want. We need translators and your English is quite good. Stay here, I'll be right back."

The officer walked up the road to a collection of tents with the red, white, and blue Union Jack flying from the center of the tallest. As soon as he was out of sight, Jacob moved to the back of the Land Rover and stuffed the rest of the sausage and two apples into his pockets, took the rest of the bread as well as a canteen of water, and joined the ragged column of people on the other side of the roadblock walking south. He quickened his pace until he was lost in the crowd.

Typhus. No, couldn't be, he thought. Mustn't be. He felt his forehead. It was warm, not hot, dry, no more sweat. It could be the Bengal Mixture that had made him sick for the last couple of days. Hope that's it. It was so foul half the people who drank it threw up.

The British had been trying to help. In India they had fought famine and disease by giving locals a mixture of dried milk, flour, sugar, and molasses. It worked well there, but here most of the inmates found the sweet drink revolting and their stomachs rejected it. Jacob sniggered as he drank from his water. That stuff made them sicker than they were before.

At dusk, as if at a signal, the refugee column moved off the road like a giant centipede and sank to the ground. For Jacob even the damp earth was a big improvement on the last few years. Curled up in a ditch he shared with two families, he slept like a baby and woke with the first light, to the shrieks of wild pigeons in the trees. He bit from an apple as he walked, while the streaking horizon turned the world pink and orange and day came. He ate the core, including the seeds.

His clothes, damp from dew, clung to him. From every side road more refugees joined the flood of people, like tributaries joining a mighty river. Some strained against carts loaded with all they owned: chairs, beds, laundry, dishes, and perched on all this, the old and the sick holding babies. Others walked alone or in groups with just the cases they carried. The only sound was coughing and footsteps, the tapping of defeat.

He was learning who was who. Those with carts were Poles, Czechs, Ukranians, Lithuanians, slave workers from the east, heading home with anything that might be of value, a pane of glass, a chicken, a dirty tablecloth. Those with only small cases were Germans kicked out of their houses by the occupiers. They were heading to their relatives until they could reclaim their homes. Those with nothing were freed prisoners of war.

As for Jews, there weren't any.

Across the wild countryside of the Lüneburg Heath, beyond the refreshing brisk breeze, there had been a thick clogging smell that at times had clung to him like a mask; it had the familiarity of death yet he struggled to distinguish the elements. It unsettled him until he understood: it was putrid corpses mixed with still-smoking pine, beech, and plants in the woods that the British had set ablaze to flush out German snipers. Like moldy rosemary in a sauna. What disturbed Jacob most was how normal it all looked. As he trudged past pretty villages with wooden homes and small farms and little churches, Jacob watched the children playing in the fields. These farm kids barely spared a glance for the ragged aliens who trudged by. They looked strong and well-fed, spared from the monster that had devoured his world. His family.

He couldn't look at them, the smug Volk.

Until at a sharp bend in the road, he saw three men in torn Wehrmacht uniforms walking with their arms linked. When the road turned they continued straight until one stumbled on the root of a tree and the others followed him straight into a bush. They stopped dead, and the two at the sides probed with sticks that they held in their hands while the middle one stretched a foot, searching like an ant's antennae for obstacles. The column moved silently by. Jacob noticed the soldiers' armbands of three black dots on a yellow background. They must be German soldiers blinded in battle. Jacob watched as they floundered into a field. I hope it's a minefield, he thought, but hurried after them and, taking one by the arm, he said, "This way," and guided them back to the road.

He thought, I should have let them get blown up.

Picking his way through the woods with a thousand shades of green and the fields blossoming with so many colors, Jacob had felt like he was waking from a nightmare. He had left a lunatic asylum, a black-and-white death machine, that had consumed his entire world, that was his entire world, a world of torturers and their victims.

Yet, what was real? Here, horses grazed, cows chewed, birds sang, church bells rang, couples strolled, children played, men plowed, women worked at their side, dogs wagged their tails, gardens grew, flowers bloomed, trees blossomed, rivers flowed, fish swam. Who knew? How could you know? And what did they know of his world? How could two such worlds share the same earth? And so close?

It wasn't till he reached the edge of the town of Hanover that it began to strike him that maybe his life in the camp had been a sanctuary of sorts. As a prisoner in the Sternlager, the Star Camp, he had been spared the worst. Because of his English mother and his relatives in England, he and Maxie had been chosen to live, they were hostages, Jews of some value, if there was such a thing, to be swapped one day for German prisoners of war in British hands. Despite everything, they had been better treated than most, until the Rat had had it in for Maxie.

Every time they'd heard the drone of warplanes they'd prayed the Americans or the British would bomb the SS guards, and cursed them when they didn't. Now, in the suburbs of Hanover, as he stepped around jagged metal beams and torn concrete boulders, passed street after street without a house standing, just a sea of rubble, he at last understood why the Allies hadn't bombed the camps. Killing Germans was more important than saving Jews.

There was the smell of decay and death, limbs and feet stuck out from mountains of bricks and timber, broken staircases hung from ghost houses with caved-in roofs, and listless Germans sat on smashed walls, looking blankly at these strange rag-people picking their way past.

Hundreds made their way through the streets, flowing over

the smashed walls and piles of bricks like swarms of rodents. The closer Jacob got to the city center, the worse it grew. Smoke curled from a pulverized basement and rags were drying. Families must live down there. As he passed he saw German survivors, with their grimy, bleak faces and their limbs wrapped in filthy bandages. In the camp you didn't feel human. Here you saw people you hoped weren't human. It stank of excrement and death.

Jacob walked by huge shell holes and craters filled with dirty water and the skeletons of dogs, picked clean for food. Unexploded shells the size of a small car were marked by colored tape and warning signs. A burned, rotting horse covered in flies lay tethered to the shafts of a wrecked cart. In one quarter every building was demolished bar one: the church, with a steeple that pointed to the sky, as if in gratitude.

As he followed the rail tracks Jacob said his own prayer, that the trains would be running. It would take a miracle. Approaching the station, carriages lay on their sides, the rear of a locomotive stuck up with its front smashed, tracks lay at all angles, and shell holes pockmarked the shunting yard. Two antiaircraft guns lay on their sides, their barrels blown off.

Jacob rested for a moment, leaning against the shell of a burned-out wooden crate. Taking in the devastation, it dawned on him: what a fool. He'd been counting on a train and now it was obvious. The railroad system would have been a key target for the bombers, so they won't be able to fix the trains for months. He'd have to turn around, get back on the road, and quick. There had been so many detours and forced halts he'd only walked about fifty kilometers in five days. About four hundred more to Heidelberg. Jacob felt his forehead. No fever . . .

He looked at his shoes, and had to smile. The left was a formal brown lace-up and the right was a dark green suede hiking boot. When the British had forced the local Germans to donate clothes and shoes to the survivors of Bergen-Belsen, nobody had thought to tell them to tie the pairs of shoes together by their laces. So when a mountain of shoes and boots had been unloaded at Harrods, the nickname for Camp 2's clothes store, it was a rare survivor who walked off with a matching pair.

They were comfortable, though. They had to be. They had a lot of walking ahead.

There was one good sign. Where the tracks ran into a collapsed shed he saw crowds of people sitting on suitcases. As he approached he saw others sleeping on the ground, mothers cuddling babies, clumps of men talking, hugging themselves, and jumping on the spot to keep out the cold. They must be waiting for something.

In a clearing of rubble there was a water truck with British soldiers in their khaki uniforms and garrison caps. A line of Germans stood patiently in single file with broken buckets, tin mugs, and dirty bowls for their turn at the tap. Jacob went to the back of the line until it occurred to him: Why should I wait? Am I still in the camp? Did a German ever wait behind me?

On second thought, maybe a dirty ragged Jew proffering a stolen British army canteen to a British soldier wasn't too smart, either. But Jacob was beyond caring. He was too tired and parched. He hadn't drunk water for two days.

The British soldier looked startled when a filthy young man in torn clothes came straight to the head of the queue, holding out his water bottle. The Germans liked to line up almost as much as the British. Who was this bloke? "The end of the line's over there, mate," he said. "And where'd you get that water bottle from?" Not that any of these Krauts spoke English.

"A British officer gave it to me," Jacob said, in English. "Because I have been in a concentration camp for the whole war.

He said I had suffered enough. I haven't had a drink in days, I've been walking. But if you like . . ."

"How come? Jew?"

"Yes."

"Well, to me you're all Germans. To the back, like everyone else."

Now Jacob looked startled. He didn't know what to say. The Germans in line didn't understand the exchange but they got the message and began to mutter. A man behind pulled Jacob by the jacket, a woman said something like "Who do you think you are?"

"But you don't understand . . ." he began.

"Oh, yes I do, mate," the soldier said. "You lot are all the same. Always want to get to the front of the line. Always did, always will. Well, there's plenty of water where this came from. Get in line like everyone else. And where'd you nick that canteen?"

Jacob stiffened. Every insult he had suffered, every humiliation, every blow, every kick, and every Nazi face that had ever loomed into his with a fist and a club and a rifle steamed up inside him like a boiling geyser. Enough! He felt his face go red, clenched his fist, knew that what he wanted to do would be a terrible mistake. But for once, for once . . .

"Don't be a tosser, mate," he heard a voice say, "give him a drink for Gawd's sake." A soldier elbowed the first away, saying, "He's on our side, you twat." The second soldier, with red hair and a sunburned face, took Jacob's canteen and held it under the stream of water till it overflowed. "Don't mind him," he said, "bit soft in the head, cooks are all the same. Let them out of the kitchen and they think they're Monty."

"Mosley, more like," a third soldier, a mountain of a man, said. "Here, come with me," he said to Jacob.

Grateful to have been spared from his own violence, and with a glare at the cook, Jacob followed the broad back past the station waiting room, which was mostly intact. He stopped dead, his mouth open, hardly hearing the soldier's question. Surrounded by upended carriages and torn tracks was a locomotive with five carriages waiting in a siding. The tracks it stood on were intact and stretched into the distance until they disappeared around a bend.

"Bergen-Belsen," Jacob answered.

"Heard about that. Poor show. Those swine. Here." He took Jacob to his Bergen bag, which lay among a pile of canvas army bags stacked against a wall. He rummaged around and pulled out biscuits, bread, a little jar of marmite, and half a bar of chocolate. "Here. You need these more than me," the soldier said. "And good luck, mate."

Jacob laid his hand on the big soldier's arm, wanting to thank him, but all that came out was half a sob. He bit his lip. He couldn't find any words.

The soldier nodded and walked away.

FIVE

Berlin,
May 6, 1945

Frau Eberhardt from upstairs wrung out a rag and reddish water dripped into the bucket. She had heated a pot of water over a wood fire and when the rag was as dry as possible, she screwed the edge up into a point, wet it again with clean, hot water, spread a little of her precious soap on the end, and slowly massaged Sarah's inner thigh and groin, dabbing at the bruises and cleaning the scratches. It stung but Sarah surrendered. The smarting pain had gone, replaced by an ache that seemed to stretch from her groin to her heart.

Frau Eberhardt tutted as she worked. "Really," she said for the tenth time, "we must find you a doctor."

Sarah lay back, her legs apart. She was exhausted, she felt empty, hopeless, and worst of all, helpless. For this she had survived? To be a prize for the eastern peasants? "What we must do," she said, "is get me out of here."

"He'll be back for sure, the big pig," Frau Eberhardt said. "There's less blood now, mein Liebchen, a lot less."

"I should hope so, it's been three days," Sarah said. "Those apples, you can take them."

Viktor had come by the next day with two bottles of vodka, had seen the state she was in, tut-tutted, kissed her forehead, and dropped off a bag of apples and some bread and cheese.

"No, no, you eat them. Well, all right, maybe I'll take one. Two, one for Stefan as well."

Every few moments Frau Eberhardt glanced at the door. She strained to hear any sound. Her husband was standing guard at the entrance to the house and would whistle if any soldiers seemed to be approaching. They were nervous. Petrified. Frau Eberhardt couldn't stop talking. If she was caught downstairs by any of those Russian swine, she'd get it too, she said. They didn't care if she was old and dry and wrinkled, as long as she breathed they'd do it, and probably if she didn't breathe, too. They'd raped half the women in the street and the only reason they hadn't raped the other half was because they hadn't found them. At least Sarah only had one. She should count herself lucky. They hunted in packs, those curs, those dogs. Trust me, enjoy the war because peace will be hell. Poor Ilse Stanger at number fifteen, the dog was so drunk he couldn't get it up so he'd used a bottle and it broke inside. And there was no anesthetic when they went in to get the bits out. Blood everywhere. And not a sound. In shock, you know. Frau Schmidt next door had hid her twins, they're only fifteen, in the water barrel in the attic, there was no water anyway. It's so unfair, how the Russians abuse them, she hadn't supported the Nazis anyway, never had, she wasn't like everybody else, she was just as much a victim as the Jews, and now they were all being treated the same, for no reason, oh, that Russian dirt, just because they kicked the Nazis out they think we owe them.

Herr Eberhardt wouldn't allow her to take Sarah upstairs,

where at least there was a proper bed she could lie on. "He's afraid that big Russian will come looking upstairs if he can't find you here. I'm so sorry, my dear, but there you have it. If he doesn't find you then we'll all be in for it. When Herr Eberhardt puts his foot down there's nothing I can do."

She left a pillow for Sarah and two blankets to lie on. She was sorry. That's all she could do. "I'll come back in the morning, my dear, see how you are. I'll bring some more water. Here's some in the pan, and a cup."

Sarah, limbs heavy, murmured, drifting off to sleep, "Thank you so much, Frau Eberhardt. You're very kind."

That evening he did come back for more, and not alone. Another man, even bigger, younger, in a gray Soviet army coat, which he kept buttoned up, entered the room with him and stood, looking at her, while Viktor laughed and introduced them and unrolled a bundle with bread and cheese and a whole smoked fish. He placed two bottles of vodka on the floor, and lit two candles. "It'll be dark soon," he said to his friend in Russian, and grinned. "Take your coat off, there's hot work here."

Sarah whimpered for a moment but was too scared to form a word. Her face puckered with despair as she looked at the new man. She shrank against the wall, her hair falling across her smudgy face, matted and dirty. She looked at the dried brown blood on the floor and the man followed her gaze. He couldn't meet her eyes.

He spoke and turned to leave. Viktor threw out his arm and held him by the sleeve. The man barked something, an order, and Viktor dropped the sleeve and stood up straight. He answered, quietly. The man looked at Sarah, said something else to Viktor, who took a slice of sausage and gave it to her. She refused to take it. The man, maybe an officer, laughed at Viktor, said something, and turned to the door.

Viktor glared at Sarah, anger in his eyes. A sob rose in her throat, a cry, he would kill her, this brute, she couldn't do it again, she just couldn't, she wasn't ready, and seeing her last chance, desperate, she cried out, "Bitte, helfen Sie mir, helfen Sie mir!" Please, help me, help me. The man seemed to pause, but she heard his footsteps continue up the stairs.

Later Sarah said she didn't know why, it had been many years since she had said the prayer, even part of it, what good did it ever do her or her family? But at the thud of those steps nearing the top of the staircase, knowing that she might not survive the night with that monster pig, she cried out in sheer panic, and from the bottom of she knew not where came those words, those holy words, those words of Jewish prayer.

"Bitte, helfen Sie mir, helfen Sie mir," she had cried in German, help me, and then she screamed, directly to God, "O, Shema Yisrael, Adenoi Elohenu, Adenoi Echad," and then again in German, "Hilfe, hilfe, um Gotteswillen, hilfe!" For God's sake, help!

The steps paused again.

She collapsed in loud sobs and fell across the pile of bricks. No, she couldn't go through it again! Her hand fell on a jagged chunk of cement. It closed on it. I swear to God, she thought, that bastard won't rape me again, I'll kill him with this or die trying.

The new man must have jumped, for she could hear him crashing to the ground. He cursed, he almost twisted his ankle in the gloom.

He appeared at the door, he filled it with his bulk. Crumpled on the floor, Sarah saw him through her tears and dropped the cement and stretched her arm toward him, pleading. "Please, don't leave me here, please."

"Sind Sie Jüden?" he said in German. Are you a Jew?

"Ja, ja."

"There are Jews left in Berlin?"

"Apart from me? I don't know. I've been hiding for years. Oh, please, help me."

"Verschwind!" the officer barked at Viktor, turning on him. "Sofort!" He realized he had spoken in German. "Out of here! Now!" he shouted in Russian.

Viktor's mouth fell open. He thrust out his chest and began to shout back but thought better of it. He was angry and spoke quickly, arguing. The younger man said something back, punching his words, emphasizing each syllable, and he moved half a step forward. Anyone in any language could have guessed his meaning. His hand was on his pistol butt. Viktor leaned down to gather up the food and the man said something else. Viktor shrugged. He took the two vodka bottles in one hand and walked out, without looking at Sarah, leaving the food.

"Bitte, stehen Sie auf. Wenn Sie können," the man said to Sarah, offering her his hand. Please, stand up, if you can.

But she couldn't. She was panting. She looked at him and shook her head. She swallowed twice. Her hand flew to her mouth, her chest heaved, and suddenly she threw herself toward the corner and vomited. Nothing came out but a guttural shriek. She was kneeling, sweating, gasping.

Between short deep breaths she said, "Entschuldigung." Sorry.

"Please," he said.

"It's horrible."

"Please," he said again. He looked around and saw a pan of water, with a chipped cup by it. He half filled the cup and held it out to Sarah. He took her by the elbow, helped her to sit, gave her the cup. She sipped, once, twice, handed it back.

"Are you Jewish?" she asked, when she got her breath back.

"Yes." He had been standing until now. With a loud sigh he

lowered himself onto the little table of bricks and pulled his knees up next to her. He was tired too. He drew his long coat over his legs. It was damp and chilly.

She drew her sleeve across her forehead, wiping away the perspiration. "How do you speak such good German?"

"We spoke German at home. My grandparents were from Germany. I'm from Balakovo. It's on the Volga. There are many Germans there."

"That disgusting man," Sarah said, looking at the door, turning to the tall man in the gray coat of the Red Army. She felt a weight lifting, hope rising. He cares, she thought. When was the last time she saw a Jew? Two years ago? A proud Jew, unafraid? Years before that. Could he look after her? Was it over, the long nightmare, the horror? The years of hiding like a rat in the cellars of Berlin. Hungry, thirsty, dirty. Her life in the hands of strangers, waiting to be betrayed.

"He won't come back. I'll make sure of that." The man began to pour himself some water when the building shook, plaster fell to the ground. It was the first explosion in days. He didn't spill a drop. They heard running feet and shouting, which faded away and it was almost quiet again. In the distance there was the faint pop of gunfire. He drained his cup.

"What's happening outside?" Sarah asked.

"It's almost over. A last bit of resistance. Hitler is dead. In his bunker. The Nazis have collapsed, they're running. A few holdouts still have weapons but we're going street-to-street, house-to-house. It's over. We're expecting a surrender today, tomorrow, this week."

"What day is it today?"

"Monday. May the seventh."

"Thank God it's over."

"You can say that again. Three years I've been away from home."

"At least you have a home," Sarah said, sitting up properly. She smacked the dust off her shirt and dress, wiped herself down. She shook her hair. "God, I must look terrible."

"Actually, yes," he said, with a laugh. "We'll have to find you a shower."

"Or a bath."

"Hot water."

"Soap. Real soap."

"That may take a day or two. How do you feel? Do you need to see a doctor?"

"I don't know," Sarah said, as he refilled the cup and gave it to her. "I think I'm all right. I need to rest. I need to get out of here. But you, tell me, who are you?"

"Me? My name is Isak Brodsky, I am from Balakovo on the Volga, as I said to you. I am an intelligence lieutenant attached to the Fifth Shock Army of Colonel General Nikolai Berzarin, who is the Soviet commander of Berlin."

"Huh," Sarah said. "So how can you let your men behave like that beast?"

He shrugged and poured some more water. "We have a proverb. Send a beast to Rome, he's still a beast. To be honest, we can't stop them. Most of them are animals. They've been fighting for years, with no women, that's war. They are sex-starved. If we tell them to stop, they tell us that's what the Wehrmacht did to our women. You think the German soldiers in Russia were any different? The only difference is we won and you lost."

Sarah looked away. "Don't include me," she murmured. "We lost before the war began."

Lieutenant Brodsky sighed. "I know." He pursed his lips and looked at Sarah, as if requesting permission, before the words fell like a hammer. "I was in Auschwitz in February, two weeks after our troops freed the Jews." He said it as if he needed to get it off his chest.

Sarah's mouth fell open. "My family was there," she whispered. "They were taken from Heidelberg to Gurs in France, in the south, and then to the east. To Auschwitz. About three years ago. That's all I know."

His eyes dropped to his feet. Sarah said, "What was there? Who was there? What did you see?" Brodsky could only answer, "What happened to you? They didn't take you?"

"No, I was here, in Berlin. Working. They took the Jews from here to Auschwitz too but I ran, I hid, I've been submerged the whole time."

Brodsky shook his head, a tear came to his eye. "Such evil things I saw," he said, and stopped. "I've never spoken about this to anyone."

She stared at him, took in his face for the first time. He was about thirty years old, with curly black hair and strong features drooping with fatigue. His brown eyes were dark and sunken. His cheeks seemed to hang from his face; his skin, where she could see through his whiskers, was red from the sun and the wind. His youth was gone and he had been aged by war. She took it all in as she thought, A sad man.

After a minute or two Sarah asked again, "What did you see there? They killed them, didn't they, I know. Who was left?" As she asked she felt they were the most painful words of her life. Who was left?

It poured out for an hour and she didn't say a thing. He needed to talk as much as she needed to hear. She didn't cry. Everything he said, all he had seen, meant one thing: the stories were true, then. Nobody could live through that for more than a month or two. Not even Hoppi. For three years? They're dead, she thought. They're all dead. I knew it. Mutti, Papi: She closed her eyes, seeking their faces. It was hard to summon them up.

And Hoppi. It was even harder to see his face. She had

promised him. He had promised her. Heidelberg. They would go there and wait for each other by the river. And however hopeless, that's what she would do. That's where she must go. Nothing would stop her. I made it, she thought. Maybe he did too. Even as she thought it she didn't believe it.

Lieutenant Brodsky broke the long silence. He sighed, shifted his legs as if he had said it all.

"Sarah," he said, taking her hands. "I am so glad that I could help you. You are safe now. I will assign one of my men to look after you. You will see our doctor."

"What?" Sarah said in alarm. "What do you mean? You are leaving?" Her heart felt like it would explode. Finally she had found a good man, a savior, a protector, and he was leaving? "Where are you going?"

"I am sorry," he said, still holding her hands. "I am a soldier, after all. I have orders. We leave tonight."

Sarah couldn't believe it. "But he'll be back, I know it."

"No, trust me, he won't be back and nor will anybody else apart from the soldier I appoint to look after you."

"But you, where are you going?" Sarah said, feeling herself sinking into mud. She pulled her arm away. *I'm lost.*

"I also speak English, in fact before the war I was a languages instructor. I am going as an interpreter with some of the senior officers to meet the Americans . . ."

"The Americans?"

"Yes, bureaucratic stuff. To coordinate. We're allies, I'm told."

"Where will you meet them?"

He laughed. "That's a secret."

"But in Berlin?"

"Oh no, they're not here. We're driving overnight. That's why I must leave. Somewhere in the west. Actually, it can't do any harm to tell you: Leipzig. To see General Bradley's Twelfth

Army Group. It's an issue of the Allied occupation zones. They've advanced too far, they must pull back."

Sarah's heart beat even faster. She could feel it banging her ribs. Her eyes widened. She squeezed his hands, pulled them to her chest. "Isak," she said. It was the first time she had said his name. "Isak, please, I beg you, take me with you. Leipzig is on the way to Heidelberg. You're my only hope. Please. I must leave Berlin. Please." Holding his hand with her left hand, with her right she covered her mouth, which was trembling. "You could take me to the Americans. Or I could take a bus from Leipzig. Or a train. Walk. Anything. It would get me out of Berlin . . ."

As Sarah spoke she was thinking, This is my first stroke of luck in years. Don't lose it. If he doesn't take me I will never get out of Berlin. A woman. Alone. Weak. A Jew. I'd have no chance. "Oh, for God's sake, take me with you."

She held his hands so tight he had to pull them away.

Brodsky looked over her shoulder, at the wall, with such intensity it was as if he were looking through it. His thoughts were in turmoil. He was imagining the consequences. Could I? Thoughts tumbled over each other, half-formed, unfinished: Auschwitz, Jews, fear, rape, borders, war, rape again, her whole family dead, they must be, she's alone, I have my own car and driver, papers, passes, I can just add her name, do it, it's now or never, after what she's been through.

Sarah watched him thinking, his eyes creased yet far away. She stroked his hand and whispered, "Please. Please. It's my only chance. Please help me."

If she doesn't leave now, Brodsky thought, it will only get harder. The lines will be drawn, the zones closed, Berlin could be cut off from the west. It's now or never. Do it. Help her. God knows she's suffered enough. Isn't it time for a good deed? In victory?

It had been a long time for him, too, since he had had a woman, had stroked one, had held one, been held. Since he had even kissed a girl. Made love? Hah! He sighed. He pulled his hand free and cupped her chin, wanting to feel his lips on hers. He thought, She's so sad. And sweet. His hands were so big and Sarah's face so small, the tips of his fingers played with her hair, her dry, dirty, matted hair. He took the tip of her ear between his thumb and forefinger, rolled it, played with it, bent to kiss it.

And stopped himself. What was he thinking? This is a mitzvah, a blessing to help her, not a chance to abuse her. Am I, too, a beast?

Another great sigh, almost a shudder, and Brodsky smiled, with as much sadness as Sarah had ever seen. His hands felt good, loving and tender and strong. With his hands cradling her face, she felt protected. Would he kiss her? What to do? She pulled back. Yet mostly she felt a deep pain, for herself, and, yes, for him. He didn't win this war, she thought. We all lost.

As if in a dream, she heard him say, "If I could, if I could, how soon could you be ready?"

"How soon?" Sarah said with a slow smile, the first he had seen from her, and it melted his heart. "Let me see. Select my clothes, arrange my affairs, pay my bills . . . I'm ready now, of course. Can you? Oh, can you take me?"

SIX

Frankfurt,
May 5, 1945

Jacob woke by a mound of bricks that were scraped, cleaned, and ready for reuse. There were piles like this every fifty meters, and by each were little shelters of brick and wooden planks where ragged people huddled to keep warm. He stretched his arms and legs, rubbed the ache from his joints, and pushed himself to his feet.

His shoulders were slumped, his eyes were dark, and he had the hangdog expression of exhaustion. He yawned, took a piece of paper from his pocket, unwrapped it, and sighed at the little dark slab. He put the last small piece of chocolate into his mouth and sucked, playing with it with his tongue, trying to print the taste in his memory. It was the last of his food.

Hanover and Kassel had shocked him but Frankfurt was like a demented Grimm's fairy tale. It had been devoured and spat out, shapeless in complete defeat. Maybe three houses were left standing in each street. There were mountains of rubble as far as the eye could see, covering every centimeter of ground. People picked their way across the debris like tight-rope walkers.

But he found the house he had been told about, near the center, one of the few houses fully intact. There wasn't a scratch on the stone angels in the elegant façade. The Americans had kicked out the owners and given it to the Jews of Frankfurt as their community headquarters.

"It'll do for now, till there are more of us," a bald man with thin round spectacles told Jacob, gesturing to a chair and handing him a cheese sandwich from the box donated daily by the American army chaplain, a rabbi. "We had thirty thousand Jews here before the war. Today, there's about fifty. We hope more will come back like you."

"I'm not from here," Jacob said. "I want to go to Heidelberg. I was told you could arrange a ride for me. That's why I came."

The man snorted. "Who told you? Manny the comedian? Rolls-Royce or Cadillac?"

"A bike?"

"Not even. I can give you another sandwich."

Jacob was too tired to be disappointed. He nodded and hunched forward, munching quietly, looking at his feet, and at the legs of the chair. He thought, When did I last sit on a chair? Or eat a cheese sandwich? Or drink water from a glass? I'm like a newborn baby, everything is new.

As for news of family, friends, neighbors, any confirmation that he was not alone in the world, this too he was denied.

"I'm sorry," the man said. "It's too soon, I suppose, maybe more will come back. I can find you a place to sleep here in Frankfurt if you like, I'm afraid there's nothing else I can do. At least you can rest. We're all staying in the hospital for the time being."

"Thank you. But I must get to Heidelberg." He took four more sandwiches and put them in his pockets.

He left the building and headed west, counting the steps, as he always did, each step seventy-five centimeters. Each day he knew exactly his progress. Thirteen hundred and thirty-three steps per kilometer. Eighteen hundred and ninety-eight steps later, almost one and a half kilometers, he reached the river and turned south.

Gray light from the gathering clouds flashed on the dark flowing waters of the Rhine, whose lush green banks exploded with white and purple magnolias and red and crimson azaleas. Steep vineyards that cascaded to the water's edge were heavy with grapes. Spring was bursting forth in an explosion of color and light along one of Europe's mightiest rivers.

For all he saw of it, Jacob might as well have been in a box.

What he did see was people like himself, in rags, trudging alone or in groups, pulling and pushing all they had in the world. And Americans. Jeeps, trailers, tanks, armored personnel carriers, field guns, and truck after truck carrying doughboys and equipment of the 10th Armored Division. Sometimes they forced him off the road, or he had to wait until soldiers at roadblocks allowed him to continue, but mostly he plodded on, head down, counting his steps, heedless of the river and its beauty, feeling he could walk forever but wondering what was the point.

The closer he got to Heidelberg, the grimmer his thoughts. The total destruction he had seen in Hanover and Frankfurt, Kassel, and the dozens of burned, gutted villages at crossroads or bridges warned him over and over: Don't be surprised. There's nothing left in Heidelberg. What is there to celebrate?

What caused most pain was that he was glad. Or at least, he thought he was. He wasn't sure. He didn't know what to think. That town that had spat out his family and their friends, led them to their slaughter, what right did the people there have to live? He hoped they were bombed to bits. Yet what right did he have to live either? Why hadn't he died along with Maxie and everyone else? Anyway, he was dying inside.

As he walked, Maxie came to him, a blurred face behind his eyes, beckoning him. Teasing. His image was hazy but his voice was clear. "I told you so," Maxie was saying, in his deep voice so at odds with his slight body. "You promised you'd look after me . . . you promised . . ." Names repeated themselves in his head, like a loop, a tightening noose: Gurs. Auschwitz. Maydanek. Belsen. All he knew was the names that had blotted out the souls of his family. "Told you . . ." Maxie had the sweetest face, if you ignored the bruising around the eyes and the open wound on the forehead that never healed but became infested with crawling white things that Jacob pulled out one by one in the narrow hut they shared with a hundred others. Maxie never complained. He didn't dare. One sign of weakness and he could be killed. Auschwitz. Dachau. Maxie again; now he's crying. Sobbing. "I told you . . ."

They hadn't played together much at home—Jacob was three years older, they had different friends—but when Maxie was bullied at school, he came to Jacob. Not that Jacob could protect him from the braying packs of Hitlerjugend, but at least he could explain to Maxie what Jewish was and why this label, which at home was most commonly used to describe their favorite soup, had suddenly turned them into some kind of Untermensch to be taunted and beaten. Together they could curse the other kids and laugh at their pathetic little swastika armbands, but they couldn't fight back. He'd always promised Maxie one day he'd beat up the Nazi bastards, but instead the bullying got worse, much worse. As Jacob trudged south, counting the steps, he heard Maxie's voice trailing off into a warning whistle: "I told you sssssooo . . ."

That bastard Hans Seeler. Where is he now?

After seeing him leave the Human Laundry, Jacob had searched the camp for days, but among thirty thousand people, with the number growing daily as more refugees came seeking food and shelter, he had lost him.

The sign showed seven kilometers to Mannheim. Seventy-five centimeters a step. That is . . . nine thousand, three hundred and thirty-three steps to go. Head down, one at a time, one after the other. From Mannheim, a left turn into the Neckar Valley and follow the Neckar along the natural terraces of the Odenwald Hills. To Heidelberg Castle and the old town and home. What was left of it.

After two days' walking, and a damp night in a rotting tool shed, he approached Mannheim just as church bells rang out their once-comforting message of welcome; it was six o'clock in the evening. He looked around but could see no steeple. It was a distant, clanging sound, like rocks hitting a tin can. The church must be far away, but with no buildings standing to block the sound, it carried far and wide. The chimes mocked the ruins and the suffering.

Just as Jacob found a burned door-frame and lowered himself to sit down, an old bent man pulled the timber from under him and loaded it onto his cart. At Jacob's protest, the man offered him a lift into town. His cart was pulled by the oldest, boniest, and weakest horse Jacob had ever seen. "Your nag," he told the old peasant carrying timber to barter as firewood in the market square, "looks like how I feel."

It was only at daybreak, after an exhausted sleep inside a bombed-out building, that Jacob took in the extent of the damage. If anything, Mannheim's city center was worse than in Frankfurt. Here, too, glassy-eyed Germans picked their way across the debris, searched for wood to burn and water to drink. Here, too, was the piercing stink of bodies and excrement, vegetal and dank.

Jacob filled his canteen at an American water truck outside the destroyed city hall. He went straight to the front of the line, and when a German with a mustache and muttonchop sideburns told him to get to the back he told him to lick his ass. That made him feel good.

Jacob took off his left shoe. It looked fine when I got it at Harrods, he thought. Especially for dancing. He'd wanted the pair, but couldn't find the other one in the pile. He massaged his heel and pulled up his foot and blew on the blister under his big toe. But for walking three hundred kilometers plus a train ride? He sniffed. What a fool. Lucky he didn't find the second one, at least his right foot is okay with the hiking boot.

Nineteen kilometers left to Heidelberg. As he walked, he counted and calculated. Twenty-five thousand, three hundred and thirty-three steps. One second per step. Three thousand, six hundred steps per hour. Seven hours and three minutes.

The G.I.s wouldn't let him walk on the Autobahn, so he had to use the narrow side roads. Even they were clogged with military traffic, horse-driven carts, and people like him, trudging this way and that.

As he reached the Neckar and caught a boat ride to the northern bank to avoid a total halt in traffic, his thoughts turned to home. He knew nobody was alive. He'd heard about Auschwitz, he knew about Bergen-Belsen, and he knew he was alive only because he'd been kept in the Sternlager to be swapped for German prisoners of war. Even there, with their extra rations and less work, most had died of exhaustion, illness, and starvation. In the real camp he'd have had no chance to survive so long. Still, where there's life, there's hope. Maybe someone is alive. He'll soon find out. His pace quickened as he thought of Papi, yet when he thought of Maxie, he had to stop. They had been so close in the camp. Looked after each other. He'd washed the wound in Maxie's head for weeks, and

Maxie would smile at him the whole time he held his head and swabbed the sore.

As he thought of Maxie, he stared at the river, logs and branches floating gently by, birds crowing and swooping, an American tug pulling a giant raft piled high with machinery.

Jacob's lips turned into a sneer as he thought: Hans Seeler, you pig, your time will come.

After walking a couple of kilometers, Jacob began to look at himself as others might see him. I can't go home like this, he thought.

He sniggered. His shoes! He sniffed his armpit. Ugh. He'd been walking for ages, his clothes were filthy and his trousers were torn at both knees and the seat. All he carried was his British army water canteen. I've got to get some clothes, he thought.

Maybe Maxie was in heaven after all, putting in a good word for his older brother. For at that moment, just past a hamlet, he saw a clothesline crowded with fluttering men's clothes. It was behind a hedge at the bottom of the garden of a solitary small house. He looked around: nobody. So what if I take some clothes? Is it thievery if you steal from a thief? They owe me. They must have many more.

Looking around, he squirmed through a break in the hedge, hid behind a tree for a moment, checked the garden really was clear, and walked straight to the line. His hands fell and rose with the speed of a woodpecker as he grabbed what he wanted. He couldn't help grinning as he pushed through the same hole in the hedge and almost ran, gripping a bundle of clothes.

A good haul, he thought, all I need. It looked about the right fit, too. He'd stolen . . . well, requisitioned . . . a pair of trousers, three shirts, underpants, a pair of socks, and two handkerchiefs. All he needed now was a jacket, and he'd keep his eyes open for one.

It was already turning hot and the sky was pristine blue. He guessed the time to be close to nine o'clock. The path along the river was pleasant, apart from the glare of walking into the sun. As much as possible he kept in the shade of trees that lined the road. Soon the trees merged into thick bushes that reached the water. I can't put on my nice clean clothes smelling like this, Jacob thought. Again, he looked around and decided not to hesitate. He was a free man, right? Who knew for how long? Enjoy it.

Without a further thought, hidden by the bushes, Jacob peeled off his odd shoes, his torn trousers and jacket, his sweaty stained shirt, his smelly underpants and socks and, shivering with the fresh breeze on his naked body, stepped carefully into the river. Gasping as the cold reached his crotch, he threw his arms forward and dived. Within moments he was floating on his back, swimming a few strokes, diving, popping up and brushing his hair from his eyes. Free as a fish, he thought, shooting a jet of water through the gap in his front teeth.

Jacob floated on his back, warmed by the sun, a smile on his lips. Even the sudden intrusion of snow, standing naked in the icy winter, blue and trembling so hard his bones ached, even the snap of the whip couldn't remove his smile. I survived. He drifted for minutes with the river until he turned and swam back, grateful that he remembered how. Stepping through the algae at the water's edge, with the mud sucking at his heels and squishing between his toes, he picked his way over the sharp roots of the tall rushes and lay down in the grass. He watched a family of startled ducks waddle in a row to the water. The grass was sharp and hard and scratched his back but he didn't care. He threw open his arms and spread his legs and felt the warmth envelop him and the river breeze dry those private places.

Relief swept through his veins: Yes. It's really over! He listened to the singing of birds settling in the nearby bush and to the little blue-chested ones that trilled and warbled back. Jacob heard himself shout to them all: I made it! I'm free too!

So what?

He felt a tightness, a band around his lungs, a noose closing. It was the memory of his promise that now he must keep. His stomach clenched at the thought.

As quickly as it came he shrugged it off and jumped up with his arms out to embrace the sun, which brought back the smile. He examined his sinewy arms; and his legs, which seemed to be adding some muscle; his hairy white belly and the shrunken prune below. Hello again, old friend, he thought.

Washed, dried, in clean clothes that were only slightly too large, Jacob set off again along the Neckar, which now looked to him more beautiful than ever, more inviting even than when he had pushed in Karl Wagner on his birthday, an existence ago before Karl donned the swastika.

I could do with some new shoes, too, he thought. Can't go home in odd shoes.

But a mile on, at the narrowest point where the hills are closest to the river, two massive American tank transporters were parked parallel to each other blocking the road. A growing mass of carts, people, and livestock waited in silence. It had been closed since the day before. Nobody knew why it was closed, or when it would reopen.

There were no river boats here and the bridges had been blown up by the retreating German army. The only way across, an annoyed matron told him, was an American pontoon bridge kilometers ahead by the historic Old Bridge: "And that's been blown up too."

Jacob wasn't going to wait. He was excited at being so close to home, at discovering who was in Heidelberg and what remained of the town. Surely at least the Old City would have been spared, even if the bridge was down.

As soon as he understood the delay could last another day at least, he set off into the hills of the Odenwald, following a trail he remembered that wound around the high ridge and rejoined the river road at the Snake Path almost opposite the Old Bridge. The trail ran through thick woods until it opened onto the last part of the Philosopher's Way, which had been everyone's most beloved picnic spot. Philosophers, poets, and painters dedicated their art to the startlingly beautiful view through the trees and across the winding river to the steeples, gables, and red roofs of Old Heidelberg, over which ruled, from its perch on the hill, the ghostly towers of the destroyed renaissance fortress of Prince Elector Otto Heinrich.

As he pushed through the overgrown trail, arms raised to protect himself from the whip of branches, his step became heavier. A cloud descended upon him. He was nearing the most beautiful city in Germany from its most beautiful approach, and all he would see was a sea of rubble, like every other city through which he had passed. He didn't want to see the medieval towers, the ancient university buildings, even the old castle, humiliated by the bombs, even if he hated everyone who lived in them.

His thoughts became grim. The trees were tall and dark and their branches spread and their foliage pressed in and his childhood fears knocked at his heart. The ogres and demons of the forest and the gnomes and elves of the fables inhabited the minds of all who dwelt in the Odenwald. And even after all he had survived, the howls of the wolves and the shrieks of the dwarves and the fiends of the tales of his childhood still prickled his skin. He hurried forward, sniffing evil spirits in the wind, and wondered with Rotkäppchen: Who is sleeping in my bed? Or did the warplanes huff and puff and blow my house down?

He steeled himself as he broke out of the forest and climbed the final hill from whose peak he would see Heidelberg, for the first time since that loud sharp knock on his door, on October 22, 1940, a date he would never forget, when the Gestapo ordered the family to report within two hours to the train station on Rohrbacher Street. Bring a hundred Reichsmarks and one small bag each with your name, address, and date of birth on a piece of paper inside.

Don't worry. To a safe place.

The crowd of Christians grew as word spread. They watched in silence: schoolmates, neighbors, their local shopkeepers. When Jacob's eyes met those of Thomas Holtz, once his bosom friend from kindergarten, Thomas blushed and looked down.

A light rain scattered the onlookers as the first train, with wooden planks nailed over its windows, pulled away from platform 1A at 6:15 in the evening. From inside, fingers poked through the slats, feeling for freedom, a woman's long black hair billowed through a crack as the wind picked up with the speed. It was the last time he saw his father.

It was just after Yom Kippur and the Jews were taken into occupied France, to Gurs, in the south, where most died of exposure that first freezing winter. The rest met their end in Auschwitz. He and his brother, after watching the first train pull out of the station, were trucked in the opposite direction, to Bergen-Belsen, to the Sternlager. His dead British mother, who he could hardly remember, had saved his life by giving him her nationality. With his last hug, with his last kiss, with his last words to his father, who was strangely calm, as if he had accepted his fate, Jacob had promised: "I will look after Maxie."

And now he was returning, alone, wearing a stranger's three shirts, and odd shoes.

Even when Maxie died, Jacob hadn't cried. His grief was so overwhelmed by his fury and frustration that he had frozen, seized up, and his friends had carried him to the hut, laid him on the bed, and when he had started to rave and yell, they had held him down, sat on him, anything to keep him away from the Rat.

He was twenty when he last saw his father, and now he was twenty-five. In those five years in the hands of the torturers he had never cried.

Maybe it was because he had expected so little that the shock was so great. When he emerged from the trees and looked down from the hill, steeling himself for the worst across the river, only to find the sun glittering on red and black rooftops, lighting rows of medieval homes in the narrow alleys, their white walls gleaming, almond and chestnut trees blossoming white and yellow in the cobbled squares, and he heard the four o'clock chimes of the Church of the Holy Spirit pealing across the Neckar from the middle of Market Square, and he could even see, counting from the left, the gabled roof of his own home, at Dreikönigstrasse 9, as if nothing had changed, as if a good spirit from the woods had laid a protective hand over Heidelberg and kept the city safe, Jacob couldn't hold it in anymore.

Alone on the hill, he sobbed with relief: his home still stood; he had come home; so others may return too. And he wept for all he had lost: his youth, his family, everything but his life. And for what he had endured. He howled across the river, and felt better for it.

Finally, trembling, with an unfamiliar relief sweeping through him, he wiped his face, and as he set off down the Snake Path toward the Old Bridge, pushing aside the overgrown bramble, he believed everything would be all right again, after all.

It was a beautiful feeling.

It didn't last long.

The beauty and the serenity of the ancient town had lulled him. It was picture-perfect down there, but that's all it was, an image, like a postcard mailed the day before an earthquake. He had been duped by the flowers and the birds and the view.

His back straightened as he walked and it all came back. Why was he here? To find family? He wished, but no chance. Friends? No. Property? No.

No.

His oath to Maxie as he died in his arms.

SEVEN

Twisted around with his arm over the passenger seat, Yonni Tal reversed the darkened jeep into a stand of pine trees. He came to a halt at the edge of a shaft of moonlight, walked to the back, pulled out two long wooden planks, and wedged them beneath the two front wheels, to give them a firmer grip. Heavy rain that afternoon had turned the grass into mud. He didn't want any surprises; they needed a clean getaway. He leaned the heavy spade against the spare wheel, to grab it quickly just in case they did get stuck.

Ari Levinsky unzipped a kit bag and pulled out two gray German army combat jackets, which he and Omri Shur put on. They adjusted their steel helmets, more for disguise than protection. They didn't want to be seen at all but if they were, they didn't want to be recognized later. In one pocket Ari put his jackknife, and in another, two thin steel cords with knotted rubber ends. Just in case, he slipped a seven-inch commando knife into the top of his boot. His stomach turned. He hated the rancid smell from his bag of raw meat and bones.

Omri detached his Colt .45 from the shoulder holster, which he didn't need, and checked all seven rounds in the magazine. He'd need only one, and hopefully not even that. He'd bought the gun from an American G.I. and liked it for his private work. He snapped the magazine inside the butt, double-checked the thumb safety, and pushed it in his belt. Ari looked around, pointed with his chin at the row of small houses at the end of a country lane. "One, two, three," he said. "The third house on the left. With the two lights."

"You don't say," Omri said. They'd cruised by six times in two days.

"Ready?" Ari said.

Omri nodded. "If you are."

Omri, as he always did before a kill, slid his hand under the German jacket and tapped his British army shoulder flash with two fingertips, kissed them, and again tapped the golden Star of David on blue and white stripes.

"Yallah," he said. "Let's go."

Omri Shur was a legend in Palestine, at least among the fighters of the Haganah. Born on Kibbutz Ashdot Ya'akov in the Jordan Valley, at twenty years old he had been a strategist and instructor for the Jews' endgame, code-named Maoz Haifa. It would be another Masada, the final fight of the Jews in the Holy Land. In 1942, with German Panzer divisions storming across North Africa, led by their greatest general, Erwin Rommel, the Jews in Palestine understood that if his Blitzkrieg crushed the British in Egypt, they would be next, and if the reports from Europe about the Jews were correct, there would be no mercy. They would all be slaughtered. But here it would be a different story. Here, the Jews would fight to the last, and the last redoubt of the last Jews would be in the hundreds of linked caves and thick forests of Mount Carmel— Maoz Haifa, the Haifa Stronghold. On these slopes, Elijah defeated the prophets of Baal. Omri Shur didn't expect to defeat the Nazis, but he would make sure he would be among the last of the last.

He was trained to kill Nazis at any price.

As for Ari Levinsky, he was born in Hamburg and left for Palestine in 1933 when his prescient parents took Adolf Hitler at his word. He was thirteen years old, newly bar mitzvahed, and thanks to generations of intermarriages with prototypes of Hitler's racial fantasies, grew into a powerfully built young man with blond hair and blue eyes.

He, too, had been part of the underground Jewish army's determination to go down fighting. They had formed a secret unit of Jews in Palestine known as the German Platoon: fluent German-speakers who could pass as Wehrmacht soldiers if the Nazis occupied Tel Aviv. They learned to impersonate the enemy: to swagger like them, sing Nazi marching songs, give correct greetings according to rank, until they could get close enough to murder senior SS officers.

In late 1944, two years after General Montgomery's Eighth Army, the British "Desert Rats," had turned the tide on Rommel, and the Nazi threat to Palestine had evaporated, the British army formed the Jewish Brigade. Five thousand Jews who would fight for the British against the Germans in Europe.

The Haganah sent Omri Shur and Ari Levinsky, and hundreds more, to join the Brigade and gain experience for the next war they all saw coming: against the Arabs in Palestine. They didn't get a chance to do much fighting, though. British commanders didn't trust the Palestinian Jews, and the war ended too soon.

But for a rogue handful of the Jewish Brigade, their own private war was just beginning. A war of revenge.

Omri and Ari trod in the shadows of trees until the track from the meadow merged with the lane. It was the very last street of Holzkirchen, a small market town in Bavaria, about thirty kilometers from Munich: Hitler country. At ten o'clock at night, most of the worthy burghers were fast asleep. All the houses in the street were dark, except for the third on the left. Upstairs, their man in British Intelligence had told them, at 10:00 p.m. Frau Inge Langenscheidt would be preparing to put out the light. Downstairs, her husband would shuffle around till the small hours of the morning, reading, writing, pacing.

SS-Obersturmbannführer Uwe Langenscheidt, of the 13th Waffen Mountain Division, special liaison with the Croatian Ustasha, murderer, torturer, rapist, had trouble sleeping.

"The fuck he does," Ari had said when they were given their target, his history, his address, his habits, his wife's habits, and the names and breeds of the neighborhood dogs. "He's a big guy, rough, be careful," the briefer, known to them only as Blue, had told them. Blue was a Jew in British Intelligence, part of a tiny underground within the Allied armed forces that gave the files of identified yet unpunished SS officers to the secret band that called themselves the Avengers. It enabled small units of killers to operate in the British, American, and Russian zones of occupied Germany.

Omri and Ari emerged from the blue-tinged trees into pale moonlight. Now that they were in the open anyway, they no longer crept but walked boldly in the middle of the street as if they had grown up there.

Two men and their shadows, with guns.

At the gate to the house, Ari clicked with his tongue, and clicked again, until Topf, the Langenscheidts' big mutt, appeared by the garden shed, alert and suspicious. They heard his low growl. Ari clicked again a few times, burrowed in his pocket, and threw a slice of raw meat toward the animal. "Kelev tov," Ari murmured in Hebrew, good dog. As Topf leaped onto the meat and gulped it down, his tail wagging furiously, wanting more, the two killers quietly unlatched the gate and walked toward the front door, avoiding the two orange pools of light from the windows.

Upstairs, the light went out. After five minutes, without a sound, Ari released the clasp on his jackknife, slid it between the lock and the door, and maneuvered and levered until with a pop the bolt slid back into its cylinder. He pushed the door. It still didn't open. He slid the blade of the knife down to the floor and then upward till he found a second lock. Again, the clasp, pressure, a sudden giving, and the bolt moved backward.

It was just a simple country door.

Omri, pistol in hand, breathed out again. Topf pinned them with his eyes and whined for more. Ari placed a bone in his slobbering mouth.

Omri eased the door open to find himself in a small hallway with a neat row of walking shoes and boots lined up beneath the coatrack. There was a set of stag horns above a mirror. He saw his reflection: coat, helmet, slit eyes, a gun. A shaft of light beneath the door to the left, the only light in the house, showed the way to Langenscheidt. Ari picked up a boot and quietly placed it against the wide-open front door, to keep it from slamming.

He looked into Omri's eyes and nodded: ready?

Omri's right hand held his Colt .45 at shoulder height, the safety still on. He didn't want to shoot. He nodded back.

Ari's left hand held the doorknob. He squeezed it gently

and began to turn. The slightest squeak and he would just throw the door open and barge in. But the more he could open the door undetected, the safer.

The knob turned all the way, both men nodded again, and it was time. Ari opened the door, Omri went in first.

It was a small room. Aiming the gun straight at Langenscheidt's head, Omri stood before him in three quick strides. The Nazi was sitting in a chair at his desk, his mouth wide in shock, color draining from his face; they saw him turn white. One hand was in the air, as if to push them away, the other on the desk. Omri flicked his gun at the hand and it was in the air too. Langenscheidt was so shocked he didn't say anything. As he began to collect himself and opened his mouth, Ari put his left index finger to his lips. He whispered in Hamburg dialect: "If you make a sound I will rape your dear wife and kill her."

At the front door, Ari looked from left to right, saw Topf busy with his bone. Behind Ari, Langenscheidt, his hands tied behind his back with the steel cord, glanced upstairs. Omri's gun pressed below his right ear. "One sound and she dies," Omri whispered.

Ari gestured, Follow me, and they moved down the garden path. Omri was tall but Langenscheidt was taller, and broader, he was an ox. In the street they were alone in the dark, Omri's gun now in Langenscheidt's back, Ari leading the way. Langenscheidt began to say something but Omri pressed the gun harder and hissed: Shut your mouth.

They came so silently Yonni started when they loomed before him. He was standing by the jeep with his Webley .38 in his hand. He looked at Langenscheidt with a face of pure hatred.

"Who are you?" Langenscheidt said, at last. "What do you want?"

Yonni said something in a strange language and stepped forward.

"What are you speaking? Who are you?"

Standing clear of the jeep, with Yonni's pistol cold against the skin between the Nazi's eyes, Omri and Ari took off their German helmets and combat jackets to reveal their brown British army uniforms. Omri stuffed the German clothes back into the kit bags. Langenscheidt took a step back. "You're not German. You're English?" he said. His voice was strong, he had regained his composure, he had the confidence of the biggest man in the room, even with his hands tied behind his back and a gun in his face. "What are you doing here, this is the American zone. You have no rights here." And then he added, placatingly, "The war is over, what do you want?"

Ari said, "Auch kein Engländer." Not English either.

Bluish light from the quarter-moon filtered through the clouds and the branches. They were all shadows, silhouettes in the woods.

"You are SS-Obersturmbannführer Uwe Langenscheidt," Ari said.

"What? Who? Of course not, I am Winkler, Kurt Winkler." Now he seemed confused. He looked desperately from man to man, and struggled with his bound hands. "I was never a Nazi. I worked on the railroads. I don't know this man. This is a mistake, a terrible mistake."

"You are SS-Obersturmbannführer Uwe Langenscheidt," Ari said.

"No. No. You are wrong. I am Kurt Winkler, come back to my house, ask my wife my name. I will show you my identity card. My ration card. My library card, for God's sake. This is all a terrible mistake. My name is Kurt Winkler. Please. You must believe me." His forehead gleamed with sweat.

Blue had shown them a photo of their target. Big, swept-back brown hair, fleshy eyebrows, a drinker's red-veined nose, fat lips.

Omri said, "You coward, and liar, and murderer. Do you speak English?"

"Yes, a little."

Ari, gripping his commando knife, grabbed Langenscheidt by the hair from behind, and yanked his head back, exposing his throat. He pressed the blade above his Adam's apple. He hissed in English into his ear, "SS-Obersturmbannführer Uwe Langenscheidt. In the name of the Jewish people, I sentence you to death."

Langenscheidt responded as if a red-hot rod had been stuck up his ass. His body jerked so hard he appeared to rise from the ground, knocking the knife away. His hands still tied behind his back, he roared and charged into Omri, knocking him against the jeep fender, which tripped him up. Out of knife range, he kicked backward with his heel and caught Ari below the knee. His leg went from under him. Langenscheidt whirled around and kicked Ari in the head, a glancing blow, for Ari managed to roll to the side, though he lost the knife. As Omri scrambled to his feet in the slippery mud, Langenscheidt kneed him in the head and began to run. He'd taken three steps and passed the back of the jeep when Yonni pointed his gun at his head from two meters. Langenscheidt froze. Yonni pulled the trigger. Nothing. The gun jammed. Langenscheidt roared in relief and began to run again, toward the lane, but Yonni spun around, dropped the gun, grabbed the spade, and wheeled it over his head and caught Langenscheidt smack in the face on the run. The force of the blow lifted the big man off his feet and stunned him. Blood poured from his crushed nose as he lay motionless.

Ari whipped out the other steel cord and garroted Langenscheidt from behind. Lying in the mud behind him, he pulled with all his strength while he pushed with his foot against the big man's neck. Tighter and tighter he pulled and the cord cut into the Nazi's throat as Langenscheidt kicked and squirmed and finally gargled and groaned until his giant body went limp. To verify the kill, Ari whipped his seven-inch blade from his boot and cut Langenscheidt's throat.

Ari lay back gasping, spent, with Langenscheidt's bulk pinning his leg. "Get the bastard off," he said. "Oh, my fucking knee."

Omri stood above him, one hand covering his swelling forehead. "Well," he said in Hebrew, "that went well."

EIGHT

Elbe River,
May 8, 1945

"Where are we? Are we there yet?" Sarah's slurred little voice barely reached the front.

"That's twenty-seven," Lieutenant Brodsky said, turning around. He saw deep into Sarah's yawning mouth.

"Oh, excuse me," she said as the yawn faded. "Oh, my neck. It's stiff, I think my head weighs more than my body."

"It probably does. We'll have to fatten you up." He smiled and touched her hair. "You look rested, believe it or not."

"Where are we?"

"Dessau. About a hundred clicks from Berlin. On the river Elbe. We're waiting in line. There's a holdup on the bridge."

"How far to go?"

"By the way, that's twenty-seven," Brodsky said. "I've been counting."

Sarah leaned out and sucked air as deeply as she could. The din was deafening: engines roaring, gears crashing, people yelling, but the night was fresh and the wind was cold on her cheeks. She strained her head down, massaging her neck. "Twenty-seven what?" she said.

"Twenty-seven times you've asked if we're there yet. You even ask in your sleep. You're like a little girl." Brodsky pushed open his door and stuck his legs out stiffly, rubbing his knees and thighs. He groaned in relief. Next to him his driver's head was slumped over his chest. Each time they'd halted for more than a minute he'd fallen asleep. Brodsky looked back. "You look comfortable," he said.

The backseat was crammed with piles of documents, box files, and maps. A blanket draped them and Sarah was squeezed between the mound of paperwork and the metal frame. She was slumped against the boxes, with the blanket providing some comfort. At her feet was a wooden ammunition box full of food.

"What is it?" Brodsky asked a driver walking back to his command car behind them. They were in a vehicle convoy with half a dozen officers escorted by soldiers in two "Bobik" armored cars. The war was not yet officially over; it was too early to celebrate. Germany's final surrender could come at any moment, but with armed soldiers from the Wehrmacht mingling with refugees on the roads, remnants of German units still wandering in the woods, and the guerrilla threat from Nazi Werewolves militias, nobody wanted to be the last person to die on the last day of the war.

"You ask what is it, Tovarich Lieutenant?" the driver answered. "What isn't it? Take a look. Everyone wants to cross at the same time. It's a mess."

There was shouting in English, Russian, and German, engines revved, soldiers stood around smoking, and even now, an hour before dawn, German children were dashing between the cars, looking for handouts or something to steal. Dessau, an industrial town on the junction of the Elbe and Mulde rivers, had been bombed to bits in the last weeks of the war and the old steel bridge destroyed. The only way across the Elbe was an American pontoon bridge that the Yanks thought gave them priority.

An American sergeant stood at the entrance to the bridge, waving, pointing, ordering, as if he owned the place. A line of American armored cars and Willys jeeps with mounted machine guns clattered off the wooden struts onto the cobbled ramp that led to the street. They gunned by, Stars and Stripes flying, their camouflage paint and olive stars barely visible beneath the caked mud and dust. There was a sudden flurry of hands and shouts, leaving a little boy jumping up and down in delight, right in front of Sarah. He was waving a Hershey bar until a friend made a grab for it, but he was too quick and whipped it away and ran off. His friend, left with nothing, held out his open hand to Sarah and made a sad clown face. She began to smile but the smile went away. Unfair, she thought. He's just a little boy.

"Kiss, kiss. Hello, beautiful," the boy said in American.

Brodsky laughed. "He's right!"

"Fuck, fuck?" the boy said, hoping to wheedle some candy out of her.

It had all been so quick. When Isak had asked in the basement how long it would take to get ready, she could only laugh. She had nothing but the clothes she wore, and one little dusty purse of documents and photos she had guarded with her life for three years. They were all that remained of her life and her family, her only link with the past. In her loneliest moments, and they were many, she would stare at the creased and cracked photos of Mutti and Papi, and Hoppi, and kiss them, and would smile. She would look at them for so long, and so intently, it was as if she dissolved into the photo with them, they were together again, their bodies merging, until slowly her hands would fall and her head would follow and sleep would take her to a peaceful place.

Get ready. She tried to laugh. It came out as a snort. Sarah could have walked straight out the front door, if there had been one, if it hadn't been used for firewood long ago, but first she went upstairs to say good-bye to the Eberhardts and to give them the last of Viktor's food. They had been kind, as kind as anyone could have been while risking death to help a Jew in hiding.

She emerged from her basement like a troglodyte from its cave, throwing her hands up to protect her eyes from the sudden light. She had cowered from the explosions of the last few days, and now she saw what she had escaped.

Houses leaned dangerously to the side with smashed roofs and ragged gaps in the walls, scarred with pockmarks from bombs and shrapnel, some with façades ripped off so you could see into the rooms. There were people sitting inside as on a stage. It made sense. Where else would they go? It stank, of sewage and stagnant water and God knows what diseases. Fat blue-black flies swarmed around a pile of garbage. There was a scarlet pile of torn, discarded swastikas. On top was a torn German poster with its stale warning: "Any Man found in a House with a White Flag will be Shot." In the garden opposite were two stakes driven into the ground, with steel helmets on top. German graves. But whereas the street had been deserted after the German army had fled, with everybody hiding in their shelters and basements, with just the booms and cracks of bombs and guns, now it was like market day.

Russian military vehicles lined the street, soldiers lounged about at a roadblock, each one of them smoking and chewing. Soon the bottles would come out and trouble would start for the girls. That's why young women searched for food and water only in the mornings, when the Russians were sleeping it off. Older Berliners, shabby and beaten, wandered among the soldiers, docile yet full of disdain for the eastern peasants, even while begging them for food and cigarettes. Sarah prayed she wouldn't see Viktor.

Her head lurched against the sharp edge of a box as they hit another bump in the road. Viktor. She felt her lips turn into a snarl, even as she felt her head for blood. There was none. She should have let Isak punish him. Why did she stop him? Isak had said he would make sure Viktor got a taste of his own medicine, he'd leave orders to beat him badly, at night, he had the authority. But Sarah had said, No. Why? Despite what he had done to her, she could not bear the thought of such low revenge. Stop him doing the same thing to another woman? Yes! But beat him? That wasn't the way. It wasn't right. It would make her as bad as him. Violence was never the answer, look at the Nazis. That was what she had thought at the time. But now? Tapping her forehead with her fingers, feeling for blood again, she wondered, Why not? She should have said yes. Beat the animal. But no. That's really not the answer. There's been enough violence, enough killing. Please, she prayed, let it stop.

She looked at the back of Isak's head, swaying with the movement of the vehicle. He meant well, she thought.

Now, this is a good man.

The lieutenant had taken her to his quarters in a solitary grand house spared by the bombing. He had issued orders and half an hour later, as she sipped hot sweet tea under a cherry tree stripped of its blossoms by bomb blasts, an orderly came and led her by the hand to a room with a bath and four, yes four, large buckets of water. Cold, but she couldn't dream of hot. Soap. A towel. And a pile of clothes for her to choose from. She wondered who had been forced to hand them over. The lieutenant had thought of everything. On top of the clothes was a red apple, a hairbrush, and a cracked mirror.

After they finally crossed the bridge, Sarah dozed. Her head slumped against the box files, it flopped with the craters in the road. A gentle warmth oozed through her, a sense of comfort and the stirring of elation. I'm going home. She could see the apple tree in the garden, could smell the Lebkuchen baking in the oven. She smacked her lips in her sleep. Mutti, on the bed, brushing wisps of black hair from her brow, smiling down at her and singing a soft song. And Hoppi. Brown curls falling over his ears. Wise brown eyes like pools of evening light. In the photo, bare-chested, pulling himself out of the pool, when Jews could still swim there, the sun glinting on his wet body, laughing into the camera. It was her favorite photo, a young Hoppi, she had stared at it for hours, for days. Yet now it seemed to lose body . . . to fade away . . . wait!

Sarah's stomach tensed, a wave of shock tore through her, she woke with a start and wanted to vomit.

The purse! She tore the blanket off the boxes, kicked the ammunition box aside, clawed at it, swung her body from side to side, crying, "Oh no, oh no!"

"What is it?" Brodsky said.

She tried to stand, to feel if she was sitting on it, patted between the boxes and the seat, but, feeling the bile rise, she knew. "My purse!" Sarah shouted. "I forgot my purse. My photos!"

Brodsky pawed under the seats, searched the front of the vehicle, made the driver lean forward as he checked under him. He understood. He'd carried his own photos ever since he went to war. Every soldier did. But there was nothing he could do. He couldn't use the radio transmitter for a personal request. And he wouldn't be back in Berlin for at least a week. Instinctively he patted his left chest pocket. Felt his photos.

"I'm so sorry," he said. "That's awful, but don't worry. I'll try to find them when I get back to Berlin." He smiled in encouragement, turned to the front, and looked at the road ahead. That's the last she's seen of that purse, he thought. They'll sell it or burn it for heat.

Sarah couldn't believe she had been so stupid. She must have left the purse with her clothes when she put on her new ones after the bath. And then they had called on her to hurry to get into the staff car. After all she'd been through. To lose them now!

How could she? She stared out of the window, at the passing fields and the farmhouses, the churches, the clusters of refugees huddled by the side of the road, with their carts piled high with bedding and all their possessions. Their photo albums?

Oh, the photos: Hoppi pulling himself, his triceps bulging, he was so strong and young and beautiful. Papi, sitting at the dining room table in his suit and Tyrolean felt hat with a feather, his stained mustache and a pipe with a lion's-head bowl, gazing at the camera as if lost in thought. Papi and Mutti, sitting on a rock by a lake, her hand in his lap, with big smiles, all teeth and hair and wrinkles. She had spent days with those photos, and now she had lost them. Just as the war was almost over and she could look for her family again, she had to lose the photographs. Was that a good omen? That she no longer needed the photos? Or a bad sign? That all was lost. How stupid . . .

Desolate, Sarah stared, trying to fix the pictures into her memory forever. They passed shattered, splintered trees; gutted cars; burned-out tanks; crushed field guns. They look how I feel, she thought. In the fields around each smoldering village were yellow-and-black posters: Beware—Mines. The sky was gray. There was a drizzle and raindrops slid across the tarp cover.

Her eyelids became heavy, her head drooped. "Where are we now?" she murmured.

"About thirty kilometers to Leipzig," Brodsky said.

"What time is it?" Sarah's voice trailed off.

"Eleven fifteen."

Sarah slipped into sleep again, curled against the piles of papers, in the back of the Russian GAZ jeep, which hooted and swerved through the narrow country roads, crowded with exhausted families pushing overladen carts. American drivers waited for the refugees to pass. The Russians drove straight through them.

Sarah had studied English and could read and write quite well. But she understood hardly a word the American soldier was saying. He spoke so fast with a whine and seemed to stress all the wrong syllables and he looked so young, too young to be an officer. She could pick out some words, though, and it didn't sound good. She kept hearing "No."

She had woken up to see the Red Army officers shaking hands with soldiers in different uniforms. They wore helmets, not the cloth garrison caps of the Russians. She saw they were Americans by the Stars and Stripes flying over a circle of vehicles in a field on the edge of the large town that appeared to have been entirely demolished by bombs.

She'd never seen an American soldier before. After ten minutes of introductions, talking, more soldiers joining them, back-slapping, laughter followed by deep discussions, most of the Russians and the Americans disappeared into a big green field tent. Outside, two American soldiers stood guard. The Russian drivers sat by a truck, smoking.

Isak walked back to the jeep, where Sarah stretched in the backseat, her leg hanging over the side. She shook her hair, wishing she had a mirror. Isak looked grim.

"Where are we?" she asked when he reached her.

"The brigade headquarters of the American Sixty-ninth Infantry, they're with the Ninth Armored Division. And I have good news and bad news. The good news is they have a jeep going to Frankfurt right now."

Sarah beamed. Her luck was holding. "And they have room for me?"

"Yes, they have room. But they won't take you. I've tried. All they care about are their orders." He tried to joke. "What do they think? They're in the army?" Not the Russian army, he thought. I'd have slipped him a ham or a bottle of vodka and she'd be halfway home by now.

"But why not?" Sarah said.

"No papers. You don't have any papers. You need some travel documents, a laissez-passer, something. Nobody's allowed to travel without a permit."

"But that's ridiculous. We've passed thousands of refugees on the road. Everyone's going somewhere."

"Millions. They say ten million people are on the move in Europe, probably many more, and wait till the war's over, that'll double. But they're walking, if they come across a roadblock they just walk around it, through the fields. Don't do that, though. People are getting blown up by land mines. They won't take you in their jeep."

The young American officer appeared over Brodsky's shoulder. He looked clean and fit but his eyes showed exhaustion. He had a fresh white bandage around his neck. "I'm sorry, those are the orders," he said, leaning down and peering into the jeep. "I'm sorry, miss," he said. "Tovarich Lieutenant Brodsky told me about you." Brodsky couldn't help but smile. The

American had even learned the correct form of address for a junior Red Army officer: Comrade Lieutenant.

Another American soldier, just as young, stopped by the jeep to eye up the girl inside. The first officer was saying, "... and then there's the no-fraternization order, can't talk to Germans ..."

The last bit Sarah understood. "But I'm Jewish ..."

The second soldier said, "All Fritz to us, sweetheart, Jewish, not Jewish, all the same."

"But I'm not one of them. Look at what happened. What they did to us."

"Those are the orders, miss," the first soldier said. "I'm sorry, I didn't make them up."

Tears welled up in Sarah's eyes.

The second American interrupted again. "Come on, John, that ain't fair. You heard what General Patton said? It ain't fraternization if you don't stay for breakfast." He winked at Sarah and laughed and walked away.

"I'd like to help, really," the American said. "But we have orders. No travel papers, no travel."

And then it dawned on Brodsky. "Wait a minute, Lieutenant," he said. "Don't look now."

He went to his front seat and took out a blank sheet of headed notepaper from his intelligence file. Head down, he quickly wrote a few lines, breathed onto a stamp, which he pressed into its ink pad and with a flourish banged down across his own signature. He took another stamp, with the insignia of a hammer and sickle within a five-pointed red star, and stamped the paper in two places, at the top across the Red Army division letterhead and at the bottom partly covering the first stamp and his signature. He stamped it twice more, for good measure, and signed it again.

He handed the document to Lieutenant Reid Gould from

Montclair, New Jersey, whose first encounter this was with Russian military bureaucracy.

"There," Brodsky announced. "Signed and approved in the name of Colonel General Nikolai Berzarin, Soviet commander of Berlin, who I have the honor, along with my colleagues, of representing in all matters pertaining to coordination with our esteemed American allies." He handed Sarah's new travel document to the surprised American, who read it slowly, shaking his head in wonder. "Especially travel," Brodsky added.

There were a few lines in Russian that Gould couldn't read and below, in English, the words,

To Whom It May Concern
This is to introduce Miss Sarah Kaufman, and to request all and each cooperation in the field of transportation, nourishment, accommodations, and medical care befitting a Jewish victim of National Socialism.

Signed, Lieutenant Isak Brodsky and on behalf of Colonel General Nikolai Berzarin, Order of Lenin, Commander, Soviet Army, Berlin.

A slow smile spread across Gould's face. "Looks good to me. That would have taken two weeks with our guys." He looked up at Sarah, seeing her properly for the first time, and couldn't help nodding in approval. Cute. "Let me take this to the chief," he said. "He'll need to sign off on this."

Brodsky put his hand on Gould's arm. "Is that really necessary?" he asked. "Here's the travel document, stamped, signed, delivered. She can travel now. Let us not look for further obstacles like a pig looking for cheese." Gould looked up sharply.

"I mean . . ." Brodsky said. He had translated directly from the Russian and realized that in English it sounded rude. The last thing he wanted. He just didn't want anyone else to see the paper—the stamp didn't match the heading. It should have been his division stamp, not a generic Red Army one, but it was all he had. To a Russian bureaucrat it would look like a forgery. On the other hand, so what? With the help of a ham or a bottle of vodka . . . "Please," he said, in a beseeching tone, "can we just try to help this young lady, after all she has gone through? Can you imagine how she has suffered, and lost her family, and now all she wants is to go home to Heidelberg . . ."

The American took his arm back. "I'd like to help, really I would, but we have our orders. No fraternization with Germans, I don't care who they are. If my boss okays these papers, then she's good to go, but otherwise she'll have to go back to Berlin with you. Can't leave her here alone."

At the mention of Berlin, Sarah looked startled. Back to Berlin? Impossible. She shook her head. She'd rather walk to Heidelberg. Everyone else is walking, why not me? The American lieutenant turned, holding the paper, and began to walk away when he seemed to freeze. When his world changed in an instant, when years were added onto his life, when six months of hard slog across the battlefields of Europe, through France and across the Rhine, where a sniper's bullet grazed his neck, leaving a burn mark that still seeped, when what seemed like days of being pinned down by murderous mortar fire near Kassel, all suddenly passed from a daily mortal threat to a free ticket home on an ocean liner surrounded by drunken mates. A roar went up among the Americans and Gould roared too. Officers and their Russian comrades pushed out of the tent, hugging each other.

It was the loudspeaker, whose bass tone boomed across the

vast brigade tent camp. An excited voice said over and over, "The war has ended. The war has ended. The war has ended. The war has . . ."

"It's over," Brodsky yelled, and pulled Sarah from the jeep. He looked at his watch to record the time for posterity. It had stopped. Damn. Shook it. The minute hand fell off. He laughed. He must get an American watch. But he knew the date: May 8, 1945. He danced and hugged Sarah and pulled in Gould and the trio jumped and laughed. Gould tried to withdraw but the Russian had him in a bear hug and kissed his cheek and Brodsky kissed Sarah, too. She looked at Gould, laughed, and grabbed his face between her hot little hands and kissed him on the nose, and gave his cheek a friendly tap. For Gould, it was love at first kiss. It was a kiss he would treasure all his life. The sweetest kiss in the most glorious moment. Now a bottle of vodka appeared. The Russian drivers, who always had a secret and limitless supply, each had a bottle to his lips and passed it around to their officers, who gulped from it and handed it to the Americans. "Oh, no," one said, "not allowed," but a Russian poured the vodka over him, shouting, "Drink! To Marshall Stalin! President Truman!" The American took a swig and spat it out. "Ugh, what rotgut!" Another Russian grabbed an American's steel helmet and threw it into the air and it clattered to the ground. The same Russian took off his own cap and planted it on the American's head. Variations of "It's over" in Russian and English were yelled across the camp. A Russian call for another toast, "Commissar Voroshilov! Secretary of War Stimson!" The Americans pulled a face. "Who?" Through the barbed wire on the street, even the Germans laughed and shouted. They hardly cared who won the war, their leaders had abandoned them months ago.

Brodsky was relentless. With one hand on his new bosom

buddy's shoulder, he clapped Gould on the chest with his other. "So when is that jeep taking off for Frankfurt, Lieutenant?" he shouted. "Come on, the war's over, she just wants to go home, be generous, do a good deed and God will reward you. Or Stalin. I will too. I'll find you a nice big ham."

NINE

Heidelberg,
May 8, 1945

The same day, across the Neckar, Jacob jumped off the U.S. army pontoon and scrambled up the slippery stone bank to the main arch of the Old Bridge. A knot of "Amis," one of the kinder nicknames for the American troops, stood smoking by a group of German men who were pulling bricks and rubble out of the river, debris from the three arches blown up by the Wehrmacht at the end of March when they surrendered the town without a fight.

Jacob hesitated at the cobbled entrance to Steingasse, which led from the historic bridge to the even more historic market square. To his right and left U.S. army jeeps lined the Neckarstaden along the river. Drivers sat in each jeep while soldiers milled around, enjoying the sunny day, snapping photos, whistling at the girls. Germans walked by as if nothing had ever happened. The hangdog faces of the refugees on the road and the misery of the homeless in the ruined towns were replaced here by what looked to be well-fed, well-dressed citizens untouched by war. They strolled in jackets and ties. Take away the Americans and it seemed as if nothing had changed. The waiter at Café zum Nepomuk on the corner even wore the same pressed black trousers and starched white shirt. Jacob stared at his salt-and-pepper sideburns and extravagant mustache; he might even be the same man. Jacob peered at the Germans walking by, almost expecting to see the swastika lapel pins and to hear their Heil Hitler salutations. Instead, they wore a different lapel pin: Red Cross.

He understood immediately. The burghers of Heidelberg had switched sides. Now it would be hard to find a man who had ever been a Nazi. They had all been Red Cross workers.

He suddenly swayed. He sat down heavily on a pile of debris, sending a cloud of plaster flakes into the air. An American soldier pointed with his gun: move on. He tottered to a café chair, feeling giddy, as if he might faint. Don't tell me I'm sick, he thought. He heard a voice. "What may I offer you, sir?" He looked up, through a haze, and opened his mouth but nothing came out. Jacob gestured with the flat of his hand: just a moment. He hung his head between his knees, breathing deeply and slowly, trying to collect himself.

Five hundred and fifty kilometers, he thought, in what? Two weeks? And now he couldn't walk the last five hundred meters.

Loneliness enveloped him, made him faint with worry. He had longed for this for years, every prisoner he had ever met had yearned for home. Alone among them, he had made it. And now what? What home? It hit him: I have nobody. If I was a German soldier, he thought, I'd have a mother and a father waiting for me, a warm home to go to, food on the table. Tears of joy, hugs and kisses.

And me? Nobody and nothing. Don't even know where to go.

He sucked in air and pushed himself up from the table, which rattled on the uneven cobbled ground. He looked around at the oblivious passersby, waiting for his dizziness to pass. The waiter was observing him with distaste. Jacob tried to smile, made a small dismissive gesture with his hand, and stepped away, with a heavy heart, down the narrow Steingasse, where soldiers sat in the sun, where the Konditorei display window was piled high with fresh loaves and buns and even a tiered wedding cake. He paused at the open door to watch a woman inside filling her shopping bag. He breathed in the sweet aroma of freshly baked bread and felt his mouth water. What would I give for a bun?

As he turned, a plan began to take shape. First he would go to Marktplatz 7, the Judenhaus where his family had been forced to live in one room after the Nazis had confiscated their home. Nine Jewish families shared eleven rooms. At first it hadn't seemed too bad, living right on the market square, only a few streets from his stolen home on Dreikönigstrasse. But it also meant that there was always a crowd outside, and in every crowd there was some dolt who would shout or jeer or throw stones at the Jews, especially on market days, and it was worst of all on Sundays, when the burghers came to pray at the neighboring Church of the Holy Spirit.

He'd see who lived there now, maybe he would recognize somebody, and then go to his real home. Dr. Berger had had the decency to look embarrassed when the Nazis had given him their home. Not so embarrassed, however, as to refuse it. Whenever his father had wanted to sit in the parlor, for old times' sake, to remember the baking smells of his childhood in the small rooms and the dark stairs, to hear the laughter of his parents, even to summon up the spirit of his late wife, the doctor had been gracious and polite, almost apologetic. He didn't need to be. Most Nazis would have kicked his father out and maybe beaten him, or more likely, would have cursed him at the door and called the police.

As he turned left behind the church, Jacob found the market square crowded with more sellers than buyers. Amis in uniform browsed at stalls that sold church trinkets of no value. What they wanted were Leica cameras, gold and jewelry cheap at black market prices. He stared at everyone, searching in vain for the comfort of a familiar face. He noticed a small American flag flying from a jeep outside a side entrance to the church. Two soldiers stood on either side, and another Willys with more soldiers was parked ten meters away, providing cover. A crowd of refugees in rags waited silently in line. Good job I requisitioned these clothes, he thought, or I'd look just like them. He walked over to see what was up.

Behind a heavy wooden table in the high-ceilinged room a U.S. army officer was speaking to each refugee individually, through an interpreter. They were holding mugs with drinks. Jacob couldn't hear what they were talking about, but it gave him an idea. This time he joined the back of the line.

As he neared the front, Jacob noticed the small crosses on the officer's jacket lapels and on his cap. A good sign. His job was to help. Jacob's hopes rose. He greeted the chaplain in English with a rehearsed question: "Good afternoon, sir," Jacob said in his best accent, "I have just arrived in town and I wonder whether you could advise me how to find accommodation. Nazis have stolen my home." As he expected, this prompted a flood of questions and Jacob gave the barest outline of his story. The chaplain, a bullnecked man with tight cropped hair who looked more like an infantry sergeant than a man of God, listened with growing horror and sympathy, but what Jacob didn't expect was his response. Basically: Get lost.

"Nothing we can do about it, not yet anyway," the chaplain said. "The only government here is military, and there's no regulation about Jews getting back their property. We just don't have the power yet. And there's no mechanism for you to sue to get it back either. You can ask at the mayor's office, maybe. But don't hold your breath. Frankly he's an old Nazi, nothing we can do about that yet either. We will, trust me, but not yet. Other things to worry about."

No, he couldn't help with an ID card. That's the local police. No, he couldn't help with a ration card. You only get it with an ID card. No, couldn't help with transport. "Look, I've got Jewish blood myself, believe it or not," the chaplain said. "I want to help. But I can't. So far, absent any new regulations, Jews are treated like any other Germans. I'm sure that will change. It has to. We know what you've been through. But until we get new orders, that's the way it is. I can't help you. I'm sorry."

Jacob thought of one more thing. "Sorry," the chaplain said. "We don't use native translators. Can't trust Germans. Don't take it personally."

Jacob forced a smile and thanked the chaplain, said he hoped to meet him again, and left, cursing him under his breath. If the Amis didn't help him, nobody would. Outside, Jacob recognized somebody at last, the postman. He looked the same, his big head on narrow shoulders, that same silly long mustache with vain twirls at the ends as if he were some kind of Hapsburg aristocrat, carrying his bag over one shoulder, hurrying as usual, except when it came to the Jews. He had refused to deliver mail to the Jews' House. They had to collect it themselves from the post office. He always made them come back at least three times for each letter. Too busy. Lunchtime. Teatime. Jacob stared at the postman's jacket as he passed and laughed to himself. Yes. In his lapel was a Red Cross pin.

A thought came to Jacob. He should have left his name and address with the chaplain in case the rules changed. But anyway, he didn't have an address. All he had was his name, and the chaplain hadn't asked.

He stood outside the Jews' House, which looked like any of the others, tall and narrow with pots of flowers on either side of the entrance door, clothes drying on the railings and a line of grimy yellow plaster cracking where the terraced house joined its neighbor. They still hadn't fixed it, he thought. Pity it wasn't bombed.

The door opened and a lady pushed a pram into the street. She wore a green-and-red dirndl dress and a hat with a flower. He snorted. Didn't look very Jewish. He had no interest in the house. He wanted to go home.

He walked past the fish market and along Unterestrasse. The streets were crowded, but with strangers. Probably refugees from Mannheim. He was happy to see that the café where he used to read the Sunday papers, until Jews were banned, was boarded up. He walked on and three minutes later reached the corner of Dreikönigstrasse.

He looked down the cobbled street, barely four meters wide, with narrow terraced houses in each other's shade. They had all lived so close they could smell each other's cooking, hear each other fighting, almost touch each other through the windows. He'd played in this street, and it got bad only when he was about thirteen, when the Nazis took over. He remembered the celebrations when Adolf Hitler, who had been chancellor only a few months, was made an honorary citizen of Heidelberg. There were swastikas hanging across the alley and flowers and street parties. It didn't take long for the cursing to begin. "Jews Out" quickly turned into "Kill the Jews," and then—well—then they were rounded up like cattle and that was it.

What happened, happened.

Has anybody else come back?

At number 9, the curtains were drawn but he sensed movement. He looked around and saw a head pull back from the window in the house opposite, where the Kohns used to live. Two Amis strolled by, taking photos of the picturesque former Jewish quarter.

He sighed as deeply as he ever had, steeling himself. This was it. He'd walked five hundred and fifty kilometers to come home. Could Papi be here? Ruth? He took the lion's-head knocker, paused as his heart thumped, rapped twice, and stepped back.

Is Papi home? Is he even now bustling to answer the door? His prayers answered too, his son here in one piece? As Jacob waited tensely at the door he knew: I can hope, but this is the end of my dreams.

His father was a tailor and had lived well on a small devoted clientele of wealthy people who appreciated his perfectionist stitching and especially his eye for fashion, a strange quality given that haute couture, at its height in Paris and Berlin, was a world away from the isolated Jewish quarter of Heidelberg. But he worked from the latest designs mailed to him by contacts in the trade. In retrospect, it had occurred to Jacob as he walked, there probably hadn't been much demand for high fashion among the professors and lawyers who frequented his father's little workshop. Anyway, they soon stopped coming to the Jew.

He glanced over his shoulder and caught another light movement at the window opposite. As he wondered who lived there now, and what had happened to the Kohns and Gustav, their nuisance little son, the door opened.

It was Schmutzig, grown up. The Bergers' boy, he must have been twelve or thirteen, eighteen or so now, with the same blank face. For a moment Jacob was lost for words. He hadn't really expected his father anyway. It was just a fantasy. He couldn't remember his real name so he said, "Hello, Schmutzig." Dirty—because the boy was always dirty. Now he looked well scrubbed. Plump even.

"Remember me?" Would he? He hadn't shaved since Hanover.

Schmutzig's mouth was open. He'd always been a bit slow. It took him a moment to close it.

It came back to Jacob. When the Jews here had been rounded up, they had waited in the Heumarkt at the top of Grosse Mantelgasse, next to the Weisser Bock restaurant. The tables outside were crowded, even though it was a cold October day, and their neighbors had laughed and toasted each other as the Jews shivered with fear. Jacob remembered because at the time a gang of young boys on the edges threw stones at the Jews until the waiter told them to stop. Schmutzig was one of them.

Schmutzig swallowed and said, "I thought you were all dead."

"Apparently not."

Schmutzig stepped into the street and gestured with his hand. "You're the only one here."

He heard Frau Berger call, "Who is it?"

Schmutzig didn't answer; he wasn't sure how to put it. Jacob waited.

She came to the door, took one look at Jacob, and shouted, "Oh, my God. He's alive," before covering her mouth with her hand.

The lady opposite shed all pretense. She stood at the open window.

"They told us you were all dead," Frau Berger shouted. "Willi, Willi," she called.

He heard careful footsteps down the staircase and the voice of Dr. Berger calling, "Ein Moment," and then he was at the door. He took in the little group of people gathered stiffly on the doorstep; his eyes lingered on Jacob and widened. "Ach, Du liebe Gott," he said.

He stepped forward with his arms raised and Jacob flinched.

"Dear boy," Dr. Berger said, throwing his arms around Jacob. He noticed the neighbor at her window staring wide-eyed at the commotion outside, and put his arm in the small of Jacob's back. "But come in, come in, where have you come from? Ilse, make some tea, or would you like coffee? Come in, come in," and he propelled Jacob through the door and into the drawing room that faced onto the street.

Jacob sat awkwardly on the hard sofa and looked around, at the framed photos on the mantelpiece, the pictures on the wall, the books and candlesticks. There was nothing familiar. It had been six years and there wasn't a trace of his family in the home they had lived in for generations. Dr. Berger kept asking questions—where have you been, what was it like, how did you get here, what have you seen—but Jacob could only answer with a few quiet words. Why, could he tell them what he had been through? Over a cup of tea? Who could believe it? They would think him a lunatic. Frau Berger offered some dry cookies while Schmutzig had disappeared. Probably to get his friends and some big rocks.

Why had he come? Did he think he'd come home and the Germans would just move out? Actually, yes, something like that. But now he understood what a forlorn hope that was. His home had become someone else's home. They'd as good as stolen it, but there it was. He thought, Maybe they'll pay for it? and he laughed inside. Now what? His only feeling was extreme fatigue. He'd reached his goal only to find a nice enough couple who didn't know what to do with him. In a town that seemed from another continent. And how strange; to be in his own home and see nothing of his own, no sign of his family's existence. What happened to their things? It was dawning on him. What does it mean, to return? If what you left no longer exists, has been rubbed out of existence, like a drawing erased leaving a blank sheet of paper. To what have you returned? And why?

Jacob sighed. "Nice cookies," he said.

"I made them. You can't get much these days," Frau Berger said. "It's been hard for us." She shook her head and sighed. "Very hard. The planes, you know. Flying overhead, we never knew if they would drop bombs on us or not. And the food. Sometimes we couldn't get fresh fish." She caught herself. "Well, mustn't complain, you know better than us, it has been hard for everybody."

"I suppose so," said Jacob. He couldn't help himself. "What happened to all our things? Our furniture? Our photographs? All our stuff?" Before she answered, he remembered: the Nazis had auctioned it all.

Dr. Berger came back, holding a pair of shoes. "Here, Jacob, try these, we're about the same size. I think you could do with these, yes?"

It was Jacob's first laugh. He had forgotten how strange he must look, his legs crossed, a torn black shoe on his left foot and a green hiker's boot on his right. "You noticed," he said.

The doctor smiled. "Do they fit?"

As Jacob took off his shoes and said a silent thank-you that he had washed his feet and changed his socks that day, Dr. Berger remained standing and said, "It is so good that you have come home in one piece. Those were bad days. It was hard for all of us who did not like what the National Socialists were doing. But now that is over, thank God, and we have been liberated by the American soldiers."

Frau Berger poured some more tea and nodded hard in agreement.

Dr. Berger said again, "It has been a very difficult time for all of us."

Jacob thought, Yes, right, for all of us. He said, "The shoes fit well, a little big but thank you, thank you very much, I would like to pay you for them but unfortunately . . ."

"Don't even think of it," Dr. Berger said. After some polite chatter he rose, "Well, it's getting on . . ."

Jacob said, "I'll find some money and come back to pay you. I would never take anything for nothing." *Unlike some.* He went on, "I wonder, would you mind if I take a look around . . ."

Frau Berger interrupted, "Oh, no, I couldn't possibly . . . I haven't dusted today, I haven't made the beds . . ."

Dr. Berger said, "I'm afraid it's getting late. There is one thing, though. I suddenly remembered." He left the room and went upstairs. Jacob could hear his footsteps above and heard him rummaging and a door closing. Frau Berger smiled at Jacob and poured more tea. "Sugar?" she asked. "Our last bit of rations."

With an inward smile, Jacob said, "Three, please."

The doctor returned with a battered dark green leather-bound book. He handed it to Jacob. "I believe this was your father's? His client book?"

Jacob started. His eyes darted to the corner of the living room where the Bergers had a side table. There, at the end of each day, Papi had sat at his desk, hunched over his accounts, noting the day's sales and measurements. He could almost see him now. How many times did his father chuckle about a loyal client, "His belly has grown and his neck has shrunk." Jacob's eyes drifted back and his hands closed around the book, all that remained of his father. He hadn't even a photo. His hands trembled.

"I only came across it last year. I found it behind the bookshelves," Dr. Berger was saying. Jacob held the volume out in both hands as if it might disintegrate, as if it were the first Gutenberg bible, the finest Meissen porcelain, a stem of delicate Bohemian glass. He tried to steady his hands as he opened it and read on the first page in black ink:

Solomon Klein
Kundenliste

He turned to the next page and the next, gazing at the columns of names and numbers, sighing. He glanced up with shiny eyes and Dr. and Frau Berger tiptoed from the room.

Tears came as he read his father's almost illegible handwriting. His father would always try to make Jacob write more clearly and Jacob would retort: You can talk! Isaak Mendelsohn; Jonas Brenner; Robert Feinstein, who taught literature at school; Robert Mueller; Wolfgang Niederland, who bought three suits each Christmas; Samuel Kohn from over the road . . . pages and pages, hundreds of names, some familiar, noting the length of their inner legs, their arms, their shoulder span, their neck size. When Jacob was a little boy, Papi would call out the precise measurements and Jacob would jot them down. He could see Papi on his knees now, with a tape measure and his bald spot.

And sometimes there was a deliberate, childish writing: here, and here; that must be his own.

Jacob wasn't much for religion but he knew that God inscribes the fate of each Jew in the Book of Life.

And Papi had written the names and sizes of each client in his own book of names. And after the Jews had met their fate this was all that remained of them: their measurements.

Jacob didn't look up. A wave of fatigue rolled over him and he began to slump. "Excuse me," he murmured to the empty room. Light was fading and his head felt heavy. He shifted on the sofa and felt his neck drooping. The book grew heavy and rested in his lap. His last thought was of God, who waits until Yom Kippur to seal his verdict. Until then, the Days of Awe, a Jew can mend his ways and seek forgiveness to avoid God's judgment. Papi didn't find a way, and nor did those in his book of names.

Jacob fell into a deep sleep, the sleep of the reprieved.

TEN

Frankfurt,
May 10, 1945

In the recovery ward of the U.S. army's 123rd Field Hospital in Frankfurt, Sarah had her own little curtained-off space. She was the only woman among dozens of male soldiers, the lightly wounded. The more serious—the amputations, the skin grafts, the multiple shrapnel wounds—were across the yard in the main buildings. Fed, cleaned, and clothed, the American doctors had tended her every physical need. Her soul was another matter.

She was straining forward, her eyes fixed and intense as she told the rabbi her dream.

"I could see her beautiful smiling face and I wanted her and I stretched out my arms but I couldn't reach her and every step I took toward her she faded away a bit more until I reached where she was but she was gone. And then I was walking into water, into a lake, I was going in up to my knees and then my chest, and then my chin, and just as the water covered my head I saw her ahead of me again, in the water.

She had silky black hair and she smelled so clean and sweet and she was smiling at me with her little round face. And I kept walking with my arms stretched before me, like I was sleepwalking in the water, it was cold, very cold, but I wasn't." Her eyes filled with tears. "I wanted my baby, but I couldn't reach her, and I called to her and then Hoppi, Hoppi, her father, he was calling and shouting my name, it sounded like an echo, Saaaraaah, Saaaraah, it went on for a long time, in the middle of a forest, I was surrounded by trees, big ones, it was dark, I was lost, and I didn't know where he was, I could just hear him calling me, and then there was a face, a big baby face, it was smiling, smiling at me, from the top of a tree, and then it was gone, it exploded, there was a bang, and then Hoppi shouted, Help, and then, and then . . ."

With tears streaming down her face, dripping from the curves of her cheeks, her eyes red, shivering, Sarah gripped the rabbi's hand even tighter. "And then, then . . ."

The curtain rustled and an American nurse pushed in a steel cart laden with meals on tin trays. "Here you are, honey," she said, "eat up for once. You haven't been touching your food. Doctor says to tell you he has the final test results, and there's just one important thing he needs to talk to you about and then you can leave in a few days. You've been an angel, you really have."

U.S. Army Chaplain Rabbi Michael Bohmer gave Sarah's hand a gentle squeeze as they waited for the nurse to rearrange the pillow and leave. "Thank you," he said to the nurse.

"It was awful," Sarah said, when they were alone again, enclosed in a box of white curtains. "I've been having lots of bad dreams."

The rabbi nodded. He was a young man, recently ordained, yet he had an older man's serious face, with thin lips, a straggly mustache, and round glasses. His hair was receding fast.

Sarah liked him. He spoke fluent German. He had learned at home from his parents, who emigrated from Stuttgart to Pennsylvania the year he was born. "What do you think it means?" she asked.

"The dream, you mean?"

"Yes."

"What kind of trees were they?"

Glancing at him, she pulled herself up to a sitting position. "That's a funny question, why do you ask?"

The rabbi stopped himself. He was about to say that Jews believe if a man appears in a dream among fruit trees then he is in paradise. But that would mean that the man in Sarah's dream was dead. And he didn't want to say the wrong thing. "I was just wondering. You know, dreams are an important part of our lives. Hisda the Babylonian said that every dream means something, apart from those that occur during fasting."

"Well, I haven't eaten much the last few days. Years, really."

"Then maybe it doesn't mean anything. In those days the most common way to prevent bad dreams was through fasting. But if you're fasting, and you have a bad dream anyway, then I guess Hisda isn't too relevant today. That was some time ago. In the third century." He smiled at Sarah. "Tell me. Have you been having this dream a lot?" In Jewish lore, a recurring dream means that it will soon come to pass.

"Yes. No. Well, dreams like it."

"What do you mean? Or rather, maybe, tell me what the dream means to you."

He had been around damaged souls long enough to know that his role was not to interpret dreams but to give hope. He had accompanied the U.S. Third Army for eighteen months as they fought their way through Europe. Much of that time had been spent comforting the wounded and the sick, soldiers of any denomination. But now that the fighting was dying out, here at least, he was beginning to see different kinds of people, with different issues. Civilians, even though this was Frankfurt's military hospital. This young woman was not the first Jewish woman he had come across. How many more like her were there, filling Europe's roads, trying to go home? He'd seen the smashed towns. And the columns of refugees traipsing in circles. They were like homing pigeons with no homes. Sarah had been lucky. He knew only that an American driver had brought her to the hospital after bringing her from the north. She had been bleeding heavily from between her legs. He never asked about a patient's medical condition unless he or she volunteered information.

Sarah had told him a little about herself. But the man in her dream. The baby. Did they exist? Who were they?

Gently, taking Sarah's hand again, he asked, "The baby . . . in your dream . . ."

That's all it took. His caring touch, his warm eyes, his gentle inquiry. Tears flowed again as she talked. All she had held in for so long poured out: the years of terror in Berlin, afraid of every stranger's glance. Her years as a submarine when she ran out of friends to hide her. And most agonizing of all, her sobs as she told how she lost her baby in the cemetery at night. Through her hand he felt her trembling, and she trembled for as long as she spoke.

The man's name was Hoppi, just a nickname, of course. She started to say how he got it, but stopped herself. She just knew he was dead, she had such a sense of absence and loss. But she had promised to meet him in Heidelberg, their home, and she had to keep her promise. It was a holy oath. Now her tears stopped, her gaze went icy, as she gripped the rabbi's hand and fixed him with her eyes, withholding nothing, recounting the rape, her desecration, her sense that her body was no longer hers. How hard it was to be alone. In her pain, without knowing, she stroked his hand, as if willing him to make things better.

As Rabbi Bohmer listened, struck yet again by how unequipped he was, despite his post, to offer real solace, another interpretation of her dream occurred to him. A more recent school held that to see a dead baby in your dream symbolized the ending of something that was once a part of you. He wondered what part of Sarah's life was over. A good part? Or a bad part? Her tragic life under the Nazis? Her happy life with Hoppi? Something to do with her baby? If the part of her life that was ending was bad, then the part that was beginning could be good. What good thing was about to happen?

Sarah was catching her breath and wiping her cheeks. She blew her nose on a hand towel that was already wet. Rabbi Bohmer dipped another towel in a bowl of water and handed it to her. He sat back in his chair, folded his hands, and waited, watching her with an encouraging smile. She wiped her brow, face, and hands and lay back with a sigh.

After a minute's pause she said, "So I can leave in a few days."

"Yes, that's what the nurse said. How do you feel about that?"

"I wonder what the doctor wants to talk to me about. The nurse said it was important."

The rabbi nodded. "It can't be anything bad. The nurse said you can leave in a few days."

"I'll go to Heidelberg as soon as I can. Will that be difficult, do you think?"

"I don't know, to be honest. There are about thirty Jews here in Frankfurt that we know of, they all survived one way or another—married to Christians, by hiding like you, a few were hidden by nuns through the whole war, an extraordinary story. Do you know how many Jews there were in Heidelberg before the war?"

"About a thousand, I think. A few more."

"The U.S. Sixth Army is based there now, they took over the Wehrmacht barracks. If any Jews have come back they'll have gone there for help. Or at least the chaplain there may know about them." He wondered how many Jews there were, like Sarah, who had survived the Nazi evil. How correct Roosevelt had been when he called on the nation to come together to defeat the Hitler scourge. Look at this young woman, so attractive, so tired, so defeated, and yet her eyes, her dark eyes, they're burning. With what? Fever? The pain of her outburst? No. She's burning with hopeless love. For a man she knows is dead and for a baby that never lived. Poor thing.

He heard himself say, "I can check, if you like. About Jews. In Heidelberg."

Sarah climbed back into bed after wandering the corridor, looking into small rooms with eight cots each, greeting nurses in white frocks and caps, and doctors with white coats over their military uniforms. A general visiting the wounded had caused a commotion by telling a soldier with no visible wounds yet kept weeping, to stop faking it and get back to his unit. The soldier had not responded but one nurse, no doubt a civilian seconded to the army, for who else would have dared, muttered so that everyone could hear, "How dumb can you be?" Even Sarah heard her from outside the room.

She hated the sharp, bitter smell of chloroform and antiseptic and cleaning liquid. Tomorrow I'll leave, she thought. But first, the doctor. What could he want to tell her? She would be seeing him in three hours, not during his regular rounds but by appointment, in his office.

In bed she dozed, a small smile on her lips. She was thinking of her home, the animals, Willi the family goat, the farmyard smells, their friends, the games they had played. And then she had gone to Berlin to study and work, which had saved her life. She became sad and wondered, yet again, why she seemed to accept so calmly the deaths of her parents, let alone her aunts and uncles and cousins. She knew they would not come back, couldn't, had known it for years, since they had been taken by the Nazis, and that in a strange way had helped her. She had accepted it long ago. It was the not knowing that must be so painful.

It seemed like only minutes had gone by when she made out a distant voice and a tapping on her shoulder. "Wake up, honey," the nurse was saying, "time to see the doctor."

But later, when Sarah had returned to her bed, it seemed that the wall clock had stopped, that the minutes would never pass. When Rabbi Bohmer dropped by on his rounds, it seemed as if she had aged by ten years, yet the clock showed she had been back in bed for barely an hour. The rabbi was smiling and held out an apple. He was thinking that maybe the next part of her life would be good, as her dream had portended. But Sarah looked different. She was pale. She didn't greet him. She stared past him, her face set.

"What is it? Did you see the doctor?" he asked, and without waiting for an answer, went on, "I heard from Heidelberg."

Her eyes flickered in his direction.

Normally the rabbi would have picked up on her change of mood. Everyone said how perceptive he was, especially for such a young man, how he always knew exactly how to talk to everyone. But now he was too excited.

"Chaplain Monahan with the Sixth sent me a message. From Heidelberg." He waited for her response but Sarah stared past him.

"The pastor did not see the person but he has heard." He waited, pleased with himself, but when he was still met by silence, he continued: "There is a Jew in Heidelberg. One."

Now he had Sarah's attention. "Who?" she asked in a tiny voice. "What name? A man or a woman?"

"He didn't know the name, just that a Jew had come for help and then left."

Sarah asked, "A man or a woman?"

"A man."

ELEVEN

"I really don't like it," Yonni said as he guided the jeep slowly around a bomb crater in Hesselstrasse. "In fact, I hate it."

"Too bad," said Ari. "Because we're doing it. That's why we came."

"It isn't right," Yonni said again.

"Yes, Yonni," Omri said from the backseat, watching the slight woman holding the little boy's hand. "I think we got the message."

The woman turned left at the pile of twisted tram tracks on the corner, while they drove straight by until they took the next left, and left again. Now they approached her from the front as she disappeared into the open stairwell of the apartment block.

"We'll do it tomorrow," Ari said. "After she drops him off, after whatever she does next. As she turns into her building, I'll come out of it."

Each morning for three days they had watched the woman leave her home, walk around the corner to Hesselstrasse, and drop her son at school. Each morning she next ran an errand before returning home. The first day, she had waited in line with her ration card at the grocery store and walked home with her little bag of food. The next day, she came out with a bucket and, after depositing her son, had collected water from the pump and taken it to another building nearby. They knew from Blue at Intelligence: She took the water to her father, who couldn't leave home. He had lost his legs in the First World War and, with all the trouble, there was nobody to carry him and his wheelchair downstairs.

And that morning she had gone to the police station; they didn't know why.

There didn't appear to be a man in her life. She lived alone with her hyperactive son, a cute blond kid about six years old. That's what was upsetting Yonni. The boy couldn't pass a pile of bomb debris without jumping on top and at every corner he played traffic cop, waving his arms and pointing, although it was two minutes between vehicles.

"Who'll look after him, that's what I want to know," Yonni kept saying.

"Who gives a monkey's?" Omri said. He enjoyed the English slang he was picking up in the Jewish Brigade.

"I do," Yonni said.

"Oh, for God's sake, drop it, Yonni," Ari said. "Do you think you're the only one with a conscience? Just remember, she isn't a woman, she's a witch." A better phrase came. "She isn't a mother, she's a murderer."

They drove to the woods where they would spend the night. Sometimes they would show their papers and travel passes and sleep in an army base, but rarely in the town of a kill. Leave no pattern, no coincidences, no trail.

Not that anyone cared if a few SS war criminals were murdered. There were thousands of them, tens of thousands who
would never face justice.

As their secret unit grew, as their reach spread, their goals
became clearer and more specific. They weren't killing the
Nazis for justice, or even morality. No. It was a matter of honor.
That's why it wasn't good enough to report the Nazis to the
Allied war criminal sections.

First, they wouldn't do anything anyway, they were too busy
with the leaders.

And second, and most important, Jewish honor demanded
Jewish vengeance.

For who else would punish the bastards, the sadists? Not
the leaders, but the cogs in the machine. Those men who
laughed at the naked women and beat them with their guns
and made them run on all fours and bark like dogs? Those
who pushed them into vast pits while they were still alive and
covered them with tons of earth so that witnesses said that for
days the earth writhed and moved and groaned.

We can't punish them all, the Avengers said, but we can
punish some so that their descendants will know forevermore
that no evil deed will go unpunished.

"But what about the boy?" Yonni said yet again. "He'll be an
orphan."

"Better to be an orphan than dead. They killed one and a
half million of our kids. And now, for God's sake, enough,"
Ari said. "Don't go on about it again. That's an order. If you
do, I'll report it to the boss and you're out of the unit. And if
you breathe a word of this outside the unit, you're next."

"A bit of advice," Omri added. "Don't think about what you're
doing. Think about what she did."

On the dot of eight a.m. the boy skipped and bounded out
of the building followed by his mother, who was carrying a

tray. Two American jeeps drove by, and then came a British one, a little more slowly. "She's been baking," Omri said.

"Her last meal," Ari said.

Her errand that day was back at the police station.

"Twice in two days. Nobody does that," Ari said. "If you ask me, she's planning something. To do with papers. Getting travel papers, or a new ID card. What else would she be doing there two days in a row? I bet she's leaving. We're just in time."

"And leave her father?" Yonni said.

"Sure. He'll want his daughter to be safe. After what she did," Omri said.

"She probably got it from him," Ari said. "Let's steal his wheelchair."

They drove to her apartment building, where Ari got out, went into the stairwell, and waited. He nodded at other tenants as they came and went. They glanced at him and quickly looked away. He wore a hat low over his eyes and a shabby suit, and over that a long leather coat. He looked like a Hollywood Gestapo agent. It would confuse her just long enough to take her. In his right pocket he held his seven-inch blade, his favorite: short enough to hide, long enough to kill.

At ten thirty-seven Yonni pushed the clutch and slipped into first gear. He had kept the engine running for an hour, to make sure when the time came there was no problem starting. Two hundred meters ahead, fifty meters from the building, the woman had appeared around the corner and was walking home. Driving slowly, Yonni depressed the clutch and moved into second gear. It would take her forty-five seconds. A slow-moving jeep was not unusual. Everyone was careful to avoid craters and debris. She held the empty tray in her hand. The metal glinted in the light. Its hard, thin edges looked lethal. Yonni glanced at Omri, who nodded. He had seen that too. He held his pistol by the open window, ready to lean out and shoot, in case she surprised Ari with the sharp-edged metal—not that anything ever surprised him.

As she turned into the drab garden, with its broken wall and dusty bomb debris piled on a flattened hedge, Ari emerged from the stairwell toward her and tipped his hat.

"Frau Adler?" he asked with a smile, in his native German. Nice touch that, she'd taken a Jewish name. "Here," he said, taking the tray from her hand, "please allow me to help you with that." She looked surprised. "We've been looking for you from the Bund." The federation. Another nice touch, this time his. Bund meant nothing at all these days, but it was generic enough to hint at the good old days when every Nazi social outfit was Bund this and Bund that.

Two women in kerchiefs and coats were chatting in the next-door garden. They looked at the man in the leather coat. Is he police? Ari nodded to them. "Guten Morgen." May as well be polite. They fell silent and watched.

With his other hand he took Frau Adler's elbow and turned her around and guided her back to the street, talking all the way. "You see, some of us are getting together, there are some changes afoot, with some travel included . . ." Keep talking. Distract her. "So of course, we thought of you, you know, because . . ."

At the street, with his arm at her elbow, he felt her begin to stiffen, she was about to resist. "Wait a moment," she said, "who . . ."

At that instant the British army jeep jerked to a halt beside her, the tailgate flew open, and Ari grabbed her around the shoulders, heaved and pushed, and fell on top of her on the backseat while Omri leaped out from the front, gave their legs a powerful shove, slammed the door, jumped back in, and Yonni accelerated smoothly away.

Her scream was muffled by a rag in her mouth and a hood on her head.

The two women in kerchiefs and coats in the garden next door covered their mouths in horror until the jeep had disappeared from view. They looked at each other and quickly parted. Their silent advice to each other: Mind your own business.

In silence the Avengers drove to their woods, past a convoy of three-quarter-ton trucks with the insignia of the U.S. 11th Armored Division, past groups of tattered refugees pushing carts and carrying cases.

The woman struggled in desperation, kicking and hitting out with her elbows, but Ari had switched places with Omri, who pushed her head down out of sight and whose one-handed grip clamped her thin wrists like a vise.

Yonni followed a road that became a trail as it entered the woods; narrowed into a beaten, grass-covered track; and ended in a clearing on the bank of the Wertach River. The grass was flattened where they had slept the night.

In better days it must have been a beautiful secluded picnic spot, perfect for young lovers.

Today it was a good place for a killing.

Omri picked up the squirming, grunting woman and carried her from the jeep to a tree. Yonni tied her hands behind her back and bound her with another rope to the trunk, with loops around her throat, chest, arms, and legs. Ari took the hood from her head. He left the rag in her mouth. She struggled against the ropes and blew through her nose to clear hair from her nostrils. A high-pitched whine came from her mouth as she tried to shout and plead through the gag.

"Lucky we tied her up," Omri said. "She's going mad."

While Yonni looked out for chance strollers, Ari peered

into her face, breathing on her, and said quietly, in German, "I have something to ask you, please be quiet for a moment."

She slumped against the ropes, her head lolled forward, exhausted by the struggle.

"Frau Adler? Frau Sophie Adler?"

She looked up, a ray of hope entering her eyes. She nodded. Yes. She kept nodding, and sounds emerged from her throat as she tried to talk. Yes, yes.

Ari said to her, "Although born Alberta Braun?"

Her head shook violently.

Yonni said, "You want to take the gag out of her mouth?"

"Not a chance," Ari said, "they'll hear her in Berlin."

He took her by the chin and forced her to look into his eyes, and breathed into her face, "Alberta Braun, Oberaufseherin, Third SS Panzer Division Totenkopf, Konzentrationslager Mauthausen."

Her jaw dropped so far that part of the sodden cloth gag slipped out and dangled like the body of a snake. She shook her head and tried to talk. Since half the gag was out of her mouth Ari could make out her garbled words. "Ich bin Mutter, Mutter, mein Sohn!" I'm a mother, a mother, my son!

But centimeters from her face he said only, "Alberta Braun, you are a sadist and a murderer. Do you speak English?"

She shook her head, her eyes wide with fear. Her body was trembling, straining against the ropes. He said to her, "We are Jews."

She went pale. She stopped struggling. She nodded, once, as if to herself.

They had sworn never to say these words in the German language. He took her by the hair, pulled her head back, and whispered in her ear, in English, "In the name of the Jewish people, I sentence you to death."

Ari put his ear to her mouth to make out what she was trying to say through the gag. It was muffled but clear, even in her terror. She kept saying, over and over, into his ear: "Please look after my son."

Ari took his knife and slit her throat. Within a minute Alberta Braun suffocated. It was terrible to see.

As her body sagged and strained against the ropes, Yonni, staring into her still open eyes, which were turning gray, like water over a stone, asked, "What did she say, what was the last thing she said?"

"Nothing," Ari said. "Nothing important."

They untied her and dumped her body in the river.

TWELVE

Heidelberg,
May 17, 1945

Jacob sheltered from the rain under a shop awning, squeezed together with a dozen other men, all hunched up in the cold. He pulled up the collar of the jacket he had bought earlier in the market for eight cigarettes. One of the shivering men said, "Good jacket, what do you want for it?"

"What have you got?"

"I've got a fever, that's what I've got."

"Where are you from?

"Alsace-Lorraine. French border. Prisoner of war."

"You got anything to give for it?"

The man stretched out his arm. Jacob took his wrist and examined the watch. "Nice," he said. "Longines. Where did you get it?"

"You don't want to know."

Jacob took off his jacket and put on the watch.

When the rain stopped Jacob walked back to the old bus station, where hundreds of refugees gathered each morning. It was the poor man's black market. With his three shirts on he wasn't too cold—yet.

He needed to make some money for another jacket. He understood how, the first time he saw a Pole selling ten cigarette butts for five dollars. The Pole was saying it was a bargain. "You can make three smokes from ten butts and sell them for two dollar fifty each. For five dollars you get three smokes worth seven-fifty!" Business was brisk.

As the Pole counted out the grimy butts from a stash in an envelope, Jacob made a quick calculation and realized: The Pole was wrong. From ten butts, at three butts a smoke, he could make five smokes, worth twelve-fifty, not three worth seven-fifty. He ran the figures through his head once more to be sure.

He looked among the boots of the refugees until he found a butt in a gutter where nobody had spotted it. It was damp from the rain but would dry nicely. He sold one shirt, the thickest, for five dollars. He had his stake.

He bought ten butts from the Pole. He made the three smokes and sold them cheap, for two dollars each, on condition the buyer smoke the cigarette while he waited and give him the butt. He also kept the spare tenth butt. By selling three cigarettes for six dollars he had already made a dollar profit. But by collecting their three butts, he made another cigarette, which he sold for another two dollars, and kept that butt too, meaning he had his original tenth butt plus the final butt, making two. He borrowed a butt, so that he now had three, made yet another cigarette and sold it for another two bucks, paying the debt of the borrowed butt with the butt from the final cigarette sold. He doubled his five dollars to ten in fifteen minutes.

Jacob did that three times, making fifteen dollars' profit in an hour, and bought another fine warm jacket for seven dollars.

Walking away with his jacket collar up, and eight dollars in his pocket, he realized two things.

The market for cigarette butts was limited to people on the move. They used cash because they couldn't carry anything. But Reichsmarks were almost worthless and dollars were limited. The real market was to barter among the German citizens whose rations were insufficient to live on—a thousand calories a day. Everyone was short on food except the American soldiers and the farmers who came into town to sell their produce.

And he also realized—these are small butts because they are small cigarettes. He should hang around the G.I.s; their butts would be longer. He could make longer cigarettes and charge more. And the G.I.s would all be looking for bargains and souvenirs, like watches and cameras, which he could get from the Germans in exchange for food.

He hurried to the Old Bridge but all the soldiers there were on duty. The side streets were full of G.I.s strolling but they were in twos and threes. What he needed was a large group of off-duty soldiers who smoked a lot. He looked up and saw Heidelberg Castle towering over the Old Town, and smiled. He took the narrow alley behind the Corn Market instead of the wider, winding road. It was shorter, but steeper, and soon he had to rest among the woods to catch his breath. He paused again at the big wooden gates by the lowest firing slits in the castle walls. For a dozen generations the town's children and lovers had carved their names into the ancient oak until now the door looked like a giant medieval parchment. Each cut in the wood seemed to mark another year, like the rings in a tree. He searched for his initials. He read, "M and H, 1832." A lover had written in 1742, "Humphrey Be Mine," and here was one, "S2 How are You?" He trailed his fingers over the rough ridges and notches, touching time, looking for his own initials among the thousands of names and letters. If only it was so easy to retrieve the past.

His hand stopped and the hairs on his neck stood. He hadn't found JK but here was MK 1937, deep and rough. Could this be Maxie?

Was this a sign?

"Don't worry, Maxie," Jacob murmured, his hand covering Maxie's rough initials, as if stroking his knobbly shaved head, "I'll find him."

He looked at his new watch. Roman numerals, a white face with a thin band of gold. The Amis will love it. It was almost midday. He had another hour and a half to get to the Hotel Schwartzer Bock.

He hurried through the gates, over the empty moat, into the arched alleys, and entered the castle courtyard. Sure enough, as he had hoped, about thirty G.I.s were there, some gazing up at Heidelberg's most ornate monument, the Renaissance Frederick building, full of weather-beaten statues and chipped friezes and a battered grandeur that suited the times.

Jacob went straight up to a U.S. sergeant who was staring at the crumbling bell tower, and waited at his shoulder. "It was struck by lightning. Twice. It burned down," Jacob said to him in English.

"Shoulda bombed the whole place," the American said, without turning around.

"Why didn't you bomb Heidelberg?" Jacob asked. Everyone was asking the same question.

The soldier realized he was talking to a German and instinctively moved a step back.

"Why didn't you bomb it? You bombed everywhere else," Jacob said.

"Dunno. They say Eisenhower's family came from around here. They also say Patton wanted his HQ here. Someone also said there was a deal that if the Krauts didn't bomb Oxford, England, we wouldn't bomb Heidelberg. Who knows? Above my rank."

Jacob leaned down to pick up two cigarette butts. Much longer than at the bus station.

"Who are you?" the sergeant asked. No fraternization didn't apply to registered tour guides.

Jacob told him.

"We were at Dachau," the sergeant said. "Cleaning up. Never thought I'd see anything like it."

A dozen soldiers gathered around, asking questions. Jacob didn't want to talk about it. Not like this. Not like a circus exhibit. Each time a soldier dropped the end of his cigarette and rubbed it out with his foot, Jacob bent down and picked it up. "It's money," he said. "Want to see the biggest barrel of wine in the world?"

"No, thanks," the sergeant said. Jacob looked up in surprise. The soldiers laughed. The sarge had kept them laughing right through France and most of Germany.

"Follow me," Jacob said. He led them along a cobbled path around the terrace into a building, and down some steep steps past a gigantic barrel. "Holy cow," a soldier said, "how much does that hold?"

"Oh, man, paradise," said another, "where's the tap?"

"This isn't even it," Jacob said, "follow me." Down some more steps, around the corner, and there in a room of its own was what looked like a round house. "It holds a quarter of a million liters of wine."

There were whoops of joy and doughboys slapped each other on the back and people swayed as if intoxicated and lifted their hands to their mouths to mime drunken antics, exactly as all tourists had done in all languages for centuries when face-to-face with the Great Tun.

"Okay," the sergeant said. "We did D-Day, we fought through France, Germany—now at last I know why . . ."

A soldier tapped the barrel. "But it's empty," he said.

"Stop whining," said another. "Geddit? Wining . . ."

"Forget about Berlin," the sergeant went on. "We've arrived."

"There was a dwarf called Perkeo," Jacob called out. Every Heidelberger knew the story. "Long time ago. He got drunk every day for many years, nobody could drink like him. One day he drank a glass of water and died."

The soldiers roared with laughter and pretended to be drunk, wrestling with each other.

On the way out the sergeant laid his arm around Jacob's shoulders and staggered as if he needed support after a night's drinking.

Back in the daylight the Americans wanted to pay Jacob for guiding them but he refused. At their insistence he grudgingly accepted ten dollars and the sergeant gave him two packs of Pall Mall too. When Jacob stretched out his arm to take them, one of the men said, "Hey, nice watch."

"What? Oh, that," Jacob said. "It's a Longines. Familienerbstück. How do you say it in English? Family longtime treasure?"

A soldier said, "Rubber?" and they fell about laughing.

Another said, "Heirloom?"

"Yes, that's it, it's a family heirloom."

"What do you want for it?"

"What have you got?"

At first the police and the mayor's office hadn't known how to handle Jacob Klein. A Heidelberger, a citizen, he had a right to an ID card. In both places people recognized him, but he didn't have any papers to prove that he was he.

"Except that you know me, right?" Jacob said to the middle-aged official behind the desk in the police station, who was in charge of the paperwork after the Nazi police had fled.

"Yes, of course, you're Solomon the Tailor's son. You wrote down my measurements once. You must have been eight, nine years old."

"So you can give me an ID card."

"But you don't have any papers to prove it? A birth certificate . . ."

Jacob interrupted. "Of course not, I told you, that's what I need from you. Some papers. It's all gone, stolen, burned, I don't know what you all did with our possessions."

"Please," the official said. "We were not all like them. I personally was a social democrat."

Once they had taken his fingerprints and given him his new ID card, he went back to the mayor's office to be assigned a room with a German family. With the town overflowing with refugees, with twice as many people in Heidelberg as before the war, and with the best homes confiscated by the occupying American troops, every family with a spare room had to give it to a homeless German with an ID card. Some people had whole families living in their spare bedroom, sharing the kitchen and bathroom, which led to jealousy and even fistfights. The mayor's office was besieged with complaints but the most bitter were directed at the former mayor, Dr. Neinhaus. A Nazi party member since 1932, his family still lived alone in their thirteen-room apartment, while everywhere else two families were forced to share two or three rooms.

So Jacob, fearing an angry outburst, was surprised by how kind the Braunschweigs at Lauerstrasse 13 were when he arrived with his accommodation form.

Frau Braunschweig, a thin lady who he never saw without an apron, gave him a towel and sheet. She brought him a cup of tea.

"Will any more of you be back?" she asked. "You know. Your people?"

The best thing about the room was that it had its own separate entrance directly from the street. It was a palace. For ten days he had been sharing a tiny room with other refugees, rotating, with six hours each to sleep in the bed. Here it was like a private studio, with a basin and a tiny bath and a small separate toilet in an alcove. It had a double bed, a low table, and a painted wooden cupboard with flower carvings around the edges and a mirror on the inside of one door. When he opened it, and saw all the shelves for clothes and the hangers for suits and shirts, he chuckled. He had one change of clothes.

On the sink he laid out his razor and cream, which with a toothbrush and paste had cost him five cigarette butts in the market.

Returning from the castle, he had unlocked his door and folded the thirty dollars he had been paid for his family heirloom, and the ten for guiding, into a square three centimeters by three centimeters. He pushed the almost empty cupboard back until its front legs came off the floor, laid the folded money on the ground and eased the cupboard down again until one leg covered the little wad of notes. After ten days in Heidelberg he had ninety-six dollars in singles, a fortune, hidden under the cupboard legs, distributed evenly so that the cupboard did not look lopsided.

Jacob stretched and hid the two packs of cigarettes on top of the cupboard. Lowering his arm, he caught himself in the mirror, and paused. Sad face.

He turned away. It made him uneasy to see himself.

As long as he didn't have time to think, he was all right. For weeks now he had been merely following his own body, step by step, walking through Germany, and the same here in Heidelberg, doing whatever needed to be done, bit by bit, to earn some money, find a place to sleep, buy some food until he got a ration card, and the days followed each other, and the nights, disturbed and fitful as they were, assumed a pattern.

It was only when he caught himself in the mirror, or his reflection in a shop window, or saw himself somehow in the eyes of others, that this odd, fleeting sense came over him, that he wasn't really here. That this shape, this vessel, this wearer of other people's clothes wasn't really him.

He didn't see what was, he saw what was not.

What made him most uncomfortable was that he knew exactly what was missing. It was himself. His true soul. Only a part of him was here, like a jigsaw puzzle with missing pieces.

Where is the rest of you? You remnant. And why are you here? There's nothing for you in this town.

He hurried away, down Hauptstrasse, and only twenty minutes later, when he took his seat in the little café down the street from the Hotel Schwartzer Bock, did he think: Oh no! Did I lock the door? He couldn't remember. What if someone comes in, finds my money? But how would they?

Jacob decided not to worry. It was too late, and anyway, he probably did lock the door. Now he had other things on his plate.

From the small round table on the corner of Kirchstrasse and Bergheimerstrasse Jacob could see the pretentious carved oak door of the Schwartzer Bock hotel entrance, twenty meters away, as well as all the chairs and tables in front, and the wooden bench made of old tree branches beneath the window. So uncomfortable. Two days earlier when he had sat on it he had lasted less than a minute before moving to a real chair. The tables were covered in food-stained red-and-white checked tablecloths and even had a Schwartzer Bock menu propped between empty salt and pepper shakers. Jacob had

had to laugh when he read the puny offerings. You got more to eat in an American field ration. And it was expensive too, ninety-nine Reichsmarks or nine dollars for a bowl of hot water with some boiled vegetable and half a potato they had the cheek to call Bauernsuppe, farm soup; followed by a mystery meatball that took all his power to chew through and seemed to be held together by low-grade sawdust; ending with a lump of pudding the size of a golf ball, a cup of ersatz coffee, and a thimbleful of colored alcohol already known as Schwindel-cognac. Still, when he finished, the plate couldn't have been cleaner if he had licked it.

But nine dollars. The thieves. The only good thing about the Seelers' hotel was that one day, for sure, their son Hans would walk through the door.

And when Hans Seeler came home, Jacob would know.

Each day Jacob sat at this table just up the street. He wore a hat low over his brow and read a book. He looked at every person who entered and everyone who left. Sometimes he went into the hotel for a drink. He didn't expect to see Hans Seeler, though it was possible. He went to sense any change in the attitude of his parents, the owners, Trudi and Wolfgang, or their dim-witted waiter, Adolf. He was looking for any sign that the camp guard had returned to the bosom of his family. Like the sudden arrival of men of Hans's age, about thirty years old. Maybe they would be deep in conversation on the sofas, maybe they would celebrate in the hotel bar, maybe a steady flow of people would go upstairs without asking for a key. Maybe older people, the age of his parents, would suddenly arrive, congratulate the owners, and go upstairs in a group. For sure, when Hans Seeler came home, his family would gather to greet him, and where else but in the comfort, the Gemütlichkeit, of the family apartment on the top floor of their hotel.

Maybe, with all his arrogance, and God knows there was plenty of that, the Rat would just walk around freely. Why not? He's at home here. Would he hide in plain sight like that, when it was well known the Americans were hunting down Nazi leaders?

Of course he would. First, he wasn't a leader, just a sadistic camp guard, there must be thousands like him. Then, he had hidden among the survivors in the camp, hadn't he? He'd seen him in the Laundry. It would be just like him to hide among the hunters, the Americans. Anyway, he'll deny being an SS concentration camp guard. Who would admit it? He'll say he's just returned from the Russian front. That he was an ambulance driver in France. A prisoner of war in Italy. One thing he won't say is the truth. The hardest person to find in Germany today is a former member of the Nazi party, let alone the SS.

He'll be back, Jacob thought, his eyes scanning the street and the hotel entrance; and I'll keep my word.

He didn't know how, but—step by step.

THIRTEEN

Heidelberg,
May 17, 1945

After several hours nursing a cup of coffee and reading old magazines, as evening fell, Jacob saw Adolf emerge from the hotel at the end of his shift. It seemed natural to follow him, which wasn't hard; he shuffled as much as he walked and seemed to greet far more people than he could possibly know. He soon entered an apartment building with a tidy little garden where two boys were playing. He saluted them with his hat and walked up the stairs. A minute later Jacob approached the boys.

"That man, does he live here, the man who just went in?" he asked.

The smaller boy, about eight years old, said, "Adolf Schwimmer? Yes."

"Thank you."

That day Jacob had recognized seven people, been approached by a former client of his father's, and spoken to two old schoolmates who had walked by separately. All three people he had spoken to said words to the effect of: "My God. I thought you were dead." To each one he had responded: "I may as well be." But the more he said it, the less he felt it. He did have something to live for.

As he walked along Hauptstrasse, a dream had come back to him, bits of it.

He was underwater, swaying with the current, like plankton. Tiny, helpless. With no control of his body, hanging in a void. That's all he remembered, but now the dream took formal shape. He could sink, or he could rise to the surface. He could leave this town, to which he had always longed to return, but found there was nothing to return to. Or he could take control of his life again. But how? And what did it all mean? Give up? Take control? Just words. What does anything mean?

Why didn't he die in the camp like everyone else? Always, the fight to live another day. But why? For this?

Yes. For this. This dream, this beautiful dream.

I'll kill the rodent.

He was strolling now, registering the changes, trying to see how he fit in. Half the shops on the main street seemed to be bookshops, yet with a difference he spotted as soon as he scanned the windows. Again, he saw not what was there, but what was not. *Mein Kampf.* Where were all the stacks of Hitler's tome in the windows, the rag that had dominated everyone's life for a decade? Burned with him, he hoped.

The lines of people outside food stores reminded him: He must get a ration book. First the officials said they didn't have enough. Then that he didn't have the right; then that he had to go somewhere else, to a "KZ Betreungsstelle," an aid center for former concentration camp inmates. The nearest one was in Frankfurt.

Hauptstrasse, once wrapped in furs and echoing to the clip of high heels stepping from big black cars, was now drab and closed to civilian vehicles. It was reserved for the U.S. military. Some civilians were dressed well, in homburgs and suits: the townspeople. Most wore rags and looked lost: the refugees. Most of these had no jobs and nothing to do but wander around and gaze at the shops and marvel at the luck of this pristine city when their own had been destroyed.

Jacob passed the Steiners' old home at number 159, where his best friend, Ulrich, had lived; they were among the first to be sent to the east. He peered at the names on the bells: strangers all. The sensation returned: adrift in a void.

In the camp, even as his senses were blunted, a sixth sense, of heightened awareness, honed to any threat, protected him. He didn't feel the cold, he didn't smell the stink, he didn't taste the blood, but he did develop an acute sense of anything unusual, looming danger, how to stay out of the way of an angry Nazi guard. As he turned the corner his nerves went on edge, and as he approached the door of his own room his blood surged. He knew the door was open before he even saw it. Just a little bit, but ajar. Someone's been inside. Or is still inside.

Jacob's steps slowed as he scanned the street. Nobody around. If they had left, they would have closed the door. It's open. They must be inside. His heart pounded, it beat against his ribs. He breathed deeply to control his panting, his mind raced. It isn't the police. They would have someone waiting outside. It must be the landlady. But she had promised never to disturb him. The money. A thief? But who would think of stealing from a refugee? Who knew he had money? Maybe someone who followed him home from the castle or the market? That could be it. Someone who saw him selling all his cigarettes. No, there would be much better targets for a thief. Anyway, why would a thief leave the door open?

Or am I crazy? Did I just forget to close the door?

His heart pounding, he prodded the door so that it swung open while he stood in the street. There wasn't a sound. He peered around the door. "Hello?" he said. "Someone there?"

Five seconds went by until a little voice answered. "Hello?"

It was a woman's voice, quavering and tentative. Jacob hesitated, and stepped into his room.

Sitting on the bed, her hair disheveled as if she had been sleeping, was a young woman with dark hair, wide staring eyes, and a frightened face. A shaft of light from the open door fell across her body, cutting her in two. She stood up, holding her arms at her sides, making her look even slighter than she was. As Jacob watched her, his heartbeat dropped. No danger here. Then it sped up again as he stared at her a little longer than was correct. Her dark hair falling from her face as she leaned forward to shake hands, the swell of her breasts, her full lips. A sweet smile. Walking along the Philosophenweg he had thought of the fairy tale and wondered about his home, Who has been sleeping in my bed? He had been thinking of a wolf. Not a beautiful girl.

How long had it been?

"Hello," he said again.

"Hello." She tried to smile.

"I'm Jacob Klein," he said.

"I know," she said. "The mayor's office told me where you live."

Jacob nodded as if it all made complete sense. He closed the door.

"I fell asleep," she said.

"Yes, you must be tired. You probably have had a long journey." Why did he say that? Because she also must have been on the road? But she was well-dressed, in a frock and blouse, and a coat lay on the bed as if she'd been using it as a blanket. And she had a little bag that was open, showing more clothes. She was beginning to look a little familiar, but she would have changed a lot. She looks about twenty-two or -three, he thought, and he'd been away for five years. Girls change a lot in five years at that age. Her eyes? There's something about her . . . I've seen her before.

"I'm Sarah Kaufman," she said. Jacob nodded. There had been several families called Kaufman.

"Excuse me. Do I know you?" he asked.

"Your sister went to school with my sister," she said. Jacob made a flourish with his hand, as if to say, that explains everything. He gestured to the bed, and she sat down again. Jacob perched next to her.

Outside, the church bells chimed seven o'clock. Jacob said, "Where is your sister?"

"I don't know. And yours?"

"Same." He pressed his lips together, sighed. "Why did you leave the door open?"

"It was open when I arrived. It isn't my room. I don't know . . . it didn't seem right."

"I forgot to lock it," he said. "Now I'm glad." She nodded with a slight smile.

Jacob looked at her. There was a heavy silence, the weight of loneliness, it draped the room. She sighed. Her chest rose and fell as she tried to control herself. She wiped away a tear. She said, "It's been so hard."

"Yes," Jacob said.

"It's been so long."

There was one pillow, and Jacob pushed it toward her and she leaned back against it. For fifteen minutes they lay beside each other without a word. Her eyes were heavy. It was awkward until each began taking comfort from the presence of the other.

Jacob began to squirm and shift and could no longer contain himself. "Umm," he began, and stopped.

"Yes?" she said.

Jacob sat up. "Ummm, sorry, but, uh, I have to go to the toilet."

Sarah jumped up. "Of course. I'll wait outside." As she took the three steps to the street, Jacob said, "It's all right, there's a door."

"That's all right, I need some air."

Jacob shook his head and smiled as he directed a strong stream against the bowl, not wanting to make a splashing noise.

He thought, And then there were two.

When he opened the door and sheepishly invited her back, they hesitated a moment, choosing between the wooden chairs and the bed. "It's more comfortable here," Jacob said, plumping up the pillow. She joined him, leaning against the wall.

"Okay," Jacob said. "Tell me, I'm so curious. What made you come here?" He sensed Sarah stiffen at the directness of the question, and quickly added, "Don't get me wrong. I'm glad you did. Delighted. But you know, what happened? How did you know I was here? I mean, we don't even know each other. Although, I'm glad we do now. And where have you come from?"

She looked away. The little room seemed heavy again. He raised his shoulders in encouragement.

Sarah answered with a shake of her head and a helpless raising of her hands.

"It's all right, I understand," Jacob said with a thin smile. What could he say if she asked? "Just tell me, how you came to my room. And why."

Sarah sighed. "Well. This morning I came from Frankfurt. I was looking for someone. A man."

"How did you get here?"

"The American army chaplain in Frankfurt, he arranged a ride with a jeep, and they took me to the chaplain here in Heidelberg. He had said there was a Jewish man here. The only Jew in Heidelberg."

"Me?" Jacob said.

"Yes. He said he had met you. He didn't know your name, though. But he took me to the mayor's office, he thought maybe you had gone there for help, and they remembered you and found your name. The only Jew to come back. I recognized your name. But my husband, Josef Farber . . ."

"I know Joe. He went to Berlin. You married him?"

"As good as."

"Where is he?"

"I don't know. I hoped it was him. We said, if we ever lost each other, we'd meet here. Afterwards . . ." Her lip quivered. "But it was you."

"I'm sorry."

She looked at him sharply.

"No, really. I mean, I'm sorry he's not here. I'm not sorry that I'm here. I mean . . . I wish he could be here too."

"So do I."

"It's early. He could be anywhere . . ."

"We promised to meet here. On a bench by the river, at the bottom of the steps."

Jacob wanted to say: Then he'll come. But he couldn't bring himself to say it. How could he know if Joe would come back? With so many dead, what good would it do to pretend there was hope?

He said, "You can stay here as long as you like."

"I didn't have anywhere else to go, you see. The chaplain wanted to send me back to Frankfurt, there are Jews there, staying in a hospital. But I didn't want to leave. Who knows when I could come back here again? But there's nowhere here for people like us. When the chaplain asked about finding me a room here, they said there are thousands of people looking for a room and I should go to the countryside."

"Yes, that's what they told me."

"You'd think the Amis would treat us differently. But they say we're all Germans."

"That'll change."

"So how did you get this room?"

"I got an ID card. They knew me, they couldn't say I wasn't from here. Although they'd have liked to."

"That's the trouble. I'm not from the town, I'm from outside, from near Leimersdorf, and I'm not going back there. I hate them, after the way they treated us."

Sarah's face hardened at the memory. "I hate them." When neighbors stole their chickens and they complained to the policeman, did he help? My foot! He stole the last one. When she shouted at a boy at school who had called her a dirty Jew, it was her they had punished for being a nuisance in class. The teacher wouldn't let her into the classroom. "And they were our neighbors."

She looked at Jacob, around the room. "And so I didn't have anywhere to go. And I thought, if you're alone, and I'm alone, maybe we can be alone together."

He nodded and imagined them holding hands. She smiled and said, "After all, my sister knew your sister."

"Yes. You and me, we practically grew up together," Jacob said.

"Exactly. We're like brother and sister."

"Well, that's not exactly what I had in mind."

"Not for long, anyway," Sarah said, "just until I find somewhere."

"Well, let's see. Everyone is sharing in town, you may as well share with me." Before she could object, not that she appeared to want to, he said, "Would you like to put your clothes away in the cupboard?"

"Is there room?"

Jacob's eyes widened and he let out a guffaw. He snorted and slapped his sides as if he had never heard anything so funny.

Sarah chuckled too, and wondered, Is he all right? He was like the clown in a circus. Would he cry next? It was catching, though, and as Jacob could not stop laughing, she began to laugh too, until they were rolling on the bed and beating it with their hands.

Finally, she managed, "Wait, wait, what's so funny?"

Jacob was panting, trying to regain his breath. He stood, walked to the cupboard, and with a gesture of triumph threw open both doors. Sarah saw two shirts and a pair of pants hanging on a wooden hanger. All the other hangers were empty.

"That's all?"

"It's more than most, trust me."

"That isn't funny, that's sad."

"Yes, you're right," Jacob said, breathing in deeply, calming himself. "Of course it's sad. But it's still a lot. What about you? Where did you get your clothes?"

"The chaplain in Frankfurt. I think he liked me," she said, taking her blouses and pullovers from the bag and folding and stacking them neatly in the drawers. "Confiscated from Nazis, I suppose. Imagine what they would think, me wearing their clothes."

"And what do you think, wearing their clothes?"

"I don't care. What didn't they take from us? Can't we take a little something back?" She hung two dresses and two skirts on the hangers, and as she turned her back to him and pulled out her bras and knickers she said, "Now please don't look."

Jacob turned away and lay on the bed and closed his eyes. The glimpse of her little underclothes, so intimate yet so distant, stirred him, but it stirred memories, too. The bad ones. His night thoughts. As Sarah busied herself at the cupboard, and wooden hangers clattered against the wooden doors, he heard different sounds, saw different things. They flashed through his mind, cackling like a witch on a broomstick, those things he saw in the dark.

Naked skeleton women defecating in the open, stripped of shame. A pack of naked women herded like animals through distant trees in the snow, their bodies bouncing and quivering. They were like silent spirits gliding through the forest. Silhouettes with guns pushing and prodding them. As he lay on the bed and stared at the ceiling he grunted, trying not to think of his sister. Julie. Oh, Julie, what did they do to you? And Maxie . . . maybe not knowing is better.

After the British had torn down the wire and set them free, breathed life into the dying, they had felt reincarnated, for they were not resuming their old lives but had been given new ones.

Some of the men and women had behaved like animals, not even seeking a private place to couple in. Most survivors were young, and after years of being enslaved and thrashed like dogs they were amazed to be alive. They rediscovered themselves and their bodies, and copulation was like taking freedom, an affirmation of life. The British soldiers and doctors and nurses were disgusted, they thought the men and women behaved like shameless whores, but they were not whores, they were just in shock at what they could do. They could do anything they liked, and they celebrated. In the rooms, under blankets, on top of blankets, in the showers, even in the open, in the fields, in the woods, by the stream, they rolled together and made love and cried freedom.

But not Jacob. He hadn't thought of a woman for months, and hadn't had a woman for years.

FOURTEEN

Heidelberg,
May 18, 1945

And now Jacob and Sarah lay in bed holding hands after a night in which their silences told more than their words. He could hear faintly the twittering of birds through the open window and the drone of a car and, through the wall, the early chatter of the Braunschweigs. Jacob turned his head and looked at Sarah dozing on her back and felt some peace at last.

Sarah sensed Jacob's gaze and as she turned to look at him her eyes drifted open and a smile began to form.

As Jacob tried to smile back he felt the faintest ebbing of his senses and deepening of his breathing and, a cloud of sweetness enveloping him, he slipped into sleep.

Through half-closed eyes, Sarah saw Jacob's face slacken, his eyelids descend, and she heard his even breathing. She gently slid her hand from his and turned on her side, away from him, and tried to go back to sleep.

She hadn't meant to tell him about Hoppi, but he'd insisted. After all, he'd known Josef, there weren't that many

young Jewish men in Heidelberg, and they were about the
same age. She had met Hoppi at a student dance in Berlin,
each passing as a Christian, and their shared ruse had brought
them together until they shared a deep love. It all came back
and it had been so wonderful. When had she last poured her
heart out? They were lying on their backs. She couldn't remember who had taken whose hand as they talked but it
seemed so natural and right. She told how they had changed
hiding places almost weekly, sometimes daily, with half a dozen
regular shelters, and then they had almost argued.

She had tried to list all the names of the people who had
helped her, and called them "the good Germans." Jacob had
said there weren't any. She had tried to explain. If there
weren't any good Germans, she would have been dead long
ago. "They are not all the same, truly," she had said. But it had
been different for Jacob. People had dropped dead around
him every day. He had not been helped by a soul, every German
had been evil. He had become agitated and she had tried to
soothe him. "Yes, you're right, everyone is evil," she had finally
said. "Feel better now?"

When she told him how Hoppi had gone out and never returned, it was his turn to soothe her. She relived the torment
of waiting, for hours and then days, and the anguish of those
sleepless nights. She had looked for him in the streets and
knocked on the doors of acquaintances, which she knew was
foolish, for anyone could denounce her, but she couldn't help
herself. When she managed to say what Wilhelm Gruber had
told her, that he had seen Hoppi being beaten and dragged
away, she had barely been able to say the words, and had wept.

But she had not told Jacob what she really felt, what she
knew: that Hoppi could not be alive. That everyone had been
taken to Auschwitz, and after Isak had told her what he had
seen she knew that nobody could survive there for three years,

certainly not someone as gentle and kind as Hoppi. And she had been glad that Jacob had not said all kinds of silly things, had not made impossible promises, that Hoppi was alive and all would be well.

When she had recounted her journey, Jacob had teased her about Isak, and she had had to laugh. Yes, she thought, he's right, Isak really was sweet. A savior. Would she see him again? Their parting was sudden because the jeep to Frankfurt was already late. He had said it was a good omen: She was going home on the first day of peace. She had kissed him on the cheek, and he had hugged her, a typical Russian bear hug, big and warm and strong, and told her to visit him in Bala-kovo on the Volga. "My mother is the best cook east of the Elbe," he had promised. "Unlikely I'll come," she had said. "You come to Heidelberg, I'll show you the castle."

Then suddenly they had kissed on the lips, briefly, and she had said to him, "I owe you my life."

"No, no," he had said, holding her from him, stroking her hair. "God sent me at the right time, that's all."

Her response had been quick and sharp and now she regretted it. "What God?"

The God who had taken everything from her? Why leave her with nothing? With no one. The man she loved, the baby she wanted so desperately, the essence of Hoppi. If it was a boy she was going to call him Josef, if a girl, Josefine. She had even lost his photos.

You're so young, Jacob had said, and so had both chaplains, they all say the same: You're so young, pretty, healthy.

What good is a long life with such memories? All the longer to relive the torment?

Jacob was a typical man, she thought. Didn't want to talk about it. He described his trek, the hard days and cold nights, the destroyed towns and villages, the little joy of stealing his clothes, and his surprise, after expecting the worst, at seeing his own town almost untouched. But when she asked about Bergen-Belsen, nothing. Silence. He talked about leaving, about his new friend Benno who had said he might come to Frankfurt, nearby. But about life in the camp, a blank.

She remembered that he had a brother and asked after him. Immediately she felt the icy blast. His body stiffened. When at last he said, "He's dead," Sarah knew not to ask more. She had squeezed his hand and said, "I am so sorry." Jacob had lain rigid, like a floorboard, staring at the ceiling. He gripped her hand so tight it hurt.

Now, lying on her side, she edged away from Jacob just a little, and pulled the blanket with her. He stirred and she felt a tug in response. She pulled back. He did the same. She wriggled back toward him until they both lay snug under the blanket. In his sleep he put his hand on her thigh. She sighed and let it lie there.

FIFTEEN

Heidelberg,
May 21, 1945

Another glorious day. The sun beat down from the blue sky and trees in the cobbled squares blossomed red and yellow and white. Their leaves rustled in the breeze.

In the shade of the thick branches, waiters set out tables and chairs, smoothed down checkered tablecloths and sealed them in place with rubber bands on the corners, and placed menus in thin metal holders. The occupiers ate and drank, the occupied served and watched.

Jacob, who guided American visitors around Heidelberg Castle, collected cigarette butts, and bartered ruthlessly, was running out of places to hide his cash. His cupboard was beginning to tilt. He needed larger bills, but they were hard to come by.

Every lunchtime he went for tea to the Schwartzer Bock, and for the first time since he found her on his bed four days earlier, Sarah went with him. On the way they stopped at one of the bulletin boards covered with requests for work, announcements of events, photos of missing people, and, his particular area of expertise, goods for barter.

"So what do you think?" Jacob said. "Anything you want?"

Sarah followed Jacob's finger, reading as he drew it down the list of goods for barter:

A pair of men's heavy shoes for pipe tobacco; a Siemens electric icebox for a Leica or Contax camera; food or cigarettes for an English dictionary or cigarette lighter of good quality; a rabbit hutch and a garden hose, both in first-class condition, for a stud rabbit; twenty Macedonia cigarettes for a pound of sugar; twenty-five cigarettes for a bottle of German brandy; tobacco for Russian lessons; a beautiful old china cabinet for an evening dress, evening shoes, and some opera music scored for a soprano.

"Leicas, that's what the Amis want," Jacob said as they walked away. "And watches. European, not Russian rubbish. Rings, bracelets . . . What did you think of when you read that?" he asked.

"I don't know, what? I don't really need a Chinese cabinet. Wouldn't mind an evening dress."

He sneered. "So this is what they got, the Nazis, for their thousand-year Reich. Twenty-five cigarettes for a bottle of brandy. And how many did they kill? To swap a pair of shoes for pipe tobacco. Look at my shoes." He was quite proud of them, they were black and polished. "A perfect fit. I got them for two kilos of turnips that I got for a tin kettle that I got for twelve cigarette butts. And I got all that for three years of law school."

"You should look out for a stud rabbit," Sarah said. "You could swap it for a garden hose and what was it? A rabbit hutch? I've always wanted a rabbit hutch."

"Don't laugh. You'd be amazed what Amis would give for a rabbit hutch."

"Yes. Two and a half cigarettes. Pall Mall."

"Hey, you're learning." Jacob laughed. He almost took her hand; grazed it with his but didn't dare. Although they shared the same bed, they had not repeated the intimacy of that first night. Hoppi seemed to lie between them. Jacob had even thought of sleeping with his head at her feet, as he had slept in the camp bunks, two or sometimes three men to a bed. And Sarah, so used to being alone, felt crowded, imposed upon, and slept at the edge of the bed.

After that first unburdening, the relief of sharing, neither mentioned the past again. Jacob tried to avoid it, Sarah couldn't bear it. She knew that to dwell on such horror would destroy her. And who knew what the future would bring? She must live for the present, today, now, and wait. That is already a great deal. To live and wait. But for what?

During the day each went their own way, Jacob bartering and guiding and earning money, and Sarah wandering the streets, hoping to meet someone she knew. She had agreed with Hoppi that they could also meet in the Church of the Holy Spirit. The Nazis burned down the synagogue, they reasoned, but they would never destroy their own church.

That morning she had risen early and gone there, as she did two or three times a day, after sitting on the bench by the river, and instead of Hoppi had run into Captain Monahan of the Sixth. She had hoped to meet him again, for even though he looked like a bull he had been so kind when she arrived. He had worried about how she would live, and she wanted to let him know that she had found a friend and where she was staying. She sent her love to Rabbi Bohmer. He gave her a big bar of chocolate, which she hurried home to share with Jacob.

"Wunderbar," Jacob had said, testing the weight in his hand. "Wonderful. I can get loads of fruit and vegetables from the farmers for this, and I know someone who wants to swap a woman's silver watch for food, and there's this American officer who is looking for a present for his wife . . ."

But with a shriek of laughter that made Jacob start, Sarah snatched it back and tore the wrapping paper and popped a piece of chocolate into her mouth and broke off another piece and waved it at Jacob's mouth.

"No, no, oh, what are you doing? It's worth more in its original wrapping . . ."

"Ummm, ummm, so smooth, so sweet . . ."

"Stop, stop . . ." He tried to grab the bar but Sarah twirled around and threw herself onto the bed, hugging the chocolate to her chest, smacking her lips and rolling her eyes.

"Yummy, yummy, too late now . . . ummmm, uhmmm . . ." She put another piece into her mouth and sucked and chewed, and then another until a chocolatey goo dribbled from between her busy lips.

Jacob threw his hands up in despair. Um Gottes Willen! For God's sake. "Imagine where we'd be if I smoked my cigarettes!"

Moments later there was a loud moan from Sarah, who clutched her stomach and bent over the sink, groaning and crying. "Ow, I feel sick. I feel so sick. Help me."

Ignoring her, Jacob patted the bedclothes for the chocolate, hoping to rescue some. Even a half-eaten bar of Ami chocolate would get a kilo or two of tomatoes.

An hour later, as they approached Jacob's lookout post, Sarah was saying, "I can't believe it, I was throwing up, in agony, and you were looking for the chocolate to sell it."

"What do you mean? You were pretending, you weren't even sick."

"But you didn't know that. What if I was really sick, you'd just take my clothes and sell them, right?"

"Right off your back. They're pretty good clothes."

They passed a group of boys running in the streets, tugging at each other's jackets, shouting and laughing. Jacob stopped to gaze after them and Sarah waited at his side. He was looking for rather too long. She said, "A penny for your thoughts."

He shrugged. "You don't want to know."

"Of course I do, or I wouldn't ask. What were you thinking?"

Jacob snorted. "As a matter of fact, I was thinking of how to kill them."

"What?"

"Well, you asked. I was thinking of how to kill them. How would I actually do it?"

"Are you crazy? Why would you think that? That's horrid."

"I don't know. It just came to me."

"I could never think like that," Sarah said. "Not even after everything that happened. They're just children. Jacob, that's horrible."

Jacob turned and said, "Here's my café."

At his side, Sarah said, "Mind you, I couldn't hug them either."

After ordering a sandwich and tea for both of them, Jacob excused himself, and entered the nearby hotel. Ten minutes later, just as the food arrived, he returned. "Good timing," he said, sitting down and pouring the tea.

"Where were you?"

"In that hotel."

"I could see that. I mean, what took you so long? What were you doing?"

Jacob wanted to tell her. But he didn't know how. She'd never understand.

In the camp life was simple. Yes, it was mindless, the beatings, the torture, the terror, the killing, the starvation, the sadism, all insane. Yet life could not have been clearer, it was reduced to its essence: surviving until the next morning, like a common housefly. We hardly saw or heard, we were automatons, fluttering flames that at any instant could be snuffed out by the slightest wave of the guard's hand. The immensity of our world could not be grasped. The scale of the evil was incomprehensible. Everything was insane. And so it made perfect sense.

The only thing worse than what he had lived through was people not believing him. When he had begun to tell people on the road a bit of where he had come from and what had happened there they had all looked at him in disbelief, as if he was crazy. It was like being violated again. And so he couldn't tell Sarah. Not yet. Not all of it. But some. He had to say something, to someone.

"There isn't much cheese in this sandwich," Jacob said, opening it and closing it, and before Sarah could answer he said, looking down, "There's something I haven't told you. Maxie, my little brother, the way he died. A prison guard killed him." He swallowed. "In front of me."

Sarah put her cup down, she didn't move.

"I looked after him for as long as I could, he wasn't very strong, Maxie. He fell sick all the time, and we always had to hide him, whenever they made us all stand to attention outside, for hours on end, in the rain, in the sun, all night sometimes, we always hid Maxie in the hut. There was a pile of wood by the stove, which never worked by the way, and even the kapo liked Maxie too, everyone did, he didn't rat him out. We built a frame and stacked the wood on top and he lay inside. As long as I could, I looked after him. Maybe you knew, he was always sick as a child. Asthma. Couldn't breathe."

Jacob chewed on his sandwich. Long after he had swallowed the last piece his jaws were still tensing.

Sarah laid her hand on his. He sighed and looked away, and shrugged as if to say, what can you do?

Sarah knew that look. How often had she felt the same? And if she told him what that beast of a Russian had done to her in the basement? Should she? What would he say? What difference would it make? But all she heard herself say, after a long pause, was "And what happened?"

Their eyes met, until Jacob looked away. "What happened was I couldn't look after him anymore. There was one guard, he had it in for Maxie. Made him stand barefoot in the snow all night, always made him carry the heaviest load, whipped his legs when he couldn't stand up, he'd take food from Maxie's plate and throw it into the earth and stamp on it. And can you imagine, when he'd gone, we'd give each other bloody noses for that dirty scrap."

If it hadn't been for Isak, Sarah thought, he would have raped me again, and not only him. He'd wanted to bring more men, that's why he'd brought Isak. What had made her cry out the Hebrew prayer? Shema Yisrael, Adenoi Elohenu, Adenoi Echad—Hear, O Israel, the Lord our God, the Lord is one. Those were all the words she knew. They saved her.

"Do you ever pray?" she asked Jacob.

He laughed. "Yes, that he'll come home."

"What? Who?"

Jacob shook his head. He shouldn't have said that. "Nothing."

He thought, See? I came home. Sarah came home.

Everyone comes home in the end. Unless they're dead. Or if there's no home. Or if it isn't the end.

SIXTEEN

Heidelberg,
May 21, 1945

It was dark when they came home and Jacob read the sheet of paper slipped under the door. "It's for you," he said. They were tired and Sarah's legs ached from their long walk.

After leaving their table, which Jacob now called Lookout Point, Sarah had gone with him to the bus station, where he wanted to sell his pocketful of butts from the castle. They were mostly Pall Mall, Americans loved them and they were the longest. But when they reached the big square that was once Bismarck Square and recently Adolf Hitler Square and was now unclaimed, they saw a tram.

"Hey, it's working again," Jacob said. There seemed to be more people hanging on the outside than sitting inside. "I wonder where it goes."

As luck would have it, the first tram to run in Heidelberg after the war stopped half a kilometer short of Leimersdorf, near Sarah's home.

Jacob elbowed his way up and stood on the back fender. He

pulled up Sarah, who wedged one foot next to his, and hung on to his arm while he held on to the roof's metal lip. She pressed his biceps and mimed: I'm impressed. People crammed against them from both sides. After five minutes they had gone three blocks. "It would have been quicker to walk," Jacob said. The tram took about twenty minutes to cover the five kilometers. Half that time Jacob spent persuading Sarah this was a good idea.

How many times, hiding in a cellar or cooped up in a room for days on end, terrified to show her face, had she daydreamed of going home? Where she had swung from a rope in the trees and helped tend the vegetables and collected the eggs? Their little cottage meant family and freedom, the two things she most missed, most wanted, most treasured. Yet what would she find? Who had stolen their home? Why go? They hate us there.

But Jacob's right. How can I come to Heidelberg and not go home?

The tram stopped when the track ended at a bomb crater.

They walked the last stretch where the brick homes became fewer, the gardens bigger, and the fields closer to the road. A chicken strutted regally before them, as if looking for the red carpet, followed by a chick struggling to keep up.

"I think I recognize that chicken," Sarah said. "I'm sure it was mine."

"Really?" Jacob said.

"No, of course not, city boy." She told Jacob about the policeman and the stolen chickens. She forced a laugh but it was too bitter to work. He nodded and they walked a little closer together. Sarah looked straight ahead. Without Jacob, she thought, she would never have come. She was born in this house but she had nothing here now. What would she say if there was anyone there? Jacob had tried to reassure her. "We have to go—maybe they know something about your family. It's worth a try." Too late to back out now.

She had not been expecting to find many people in her hamlet just outside Leimersdorf; instead, it was crowded, with foreign refugees not permitted to stay in town.

At the end of a lane, Sarah came to a halt. Her eyes fixed on a low house a hundred meters on, one of three by a giant elm tree, with a garden bursting in color. "It's spring, it's always beautiful in spring," she said in a wondering voice. "Most of the year, actually."

"Which is yours?"

"The middle one."

Sarah went silent as a couple approached. The strangers walked by without a glance, but after they passed the man looked over his shoulder at Sarah, who had been studying the woman. Jacob glared at him.

Jacob set off but Sarah stayed him with a hand. He looked back. "Let's go and have a look."

"No. No." Sarah's eyes were red, she seemed about to cry. She shook her head.

"What is it? Are you afraid?"

"I don't know. It isn't that. I saw something . . ." She turned around. "Let's go. I knew I shouldn't have . . ."

"After coming all this way? Go back now? No way. You stay here, then. I'll go and have a look."

Sarah looked after the couple, and turned back to her house as if it would bite. "Wait here," Jacob said.

Jacob walked up to the house and put his hand on the gate. At that moment the front door opened and a stout blond middle-aged woman in an apron walked out with a trowel in her hand. She had a square blunt face and thin lips that spread into a smile. "Hello, can I help you?" she asked. Jacob was taken by surprise and all he could think of was "It's a nice garden you have."

"Thank you. I'm just going to pick some tomatoes. It's a bit early but some of them are ripe. They're delicious. Sweet. Would you like one?"

"What do you want for it?"

"I beg your pardon?"

"What, for nothing?"

"Of course. We have lots." She was talking as she bent down to work in the garden. "I can see you're not from around here, are you?" She turned the earth around some plants. "Don't open the gate, please, we have puppies, they're always running away. I'm just moving this cucumber plant to get more sun . . . it's strong, my best one."

Jacob looked up the lane at Sarah, who was watching, sitting at the foot of a tree.

"I was just wondering," Jacob said. "Do you know Sarah Kaufman?"

The woman was digging a hole for the cucumber and continued for a moment before looking up. "The people who used to live here?"

"Yes."

The woman placed the plant into the hole, patted earth around it, watered it from a pail, stood, put her trowel into her apron pocket, walked into the house, and slammed the door.

Jacob felt his heart race. What a cow. He turned but couldn't leave. He opened the gate and walked up the little path and knocked on the door, gently at first, then sharply, three times. The door opened slightly. "What do you want? We live here now. Go away."

What did he want?

"What about my tomato?"

She pushed the door shut in his face. He banged on it with his fist, trampled her best cucumber plant, and held the gate open until the puppies ran away.

When Jacob described the woman, all Sarah said was: "Frau Schubert. The cleaner."

There was no return tram so they walked home. After fifteen minutes of strained silence, with Leimersdorf well behind them, Sarah said quietly, "Jacob?"

"Yes?"

"You know that couple, the people walking up the lane near my house? When we stopped."

"Yes?

"Remember the woman?"

"No. Why?"

"She was wearing my mother's coat."

When they reached home it was dark. That's when Jacob found the sheet of paper under the door, read the few lines of poor German, and handed it to Sarah. "It's for you."

It was from Captain Monahan, the chaplain. "I came to find you," it read. "I waited thirty minutes. Please come to the church in the morning, I have something important to tell you."

Sarah slept poorly that night, thinking about her family. Wondering what happened to them. Well, that wasn't new. But what about the chaplain? What could he want? Jacob thought it was about a job. Maybe someone needed a maid? An American officer? In a grand house? When she had told the chaplain she was looking for work she hadn't told him that she had studied bookkeeping. She should have, but anyway, that was so long ago, she hardly remembered any of it. She'd liked it, though. She should carry on with it, as soon as she could. Jacob said the U.S. army base was growing by the day, he knew that from the soldiers he guided at the castle. The

Amis had everything, every possible comfort, but what they didn't have were Germans they could trust. Jews should get preference. It was obvious, Jacob said. First, we suffered most, so morally they should help us, and second, at least they know we weren't Nazis.

Yes, it must be about work, they agreed. Or maybe he wants help in something? The Amis had collected tons of clothes, maybe they needed volunteers to distribute them, and as she had already been given clothes, maybe they would want her to help?

What could it be? What was so important that the chaplain himself had come to their room, and even waited half an hour? Maybe he wanted to give her a gold ring? The Nazis had stolen gold wedding rings from the Jews and the Americans had discovered cases of them, thousands of wedding bands, and were giving them to women who had lost theirs. A gold ring? You think? No, Jacob said, the note says he wants to tell you something, not give you something.

Jacob made tea to calm Sarah and she lay back against the wall, sipping from her cup. Soon it began to tilt. Jacob took the cup from her, and she wriggled down with a sigh and closed her eyes, and a few moments later her breathing became gentle and deep and even and finally she was asleep.

Jacob stood staring out the window, looking at nothing, until he found himself following the black shadows of the night clouds moving across the top of the dark building opposite. I wonder what's happening in my house, he thought. I should go visit Dr. Berger. I'm going to make a claim to get it back. It's ours. Or rather, mine. It's stolen property. I'll ask the Americans what to do. So far they think we're all the same: "Germans, all same, all nix gut." But that will change soon.

No sign of the Rat yet. Jacob drained his glass of water. He'll come. Everyone goes home. One day. Where else would you go when the war ends? When the camps shut down. You'll come home. And I'll find you. He had been waiting at Lookout Point for an hour or two every day. Whenever the owners left the hotel he had gone inside and looked it over. Adolf was slow, to put it kindly, and would never remember him. In his ponderous voice he told Jacob that he worked from seven thirty in the morning to six in the evening.

He checked the dining room, the little bar with all the silly hunting trophies, looked at rooms, checked out the bathrooms, which smelled, and all the while an idea was forming, the outline of a plan. What to do when the Rat creeps back to his hole.

As the first light turned the rooftops gray, Jacob eased the blanket up and slipped in next to Sarah, who shifted to make room. He watched Sarah sleeping, the blanket rising and falling, tracing her curves, her bare shoulder by his chin. His thoughts winding down: Lucky she didn't go to her house. One day I'll go back and sort out that woman. He chuckled. Glad I ruined her cucumbers. I hope the puppies got lost. I hope the chaplain has good news, Sarah needs it.

He kissed her hair and fell asleep.

The room was bathed in light when Sarah yawned and rubbed her eyes and remembered. She jumped up, threw water at her face, brushed her teeth, and eased the door shut, not to awaken Jacob. Clutching her coat to her throat, she hurried to the church. In case she would go straight to work somewhere, she wore her good clothes: a burgundy pleated skirt with a white blouse and a double string of what may or may not have been genuine pearls, that Jacob had obtained. Over this, a long gray woolen coat, and a mauve beret. She shrugged off a twinge of guilt at wearing confiscated clothes and bartered jewelry, loot from the defeated. Well, I'd happily wear my own clothes, she told herself, if the newly defeated hadn't stolen them. She still didn't like Jacob's justification, that by exploiting the Germans' misery he was simply correcting the wrongs they had done to him—not that it would ever be possible. She had told him, two wrongs don't make a right.

He had laughed, said no, but it puts food on the table. A lot. He had several hundred dollars already, much of it in tens and twenties, which made it easier to hide.

Sarah stopped outside the church and paused to collect her breath. She adjusted her beret, smoothed down her collar, patted her coat, crossed her fingers, and knocked on the door of the anteroom facing the street. She waited. No answer. She knocked again, and still nothing. She tried the heavy metal door handle. It didn't turn.

Sarah looked around. He isn't here. She had rushed for nothing. She thought, I could have been sleeping right now. Now what? A man carrying a heavy bundle pushed by her. People were setting up stands, opening boxes, placing colorful religious trinkets and bottles of village wine and jars of jam on tables, bustling and shuffling around, and Sarah stood among them, desolate. I'll have to wait, she thought. At that moment a U.S. army jeep drew up, and Captain Monahan stepped out.

The driver backed the jeep under an awning while the chaplain strode toward Sarah, his hand outstretched. "I'm so sorry I'm late," he said, "have you been waiting long?"

"No, not at all, I just arrived," Sarah said. She seemed even slighter than usual next to the bulk of the captain, in his army greatcoat.

"Please come in," he said, unlocking the door and taking off his coat as he spoke. He took Sarah's coat and hung it up.

"Coffee, tea, apple juice?"

"Apple juice?"

"Why, surprised?"

"I used to love apple juice. It's just that I haven't seen any for so long."

"Well, this is your lucky..." He stopped himself. "Here, take as much as you like." He filled a mug and left the carton next to it. "All yours," he said.

Sarah sipped and smiled, and sipped again and then took a long slug. "Mmmmm..."

Captain Monahan shuffled some papers and opened and closed a file as if he were looking for something. His brow was furrowed and he frowned, as if he had mislaid an important document. "Have you lost something?" Sarah asked, looking around.

"No, no, I have everything right here. Would you like some more juice?" He stood to reach for the carton but Sarah said, "That's fine, thank you, that's enough for now."

"Tea? Coffee?"

"No, thank you."

He sat down, inspected his hands, glanced at Sarah, and said, "Thank you for coming."

"That's okay."

"I went to your room yesterday, I was looking for you."

"Yes, I know, I saw your note."

"Yes, yes, of course. Well... there's something I want, something I need, uh, to tell you."

Sarah watched him fidget. It didn't sound like a job.

The chaplain coughed and took some tissues from a drawer. "Sarah, I have received some information from Rabbi Bohmer in Frankfurt that he has asked me to pass on to you. It refers to a report he apparently requested from Berlin." Sarah noticed a difference in his tone. He had always sounded friendly and informal. Now his voice was deeper. He sounded as if he were delivering a sermon.

"He would have liked to have given this news to you in

person, but as he can't be here he asked me to tell you what he has discovered."

Sarah sat stiffly with her hands folded in her lap, holding her beret. She was beginning to get the message. A knot was forming in her stomach. She nodded. Yes?

"Well, it's like this, Sarah." He cleared his throat. "The occupation authorities in Berlin have obtained the police and hospital records for the local districts and the Germans have kept their usual immaculate records. Everything is in perfect order and cross-referenced according to family names, dates, geographical locations, civil reports, crime categories, and, in the case of the hospitals, causes of death."

Sarah squeezed her beret into a ball. Captain Monahan could hear her breathing from across the table. Her chest was heaving, her eyes fixed on his. It was unnerving. He took a deep breath and continued. "Sarah, when Rabbi Bohmer asked our people in Berlin to check the records for your husband, Josef Farber . . ."

"We never really married. We didn't have time."

". . . we found his name, with his age and official address, in a police file that was closed. Now . . . I'm sorry to have to tell you . . . that the file shows that Josef Farber drowned in the Grosser Wannsee lake on . . ."

Sarah threw her head back, her eyes closed, and she gasped in relief. She beamed with a smile that could have lit up the room. "That's it? Let me tell you a story," she began. "Hoppi had a wonderful idea that . . ."

But Captain Monahan silenced her with a wave. He looked grim. "That isn't all." He picked up another sheet of paper.

"The strange thing is," he went on, looking at the second sheet and then up at Sarah, "that seven months later, on June sixteenth, 1942, in the hospital records of the Charité Hospital, Josef Farber, of the same age and address, is shown to have been admitted suffering from severe head and brain trauma and that the same day he succumbed to his injuries. It seems the drowning must have been some kind of mistake, because in the hospital his body was positively identified by two people. It's conclusive, I'm afraid. Josef . . ."

He looked up. Sarah seemed to have shrunk into her chair, she was a crumpled heap. "I'm so sorry," he said, pushing across the box of tissues, but Sarah's eyes were dry. She was staring at the floor, her head moving slowly from side to side as if she couldn't believe it. Instead it was Captain Monahan who needed the tissues. Is there no end to their suffering? he thought. What a sweet and lovely girl. If only he could help her. He wiped his eyes.

Sarah was thinking: So he didn't even go to Auschwitz, thank God he was spared all that. But all the time I was hiding in Berlin, he was there too. I could have visited him, hidden near him. We could have been together. I could have slept by his grave.

She had always known. But now she knew. "Does it say where he is buried?" She couldn't think of anything else to say. She felt all her energy drain from her.

"No. No, it does not. Sarah, I'm so terribly sorry to have to be the bearer of such news."

SEVENTEEN

Heidelberg,
May 22, 1945

When Jacob returned from the castle at midday he found her clothes strewn across the floor and Sarah in bed. The room stank. She had thrown up in the sink and left the mess. "Ugh," he said to himself. "Yech." He opened the window and left the street door open. He took a piece of paper and wiped all the hard bits from the sink, and scrubbed it with more paper. He worked quietly, trying not to wake her.

Couldn't have gone so well with the chaplain, he thought. I was right, it must be news about Joe. Or her family. He'd only talked about possible jobs so that she wouldn't worry. If the chaplain had waited for half an hour he knew it could only have been very good news or very bad news. And there wasn't much chance of good news. He picked up her clothes and hung up the dress, coat, and blouse. He tried to smooth out the creased beret and stuffed some socks in it to give it shape. A tiny voice came from the bed. "Sorry."

He sat next to her and stroked her hair. He waited for her to add something, but she didn't. He cupped her forehead with his hand. "Whoa, you're hot," he said. "I think you have a fever, how do you feel?"

He felt her body tense. "I want to be sick." She rolled to the side and retched over the floor, but nothing came up but spit and bile. She lay back panting, wiping her face with both hands. Jacob held a washing-up rag under the cold water and held it to her forehead and dabbed her cheeks and neck. "I'm sorry, this is all I can find."

"Thank you." A feeble Aaiinnkhuu.

"That's all right. Did you sleep?"

"I tried."

"When did you get back?"

"Don't know. What time is it?"

He looked at his watch. "Three twenty."

"Oh. Head hurts." Eehhuurrrtss.

"Don't talk. Try to sleep."

Sarah slept for the best part of three days. She sat on the toilet with her head leaning against Jacob's chest. Jacob found the chaplain, who brought a doctor who examined her in her groggy state. "There's nothing seriously wrong with her, the fever will come down by itself," the doctor said. "She's just exhausted, that's all. After everything she's been through, the body is just catching up. The more sleep she gets, the better. You must keep her hydrated, though, make her drink lots of water, ten glasses a day at least. The dashing of hope can be debilitating. What about you?" he said to Jacob.

He shrugged. "I feel fine."

"Huh," the doctor said. "After three years in Bergen-Belsen, you feel fine?"

"I didn't have any hope in the first place," Jacob said.

"Hah, that's a good one," the doctor said, "I'll remember that. Well, if you need me, Captain Monahan knows where to find me, I'm never more than an hour away." He glanced at Sarah snoring in the bed. "And don't worry, she's a strong young woman."

"Thank you doctor, and thank you very much, Chaplain. Also for the chocolate. I'll keep it for Sarah."

"I doubt it, from what she told me." They laughed.

Days and nights were as one. Sarah slept curled like a fetus until she would suddenly stretch and moan and throw her hands out as if calling for help. She would lie on her back and abruptly toss herself to the side and mutter, groaning and talking to herself. Jacob made out the odd words: Stop it; come back; Hoppi. Several times she shouted "No!" and her whole body twitched. She slept best when curled on her left side, facing the wall. In that position her breaths were long and even, not short and fast, as if she were panting. Then Jacob would lie next to her on the dank sheet, hugging her from behind, but mostly he slept on the floor wrapped in a sheet.

Whenever he could, and that was when Sarah was at her most restless, he would pull her up and hold a glass of water to her lips. Sometimes she gulped it, other times he had to push the rim between her lips and tilt her head back and pour in the water. Some would dribble down her chest, and he dabbed her dry so that she wouldn't lie in a cold damp pool.

Frau Braunschweig knocked several times a day, bustling in with cleaning rags and advice and twice, until Jacob asked her firmly to desist, with pots of foul thin gruel. She called it meat soup: "Good for you." There was more meat in the soup in Bergen-Belsen. He'd said to her, "I wouldn't like to deprive your family of your food." And she'd said, as he expected, "Oh, it's all right, I made this especially for you."

It was never quite clear to Jacob. Was she concerned about the health of a sick girl or was she worried disease would seep through her walls? She kept her distance from Sarah, looking at her as if assessing a lettuce in the market, standing by the door or walking in a loop to the bathroom to hang up the towels she found on the floor. Once she washed out a couple of rags and commented on the weak water flow. "We'll have more water soon, they said so. Hot water too, the boiler's back up in a day or two. Things are looking up."

On the first day, Sarah had turned a waxy yellow and when she opened her eyes they were dull like stone. Jacob had tried to ask her how she felt, what was wrong, what had happened, and in a few barely lucid moments, that first night before the doctor came, he had been able to exchange some words with her. "Hoppi," she said, as if that was all he needed to know.

It was. He understood that even though she had known he was dead, had lost hope, still, there must have been a ray, a final glimmer, that had not yet been extinguished, like the very last pink rim of the sun before it finally sinks over the horizon.

We all live with delusion, he thought; it is our best weapon of survival. If we don't delude ourselves about ourselves, how can we live with ourselves? In the middle of one night she told him what she knew, as she squeezed his hand, and once said, "Hold me," and he did, even though she was hot and clammy and smelled of musk.

On the second day, he had spent six hours searching and bartering until he found a reasonable set of sheets in a shop. It would have been easier if Frau Braunschweig had given him some but she shook her head, she didn't have any spares.

Jacob gave Sarah weak tea and helped her to the bathroom, where she sat on the toilet, and once, instead of supporting her, he spread her feet on the floor and left her to slump forward with her head on her knees. He stripped the bed of the sodden sheets and threw them into a corner, and as he turned the mattress over, Maxie came to him. He wished he had been able to care for him like this. Maxie was sick most of the time, he became so frail. Yet instead of calling for a doctor they had to hide him from the Rat. And here I am, in my private room, complaining about Frau Braunschweig's meat soup and that it took me six hours to find some sheets. How quickly we get spoiled. In Bergen-Belsen half the people had fever and disease and slept in the dust on the floor, and if they complained they were kicked and beaten. He sighed. Oh, Maxie, I tried to wipe your brow but I didn't have any water.

When Sarah was ready he helped her out of her shirt for the first time, unbuttoned the front and pulled the sleeves from her arms. She sagged forward, uncaring, as he removed her bra and freed her breasts. He wet the old sheet from the tap and in gentle circles wiped her shoulders and back and arms and stomach and, finally, her chest, with the cold wet cloth. Then he helped her into a clean shirt and took off her panties. He wet another part of the sheet and washed her feet and ankles and legs up to her knees. He wet it again and did the same to her thighs as high as he could. Now Jacob helped Sarah to her feet and supporting her with one arm around her waist, with her head lolling against him and her hair across his chest, he spread her legs and slid the damp cloth across her bottom and between her legs and wet it again until she was clean.

She groaned with fatigue as he helped her into a pair of clean knickers, laid her on the clean bed, and covered her with the fresh sheet up to her neck. He sat by her, holding her hand, as she sighed, and within moments she had turned on her side and fallen into a deep sleep. He arranged her hair, each strand a bewitching memory of her silky skin, her helpless womanhood.

Jacob kissed her fingers and let them go. He walked to the window, opened it to smell the night air, and stared out into the street. It was raining and pools of water glinted in the moonlight, raindrops dancing in them. He saw a man's shadow with a ball on top followed instantly by a man in a hat walking by with an umbrella. He was out in the curfew. He must be some kind of official. Jacob leaned out and looked after him. Who is he? What does he want? Where is he coming from and where is he going? A grim smile came to Jacob's lips. Good questions. Who among us knows?

He looked over his shoulder at Sarah, who turned with a groan. Jacob sighed, his thoughts confused.

On the afternoon of the fifth day, Sarah woke to feel Jacob's hand caressing her, his fingers trailing gently from the nape of her back the length of her spine and at the last moment lifting his hand and doing it again. And again, and again. She shivered. Lower . . . please . . . After a few minutes she turned around to see Jacob lying facing her, smiling. Their noses almost touched, and she winked.

"You're back?" Jacob said. "Good afternoon."

Sunlight streamed in at an angle, forming a triangle of glaring light on the whitewashed wall. Sarah raised her hand to protect her eyes and said, "And good afternoon to you, sweet nurse."

Jacob jerked back. "Uffff."

"What?"

"Excuse me, but I think you need to brush your teeth."

Sarah jumped up and fell down again. "Oh, I'm so dizzy."

"You've been out for five days."

"What? Really?"

"Let me check." He placed the inside of his wrist against her forehead and held it for a moment, then nodded in satisfaction. "It's gone. The fever."

Sarah sat up and stood slowly, deliberately, waiting for the floor to stop rising and falling, and walked carefully to the bathroom, where she closed the door and locked it. Jacob walked over and called out through the door, "It's a bit late for modesty, you know," and laughed.

He heard the lock shift and the door opened a crack. "What do you mean?"

"Nothing."

The door closed but there was no locking sound.

He heard the sound of flushing, and running water from a tap, followed by a shriek. He pushed the door open. Sarah was kneeling by the bath in her shirt, holding her hand beneath the tap. "Guess what? It's hot. There's hot water. Can I have a bath?"

"I guess so. Sure, why not? If there's enough water."

Even in the hospital the only hot water was in the operating rooms or brought by the nurses in little pans. "I haven't had a hot bath in years," Sarah said. "Years!"

"So it's all yours."

Jacob closed the door with a tender smile. She's so beautiful, he thought. It was all so fast. She had suddenly fallen sick, slept for nearly a week, and just as suddenly woken up like a bear from hibernation. The doctor was right. A strong young woman. And what a woman. So beautiful in just a shirt. Even better without it. He smiled at the thought of washing her soapy breasts.

And what about me? When was the last time I had a hot bath? he wondered. A real bath, not that torture in the Human Laundry. The face of Hans Seeler intruded for the briefest instant, but he banished the image. My last bath? he thought. It must have been before we were rounded up. In October 1940. That must have been his last hot bath. October 1940. Almost five years ago. But come on. Think of Maxie, and all the others. And I'm whining about a hot bath. I'll never be able to complain about anything for the rest of my life.

He sighed, emptying most of his lungs. He knocked on the door. "Please don't let the water out when you finish. Save the water for me."

"Pardon? I can't hear." The water was running. He opened the door slightly and put his lips to the crack, "Don't let the water out when you finish. I'll have a bath after you."

He felt the door tugged from his hand, revealing Sarah in all her shirtless glory. She tried to raise a coquettish eyebrow like Marlene Dietrich. "I have a better idea," she breathed. "Don't have a bath after me. Have a bath with me."

EIGHTEEN

Heidelberg,
May 26, 1945

Jacob stared at the closed door in disbelief. No. No! What an idiot! Why did he say no? What did he actually say? "Oh, uh, that's all right, you go first." What a cretin! "Oh, uh . . ." And then he'd closed the door.

In her face. She'd never forgive him. That was it, he had had the chance, and he'd blown it. She'll be hurt, insulted, who wouldn't be? She'll think I don't really like her, not in that way, but like a brother. My sister knew your sister. You nincompoop!

Would you like to have a bath with me? Yes. Yes! A thousand times, yes!

Jacob backed away like a supplicant in a Turkish court, never taking his eyes from the shut door, and fell onto the bed.

Get up, you moron. Knock on the door, say you've changed your mind, yes please, actually you would like to share a bath after all. Do it, you cretin! Get up. Take your life in your hands for once. Don't be a victim anymore. She's waiting for you.

She's insulted you didn't jump on her and hug her and kiss her, that's what she wants.

That's what you want.

Oh, so much.

Jacob lay down on the bed and stared at the ceiling. What's wrong with you! Shy? He sighed at the memory of washing Sarah, her surrender in her weakness. The calm thrill of her silky skin, oily with soap. The gentle undulations of her sleek, firm body.

And now, shy? Is that it? You infant.

Or afraid. Of what?

You know what.

In the camp nudity had been so commonplace it had no meaning, no value, it was more a sign of bestiality and cruelty and abuse than anything else. There was no such thing as beauty there, just pathos and pity. There it was better for a girl to hide her beauty, for it would only lead to immediate violent rape. There girls rubbed dirt into their hair and faces, not that they needed to, hunched their shoulders to look flat, walked in feces to smell bad, anything to keep the beasts at bay.

He put his hands behind his head and sighed. The worst feeling was of being so helpless, so useless, so unmanned. But that was then and this is now. If I want one thing right now, he thought, it is to get up and open that door.

Not that it'll do me much good. Or her.

Jacob tensed. His heart sped. He raised himself to one elbow and looked at the bathroom door. It began to open. How? he thought: How do I always sense things?

He heard Sarah say, "Now you listen to me." She was standing naked in the doorway, dripping on the floor. His eyes popped. She had his full attention. "I have considered the matter, and I must make the following demand. You will take your clothes off and you will get into the bath with me. Now.

Come along immediately. Be a good little boy." With that she turned around, slowly, leaving the door wide open. She raised her leg onto the top of the bath, wiggled her bottom, and slipped into the water.

If Jacob was indeed a little boy he'd have burst into tears. He certainly felt like it. A flood of warmth and gratitude surged within and a smile took over his entire face.

It was a big bath and there wasn't much water. It barely covered their thighs as they faced each other. But Jacob's smile was so wide and his eyes so bright that Sarah couldn't help laughing. He looked like a mischievous child caught by the teacher. She scooped up water and dribbled it down Jacob's chest, and he did the same over her breasts. When she giggled, Jacob did too, in a stuttering sort of way, as if remembering how, and soon they were fairly helpless with laughter. Jacob was gasping, Sarah laughing and coughing at the same time, so that Jacob put his arms around her to smack her back and they rubbed noses. The water rocked back and forth in waves. They held hands as they laughed and finally were able to sputter to a stop and lay back, spent, smiling contentedly at each other, their knees up, their legs hooked around each other.

Now Sarah leaned forward and scooped more water onto Jacob's chest and rubbed soap on him and onto her hands and washed and stroked his shoulders and his chest as he lay back with closed eyes and purred.

So, he thought. Dreams do come true.

Then she turned around, leaned back against him, and took his hand and placed it on her belly. He encircled her with his arms and soaped her stomach and thighs gently for a long time with bubbles oozing between his fingers, and then he soaped her breasts for an even longer time. The only sound was their breathing, as the water cooled.

Until, her back against his chest, his legs wrapped around

hers, hugging her, his head resting on her shoulder, he felt her tremble and thought she must be getting cold. He felt her breathing become short and fast. Her shoulders rose and fell, and her head flopped forward and she sat up, away from him, and he understood she was crying.

She wept without a sound. Jacob tried to pull her back but she shrugged him off. Her hair was wet, clinging to her long neck, and her skin was red where she had lain against him for so long. He put his hands on her waist and said, "What is it? Sarah? Shall we get out?"

She took his hands and pushed them from her body. As she stood and he absorbed her long lines and curves, and she stepped out of the bath and took a towel and dried herself, and went into the room, where she pulled on a shirt, Jacob thought how little he knew of her. Sarah had told him what happened to her, where she was from, about Hoppi and the baby, but she had never said a word about how she felt. Or any of the details of her war. Just the hard outline. Like a picture frame without a picture. On the other hand, he thought, neither had he. He hadn't told her anything. Nothing at all.

He dried himself, feeling sad, looking at Sarah in bed.

A moment after he lay down next to her, both lying on their backs, Sarah said, "I'm sorry."

"For what?"

"You know. For crying like that."

"Don't be sorry, please. I understand." And he thought he did. She was crying for Hoppi. She had only just heard that he was dead, she had fallen sick in her pain, and now she was weakened, and he had taken advantage of her. She depended on him, she had nowhere to go, she had been sick, and he had . . .

"No, it's me who should say sorry," he whispered.

"Why?"

"You know. Well . . ."

"What?"

"Well, Hoppi . . ."

She turned onto her side, away from him. "I've tried so hard not to cry," she said. "It's been so hard. So alone . . . for so long . . . I'm sorry . . ." Sarah wept and sobbed her heart out, and the sheet was wet around her. Jacob held her to him and stroked her and didn't know what else to do or say. He held her until she had no more tears and her panting became heavy breathing and she seemed to have fallen asleep in his arms.

Not that Jacob didn't have his own tears. He had wanted to whisper to Sarah, to soothe her, to tell her not to worry anymore, that things were different now, that he would look after her, that he loved her, but how could he say any of that? How could he know what would be? He didn't know anything about the future, how could he promise her anything? They were caught in a maelstrom. Yes, they had survived. But for what? And above all, why?

Why live? And why them and not Maxie or their sisters or their parents or anyone else? Why were they, of all people, still alive?

What did they do to us? And why did they do it?

Jacob felt his eyes warm and stinging. He tried not to cry, he did his best, hugging Sarah, beneath the blanket, in their tiny cocoon of warmth and safety, and in his gratitude for this moment, this precious person in his arms, this lovely girl who was so lost and alone and in such pain . . . Jacob felt tears course down his cheeks. He felt so sorry for her, and for himself.

Now that he finally had someone, he had never felt so alone.

Sarah gently disentangled herself and wriggled around to face him. "You're crying," she said, putting a finger to his eye in wonder and tracing a tear to the corner of his mouth.

"No, I'm not," he said.

"Yes, you are. You are. You're crying."

"Course I'm not," Jacob said. "I can't be. I'm a man."

"Come here," she murmured, and she put her hand behind his head and gently brought him to her, and as it wasn't far their lips soon met. It was a sweet and gentle kiss, their very first.

It was sweet but it didn't stay gentle for very long. Urgency crept into their embrace and they pressed against each other and they caressed each other, they murmured and sighed and moaned. Jacob pulled off Sarah's shirt as she pulled off Jacob's shorts. Now they held each other's naked body and kissed and touched each other. Sarah sighed. "I want you." She took him in her hand and he kissed her and pulled away and rolled his tongue around her stomach and lower, until she took him in her hand again and said, "Jacob, now, I want you now."

Jacob pulled away, tried to go down on her again, but she pulled him up, kissing him. "Jacob, please, now . . ."

Jacob rolled onto his back and covered his face with the pillow.

"Jacob, Jacob, what is it?"

He groaned, in pain, in embarrassment.

"What is it? What's wrong?"

Another groan until he almost shouted: "I'm sorry. I'm no good. I can't."

Sarah was breathless, her breasts heaving. "What do you mean?"

"I mean I can't, that's what. I want to, but I can't. It won't work."

She fondled him in her hand. He said, "I can't remember the last time I could." He hated himself. He felt like half a man.

They held each other quietly. "It doesn't matter," Sarah said.

"Of course it does."

"It doesn't. It really doesn't."

"It does, it really does. But thank you."

Jacob tried to touch her but hardly knew how. It had been so long and he had never really known anyway. And Sarah kept pushing him away. "Let me hold you," she said, "it's what I want, it really is."

So they hugged, and talked, and made sandwiches and tea, and talked all the time until they fell asleep at night. Sarah told Jacob about Hoppi and the baby and the cemetery and she cried as he held her, and she laughed at the strange hiding places they had found and the suicide trick. And the Jewish Russian officer who had helped her. But she didn't say how she had met him and Jacob didn't ask. If he had, what would she say? That he had saved her from an animal who had punched her, kicked her, almost pulled her hair out by the roots, burrowed and bashed around inside her like a demented ferret in a tunnel until she had blacked out and woken to find herself alone in the dark and bleeding from every orifice, barely able to move a limb? Crumpled in the dirt like a used rag?

She could never tell him that. She could never tell anyone.

As for Jacob, as if to make up for his failure of the flesh, the words poured out, at last. The camp, his brother, the Rat, everything that tried to, and nearly did, but in the end, didn't, destroy him.

He told her everything, except for what mattered most: that after the Rat killed Maxie it was only Jacob's oath, the final words that Maxie ever heard, his oath of revenge, that had given meaning to Jacob's inexplicable survival. Had Maxie understood, with his last breath? Yes. He knew from the shine in Maxie's eyes as his spirit fled his corpse. Jacob was sure: Maxie died crying for revenge.

NINETEEN

It wasn't clear to Yonni because it happened so fast, but he thought it was an elderly man, with a cap on his head. Ari said it was an officer in uniform. Omri didn't see because he was asleep in the front passenger seat when the sudden swerve threw him against the door and the impact made him shout out. He thought a bullet had hit the jeep.

It took Yonni a moment to register what Ari had done. He jerked around in the backseat just in time to see the bicycle smash into a tree and the rider and one wheel crash down the slope into the bushes.

"Stop!" he yelled. Ari pulled his eyes from the mirror to the road ahead and accelerated into a long bend. Coming out of it, he pulled out sharply to avoid a tractor, and floored it again, his knuckles white on the wheel.

Omri, thrown first to the right and then to the left, shouted, "What the hell's going on? Slow down!"

"This maniac just killed someone, that's what," Yonni

shouted. "What the fuck are you doing? We gotta go back. Why did you do that? You did that on purpose!"

Ari glared ahead, trying to control his breathing. He felt his heart would explode. "Slow down, for God's sake," Yonni shouted, "you'll kill us, too." He banged Ari on the shoulder. "What's wrong with you?"

Ari was thinking, That was crazy. Not that he had killed the cyclist—he hoped he had. Fucking Nazi. No, what was crazy was how close he came to killing them all. He hadn't thought. He saw the guy, the empty road, and just did it. Lucky he just caught his leg. If he had been a little more to the left, just a little bit and caught him head on, a matter of twenty centimeters, the man wouldn't have gone shooting off to the side, he'd have shot straight through the window, bike and all.

Next time, think first.

With Yonni yelling and Omri rubbing his head where it had hit the door, Ari raced along the straight, narrow road. He saw a clearing ahead and pulled into it, a semicircular road stop lined by trees. He got out and walked round to inspect the left fender that hit the cyclist. As he suspected, there was hardly a mark, only the slightest dent, and you had to be looking for it. He must have hit the cyclist on his knee, maybe caught the handlebar. Perfect, actually. Lucky, but perfect.

"Five minutes' break," he said, unbuttoning his pants and stopping by a bush.

"I can't believe you did that, why did you?" Yonni said, holding the handle of the pot on the gas fire, so that it wouldn't topple over. He changed hands and blew on them as the tin became too hot to hold.

"Just did it," Ari said. "Why, do I need a reason? They're all the same."

"Did they need a reason for what they did to us?" Omri said.

"That's ridiculous," Yonni said. "How many can you kill? And what good does it do?"

"It does me a lot of good, I can tell you that," Omri said.

"What would you do, nothing?" Ari said.

Yonni poured boiling water over the coffee and mixed in sugar and handed around the cups. "I'd rather save Jews than kill Germans," he said. "I'd rather build a town in Palestine than destroy a town here."

"Noble you," said Omri.

"Yes, exactly," Yonni said. "This is my last job. I want to help with the Bricha." The Jewish Brigade had been smuggling thousands of survivors across Europe to Italian ports and loading them onto hired boats to break the British naval blockade of Palestine.

"That's our future," he said. "This is our past. We're fighting yesterday's war."

"Yesterday's war. You're so good at phrases, but they're empty. You're an idiot if you think the Nazis are done killing us," Ari said. "And it isn't only them. What we're doing here is showing the Arabs what will happen to them if they mess with us in Palestine."

"Oh, smart. So why are we keeping it so secret then?"

"They'll get the message, trust me."

"Okay, children," Omri said. "Let's focus on what's here and now. What's next. What's the plan, Ari?"

Omri and Ari hugged the walls in the darkness, their faces blackened with charcoal. The sliver of moon faded their weak shadows into the gray street. Their steps were slow and silent, muffled by cloth tied around their boots. No guns, just knives. In the center of Stuttgart's poorest neighborhood, on Karl Blucher's home territory, any screwup and there would be nowhere to run. They had to be fast, silent, deadly.

They didn't like to do it this way. They were too committed, there was no way to talk their way out if caught. But Blucher, Untersturmführer in the 5th SS Panzer Division Wiking, was too juicy a target. Only two months earlier he was still murdering Jews any chance he got, before he made his own run for it. His specialty was to form his men into a gauntlet, make Jews run through their clubs and rocks, and if they made it, beaten and bloody, bury them alive in the forest, just for the fun of it.

The Americans knew he had come home but didn't act. So the Avengers would.

A hundred meters behind Ari and Omri, Yonni followed in the jeep, without lights and engine off, gliding down the hill. No Allied vehicles ever entered this side of town, so their jeep would ring immediate alarm bells. It was a gentle slope and Yonni used the brakes to keep his distance. He saw their shadows stop moving, and stopped too.

Their plan was so simple it was barely a plan. When Blucher left his drinking club to walk home, Ari and Omri would emerge from the shadows, subdue him, and kidnap him. If it was easy, Yonni would glide up quietly. If there was any doubt at all, they would knife him on the spot. If there was trouble, Yonni would switch the engine on and roar up fast. Yonni wasn't happy with the plan; his nightmare was always that just when he needed it, the engine wouldn't start.

Even though the Germans here ignored the curfew, and there were no occupation troops to enforce it, they hoped there wouldn't be many people around, and that those who were would ignore the jeep. If worse came to worst, Yonni had an automatic weapon on his lap, two pistols on the passenger seat, and two hand grenades between his legs. If the cavalry had to come over the hill, it would blow up the mountain.

They couldn't wait long though. Every extra moment was

an added risk. One yell and the street would be swarming with hard guys.

They'd been told Blucher would leave at eleven p.m. sharp, alone. He would be easy to recognize, Blue, the British Intelligence officer, had told them, handing them three photos. Blucher was exceptionally short and very broad, with a red face and shaved head, and never wore a hat. Blue had said: "Think of an angry boiled potato."

Ari and Omri each gripped ten-inch commando knives. When they left the doorway and started walking, Yonni would release the jeep's brake and glide after them, slowly catching up.

"That's the plan?" Yonni had said.

"That, plus God is on our side," Ari had answered.

"He better be," Yonni said. Nothing works every time. It's the law of averages. "Not so sure about this one," he added.

And he was right.

Because Blucher did not come out at eleven. He came out at ten of, before they were psyched up. He did not come out alone, he came out with two other men. And just as they began to walk the thirty meters to where Omri and Ari hid in the dark, just when Yonni was supposed to release the handbrake and let gravity do its work, another man stopped by the jeep and looked inside. "Who are you?" he said. At least Yonni presumed that was what he said, because he didn't speak a word of German. Yonni was focused on the dark shapes of Ari and Omri. They hadn't moved. What are they going to do? He knew it was a shitty plan. Will they wait and take all three? Or just let them walk by? Call it off?

Yonni thought, I shouldn't have left the flap up. But he had to in case Ari and Omri called him for some reason. Anyway, it was too late now because the guy was leaning forward and had put his elbow in the window and said something else in German, something different. Yonni couldn't risk any sound in case it warned Blucher and blew the kill.

Yonni smiled at the man and gestured that he wanted to open the door. He turned his shoulders to hide the two pistols on the passenger seat, and as he told the story later, it was only then, as he tried to hide the pistols, that he remembered he had a semimachine gun on his lap. He put his index finger to his lips and took the gun and pointed it into the man's face. He told the man to turn around by spinning his finger. He stepped out of the car, and it was while he was knocking the man on the head with his gun, and catching him and lowering him quietly to the ground, that all hell broke loose down the street, and he had to drop the guy, jump back into the jeep, start the engine, and put his foot down, and that was why he was slow to reach his friends.

The cavalry was late over the hill, but it did make one hell of a mess.

Ari and Omri let the three men approach, closer and closer. The odds had changed but they nodded to each other: Let's do it. No way Blucher would live. Ari made a stabbing sign. Omri nodded. He understood. No time for a speech. Just do the job. Blucher was on the inside, closest to the wall. They'd been trained for this. Both of them would go for the kill. The other two men would be so surprised they wouldn't be a problem. They would either run or, if they stood and fought, they would be so shocked they'd have no chance.

Speed and aggression.

Ten meters away. Five. One.

The two killers stepped into the light and both uppercut Blucher in the heart. Karl Blucher was dead before he hit the ground. As the other two men froze in shock, Ari pulled out his knife and swung around. Where was the jeep? In that moment two more men left the club and saw a man on the ground. One of the men by Blucher shouted, and the two men at the club shouted back and within moments a swarm of men appeared at the club's steps and next were in the street, lit up by a lamppost, running toward Ari and Omri, whose knives were out and dripping red. Blucher's blood pumped into the gutter. His leg twitched, catching Ari in the shin. The man who had shouted first backed away, still yelling for help. The first man from the club had a pistol in his hand, and now he was fifteen meters away. Uncertain, he slowed to a walk.

"Yonni," Omri yelled. They couldn't run to Yonni, they'd get shot in the back. The only way was forward. Attack. Omri grabbed the shoulders of the first man who was so shocked he hadn't moved, and ran him toward the man with the gun, using him as a shield.

The second man ran away, leaving Ari alone by Blucher's body, screaming for Yonni. He heard a roar as the jeep shot forward. But Omri was alone, meters from the crowd. There was a gunshot, and another. Ari saw Omri stagger and shouted, "Omri!" There was a shout in Hebrew from Yonni, "Get down! Get down!" followed by an explosion, a ball of flame, a rush of air, yells, screams, and rapid fire from an automatic weapon. The jeep drove straight into the crowd and Omri jumped in, as Yonni sprayed the street with gunfire and hit the brake, waiting for Ari to run up. The engine roared as Yonni flattened the pedal and raced away with Ari hanging on to the back fender. Three hundred meters away, Yonni jammed on the brakes and Ari fell through the door Omri had opened from inside. Yonni turned at the next right and then right again and drove slowly, not to draw any attention.

"Everyone okay?" Ari said.

"Yes," said Omri.

"Yes," said Yonni.

They continued in silence through the streets, Yonni following a map that he had memorized, until a U.S. army foot patrol appeared from nowhere, blocking the street. Yonni braked hard and swung to the side, coming to a halt by two doughboys on their knees aiming their automatic rifles at them.

"Where you boys heading? Where are you coming from? Papers," an officer said.

Ari leaned out of the window. "Good evening, sir. British army." He handed him a sheet of paper with their orders. "Heading to U.S. Sixth Army HQ."

"ID."

They handed them over. The Americans made a note of their service numbers and waved them on. "Be careful," the American said. "There's been some shooting."

At the edge of town they stopped by the side of the road.

"So, Yonni," Ari said at last. "Where the fuck were you?"

Yonni told him. He couldn't risk the guy making a sound.

Ari listened, his lips tight. Omri said, "That's fair enough."

"Of course it is," Yonni said. "What do you think I was doing, picking my nose?"

Ari said, "That was very, very bad."

Omri said, "Was that one or two grenades?"

"One."

Omri sighed. "I thought I'd had it. The guy shot my guy twice. I couldn't hold him up. One, two more seconds, I'd have been toast."

"We better get out of town fast," Ari said, putting a water canteen to his lips. He half drained it and passed it to Yonni. "They got a hand grenade, dead and wounded. As soon as they work out it's a British grenade, and who the target was, they'll know who did it. The false IDs will slow them down, but not for long."

"Well, we got him," Omri said. "That's what counts. Bastard."

"And they nearly got you. Great plan, Ari," Yonni said, releasing the hand brake and driving off. "Maybe you should stick to knocking old men off their bikes."

TWENTY

Heidelberg,
May 30, 1945

A single ray of sun pierced the grayness and lit up a clump of weeds struggling through the marble cracks on the synagogue corner of Lauerstrasse and Grosse Mantelgasse.

In her village, little Sarah had been spared the terrified screams and the pounding of boots and the triumphant yelling of Kristallnacht, that November night in 1938 when the Nazis beat the Jews, set alight every Jewish house of prayer in Germany, and burned their holy books. Yet before the ashes cooled every villager knew: It was over for the Jews.

Now seven years older, she perched, legs crossed, on a pile of bricks and debris stacked in a corner of the smashed marble synagogue floor, studying the sun-washed weeds. She was thinking: This is all that's left, a gap among the houses, like a missing tooth. All that's left of Jewish life here are these weeds. And in all the grayness, the sun shines only upon them.

Those weeds are Jacob and me, she was thinking, not the weeds the Nazis saw, to be torn out by the roots, but two shoots of grass growing together, seeking the sun through the cracks. Jacob. A smile came to her lips and a tear to her eye. Hoppi. There was nothing left of Hoppi, not even a photograph. He was gone, destroyed, like the synagogue. One day there will be a new house of prayer. But a new Hoppi? More tears came, of frustration, because she could hardly see him, she could not fix his face, just a blur of shifting lines, watery eyes, a soft mouth, adrift, washing up against the banks of her memory, and out again to sea. She had always known he was gone, as soon as Wilhelm Gruber saw him dragged away and beaten. He would have resisted, struggled, they would have kept beating him, she had known that he was dead for years. Yet now she knew he had been spared the worst. Maybe that was why she accepted it so calmly? Knowing that somewhere he was buried peacefully in the ground and had not suffered for years in a camp after all. But it was also why her return to Heidelberg had meant so little to her. It was as much an escape from the terror of Berlin as a return to the emptiness of Heidelberg. She had come, with no hope, to keep a promise that offered none. But then, where else would she go?

Not to her own village, though everything was familiar, the trees, the river, the neighbors; but was it home? How long had they dreamed of home only to find there was no such place.

Until . . . Sarah closed her eyes and was filled with warmth. She could feel a wave of affection and love wash through her, like hot sun caressing her bare skin. For now they had their little room. And even hot water in the bath. And their soft bed. They were creating their own little home, together, their cocoon of love.

She smiled at Jacob's embarrassment. He had been so sweet. So upset that he couldn't satisfy her. If only he could understand how much it meant just to hold him and stroke him and to be stroked. She, who had shared not an instant of affection for three years. And now with Jacob, who didn't remember when he had kissed someone, or been kissed.

She had held him and stroked his face and kissed his nipples and he kissed hers, for hours. They had fallen asleep in each other's arms and when she awoke in the middle of the night they were still hugging. She felt his heat and smelled his maleness and she fell asleep again, and in the morning his arms still held her and their legs were intertwined.

They had spent that whole day in bed and at every failure Jacob had become angry and bitter, and Sarah had told him again and again that it didn't matter, that she loved him, that it would be all right, that there was no hurry, and he had cursed and hidden his head and struck the bed, as if it should pay for his pain, as if beating the bed would make him a man.

They had walked along the river and held hands like a dozen other young couples that evening who didn't need to speak, and as they had kissed, a tug pulling a barge full of Amis had glided by. They had cheered and applauded the passionate couple, and Jacob had called back and laughed, and Sarah had curtsied and blown them a kiss, which won them another roar of approval.

They had laughed and stopped for a glass of beer, which they shared, and a pale stringy sausage, which Sarah refused to touch, even after Jacob coated it with ersatz mustard. "What's in it? It could be anything."

"I happen to like cow's toenails," Jacob had said.

"With eyelids?"

"My favorite."

It was early the third morning that Sarah woke to feel the sweetness of Jacob's lips on hers. He supported himself on one elbow and with his other hand was combing her hair from her mouth, as he gazed into her eyes in wonder. Pale shadows moved on the wall and shaded Jacob's face, which he buried in the crook of Sarah's neck. His rapid breathing tickled her and now at last she could feel him against her, growing, probing, slowly, carefully, opening her legs with his. He put his lips to her ear and whispered, "I love you, I love you," as he pushed gently, at the edge of her, around, seeking, and she said, "I love you, too," and bit his throat and with her hand felt him, a miracle, and guided him into her, deep inside her, at last.

Jacob's tears wet her cheeks as he held her so tightly she had to wriggle free. She pushed up against him, with him, arching her back until his cry at the end was from his very soul.

"This is how I want to wake up every day, please," Sarah said minutes later, as Jacob entered her again. And the next time he did it she said, "Afternoons, too."

That third day in bed was a day of wonder for them both, as if they were wiping from their bodies' memory the fear and loneliness that had consumed them both for so long. They emerged from deep holes. They made love with gratitude, they said thank you with their bodies. They could have been bones in the ground or ashes in the wind instead of lovers in bed, and they didn't need to speak a word of it for they were never alone in the room but were accompanied by the spirits of all their loved ones who were gone, and they knew they were blessed by their approval. The spirits smiled upon their passion.

"What is that actually on your face?" Sarah said. "Would you call that a smile? A smirk? A leer? My goodness, you do look smug."

"All of those. And with good reason." Jacob pulled back the sheet and looked at himself in wonder. "I mean, look. I thought I had lost it forever. Now it won't go away."

Sarah laughed at Jacob's pride until a cold shiver shot through her. She closed her eyes and turned away. Her body went stiff. Hoppi had come to her. He did that sometimes. She had whole conversations with him, as if he were an invisible presence walking in the street with her, and she described to him what she saw and how she felt. He comforted her, but not this time. Now he was looking at her looking at Jacob's nakedness. There was no expression on his face. He didn't look angry, or hurt, or happy for her, or anything. Just his face, immobile, looking at her. Was he judging her? It isn't fair, stop it! She felt like crying. An eternity, an infinity suddenly separated her from Jacob. She moved away. And then Viktor's ugly face. The big brute, the disgusting animal, standing above her, laughing, and just as suddenly Viktor vanished, and Hoppi slowly faded away, leaving Sarah on her side, and she heard Jacob say, "Sarah, Sarah, what is it, are you all right? I was only joking. Please, come back here." And he had moved to her and held her, and at first she wanted to push him away but slowly she came back and whispered, so softly that he had to put his ear to her mouth. "Just hold me, Jacob, please, just hold me quietly," and he did, and in this manner they took their breaths together, feeling their chests rise and fall, until sleep took them both.

She awoke in darkness and felt Jacob beside her and pressing against her, and Sarah turned and took him in her hands and kissed and licked him. He stroked her head in his lap and sighed and moaned until he fell back and pulled her up onto him. With a shrug of her hips he was inside her and again they rolled and shifted and thrust as one and caressed each other into a frenzy, and again the spirits smiled upon them. They were never alone in that room, it was more than the joining of two lovers, of all their sinews and nerves and energies, it was the union of past and present and future, of all their memories and hopes and dreams, of all the good and the bad and the evil, all held in a tender ball of perfect love.

"Ouch!" Sarah had banged her head on the wall. Jacob

pulled her down the bed and turned her around. He bit and licked the back of her ears and neck, pulled her to her knees, and spread them. And so it went, till they fell asleep again, taking in deep breaths of each other.

The next morning, the fourth in bed, Jacob wanted to go for a walk. "You must be joking," Sarah said, holding herself between the legs. "I don't think I'll ever walk again."

"I'm starving, come on, I'll walk slowly, let's get something to eat."

For four days they had lived on cheese and egg sandwiches and apples.

"No, don't go yet. Later. Come back to bed. Let's sleep a little."

Jacob smiled at Sarah, who was lying on her back under the blanket with her legs pulled up and wide apart, her knees like tent poles. Her hair flowed across the pillow; she had one hand under the blanket and her other thrown back. He sat down and tickled her under the arm. She jerked away.

Suddenly he felt sad. "Thank you," he said.

"Thank you? For what?"

"You know?"

"Ah, of course. For being such an amazing lover."

"That, too. But you know. Thank you. For being here with me, I suppose. For saving my life. For walking through the door of a complete stranger."

"I didn't have anywhere else to go."

"Well, you can make it sound a bit more romantic than that."

"Actually, if you have to know, I knew where you lived. I followed you. I had seen you and found you the most attractive man I had ever laid eyes on and knew, just knew, that I wanted to spend the rest of my life with you, and only you." Jacob's jaw dropped, he listened with wide eyes. "I knew it as soon as I saw you walking across the square outside the church. So I followed you home. I didn't have the courage to knock on the door so I waited on the other side of the street and when I saw you go out, and that you had left the door open, I came in and waited for you. I was in love with you from the first moment I saw you."

"Really?"

"No."

"You silly!" Jacob said, and fell across her and kissed her and pulled back the blanket to see her naked body, but Sarah pulled the blanket over herself and said, "No, really, not again, I can't, not yet, please, later . . . go for your walk already!"

After two hours and Jacob had still not returned Sarah began to imagine every possible accident that could have befallen him. She was sure he had been beaten by a mob of Nazis. Or slipped into the river. Could he swim? She didn't know. Could a car have hit him? Was he in the hospital? Should she go there? She had an image so clear it was as if it was happening right now, of Hoppi waving from the door. Why hadn't she stopped him? Oh, why? Jacob had waved too, a cheerful goodbye, a mirror image of Hoppi. She shouldn't have let him go. Where was he? What was he doing?

Sarah couldn't bear it, she had to go out too. She washed and dressed and walked to the remains of the synagogue. She had never been there before it was burned down; her parents were about as religious as their goat. The only time she really felt Jewish was when she was cursed and threatened for being a Jew. And now that all the other Jews were dead, as far as she knew, the carcass of the synagogue held some kind of attraction for her. She just sat, and brooded anxiously, like a hen with no chicks.

Jacob had claimed he needed some fresh air but the truth

was that Lookout Point was calling. He shouldn't have missed a day, let alone four, it was a risk. The Rat might come back for good or he might come back just for a day or two. It never occurred to Jacob that he wouldn't return at all. Yet as he walked to his table in the café near the Schwartzer Bock hotel, he wasn't thinking of the Rat but of Sarah.

He walked past the shops of Hauptstrasse and American soldiers by their jeeps and knots of Germans chatting on the benches without looking for a single cigarette butt or noticing any bartering opportunity. He was in a daze, floating on four days of pure fantasy. Part of him thought, If only there was somebody I could tell! Before Sarah there had been a couple of girls, briefly, in his teens; he'd been a late starter, an amateur. But what could he do? Tell who? Go to his old home and knock on the door and say to Schmutzig: "Schmutzig, in a hundred years you'd never guess what I've been doing for four days straight." And with such a beauty.

And what if Frau Berger answered the door? Would she notice something? Flushed skin? Sparkling eyes? His stupid grin? A couple walked by and looked at him. Do I look different? Can they tell? Do they know? Is it so obvious that I'm in love?

How can life change so suddenly? He could still feel Sarah's skin, her touch, her wetness, he could taste her . . . "Oh, sorry!" he said as he walked into an old man with a cane. And the way she opened up to him, so easily and freely and yes, to be honest, almost desperately. But not as desperately as he. Their very desperation meant they couldn't stop. Who knew when it would end? When they would be taken from each other? They made love as if there were no tomorrow, because they didn't know anything else.

To have nothing, nothing at all, and then have so much, within moments, it didn't seem possible that life could hold such pleasure and such surprises. On the other hand, he knew what evil it held, what horror, oh yes, this he knew in intimate detail, and yet, even that seemed to be fading. Not Maxie, never, but the cold, the hunger, the desperate thirst, the pain, the sickness, the stink, the fear, the mindless bullying, the endless itching and scratching, the hunting for any scrap of food, for any advantage over the others, for the slightest favor from the guard, anything that would give life the slimmest edge over death. This he knew well. In this he was an expert, no amateur, he was a doctor, a professor.

He waited on the corner of Hauptstrasse and the orphan square that had been Adolf Hitler Square. A convoy of American trucks blocked the road and only when the military policeman blew his whistle could the pedestrians cross. Jacob was jostled and nearly tripped but passed over into Bergheimerstrasse. He was thinking of the tingling of his skin and Sarah. How she had brought him to life. Just the thought of her made him have to put his hand in his pocket and rearrange his pants. He had hardly thought of loving a girl for years, or even thought himself capable of fulfilling his role as a man. Everything was too dirty, too evil, he was surrounded by too many sick and dying people. Other inmates had thought of little else, and found ways to meet up with female prisoners, but not him. He just couldn't.

He smiled as he turned into Kirchstrasse, and an elderly woman walking past him smiled back. Jacob was thinking of Sarah lying on her side and him pressed against her from behind, stroking her. He shivered as he remembered the surprise of her softness among her firm lines, her silky roundness, and the straining hardness of her nipples. It irritated her if he played with them too much, and she had pushed her bottom back into him, which had instantly turned him harder than her nipples. When she turned to touch him there he had said, "It doesn't irritate me at all."

He smiled as he pulled out his usual chair at Lookout Point. Sarah had kissed each toe and every centimeter of him, as if worshipping him, and he had done the same to her, only with his tongue, licking and lapping at her skin until she had told him, begged him, to stop, it was too ticklish. He grinned as he remembered where he had been when she cried, "Please, no more," and then, "Please, no," until she was moaning, "Please."

That's him!

Every nerve in his body screamed, every hair sprung up, every sinew and muscle went taut as steel.

He sat stiff in his chair. That was him. He just went in. That was the Rat. He only saw his back and he wore a hat over his ears. But no mistake. Jacob's heart thumped, he could feel himself flushing.

"Are you all right, sir?" the waiter asked, bending near Jacob with a tray of drinks balanced on his open palm. Jacob nodded.

"Can I get you something?"

"Coffee."

"Yes, sir. Something to eat? A sandwich? A salad? We have cucumbers today."

"No."

"Very well."

Jacob never took his eyes from the door. He thought his heart would explode. Was that the Rat? He was sure it was. But was it? He hadn't seen his face. He put two fingers on his wrist to time his pulse but stopped counting after five seconds. He could hardly count that fast. That's strange, he thought, why did I do that? Yes, for sure, it was the Rat. He's come home. Jacob knew he would. Everyone does. Eventually.

PART TWO

TWENTY-ONE

Heidelberg,
May 31, 1945

The next morning, Sarah murmured, "Jacob? Jacob?" Feeling for him, she turned and her arm fell across his side of the bed onto the sheet. "Sweetie? Where are you?" A shiver ran through her . . . Is he gone? Will he come back? Did they take him? . . . and she jerked awake. It was the terror, always there, barely suppressed, of losing everything, everyone, in an instant. "Here, darling," he said. He was sitting on the bed, dressed and putting on his shoes.

She felt herself sink into the sheet in relief. "Sweetie? What are you doing? Come back to bed. Don't be silly."

"No, don't worry, I've got to go somewhere."

"Come back. Look." She edged back the sheet to reveal her bottom. "Stroke me."

"No, really, I'll be back later on."

"You aren't still sulking, are you?"

"No, of course not."

A faint smile came to Sarah's lips as she drifted back to

sleep. It really didn't matter if he couldn't do it. Four days was enough anyway, she had waddled to the synagogue like a duck and when she came home again needed a cold compress between her legs. "Come back soon," she managed to say. Behind her eyelids an outline formed and faded. Oh . . . Hoppi, I know you don't mind, I know you're happy for me. Hoppi came back and smiled and nodded and stretched out his arm; Hoppi, I love Jacob now; I'm so lucky; I was so . . . unnecessary. And now, I'm so needed. I need him and he needs me. Oh, how lucky we are. She sighed as she drifted and thought of Jacob, her lover, her friend, oh, Jacob . . . She was almost fast asleep when she heard the door close. "What time is it anyway?" she heard herself whisper from a faraway place.

Jacob reached Adolf's apartment building at seven in the morning, expecting him to leave for work around seven fifteen.

He walked in fast circles to keep warm, keeping the entrance to Adolf's house in sight, thinking of Sarah. Last night his body had failed him again. Each time he felt close, the Rat intruded. Was it really him? He'd only seen his back, he could easily be wrong. But he had that feeling, he just knew it was him. Maybe he had come for one night, and he'd be gone, on the run, never to be seen again? But then, where would he run to? No, if it's him, he'll stay at home and lie about being in the SS.

He had tossed and turned and squirmed, and when Sarah had wanted him again, he couldn't get Maxie off his mind. His face, all that blood, the squashed nose and the dent in his skull. Even now, Jacob wanted to puke.

At seven fifteen, as he expected, Adolf came out, dressed in the same coat and hat, walked through the little garden, and turned right along the street. Jacob caught him within a minute.

"Good morning, Adolf, and how are you today? Bit more chilly than usual."

"I am very well, how are you?" Adolf said with a smile to the stranger.

Jacob fell in step with Adolf as with an old friend. "And how is work at the hotel? How are the Seelers keeping? They are such nice people."

"Yes, thank you."

"Anything new?"

"No, business as usual."

"Yes? And how is Hans? It must be nice to have him back."

"Yes."

"How is he?"

"He is all right. He was fighting in France and Italy. He is a hero."

"Yes, I heard that. When did he come?"

Adolf calculated. "Two days ago."

"How long will he stay?"

"I do not know."

"What will he do?"

"He will work in the hotel."

"Where will he live?"

"He is living upstairs in one of the suites."

"Which one?"

"Number nine."

"Do you keep the key downstairs? Behind the desk?"

"I have all the keys," Adolf said proudly.

"Well, have a good day today, Adolf, I'll see you again soon."

"Good-bye." Adolf walked on as Jacob took the next right.

That was easy, Jacob thought.

Now what?

Jacob walked to his café and ordered a coffee. He watched

the hotel door and imagined Hans "the Rat" Seeler sniffing around in suite number nine. He'd always been called the Rat, even in school, because of those long, round stick-out ears. It was only in Bergen-Belsen, though, as far as Jacob knew, that he had really earned the nickname. If you're called the Rat all your life, does that do something to you? What comes first, the nickname or the person? Was Hans always a rat or did he become a rat?

And when did the rat become the Rat? And what's wrong with rats, anyway, did Hans give rats a bad name? He'd eaten many, they tasted quite good, a bit stringy and tough, although you had to be starving to death to eat one. They had caught them by blowing smoke from a fire, when they could make one, into rat holes and after an hour or two the rats poked their heads out to breathe. As a matter of fact, they'd even boiled the head and ears. It was better than dying of starvation. Protein. Very important.

Hard to catch, though. They're smart and fast, and when cornered, they stand and fight.

Hans Seeler. Jacob didn't really remember much about him before the camp. Only that he was about five years older and went to a different school. He hadn't had many friends, or belonged to any of the drinking or student clubs. The townies had their own sports and social clubs and bars, no fancy duels and polite scars for them. They mostly involved getting shit-faced and shouting at students and fighting with them in the street. Jacob remembered Hans at the edges but never being a leader or even particularly liked. It was only when he joined the Nazi party that Hans had become a bit of a figure in town, strutting and saluting and conniving, but even then he kept mostly to himself.

He didn't know Jacob. Jacob was too young to be noticed. That was what had saved him in Bergen-Belsen. He knew Hans

but Hans didn't know him, or Maxie. If he had, it would have
been worse, far worse, for Hans wouldn't have wanted witnesses from home.

Hans was the worst of the worst, he was a sadist and a pig
and a maniac. He couldn't pass a Jew without whipping him,
and as there were thousands of Jews, that was a lot of whipping. He had a special whip that he kept in his boot. It had a
thick leather handle with eight leather thongs and at the end of
each thong were smaller thongs with half a dozen tiny metal
balls each. He could eviscerate a man with three lashes. Jacob
remembered his harsh laugh when he saw prisoners flinch as
he approached. It was a snort, like a pig's, full of scorn and
contempt. Every mealtime he decided who would miss food
that day, and taunt them like a dog, leaving a plate of food just
out of reach. And then he'd make the victim of the day carry
the heaviest loads, stand outside in the ice, try to break them,
one by one. They heard the stories about the Rat and his two
women. They were his slaves. All the SS officers had sex slaves.
But the stories of what the Rat did . . . who knew what was
true? If he was a sexual sadist the same way he was a sadist to
everyone, well, then it probably was. Hans the Sadist Rat. He
should write a musical one day. Good title.

Jacob sipped his coffee, and shook his head. Two months earlier, his life was in the Rat's hands. A month before that, the Rat
had killed his little brother. Now . . . well, now . . . we'll see.
Jacob looked at the hotel door.

Jacob still didn't have a real plan, but he had dreamed of
this moment for so long he knew he'd work it out.

He turned his collar up. The day was gray with a biting south
wind. Jacob pulled down his hat and, leaning back in his
chair, eyes on the hotel door, he plotted . . .

Suite nine. Easy. I wait for Hans and his parents to go out.
I go in, get the key somehow from Adolf, or just take it when

he's not looking, when he's delivering a drink. What if Adolf notices the key is missing? He won't. I'll take another key and hang it on the Rat's hook. Then I'll leave the door open a bit and return the key when Adolf isn't around, and go back upstairs and wait in suite nine. When he comes in I'll shoot him in the face. I'll need a gun. No problem on the black market. Too noisy, though. Smother the shot with two pillows? Find a silencer?

Or a knife. Wait behind the door and when he comes in cut his throat from behind. That may be tough, he's much taller, I'd have to reach up and that would make me lose leverage. Hit him first with a hammer and then cut his throat?

Yes, a hammer to the head first. Knock him out. Or stab him in the back. Where? The kidney? Keep him quiet or I'll be caught.

As he put his cup to his lips he noticed his hand was trembling. He held up his left hand and it held still. Strange, just the right one. The cup clattered as he put it back on the saucer. He steeled himself by thinking of Maxie when he was young, when they played together in the staircase. Maxie's lifeless eyes when he closed them with his fingers. They looked like wet gray stones.

The Rat. What if he comes in with someone else? His mother? What if two people come into the room?

Could be best not to do it in the hotel. Too many people may hear, get caught.

Maybe in an alley at night. Follow him and beat him over the head with a club? Or stab him with a knife? When he's alone. A gun would be best, in the head, two shots to be sure, but too loud, could be caught. Can't walk through the streets with two pillows. Can I get a silencer?

Hit and run with a car? Too messy, uncertain, and anyway,

no car. A hunting accident in the woods? Does he go hunting? Push him off a cliff? Drown him in the Neckar?

How about getting some help? Kidnapping him? Torturing him. But who? And where? Somebody with a car. In the woods, outside town.

What will the Rat do, anyway? Stay inside? Go out with old friends?

Or will he leave, go somewhere else? But where? There's nowhere to go. No, there's time, thought Jacob, he's not going anywhere.

So here's the plan. Wait. Follow him. Decide. Do it in his room or in an alley. In the meantime, get a gun, maybe a silencer, and a knife. And a hammer.

Jacob knew where to go for a knife. The Amis loved German bayonets, commando knives, hunting knives, SS daggers and swords. On the road to the castle Germans sold dozens of them to American soldiers looking for souvenirs. These were the support troops. American combat soldiers had captured more weapons than they could carry but the cooks, the drivers, and the cable layers paid through the nose for anything warlike. Jacob had seen an Ami pay twenty-three dollars for a ceremonial SS fighting knife with the words "Blut und Ehre" engraved on the blade—Blood and Honor. It didn't even have its sheaf. Germans weren't allowed to sell guns but everyone knew they were for sale too. They'd sell their sisters if they could, and many did.

After three hours waiting for Hans and a quick purchase in a general hardware store, Jacob walked to the castle, where he bought a seven-inch Wehrmacht fighting knife with original sheaf for a hundred Reichsmarks. "It's a TS-136-A," the seller had begun, hoping to get top dollar from Jacob, "it's worth more than the 137 because—" But Jacob interrupted,

"I couldn't care less, no dollars, a hundred marks, take it or leave it."

Jacob was almost home when it suddenly occurred to him that Sarah might ask why he had bought a fighting knife, so he took off his jacket and hid it carefully in the sleeve.

Sarah, who was chopping vegetables, looked over her shoulder as he came in. "It's freezing outside, why aren't you wearing your jacket?" she said. "And what's that you've got wrapped up in it?"

Jacob looked at his jacket in surprise. "Oh, nothing. Just something I got cheap, I can make ten dollars on this."

"Whenever you say it's nothing, it's something. What is it?"

"Oh, just a military souvenir, Amis collect them."

"But what is it?"

"Just a little knife."

Sarah stretched out her hand. "Can I see it? This one is so blunt."

With a sigh, Jacob unfurled the sleeve and pulled the seven-inch dagger from the sheaf.

"Goodness," Sarah said. "What is it?"

"Just a knife, what does it look like?"

"It's like a razor," she said. "And the point, be careful, you can kill someone with that. Take it back. I don't want to touch it."

Jacob slid the knife back into the sheaf and put it under the bed. He waited for the right moment when Sarah wasn't looking to take the hammer from the other sleeve and hide it next to the knife.

He smiled as Sarah placed two plates of hot food on the table. "It smells so good," he said, slapping her bottom. "The perfect Hausfrau."

They had fried potatoes and onions, two fried eggs, and cucumbers, and drank ice-cold water. They ate in silence until Sarah said, "Jacob?"

"Yes?"

"Why did you buy a hammer? And why did you hide it with the knife?"

"I didn't hide it."

"Yes, you did."

"No, I didn't."

"Then why did you look so guilty and wait till I wasn't looking to put it under the bed with the knife?"

"What do you mean? I wasn't hiding anything."

"You were, I've never seen a man look so guilty."

"Anyway, if you weren't looking, how do you know I looked guilty?"

"I saw you in the mirror."

"Oh."

"So?"

"I honestly wasn't hiding it. I just forgot I had it and then had to put it somewhere so I put it under the bed too, that's all. Is there any pudding?"

"Rice pudding. With milk, or rather, milk powder. And there are more breadcrumbs than rice. Rice pudding sounds so much better than breadcrumb powder. But it's really good."

And it was. By now it was three o'clock in the afternoon.

"Bedtime," said Jacob. "I'll do the dishes later."

"Oh, thank you. The dish."

"Did anyone tell you that you are quite a cheeky girl?"

"No, never."

"Well, come here and let me whisper it into your ear." Jacob took off his shirt and sat on the bed to remove his trousers and underpants. "Don't look."

Sarah placed her hand over her eyes with her fingers wide apart.

"I'm not looking," she said.

"Oh, good. Because we're not married."

"That reminds me. Will you marry me?"

"I beg your pardon?"

"Nothing."

"You did. Did you ask me to marry you?"

"No, of course not. I would never say that, a girl never says such a thing. That would make me a very forward girl."

"Oh, right, of course, I forgot, you are a shrinking violet."

"A what?"

"A demure maiden. A coy damsel. A bashful maid."

"Exactly. So?"

"So? What?"

"So, will you marry me?"

Jacob lay naked on the bed, propped up against the pillow. He considered Sarah through half-closed eyes. He was thinking, There's a slight stirring, please, please, God in heaven, give me an erection this time. "Isn't the man supposed to ask?"

"What man?"

Jacob closed his eyes and half-smiled. He nodded, as if all had been revealed. He turned onto his side and slid under the blanket and with a sigh laid his head on the pillow.

Sarah undressed and got into bed. "Jacob, you've gone all silent. What is it? Are you all right?"

Jacob wriggled away from her.

"Jacob. What is it? You don't want to marry me? It's all right, I was only joking. Come here." She snuggled against his back. "I'm cold," she said, hugging him. "Do you just want to go to sleep?"

No, he didn't. He wanted to make love. But he felt nothing, the brain's message had gone AWOL. It didn't reach its destination. They lay there, Sarah hugging Jacob from behind. Finally he murmured, "Why do you want to marry me?"

Sarah smiled and whispered into his ear. "My mother always wanted me to marry a Jew."

"But why me?"

She couldn't help herself. "Because you're the only Jew."

Jacob laughed out loud and turned around suddenly. "Now that's a good one," he said, "I like your mom." Now Sarah went quiet, and Jacob said, "Sorry. I'm sure I would have. Tell me about her. Would you?"

Sarah sighed. "Or later," Jacob said. "It doesn't matter." They lay face-to-face, holding each other's naked body, and they kissed, and with his index finger Jacob traced the tear that traveled down Sarah's cheek, following the curve, and dripping to the pillow, and another one that followed. He smiled gently and kissed the corner of her eye. "Salty," he whispered. Sarah nodded and tried to smile. She kissed the tip of his nose and his lips and he kissed her back. Jacob's hand followed the line of her back to the silky down of her bottom and caressed it until Sarah gently pulled his hand away.

"She loved to knit and embroider," she said. "Every evening after dinner she sat by the window. Socks, gloves, pullovers. Tiny ones in bright colors, with little animals on the collars, deer, ducks, or roses. She always said to me and Ruth, it's for your babies. She always said, 'B'zrat ha Shem,' with God's help, that's about as religious as she was. She wanted so much for us to be married and happy, to be a grandma. And now she's gone. And Ruth, too. And Daddy. Maybe it's better that way. She would be so disappointed."

Sarah began to weep and Jacob held her to him. He whispered into her ear, "Disappointed? Why? She would never be disappointed. Sarah . . . I love you. Of course I want to marry you. Will you marry me? Please? I love you, my baby Sarah, I love you," and he stroked her hair and caressed her body as she wept in his arms and she cried out loud, "You don't understand," and Jacob said he did and she cried, "No, you don't, you really don't." Jacob hugged her and kissed her and as they were folded into each other he felt himself stir and harden and he pressed and moved against her until she opened her legs and he probed and pushed inside her, all the way, as far as he could, and they rocked slowly together as she sobbed in his arms, until the sobs turned to moans that merged with his.

"Sorry," Sarah said.

"No, no. That was beautiful, the most beautiful ever." Jacob was lying on his back, Sarah on her side, snuggling against him as he held her close, his hand cupping her breast. They lay in silence, as their breathing quieted and the heaving of their chests slowed until the sheet barely rose, and even the rhythm of their breathing was as one and they fell into the deepest of sleeps.

It was dark when Jacob jolted awake. One arm was numb, under Sarah's body. He extricated himself and wiped his brow. He was sweating. He breathed in deeply and blew out all the air, as if trying to banish the thoughts that had awoken him so harshly: What was that in his dream? It left him feeling ashamed of himself, humiliated. The Rat? Maxie. Outside . . . he was helping Maxie carry something, the Rat was shouting, he said to Jacob, If you're so strong, you carry it. He'd flicked his whip at Maxie, who screamed and fell to the ground, and Jacob took the full weight of the bag of earth. Yes, that's it. Hans was making the two of them carry a bag of earth up and down in the snow, from the trees to the first line of huts. For no reason, the bastard, the filthy scumbag. Maxie collapsed. Naked, that's it. He was naked. Hans had made Jacob strip naked in the snow too and carry the huge bag of earth alone, there and back, sinking into the snow to his knees, stumbling and clawing at the ground until he, too, had collapsed, barely able to breathe, gasping for every breath, rasping and croaking, his lungs exploding, sweating like a pig in the ice, with Hans cursing him and lashing out with his lethal leather whip and missing him by centimeters.

Maxie was lying in the snow, vomiting blood, watching his big brother, who was naked and screaming for mercy.

Was it a just a nightmare? Did it happen? Jacob tried to remember. It had all been so horrific it didn't seem possible anymore. Did these things really happen? Oh yes. That was nothing. Nothing at all. Just one more day in the sick mind of the Rat. Yes, Jacob remembered now. Of course it happened, and worse things happened every day.

A wave of humiliation and shame and hatred washed over Jacob. He edged away from Sarah. If she knew. If she knew. It made him sick to think of her knowing what the Rat had done to him. I have to kill him, Jacob thought, I'll go mad if I don't.

He heard Sarah's gentle, peaceful breathing, saw her chest rise and fall, looked at her relaxed face, her closed eyes. He had stroked her tears away. Kissed those eyes when they were clenched in ecstasy. And now she rested.

I'll never tell her what happened there.

He laughed to himself. She really did say it, didn't she? She asked me to marry her. He laughed aloud, and turned, hoping not to have awakened her. In his home, sleep had been holy. If someone was sleeping, everyone had to tiptoe and whisper. And food. No talking at mealtimes. That was holy too. Sleep and eat, work and study, that had been the family rhythm, until Mutti died. Jacob tried to see her face. He couldn't, he had no memory of how his mother looked, and all the photos were gone, as far as he knew. He would gladly have given everything, even his home, for some photos. He had nothing left. Nothing. It was as if his family had been swallowed by the universe. Gone. Where? If only he believed.

He should go to the Bergers, maybe they would have something.

He looked at Sarah again as she slept, and turned onto his side so that he could watch her. She was facing him, her mouth slightly open. She was dribbling, there was a damp spot on the pillow by her lips. What has happened to us? Damp spots from dribble; from tears; from sex. He smiled, full of love. He hoped nothing would change, but who knows, he thought. He had lost everything. She had lost everything. Now they had found each other. And in a world where everything can change in an instant, you hold on to what you have as hard as you can. Sarah wouldn't even throw away a crust of bread, let alone a paper bag. She hoarded everything. A phrase ran through his mind, again and again: You have nothing, I have nothing, let's have nothing together.

And then it occurred to him: If I kill Hans, will I lose Sarah? The thought left him breathless.

Could he really kill him and get away with it? What could they do to him? They could put him to death, that's what. Who would look after Sarah? What would she do? Where would she go? He snorted. Why would they catch him? He'd plan it properly, he'd be careful, and if, God forbid, there was a chance of getting caught he'd go straight to the Amis and confess. Better the Americans than getting beaten to death by German prison guards, they're all Nazis anyway. That's it, any danger, straight to the Americans. How can they punish a Jewish concentration camp survivor who killed his SS guard, after they hear what he did to Maxie?

But for sure, he thought, don't get caught by the Germans.

TWENTY-TWO

Heidelberg,
June 3, 1945

The next day, and the next, and the next, Jacob went to his café down the street from the Schwartzer Bock hotel. He didn't want to draw attention by sitting for hours, so sometimes he walked slowly up and down, until the third morning, when the café owner approached him. "Lost your wallet, have you?" he said. "Don't worry, you can sit here as long as you like, makes us look busy. Empty tables are bad for business." Jacob laughed and ordered a coffee. The owner joined him with a cup of tea and a plate of cookies, "Baked by the gracious lady"—his wife. There was no German newspaper yet but the owner didn't need one, he knew all the gossip. "There's a new tax on dogs, can you believe it?" He shook his head as if to say, losing a war is bad enough, but a dog tax? Two members of the Hitler Youth were shot for spying. Don't they know it's all over? Thank God. He was short on rolls, there wasn't enough coal for the bakeries to bake bread. The good news was that the railway line to Frankfurt was running again, two trains a day, there and back. The Maggi soup cubes factory had reopened and was hiring. City hall was looking for garbage workers, cemetery staff, and kindergarten teachers. "Do you need a job?" he asked Jacob.

"Not yet. But I will soon." He hoped the owner, Karl-Friedrich, wouldn't ask any more questions and he didn't. He was too busy in his role as town crier. Former prisoners of war had to register within two days or they wouldn't get any ration cards, and if men didn't report for work they could be arrested. "We need every hand there is to rebuild, especially the bridges. Jews, too," he said, "if there are any. Not that they know what work is."

"Why, don't Jews want to work?" Jacob asked.

Karl-Friedrich snorted. "Why, did they ever?"

Jacob laughed. What he wanted to say, but didn't, was Fuck you. What Jews? First you try to wipe us out, now you want us to rebuild your country. Build your own bloody bridge. Instead, he changed the subject.

"What else is going on?"

"There's a busload of Jews coming soon, from Theresienstadt."

Jacob froze.

"Eighteen. Eighteen too many. And did you know there are six thousand Russian workers here? Workers, that's a joke. You know what the Russians say? A cigarette shortens your life by two hours. A vodka by three hours. And a day's work by eight hours. Ha!" He slapped the table. "That's a good one! They're all going back home, not that they want to. I wouldn't either. Better off here, except there's no room."

Theresienstadt? Where's that?

"There's a new curfew time too, from tomorrow. At home by nine thirty instead of six thirty. Better for business."

Karl-Friedrich drained his cup and stood. "Well, back to the grindstone. Nice talking to you. What did you say your name was?"

Jacob's jaw dropped, he went rigid. *There's the Rat!* His neck hair stood, like a cat before a Doberman. As if in a trance, eyes fixed on Hans, Jacob pulled a note from his pocket and held it above the table before putting it down. *At last.* His heart raced. Three men, about the same age, had come out of the hotel door and were walking up the street toward the café, on the other side of the road. The Rat was in the middle, the tallest. They all wore hats. "Thank you," Jacob said with a wavering voice and started walking, slowly, allowing the three men across the street to overtake him. The café owner looked after him and shook his head, as if he had another good story to tell, about the man who saw a ghost.

Jacob kept thirty meters behind. He had stopped trembling, but although they were just ambling along, now he was almost panting, short, shallow breaths, and when the Rat turned to look at something Jacob looked away so sharply he felt his neck creak. He realized: That bastard still scares the life out of me. Could he have his leather whip under his coat? A pistol? He hadn't considered that before. Of course, he'd have a weapon, maybe a knife. Could the other two be bodyguards? No, he wasn't that senior. They all walked the same. Confident. Rolling along. Military? But then, what young man isn't these days? Friends? Maybe, he'll find out soon enough. Just don't be seen.

In Heidelberg all roads lead to Hauptstrasse. They entered the long main street but took a left after two hundred meters. Jacob almost lost them. He'd heard somewhere that people have a sixth sense and that if you look at them for a long time they'll feel it, even if you're behind them. So don't stare at them, keep them at the edge of your vision and even then, not all of the time.

Also, when people walk on the long main street, the assumption is they'll keep going straight. After taking his eyes off their backs for twenty seconds, Jacob was shocked not to see them. He scanned the people walking in both directions, disappearing behind moving jeeps, going into shops and coming out. He quickened his steps, cursing himself, looking into the shops, into the yards of the houses, until he came to the left turn and there the three men were, fifty meters away, walking on the left hand side. It was a quiet side street, so Jacob kept a greater distance, but this time he didn't take his eyes from them. When they turned onto another main street and followed it for half a kilometer, Jacob had an idea where they were headed, and he was right. That was why they were dressed so well. Coats, hats, proper trousers. They wanted something.

The police station. A thought flashed into Jacob's mind, to be dismissed as fast as it came. Denounce them. Go into the station and shout, "He's a Nazi, SS, a prison guard, a murderer, arrest him now!" Yeah, right. When that didn't work, go to city hall, fill out a complaint form, and stick it up your ass.

Everyone knew. The only place where there were more Nazis than in the mayor's office was in the police station. The only place you couldn't find SS was in prison.

He could go to the Americans but they'd just take notes, maybe begin an investigation. At best, arrest Seeler. Even jail him for a bit. But so what? Revenge? That wasn't what Jacob meant by revenge. It would just stop Jacob from getting his.

So what to do? How to get close? Without being seen? He couldn't hang around outside the station, somebody would notice and he needed to keep a low profile. An SS guard is killed and one of his Jewish prisoners is seen nearby. They'd string him up in minutes.

Jacob decided to wait at the end of the street, well away from the police station, and follow the Rat as long as he could, all day if necessary; to see where he went, who he met, how long he stayed, anything that would give him an idea of how to kill him. Because it was dawning: It wouldn't be so easy. In all his fantasies of torture, revenge, and murder that had consoled him in the camp and maintained him on his journey, he'd never actually asked himself: After he did it, how would he get away?

Because he had never cared. Living, dying, what was the difference? If anything, death was preferable. It was inevitable, so just get it over with, the only question being how miserable would be the dying? It was only when Hans killed Maxie that Jacob had a reason, a manic drive, to live until he had fulfilled his promise to his brother. Live after that? Why? He had died so many times in the camp already, what did it matter, one more death?

But now? There's Sarah. He hadn't counted on Sarah. I love her, he thought, I truly love her. He smiled. My first love. As he looked into shop windows, waited in shop awnings, strolled up and down the street seventy meters from the police station, eyes open for the Rat, Jacob kept smiling, as he kissed Sarah in his mind. He laughed as he remembered her whipping the sheet back to display her naked bottom, which seemed to wink at him, and how she had wiggled it, and that had spoken more eloquently and urgently than any words. What a brazen hussy. He loved the sound of that. Let's hear it for all the brazen hussies. He should go back soon. She was waiting for him. He had never imagined he could have met somebody so beautiful, so quickly, who loved him as much as he loved her. Who would have thought?

He was so absorbed in Sarah that Hans Seeler was twenty meters away and walking straight toward him before Jacob noticed. The three men walked abreast and Jacob had to step aside. He looked away and brought his hand to his face and coughed into it. He didn't think Seeler had noticed but Jacob had stayed on Seeler's face, in that first moment of recognition, a shade too long. Did he see me? Did he recognize me? Jacob crossed to the other side of the street, turned, and followed Seeler and his two friends.

He looked good, Jacob had to admit. He'd even put on some weight in the face. He still had that lean, sallow, aggressive look, and with his strange pointy-round ears, which Jacob hadn't seen under the hat, would look more like a rat than ever, especially with those whiskers. He had always been unshaven but now he was growing a mustache. Just when everyone else had shaved off their Hitler toothbrush excuse of a mustache, the Rat was growing one, but longer.

The men turned into the Bierkeller. After five minutes Jacob went in too, walked through the bar, and, as he had expected, there they were in the garden. He took a small table by himself on the other side, facing a bizarre wall frescoe of a naked woman and a dirty old man. He could see the Rat and his friends in a mirror, across the heads and shoulders of a full house. Where did all these customers get the money from? Same place as him, he supposed.

He thought of the camp; of Sarah; he wondered where Theresienstadt was. Karl-Friedrich at the café had said that a bus with eighteen Jews was on its way. How did he know, anyway? Who were they? From Heidelberg? Would he know any of them? He thought about his cigarette butts. He had a couple of hundred now, wrapped up tight in a shirt, but he'd moved on. The day before, he'd exchanged a bicycle wheel for a Soviet army whistle on its leather cord and sold that, plus a Wehrmacht bayonet he had bought five minutes earlier, to an American G.I. at the castle for twenty dollars, a profit of twelve. He thought of his journey and how sure he had been, he had never wavered, that the Rat would come home.

And there he is. In shirtsleeves, with his friends, on his second liter of beer, white foam dripping fom his mustache, talking and laughing and probably telling war stories he stole from someone else. His forehead was sweating, or was that just the reflection in the mirror? His ears really are round with a point and do stick out. They really are just like a rat's. Who came up with that name first? Funny that that was his nickname as a kid, and then in Bergen-Belsen, quite independently, that had been his nickname there, too. It must say something. That he really is a rat.

Three hours later, Seeler and his friends and two girls they had met staggered out and Jacob, barely awake, followed. He followed them all the way back to the Schwartzer Bock and that's when it occurred to him. He'd never get to him outside. Not secretly. He should do it from the inside. Rent a room there too. Do it at night.

That night, Sarah was angry, preoccupied, nervous with Jacob. She couldn't stop thinking of one question, it had colonized her mind. It nagged her as she sat on the pile of debris at the synagogue. And while she was cooking. And now in bed.

Why am I here? Really? No Hoppi, no baby, no family. No home, just this tiny room, for which she knew she should be thankful. The worst, she was beginning to realize, was being among these Nazis. Lining up for rations, she couldn't look them in the face. They all looked so normal, out shopping, well-dressed, healthy, gossiping, whining about how hard their life was, how the butcher had run out of garlic sausage, how the town was full of foreigners. There were good ones, yes, they had sheltered her, had saved her life, but they were so few. Even half of those she had to beg from.

That's why now she stayed at home so much, had hardly

met a soul. How could she be here, a sheep among the wolves? But where else could she go?

She had wanted so much for Jacob to sit with her at the table, to share the little meal she had prepared for the two of them, but the louse had come home late, after she had gone to bed. He stank of drink and cigarettes. Sitting alone in a beer garden till the curfew, after leaving in the morning? Sure. And I've been dancing in the palace. Where had he been all day? What was he doing?

His answer to everything was to hug her and caress her till she pulled him into her, and this time somehow they found themselves on the floor underneath the table, laughing hysterically.

"Ow, move the chair," she said, "it's in my back." They had knocked it over. "How did we get here?" she said, looking up at the underneath of the table. Jacob was panting so hard he couldn't answer. He staggered to his feet and pulled her out by the leg. "You were so noisy," he finally said with a laugh.

"No, I wasn't, you were."

"Well, that's possible. Both of us. You were noisier, though. We'd better be careful we don't get thrown out."

There was a demon in Sarah that night; she couldn't sleep, she turned and tossed and kept Jacob awake too. They kissed and hugged but mostly Sarah sighed and muttered.

"I don't know either," Jacob said, when he finally understood what was bothering her. "How can anyone know, there is no answer."

Why are we here? Is there an older question in the universe? Yet—was there ever a more painful time to ask it?

Were we spared for a reason? she had asked, again and again.

"Sarah, how can we know? Did God mean this to happen? Let's say maybe he got a bit carried away. Fell asleep. Which is what we should do." He held her close, in silence, as they stared at the dark, at the grayness at the edges of the curtain, at its billowing folds by the open window, at the faintest shadows that played on the bedding and across the walls. They lay on their backs. Jacob's left hand rested on Sarah's thigh, her right hand rested on his stomach. We've got to buy another pillow, we've shared this one for two weeks, Jacob was thinking.

It must have been three in the morning when a thought came as he dozed and he whispered, "Were you serious about marrying?"

Sarah heard him, barely. "Yes," she murmured back, "very serious. I love you."

"I love you, too. Sarah?" He turned on his side, rested his head on his elbow. "Sarah . . ." He kissed her, felt her soft full lips warm and tender and moist. "I want to marry you, yes I do, I want to spend my life with you. We'll find a place. I promise. Maybe not here. Maybe not even in Germany. I don't know where. Palestine? America? Who knows? But Sarah, I want to spend my life with you. I love you so much." He kissed her on the lips, gently, long, and caressed her breast and laid his head on her chest. "I love you, Sarah."

"I love you, Jacob. But you don't think we've just been thrown together because there is no one else?"

"Sarah as life raft?" He cupped her mound and pubic hair. "No. I don't."

He lay there for long minutes, feeling her chest rise and fall, her breath on the top of his head, and laughed and stroked her tummy when it growled. "Hungry?"

"No. Happy."

"Your tummy rumbles when you're happy?"

"Yes. And not only my tummy."

He kissed her navel and stroked her thighs and everywhere else and tasted her wetness until their passion united them and they moved together until that moment when for the first time they groaned together and shook together and fell apart with utter satisfaction.

"When shall we marry?" Jacob said when he had regained his breath. "My father would have loved you."

"And my parents would have loved you, too." She saw their faces, heard the clicking knitting needles, the clucking of the hens, the call to dinner.

Jacob heard screams and saw blood.

"It's all over, it's behind us, we'll start again," he said. "That's what they would have wanted. That's what we'll do. It doesn't matter where, it just matters that we will be together. You and me." He kissed her again, on her lips, on the tip of her nose, on her eyes and her ears.

"Ouch, that tickles."

He licked them instead. "I love you, Sarah."

"I love you, Jacob."

"We'll start a family. Soon. Have a baby. We'll start again, lots of babies, if it's a boy we'll call him Solomon, after my father. And if it's a girl, Anneliese, after your mother. That's what we'll do. They tried to wipe us out. We'll show them. Lots and lots of babies." Jacob laughed and threw himself onto his back. "We'll show the bastards!"

He was earning very good money on the black market but that couldn't last. He would have to find a real job. He could go back to law, finish law school. Or he could start a business. The occupation authorities were already talking about business licences and one of the first conditions was to prove you weren't a member of the Nazi party. That would give him a quick advantage. He could be one of the first. But what business?

"Sarah? Sarah? You're very quiet. Don't you want to marry me?"

She had turned away from him. "Sarah? Sarah, what is it?"

He leaned over her, tried to pull her onto her back, back to him, but she pulled away. With his hand on her shoulder, he felt her crying. Is she happy? Tears of joy?

No.

"Sarah, Liebchen, what is it? Why are you crying?" He rested his head on her arm. "Baby, what is it? Please tell me? I love you, we'll marry, have a baby, lots. Darling, what?"

He felt her body stiffen and suddenly go limp, as if she had collapsed into herself. She was weeping now, catching her breath between sobs. Jacob went cold. What is it?

"What is it? Sarah, please, you're scaring me, what's wrong?

"What's wrong?" he said, again.

He tried again to pull her onto her back, toward him, but she pulled away and her body shook.

Jacob lay on his back, staring, his hand on Sarah's waist. They have ruined us all, forever, he thought. She had gone quiet now. He knew she wasn't sleeping. After a long silence, he said, "Sarah?"

"What."

"What is it? Please tell me."

He felt her chest rise and rise and rise before it fell in a great sigh. "Jacob?" she said.

"Yes."

"The thing is, there's something I didn't tell you before."

He went cold. He knew there was a lot she hadn't told him. She had told him almost nothing. He had done the same. Was there someone else?

"Yes? What? Sarah, you can tell me anything."

"Anything?"

"Of course." Wait for it, he thought. Will it ever be over?

She sucked in her breath. "When I was in the hospital in Frankfurt, the American hospital . . ." She stopped and squeezed his hand. He could feel her trembling.

"Yes? It's all right, Sarah, really, tell me, what happened?"

She thought, Say it. Just say it! She would have to sooner or later. We can't start with a lie. Not about this. He has to know. Oh, how much she wanted a family of their own. A sob rose to her thoat, her chest heaved. Get it over with.

It came out in a rush. "Jacob, oh, Jacob." When she finally said it, it was almost a shout. "I can't have a baby. The doctor told me, he said that I would never be able to have a baby." It came out with a sob, a shouted sob, and her body shook but just as suddenly her tears stopped and she went silent.

Jacob felt the blow in his stomach. Bile rose. He wanted to vomit.

It sank in quickly. It wasn't complicated. So. No babies. No family. After all. They'd all said, When we get out, we'll have lots of babies. Those Nazi swine wanted to wipe us out. We'll show them. We'll multiply like rabbits, Jewish rabbits, and every baby we'll name after Mommy and Daddy and brothers and sisters and everyone, their names will live on, in our babies. Jews never call a baby after a living relative in case the angel of death takes the wrong one. But the angel of death had the last laugh. He'd taken them all.

"Jacob, forgive me." He felt Sarah's body heaving and heard her gulping as she tried to stop more sobs.

It had never occurred to him. Not for a moment. In all their lovemaking they hadn't taken any precautions. He had thought a baby would be a blessing, the fertile earth replenishing itself. They hadn't mentioned it, but he had thought she must be thinking the same. Now he understood why she hadn't talked about being careful.

What a cruel, final blow. Jacob hugged Sarah and thought: So. They won after all.

My line will finish here, just like they wanted. It'll just take a bit longer.

When I die, it's over for the Kleins. He killed Maxie. And now, without even knowing it, he killed me, too. Oh, you rat, I'll tear you apart with my bare hands.

"Sarah, how do you know? Maybe the doctor is wrong. How can he know? Please don't cry. Anyway, it doesn't matter. Really, it doesn't. We have each other, we'll always have each other. You are everything to me. Anyway, we'll adopt. We can adopt a baby. There must be so many orphans, we can adopt one. Or two. Five. Ten! Sarah. Sarai. Saraleh. As many as you like, please don't cry."

TWENTY-THREE

Heidelberg,
June 4, 1945

Two men slid tin trays of pastries and bread from the back of their van and carried them into the hotel lobby. On the van's side was the legend *Backerei Eichl*. That's another way, Jacob thought, watching from the café down the road. Poison the bread. Kill them all. I could get a job in the bakery, I did cooking at school, get some poison from somewhere and inject it into the rolls. Or I could poison the water supply. Kill the whole town. He sniggered. No, not really. Although it wasn't a bad idea.

He had followed Hans three more times, once back to the police station, once when it seemed like he'd taken an aimless stroll alone, and the third to the beer garden. But the times were random. Nothing on which to base a plan. What about taking a room in the hotel, then? Extremely risky, first because the Rat might spot him, and second because he'd leave a trail.

And he didn't want to get caught. Not now. Not since Sarah. She said she was feeling so much better now that she had told him. It was too much to carry alone. He'd joked, it didn't matter that she couldn't have babies because anyway he couldn't get it up. A fine couple they were. She had laughed. Yes, they could adopt. "No secrets," she had said. "No more secrets, we tell each other everything, right?" Jacob had nodded and smiled and held her. "Right. No secrets."

And here he was, with the biggest secret of them all. He was going to kill a man. Or rather, a rat.

But how to do it without getting caught? That made it much, much harder. Jacob was something of a fixture by now, the only Jew in town, apart from Sarah, who was less well known. And if Hans Seeler is murdered and the police work out that he was an SS guard at Bergen-Belsen, and they know that Jacob was a prisoner there, well, they'd soon be knocking at his door.

Every day there seemed to be more people in town. German refugees streamed in and with their identity cards had the right to a room. Buildings had two to three times the number of people they were built for. Families shared rooms. Punches were thrown as refugees who had been given spare bedrooms were thrown out when the boys came home from the war.

The street was getting crowded and Jacob was no longer the café's sole client. He liked it in the morning when the sun fell onto his side of the street and warmed him in the chilly morning and there was soft music in the background. At eleven o'clock Jacob leaned back in his chair with his legs stretched out and his shirt open to the third button. The sun was soft on his face. Two hours earlier he had already reached his goal of fifteen dollars for the day. Now he was spending a couple. He had a plate of cookies with his coffee. Apricot jam. Every day Karl-Friedrich gave him some of his wife's latest batch, one to taste, five to buy.

It was all looking pretty damn good. He had lodged a complaint about the Bergers. The Americans had told him that there was no mechanism to return the property of Jews to its rightful owners. Yet. Surely it would come. And when there was a law, Jacob, the first Jew back in town, would be the first to get his home back. They had promised.

All was going so well, in fact, that impure thoughts had entered his mind. Such as, what if he didn't kill the Rat after all?

Don't be mad. But he forced himself to think it through. He was in love. He was making money. Babies? They'd adopt. He had something he thought he had lost: a future. The country would have to rebuild, from scratch. There would be endless opportunities for a new business, maybe something to do with construction, Germany would be rebuilding for decades. He could get a business license quickly and get a head start on everyone. Import raw materials. He could be rich within a few years, very few. Then leave Germany. Go live somewhere else. As soon as he could afford it.

Did he really want to throw it all away by murdering one lousy camp guard, when there were tens of thousands of the bastards who nobody cared about? His anger said: Kill. Revenge. His love for Sarah said: No. Move on. It was the past versus the future. Love versus hate. He shook his head to banish the thoughts.

Okay. So I kill Hans Seeler. And I ruin my life. And Sarah's. Is that really what Maxie would have wanted?

Oh, yes. That's what Maxie would have wanted. Not the ruining-my-life bit. The killing-the-Rat bit.

So it was simple. Kill the Rat. Don't get caught.

But how?

There he is. Hans was dressed warmly, a coat, a scarf, and a hat, and he walked with confidence, determination, as if he had a purpose. He turned left and it soon became clear he wasn't going to the police station. He went there so often, though, he must have friends there. All the more reason to be careful.

His direction was taking Hans toward the beer garden. Jacob hurried along a different route and got there first.

The only free table was by the wall, beneath the fresco that had so fascinated him last time. It was a wall-sized painting of a German peasant dressed in green Lederhosen, green jacket, and green hat, wearing long flippers on his feet, hanging on to a naked damsel by the crotch. His gnarled face looked out at the viewer as one huge hand grabbed her between the legs. They seemed to be in a rowboat sinking in a raging sea while a full-maned lion looked on. As Jacob looked up he wondered, yet again, what on earth it all meant. Her left breast swung to the side and appeared to knock his hat off. Her right arm was raised above her head so that her right breast rose pertly, and the other hand gripped the oar. She, too, looked at the viewer, as did the lion.

Altogether very strange, Jacob thought; all German allegories were the same—rude, violent, and pointless. He looked down again to see that the people at the next table had left, a waiter was clearing up, and a waitress was leading three men to it. Jacob's skin crawled, his pulse raced. Hans and his two friends. He looked down but it was too late to hide. They were walking straight to him. Hans was thanking the waitress. He was smiling. He said she should join them if she had time. She laughed and said she couldn't drink while working. Later then, possibly? She laughed gaily and took their orders. Three beers and three schnapps.

Jacob tried to calm himself, but his heart was pounding. He moved his hand from the table to his lap. It was trembling. He was supping with the devil.

The beer garden was noisy, alive with chatter and laughter and accordion music that seemed to bounce off the wall, yet Jacob could hear their every word. They were so close he might as well have been sitting with them.

He should leave, not risk being recognized, but he was stuck to the chair.

Hans had removed his hat. He looked exactly the same, apart from the stupid mustache. Slowly Jacob dropped his hand from his face. He couldn't hide it forever, it would draw attention. Anyway, he looked completely different, or so he hoped. He was clean-shaven and his hair reached his ears. In Bergen-Belsen he had been a different person, miserable and cowed. Unshaven, cropped hair, runny red eyes, bruises or welts or open sores, scratching endlessly, hunched over to avoid drawing attention. Dressed in rags.

He sat up straight as if he didn't have a care in the world, adjusted the collar of his shirt, and smoothed his woolen jacket. He drank from his beer and when he caught the eye of the waitress ordered a plate of sausage and sauerkraut.

Hans called one of them Kristoff. They were talking about women. Kristoff was eyeing up the waitress, smirking in approval as she brought another round of schnapps. As she walked away they all followed her with their eyes. "Nice haunch," the third man said. They moved on to the war. Kristoff was clearly an old pal whom Hans hadn't seen since he was shipped off to the east. The music became louder and a man with a foghorn voice sat nearby, making it harder for Jacob to make out what they were saying. He could understand about every third word. The other man had been some kind of infantry soldier. Lucky to be alive. Sixty percent of his draft had been killed and seventy percent of the survivors wounded. He didn't have a scratch. They drank to that and ordered more schnapps and beer.

Jacob sat half turned to them, so they could see only his profile. He ordered a second beer. Hans was talking, drawing on the table with his finger. He moved an empty schnapps glass and then moved two more. He pointed from one to the other and shook his head. Jacob strained to hear. He moved his head closer, stretching from the shoulder. The bastard was telling some war story. Something about tanks and the British. They advanced. We fell back. An ambush. Who ambushed who? Jacob couldn't quite hear. All three burst into laughter and toasted Hans, who made a joking modest shrug and drew his thumb across his throat.

Oh, yes. Hans, the Wehrmacht war hero. Lying through his teeth. Funny. The whole nation had joined the Nazi party and now you couldn't find a Nazi if you had a thousand dollars to give away. An SS guard? No such thing.

Jacob felt his anger growing. At first he'd reacted with terror at being so close to the Rat. He'd looked away, hidden his face, hunched his shoulders, had the shakes. But as he listened to his lies, saw him laugh, drink, pound one friend on the shoulder as he told a joke, throw his head back and survey the garden, lick his lips and leer at the waitress, Jacob was filled with contempt and fury.

He thought, I could hit him right now with a jar of beer. He looked away. He was so tempted to stand up and scream at him that he had to bend over and pretend to tie his shoe, to calm down. Calm down, he told himself. This is not the time or the place.

The three men put their heads together and looked around as they spoke. Hans was doing the talking, quieter now. There was an unexpected lull in the noise level while the man with the booming voice chewed his sausage. Jacob made out the words "police station," and "papers," and "train," and as he leaned toward them and strained to hear what Hans was saying he turned his head toward him to hear better with both ears, not just the one, and now he heard quite clearly. Hans said, "In ten days we'll be ready, I'll be gone."

Gone? Where? Ten days? The Rat is leaving in ten days?

Now Jacob's whole body was turned toward the three men, he was looking at the floor, straining to hear what the man called Kristoff was saying; something about meeting other people, a boat, did he say Hamburg?

Ten days? Jacob raised his eyes and saw the Rat staring right at him. Their eyes met. The Rat's eyes were small and hard and they narrowed and Jacob could see and almost hear the wheels creaking in his mind. Jacob looked away but the Rat was so intense Jacob felt himself drawn back. His heart slammed against his ribs like a hammer and he felt the heat on his skin.

The Rat was looking in his eyes, straining to remember.

Jacob shifted and looked away again. He had been so dirty, unshaven, he must look quite different now. And then he froze. He remembered. The last time the Rat had looked into his eyes he had looked just the same as now. A bit thinner, that was all, less hair. On the metal table in the Human Laundry. Shaven, like now. Clean, like now. Slowly his eyes turned back toward Hans, he couldn't help himself.

And their eyes met. The Rat slowly nodded. His thin lips turned down in the faintest show of scorn. Jacob was transfixed, he couldn't take his eyes from the Rat's and he felt himself break out in a sweat. He smelled his own fear. He felt his heart would explode. The Rat stared at him until his two friends followed his stare and looked at Jacob too. The third man said, "What is it, Hans?"

Hans's eyes flickered to him and back to Jacob, whose lips were trembling. He felt tears coming, tears of pure terror. He felt his nose quiver, he could hardly breathe.

Hans Seeler turned back toward his two friends. From far away Jacob heard him say, "It's nothing. It's nobody."

TWENTY-FOUR

Heidelberg,
June 4, 1945

Sarah knew something was wrong as soon as Jacob came through the door, closed it with great care, and took too long to take off his jacket. He tried to smile and went to wash his hands.

Sarah said, "You won't believe it, look on the table."

"What?" Jacob said over his shoulder as he rubbed his hands under the water. They were still shaking.

"Look."

"I said what. What is it?"

"Cherries. Fresh cherries. I'd forgotten how delicious they are."

Jacob held one up to admire and pulled the dark red fruit from its stem. He separated the pulp from the pip and crushed it slowly in his mouth, savoring the rich fresh taste, like sweet meat. He spat the pit onto a plate.

He took the little bag and sat next to Sarah on the bed. Soon the plate was full of pits. Their hands met in the bag, on the plate, grazing each other. Sarah sighed with contentment, but not Jacob.

"So, are you going to tell me?" Sarah said.

"What?" He'd been thinking of this all the way home. Could he tell Sarah? How much could he tell her? Would it help? Did he have to now? No secrets.

"Well?"

"Don't worry. There's nothing to tell."

"Darling, I can feel it. Please don't lie to me. Remember? No secrets?"

"Really. Nothing."

"I'll guess then. You bought a watch that doesn't work. You found ten Pall Mall cigarette butts and it rained and they got all soggy and are worthless. You wanted to get our bread ration and they ran out just as it was your turn." She took his hand and laid it on her chest. "Yes? One of those? No! Not all of them?"

Jacob had to smile.

"You know what that smile is?" Sarah said. "The word is 'bleak.' It is a bleak smile. What is it, what happened?"

He looked away and chewed on another cherry.

"Be a good boy. Tell Auntie Sarah."

Jacob rose and went to the toilet. Through the closed door she heard him spraying the bowl.

"Is the seat up?" she shouted. "And put the lid down afterwards. You always forget."

"Who gives a shit," he muttered. On the way home he had realized he would have to tell her. He had made a huge mistake. He should never have taken the bait. He was an idiot. Now everyone knew, so he might as well tell Sarah.

But how? What to say? Where to begin?

"Just tell me," Sarah said as he came out of the toilet. "I felt so much better after I told you. You can tell me anything. Is it something that happened then?"

Then. The Great Unspoken. The Never to Be Mentioned Yet Never to Be Forgotten.

He flinched. That was Maxie's voice. He swore it was. Calling his name . . . Jacob. He looked around in alarm, at the window, the door, he could have sworn he heard Maxie call.

But he knew he didn't. It must have been the wind, or the whispering of the curtains. Or maybe he was just going crazy.

Jacob sat and closed his eyes with a wavering sigh. "Something just happened," he said. He leaned back against the wall in a dark world of his own.

He couldn't bear to look at Sarah as he told her about Maxie, how he had been beaten by the crazy SS guard until he had died in Jacob's arms. As he recounted that moment, in a dull voice, in agonizing detail, she gripped his arm in growing horror. Through clenched eyes he told her the Nazis had thrown Maxie's body onto a pile of corpses, and he had lain there, in plain sight, going rotten, for weeks. At the end, when they had separated the prisoners in the Sternlager and taken the elite ones away on a forced march, he'd hidden in the pile of firewood in the hut. Because he had seen that the Rat had stayed behind among a last contingent of SS guards. Then he hadn't seen him for weeks, he thought he'd lost him, until that time in the Human Laundry.

When he told her that Hans Seeler, the Rat, came from Heidelberg too, she gasped so sharply her whole body jerked. And when he told her that he had already seen him, he had to remove her hand from his arm, her grip was so tight it seemed to stop his blood. He opened his eyes and saw her tears.

She was white. *Does she know what's coming?* "The thing is . . ." He hesitated, plucked up courage, there was no holding back now. "The last thing I said to Maxie, the last thing he heard before he died, was my oath. I promised, on his life, to kill the Rat."

That's it, it was out. He had sworn never to tell her, to protect her innocence in case he was caught, but now he had no choice. He had to tell her. Because now everyone else knew. What a fool.

He closed his eyes again, pressed himself against the wall, as if to hide behind a screen. "So this is what happened," he went on. "Tonight . . ."

He had sat down, the Rat was at the next table, he could hear them . . . he told her everything except the Rat's taunt: "It's nothing. It's nobody."

He had lost it. He had jumped up and pulled the Rat's arm. Tried to punch him. But the Rat was taller, stronger, quicker. And so were his friends. They had pushed him against the wall, pinned his arms, shouted at him. The biggest one, Kristoff, had pulled back his arm to punch him but the Rat had stopped him. And as two waiters pulled Jacob from the garden, he had turned and yelled, "You bastard, you rat, you Nazi pig, I'll kill you, so help me God, I'll kill you."

Stretched out on the bed, eyes shut, he swallowed so hard his Adam's apple traveled the length of his throat.

Sitting next to him, Sarah stared blindly into the distance, her mouth open. Finally, she spoke.

"We were too happy."

TWENTY-FIVE

Heidelberg,
June 4, 1945

It was dark but for the warm glow of a candle that Sarah had bought that day. She had intended a romantic meal by candle-light and a loving romp in bed. Instead she had made tea three hours earlier and they hadn't stopped talking. Mostly she had listened, sitting on the edge of the bed with her legs drawn up to her chin. Walking in circles, shaking her head. Examining the torn wallpaper in the corner.

Jacob had stretched out on the bed, resting his head in his hands. He had also walked in circles and kicked the bathroom door twice. He had agreed that it didn't help. He had sat at the table with his head in his hands. He had wanted to punch the wall but thought better of it.

For the tenth time Jacob said he would get a gun and shoot him in the head and for the tenth time, Sarah had said, "No, you won't."

The only light was from the candle, which threw a pool of golden light until it fluttered and burned out.

They sat in darkness until Sarah said, "It's getting cold, let's go to bed."

"Put the light on," Jacob said. He turned the switch and the room was flooded with glaring light. It was quiet.

"What time is it?" Sarah asked. Jacob shrugged. She turned the light off and took his hand. "Please. Come to bed now." They undressed as they walked to the bed, and covered themselves with the sheet and blanket. Jacob turned away from Sarah and she hugged him from behind. They both sighed at the same time.

"We have to leave," Sarah said. "Really. Let's not talk about it anymore."

"Exactly, let's not talk about it anymore. There's nowhere to go."

"We'll find somewhere. America. Palestine. We'll get out of this damned country."

"You go. I'll come later."

"Don't be ridiculous."

He had shouted at her, nearly hit her. It was horrible.

"I promised! Don't you understand?" He had thrust his face into hers and she had pushed him away. He had raised his hand and she had jumped backward and he had brought it down on the table in frustration. "Do you know what that means? My brother died in my arms, for God's sake, and I promised. I have to keep that promise. Don't you understand?"

She had tried to shush him. "People are sleeping, be quiet." He had shouted louder until she had put her hand over his mouth and held him like a baby and he had trembled until he pushed her away.

"The trouble with you," he said, "is you don't know how to hate."

"They're not all bad. They looked after me. They saved my life."

"Well, good for you. They didn't look after me," he said, his voice rising. "All I saw was them beating and killing us. Okay, you had a different experience. Good for you. But don't speak for me, don't talk about things you know nothing about."

"I know nothing about? How dare you." All those years of hiding and terror, and hunger, thirst, nightmares. Her baby. Now she was shouting. "Do you have any idea what I went through? What I had to do to live?"

"No, I don't, because you won't tell me and you know what? I don't want to know. Keep it to yourself. You think I can't guess? You filthy whore!"

Sarah went icy cold, her jaw dropped. She slapped him in the face. Hard. She fell on him and kicked him. Sobbing, she beat him with her fists. He pushed her away. She threw herself down on the bed and wept in frustration and anger. "You bastard," she said between sobs. "You absolute bastard."

He looked at her, crumpled shadows on the bed. It's so easy for you, go on, cry.

She didn't deny it, though. Was it true? Why did he say that? Oh, why?

Jacob knelt by the bed and begged her forgiveness. She pushed him away with her foot.

He tried to stroke her. "I'm sorry, I didn't mean it . . ." She kicked out and caught him in the head. "Ouch!"

"Good," she said.

"That hurt."

"Good, it was meant to."

"I didn't mean it. I don't know why I said that. I'm sorry, really I am, I know it's nonsense," he said, holding her feet so she couldn't kick him again. He stroked her legs. "I'm sorry, really sorry."

"It was a very stupid thing to say, even if you're angry. And by the way, you aren't angry with me, you're angry with yourself. So don't take it out on me."

"You're right, I love you."

"Say you're sorry."

"I did."

"Say it again."

He held her tight and she held him, too. She had said, "Killing him won't bring Maxie back." She shouldn't have mentioned Maxie. She felt him grow stiff in her arms, but she went on. "Killing all the Nazis won't bring back a single Jew. And hating like this won't do you any good. Hatred will destroy you. It will destroy us."

Jacob had tried to make her understand. He didn't have a choice. Maxie had died, dozens of friends had died, many thousands more who he had seen every day—all dead now. Only he lived. So he should forget them? Like it never happened? Do nothing? What sort of a man would that make him? Of course killing one man would be like a howl in the darkness. But not killing him? How could he live with himself?

Sarah kept trying to make him understand. "What, you'll always hate? Don't you see, if you kill him you will destroy yourself, too."

"No, *you* don't see," Jacob had shouted. "It will destroy me if I *don't* kill him."

Sarah had run out of arguments, and patience. He was as stubborn as a mule. As he ranted on and on about his oath to his brother, his debt to his friends, his duty to mankind, that asshole rat, she whispered her own deepest thought, so low he didn't hear: You will destroy me, too.

She saw it slipping away. In three weeks they had done something she could not have dreamed of: they had built a little paradise, a safe haven in the insane world around them, and now she realized it was a fool's paradise. We can't escape what happened, it will forever follow us. We can never forget. We can try, we can rebuild, but we are all damaged goods. We cry out at night, we shiver under the sheets, we wake up soaked in sweat. There is no escape.

But no. She shook herself. Don't think like that. We aren't victims anymore, we can live our own lives, we are not hostage to the evil people who slaughtered us. Do not let Jacob kill Hans Seeler. It will ruin him, ruin us, and for nothing, nothing at all, there are tens of thousands of Rats running around, all trying to hide. Let them. Who cares? It's too late now. What counts now is the future, not the past. We have each other, that is what counts. Our love. Looking at Jacob, lying facedown, his face molded into the pillow, she said slowly to herself, stressing each syllable: *I will not let him ruin us.*

Because if he kills the Rat, he will be caught. Obviously. And they would both lose everything. Again. Hoppi. Sarah suddenly realized she hadn't thought of him for days. If only she hadn't lost her photos. She hadn't even thought of the worst time of all, that night in the cemetery. And that was good. She didn't want to forget but she didn't want to remember all the time, either. She was rebuilding her life, and now Jacob was threatening to tear it apart, from hatred, from an insane need for so-called revenge, from, let's face it, pigheaded male pride. She wouldn't let him do it.

Hoppi was the same. She'd told him not to go out. And look what happened.

Not again.

As the very first hint of dawn lent a blue-gray hue to the black gables across the road, Jacob turned his back to the window and, with a sigh, sat in the chair. Sarah's breathing was even and quiet, at rest at last. With her last ounce of consciousness before drifting to sleep she had murmured, "So that's decided, then, we're leaving Germany. Good night, baby."

But he still hadn't been able to shut down. In all the drama, he hadn't been able to think about what he most needed to think about.

Ten days.

The Rat was leaving in ten days. Ten days to kill the bastard. But how? That's what had kept him awake the last two hours as Sarah slept.

He really wasn't any closer to a plan. Further, actually. He had made a list in his head of all the obstacles. The Rat is strong and quick. He's usually with his two friends, who are just as big. He'd have no chance against them. He couldn't take a room in the hotel, he could too easily be recognized. He had lost his only real weapon: surprise. And by threatening him in such a public place he would be the first suspect if the Rat really did turn up dead. He'd never get away with it.

He had looked at the plus side, too. And come up with zero. Absolutely nothing in his favor. His only way to do it was to buy a gun and shoot him dead, and then be put to death himself. He realized if he committed murder, however justified in his own mind, in a public place, there was no way the Americans could get him off the hook. They would need to show the law applied to everyone or risk anarchy.

And time was running out.

TWENTY-SIX

Heidelberg,
June 5, 1945

At seven o'clock in the morning Sarah was dozing, with fragmented thoughts jumbled and jumping between lush cherries and being lost in crowded Berlin streets, people bumping her, forgetting where she lived, Hoppi's head disappearing in the crowd, looking, looking for him, and the long jeep ride where there was no room for her legs and Isak turning around and looking at her, and the hospital, the sickly smell, the awful news. She wanted to wake but dozed off again and had horrid thoughts about their fight, she had a bad feeling, she wanted to come out of it, but was sucked back into drowsiness until, after struggling between sleep and consciousness for what seemed hours, she finally pulled herself up with a start.

Jacob? "Jacob?" she called.

The bathroom door was open. He had gone. So early? Where? Why?

She had a sinking feeling. When did he leave? What is he doing? She looked around. There was no sign that he had slept in the bed. She brushed her teeth and put the kettle on. He's gone, she thought. He's angry. He's left me. She checked the closet; his clothes were still there. She went back to the bathroom. So was his toothbrush. So where is he, then? What is he doing? Why did he leave so early?

At seven twenty, just as she had talked herself again into fearing the worst, there was a knock on the door. A sharp knock.

A few minutes earlier, Adolf the hotel worker stopped at the exit of his building, sniffed the air, put a hand out to see if he felt rain, and decided he didn't need his hat that day. He went back inside and after two minutes came out again, hatless, dragging his hand along the bush that lined the garden path, and turned left to walk to work.

Jacob fell in beside him.

"Good morning again, Adolf," Jacob said.

"Good morning to you, too." They walked side by side for a couple of minutes.

"Anything new at the Schwartzer Bock?" Jacob asked.

"We're hiring a new staff person," Adolf said. "Maybe you can apply." Jacob's heart jumped for a moment before he realized how impossible this would be. He had come to talk to Adolf out of desperation, hoping he would get an idea. "Who knows?" he said. "What's the job?"

"Waitress." Adolf laughed as if it was the funniest thing he'd ever heard. It was a jolting laugh, as if he didn't have the breath for it. "Sorry, I was just making a joke."

Jacob duly laughed. "Waitress. Funny one. Tell me," he said. He didn't have time to waste. "Hans. How is he? I hear he may be leaving soon, is that right? Do you know where to?"

"I don't know. He doesn't really talk to me. He says I'm a village idiot." He laughed again.

"I think you're very smart."

"Thank you. I think the same about you."

"Thank you. So tell me, you don't know if Hans is leaving or you don't know where he is going?"

"I do not know where he is going. He is leaving next week. That is why we need more help. Frau Seeler thought he would work there, but he will not."

"So he's leaving next week."

"Yes. I said that."

Nine days.

No plan, no ideas. No time.

Sarah shrank from the door, out of habit. Who would knock so early? Only the police. Trying to catch people off guard. They always did. But why? What did they want? Oh no. Jacob . . . Had something happened to him? Did he do something stupid? So quickly? She cursed herself. Oh, why didn't I think of that, I should never have fallen asleep. Where did he go? What did he do? Her stomach churned.

Another knock. "Open up, police." A sharp rap-rap-rap.

Her heart jolted. How she had feared this moment in Berlin; there it was a death sentence. What did it mean here? If the window had not opened onto the street by the door she might have climbed out of it. As if in a trance, she pulled a coat over her nightclothes and heard her quavering voice say, "Just a moment." She reached the door, drew a breath, and with a trembling hand turned the knob and opened the door a fraction. A big man stood on the doorstep, in uniform.

Sarah's lips quivered as her hand flew to her mouth.

His smile was huge as he produced a bunch of flowers.

"I don't understand," she said. Her legs began to shake. "Oh . . . my God . . . Isak . . . is that you?" She thought she would fall. "You said the police . . . I thought . . . you have no idea . . ." The room spun and the ground rose as the blood drained from her brain and she swooned.

"Oh no, I was joking, it was a joke," Isak gasped, dabbing his handkerchief into a glass of water. He wiped her face as he picked her up and carried her to the bed, all while struggling out of his coat. "Sorry, sorry, sorry, joking, I was joking. Bad joke." He wet the cloth again and wiped her brow and cheeks. Her eyes rolled back into focus, a blush of pink returned to her cheeks.

"Oh, my God," she breathed. "With comedy like that, who needs tragedy."

"Are you all right?"

"Yes. Yes. Well, no. Not really. Not at all. Oh, I don't know. Anyway, I am better now that you're here. Oh, Isak. You scared me. So much has happened. How did you find me? Would you like some tea?"

"I'll make you some. But first . . ." He put a flask of vodka to her lips. "This is what you need now, though." She sipped, coughed, and sat up.

"That's better," she said. "I think. What on earth are you doing here?"

"I'm on a liaison team with the Sixth Army. General Patton. A fine soldier. An anti-Semite, but a fine soldier. I have brought you something."

"Not more vodka, please."

He chortled. "No, not vodka. Something better. And not chocolate."

Sarah watched as he reached into his satchel. He smiled, ready to enjoy her reaction, as he slowly, tantalizingly, slid out a small brown velvet purse. His mouth matched hers as it widened in surprise. She sucked in her breath as she understood. She took the purse and pressed it to her chest and looked at

Isak with tears streaming from her eyes. She shook her head in wonder, could find no words. Her cheeks glistened. Silently she stretched out her arms, still holding the purse, and he came forward and she embraced him and the sobs wracked her body. She held on to his great frame and he pulled her shaking slender body to his and stroked her hair and patted her back as she wept.

"So, sweet Sarah," he said as he kissed her brow and pushed her gently from him. Her eyes were red and wet and her cheeks glowed and she wiped away her tears. "I must look terrible," she said.

Sarah opened the purse like a medieval manuscript that could disintegrate in her fingers. She drew out a picture of Hoppi and held it to her lips and cried some more. She cried over her mother and father and the baby photo of her with her sister Ruth, while Isak stroked her hair. When she stopped crying he gave her tea. Its heavy, sweet aroma filled the room.

"So," Isak said, and tilted his chin toward the cupboard, "who do they belong to?" Sarah followed his gaze to Jacob's spare shoes. Their eyes met. She blushed to the very core. "Not you, I take it," he said. The bathroom door was open. She saw the two toothbrushes, Jacob's trousers thrown over the chair.

"You always turn up when I need you most," she said with a gentle smile. "You are my savior, my knight in shining armor."

He looked down at his shapeless Soviet army uniform with its leather belt and brown jacket. "Hardly."

"Thank you for this," she said, hugging the purse.

"It belongs to you."

"That doesn't mean much these days."

Isak nodded. "Sarah," he said, raising his bushy eyebrows,

"you're avoiding the question. What is a beautiful girl like you doing with a pair of black men's shoes in dire need of a polish?"

Four hours later, Jacob walked in to find Sarah and Isak lying on the bed, holding hands, her head against his shoulder. Isak's army jacket with the red star in the lapel was hanging over the back of the chair, his big army boots lay on the floor, and his shirt was hanging out. On the table were cups, a plate of nuts, the remains of a sandwich, and a flask of vodka. Jacob took it all in before he had shut the door.

"You're Isak Brodsky," he said. "Because if not, I'd have to kill you."

"You're as smart as Sarah says, then," Isak said with a laugh that shook the room. He threw his feet to the floor and stood to shake Jacob's hand. Even in socks he towered above him. His broad shoulders made Jacob look frail, and as he took Jacob's hand he pulled him into a hug. "I feel I know you as my brother," he said. "A drink?"

Jacob looked at the flask and smiled. "For once, why not? Sarah?" She shook her head.

"I've told Isak everything," she said. "Everything." She got up. "I'll make some more tea."

"Everything? I hope not."

"Everything he needs to know."

"Needs to know?" Jacob threw an inquiring glance at Isak. Isak raised an eyebrow—it formed a perfect arch—and he opened his arms as if to say, What can I do?

They pulled the table to the bed so that Jacob and Isak could sit on the two chairs and Sarah on the edge of the bed. Jacob's instant suspicion had faded. Sarah had never gone into details but this man had saved her life, spirited her out of Berlin, got her a ride to Frankfurt, never asked for anything, and now he had even brought her precious purse with all its memories. He wished he had even one photo. He would go home today to ask Berger. He looked at Isak and remembered the hug. He's all muscle, too. These Soviet officers, no wonder they won. He took another slug of vodka.

Sarah had made sandwiches and tea. As she poured it and stirred the sugar, she glanced at Isak. Jacob caught it. He stiffened. Oh yes? What's this all about? He looked sharply at Isak, who noticed. "It isn't that," Isak said, "don't worry. Look, I've got to go in a moment, we were hoping you'd come home, I have a meeting to go to, I've already been away too long. Now listen, Sarah told me what you are up to."

Sarah's eyes met Jacob's. She nodded in encouragement. Jacob opened one hand. "What? Bartering? Or something else?"

"Something else," Isak said. "The Rat."

"You're a man of few words," Jacob said.

"Ha! Tell that to my wife," Isak bellowed and smacked the table, which shook. "She would be very surprised to hear that." His laugh was short. "But work? Yes. Few words. Don't talk. Do. My brother. I will take care of the Rat for you."

Jacob's eyes went wide. He felt himself go cold. Sarah took his hand. "Isak can do it," she said.

"Not me," Isak interrupted. "Don't get me wrong. I will get it done. Not me. But I know people. They will do it."

Jacob sat in shock. Really? He was looking down, he couldn't meet their eyes. Suddenly there was light. All the way home he had been telling himself how impossible it was becoming, how he could never get close enough, how torn he was between killing Hans and losing Sarah, losing his future. In the camp, awaiting his moment, there was no either/or. There was no context, no background, no choices. Simple revenge. He was going to do it, one way or another, he knew he would, but the price he would have to pay was increasing every day. But now . . . now . . . is this really possible . . . has this man saved Sarah again, saved me? Saved us? Who is he, this angel from heaven?

"How? How can you do this? Who would do it?"

"If I told you I'd have to kill you." Isak threw his head back and roared. "Really," he said, settling his chair on all four legs again. "I'd have to kill you."

He stood and pulled on his jacket and buckled his belt. "Jacob, seriously. Sarah has told me his name, the name of his hotel, and especially, who he is and what he did. That's all I need to know."

"There's something else you need to know," Jacob said. He could hardly believe what he was hearing. Would his oath really be kept, and he'd be safe at the same time? Had his luck finally turned? He looked at Sarah with utter love in his eyes, and a tear formed in the edge of hers. She squeezed his hand. His mind was working feverishly as he tried to get his head around what he was hearing, before the Soviet officer left.

"There's something else. If you really do it, everyone heard me threaten him. I'd need an alibi. I'd need to know when it happens so I can be somewhere else, in a beer garden. In the police station getting some papers, that would be perfect. Right? Otherwise I'd be picked up immediately. I need an alibi, so I'd need to know when, is that possible?"

Isak sat down again. "I don't know. I have to see if that is possible."

"It has to be," Jacob said, and Sarah agreed. "Yes, he's right, everyone heard him say he'd kill him."

"Look, I'll be honest," Isak said. "I don't know if that's possible. Let me tell you what I can." He paused, took a breath, and let it out without saying anything. He was measuring what was safe to say. He spoke slowly, deliberately. "Look. I am an officer in Soviet Intelligence. I am a translator. But maybe a little more than that. Never mind. Liaison with the American and British armies. Intelligence. That sort of thing. I know things. I am Jewish too. I know things about the Jews. There is a group of Jews, I won't say anything more about them, but let's put it this way. Jacob, you are not the only Jew who wants revenge. And Hans Seeler is not the only Nazi out there who needs to be destroyed. Let's just say that there is a way to put his name in the hands of the right people. It will be done. I can guarantee it. But those people must be protected. Zero risk. Zero." He poured himself a glass and drained it. "Now I must go. Jacob, it is over for you. It will happen. But I should tell you now. They will not want to widen the circle, not even by one. They are complete professionals. I don't know what you will do about an alibi."

Jacob nodded with pursed lips. The main thing was revenge for Maxie. That was all he cared about. What a stroke of luck. Then he remembered. "There's one more thing."

"Yes?"

"He will leave Heidelberg in nine days."

"Who, the Rat? Nine days?"

"Yes."

"From what I know, that is enough time. More than enough."

"Why, are they already here?"

"Jacob, oh, Jacob, you are too smart for your own good. I may have to kill you anyway." Isak stood again and poured himself another vodka and drained it and pushed the flask toward Jacob. "The rest is yours. Sarah, I came to give you your photos, and look what you've got me into. Come here."

Sarah stood and hugged Isak. She put her head against his chest. She trembled. "I have no words."

She felt his words rumble through his body. "Just remember. You will come to Balakovo for dinner. Both of you. I have told you before, Sarah. My mother is the best cook east of the

Elbe. And my wife is the best hostess. She will love you, like I do. Anyway," he said, letting Sarah go, "I will see you again. In a few days I will be back in Heidelberg. Sarah knows how to contact me. Dosvidanya tovarishchi." Farewell, comrades. He swept his cap from his head, threw out his arm with a flourish, bowed from the waist like a hussar in the court of the tsar, and the door closed after him.

Jacob and Sarah stared at the door, shaking their heads in wonder. "You were right. That man," Jacob said, "is a force of nature."

"I told you. A whirlwind," Sarah said.

"Can he really do it?"

"He says yes. So far he's done everything he said he would. And more. I believe him. Absolutely."

"Can it really be so simple? Just like that? Problem solved?"

Sarah poured a small glass of vodka and put it to her lips. "Aah." She spat it out. "Horrid."

"You know," Jacob said, "I really don't know if I could have done it anyway. I know what I wanted to do but I don't know if I could have done it. Kill a man? Even the Rat? It just isn't me. Shoot him with a gun? Maybe. Stab him? Hit him with a club or a rock?" He shivered at the thought. "I could never have done it. Inside, I think I always knew it. The very idea gives me the creeps. How do people do things like that? I just don't know. It just isn't me. I wish it was. But it isn't."

"I know," Sarah said. "That's why I love you. Anyway, let's just wait." She hugged him. "We have so much to wait for."

Jacob took a sip of vodka and waited for the burn to fade before swallowing. It burned anyway. "Ugh. What time is it. Noon?"

Sarah smiled. "Bedtime."

TWENTY-SEVEN

Heidelberg,
June 8, 1945

Frau Trudi Seeler sat on a high wooden stool behind the bar that doubled as hotel reception. She held a wineglass to the light, breathed on it, polished a bit more, examined it again, and went on to the next. She brushed crumbs of almond cake from her apron and put another slice to her mouth. On the wall behind her was a carved wooden box in which room keys hung on numbered hooks. Two keys on each hook, round one for the guest, square one for the maid. She was smiling to herself. For the first time since 1939 all the round keys were out to paying guests. Not freeloading National Socialists or occupation troops, or refugees, but actual, bona fide, paying guests. She had let the last suite yesterday, even though she had given it for the price of a double room. It was only for two days and she gave it cheap just so she could say the hotel was full. At least the nice man had paid in advance.

Wolfgang had hung out the sign right away. A beaming fat man lying on a bed with the word "Voll" painted across him.

That would show the neighbors. What a feeling. Things were really looking up at last. But nothing was perfect. Such a pity that Hans would have to go in a few days. He wouldn't say why or for how long, but she trusted him. These were difficult times. He was such a fine young man, any mother would be proud. If only he could find a nice young girl.

She looked through the arch to the dining room, where Fritz von Schuhmacher, who had taken suite eight, was eating lunch. He had slept late. He looked up and she smiled at him. "Ist gut?" she mouthed silently, stretching her lips like a clown. He smiled in appreciation and rubbed his stomach. He toasted her with his glass of wine and she raised her polished empty one to the elegant young man.

Nice woman, he thought. Pity about her son. The strudel was so light and flaky he ordered a second slice with cream, and sighed as he tilted his glass to savor the last drops of wine. Gewürztraminer. When he did the "Nazi officer" course they had even had wine-tasting sessions. But not this one. Probably couldn't get it in Palestine. He'd have to remember it. He signed to put the lunch on his room bill and left a few coins for a tip. Outside the hotel he turned left, walked a block, and as he passed the café over the road, von Schuhmacher, aka Ari Levinsky, pulled out a handkerchief to blow his nose.

Sitting at one of the wooden tables, Yonni Tal responded by dropping the menu to the floor.

They were in business.

Ari finished his short walk and returned to the hotel to find reception empty. He reached across the bar, took his key off the hook, and went to his room. The stairs to the guest rooms were through a narrow swing door off the Stammtisch, the group table that was closest to the bar. He counted the curving steps. Ten to the first floor, where a polished brass sign showed an arrow to rooms one to five. Ten more steps. Another brass sign pointed the way to rooms six and seven and the two suites. "Next to my son," the owner had said when she offered him the room. He'd said he could only pay for a single or he'd have to look elsewhere, so she upgraded him. Must be because I look like a Nazi poster boy, he thought.

The first two rooms on the corridor were six and seven, then came his suite, which was just a room and an alcove with the bed, and at the end of the corridor, facing west and south, was the larger corner suite with Hans Seeler. Locked double doors connected the two suites and both faced the road. At the end of the corridor was a low niche with a decorative brass coal bucket and poker. When it was showtime, he'd hide the poker, just in case. The bucket, too.

Otherwise, a piece of cake. Which reminded him. He bought two pieces of strudel for Omri and Yonni.

"Too good to be true" was Yonni's reaction as they leaned against the jeep, after visiting the ruins of the old synagogue.

"The cake?" Ari said, licking the last cream from the paper bag.

"No. The plan."

"Well, simple is good," Ari said, looking over Omri's shoulder.

"What are you looking at?"

Ari raised his eyebrow and inclined his head. Omri turned and stared at a girl sitting on a pile of bricks in the corner. "Cute," he said.

"Beautiful, you mean." Ari smiled and greeted her. She looked away sharply.

"Anyway, again," Ari continued. "Just wait up the road in the jeep. When my light goes on and off again, it means I'm going downstairs to get his key. I'll do that when his light has been off for two hours. I'll see that from the crack underneath the connecting door. I'll unlock his door, do the deed, close it quietly. When my light goes on and off a second time, you pull up outside the hotel. Yonni, you have the curfew pass?"

"No, I forgot it. Of course I do. What happens if he doesn't go quietly?"

"He will. It isn't a big room," Ari said. "And I've already been inside. It's the smallest suite I've ever seen, apart from mine. The bed is to the left of the door, less than a meter. All I carry is a flashlight and a knife. I open the door, light him up, and cut his throat."

"Wouldn't it be better if I was inside too?" Omri said. "Just in case."

Ari considered this.

Yonni nodded. "Many hands make light work."

Ari said, "You stick a pillow on his head, keep him quiet, I'll cut his throat?"

"Good."

"So when the light goes on and off the first time, I go down, get the key and open the front door to let you in."

"Yes."

"Okay. I'll bring the pillow."

"What do we know about him?" Yonni asked. "And it isn't from Blue this time?"

"No," Ari said. "From Red."

It had taken Lieutenant Isak Brodsky of the Red Army a day to get the coded message to the Avengers, and because the team was already near Mannheim, it took them an afternoon to reach Heidelberg. The Rat had gone straight to the top of the list. They knew they had to act fast. Hans Seeler was leaving within six days and nobody knew where he was going. It was now or maybe never. They'd been worried about doing a job in the town center. But as Seeler lived in a hotel, and by a stroke of pure luck Fritz von Schuhmacher had been given the room next to his, SS-TV Unterscharführer Hans Seeler was about to get his reckoning in record time.

TWENTY-EIGHT

Heidelberg,
June 8, 1945

An hour later, five hundred meters away in the lookout tower on the Scheffel Terrace of Heidelberg Castle, the photographer moved Jacob a little to the left and pushed Sarah toward him until they were perfectly framed in the window, with Sarah nestled in Jacob's arms, their left shoulders toward the camera. In the background, far below, Heidelberg sparkled in all its sunlit glory. The destroyed arches of the Old Bridge broke the waters of the glittering Neckar, which flowed around and beyond into the open plain at the edge of the Odenwald forest, whose green canopy reached the river's banks. Soaring above the ocher roofs of the university and the Old City, the sharp steeples of the Church of the Holy Spirit and the Jesuit Church pointed the way to heaven.

They smiled at the camera and again and yet again as the photographer gestured to them that now he wanted a profile shot. "Enough, Michael, enough," Jacob said. "Who do you think I am, an American officer?"

Michael laughed. He knew Jacob as a guide and translator in the castle but he had never met his girlfriend.

"This one is free. For the lovely lady." He adjusted the fill-in light to compensate for the shade in the tower against the bright sunlight in the background and took two more photos. "Tomorrow," he said. "Come in the afternoon and choose."

"How much each?" Jacob asked.

"Oh, for you, five Pall Mall."

"Three."

"Four and two butts."

"Three and one butt. Camel."

"Stop it, you two," Sarah said with a smile.

Holding hands, they walked down the steep cobbled alley shaded by overhanging trees to the Corn Market, where they found the perfect table, beneath the white blossoms of a spreading almond tree and next to three large pots of flowering geraniums. They ordered two teas and shared a slice of cheesecake. As their forks met on the plate their eyes met too and they smiled, content.

They had woken late and for a change had not made love. Jacob had kissed Sarah's puffed eyes and sighed, and she kissed his lips and turned around. He hugged her as she held his hands on her stomach. Like the quiet river below the white water, it was enough to hold each other and to drift in silence.

The frenzy had passed. The uncertainty, the tumult of it all. Leaving in its wake the eternal question: Why me? Of all the men in Hut 28, Square 9, Block 2, why was it he lying in a warm bed with a beautiful woman who loved him? The devil had destroyed them all, apart from one. One weak and undeserving man. Why was he spared? It was a question Jacob dwelled on everywhere, waiting in the bus station, working in the castle, drinking at the table by the Schwartzer Bock.

Surely he was not left alive just to kill a man? There must be a greater purpose to his life than murder.

Finally, he had found an answer. To love Sarah.

Sarah turned and kissed Jacob and hugged him to her. He didn't need to say a word. She knew. She had also fought and suffered and in the end survived. She had lost everything, her family, her lover, her baby, but never her will to live. In the coldest, most freezing moments, when her bones ached, without water to drink or food to eat or a blanket to cover herself, she had stamped all night in the woods, in circles, hugging herself, fighting off the siren call of sleep, to make sure she would still be there in the morning. It rained and hailed on her. When she had run out of friends she had lived like this in the Berlin woods for two months. Hiding by day, foraging for food by night. Why? She never really knew. Less to live, more to deny them the pleasure of killing her. She just wouldn't allow it.

And now here they were, the two of them, holding on to each other as if holding on to life. A reprieve at the gallows. She swore she would never let go again. She would never lose Jacob. She would never lose her love again.

A long sigh shook her body. If only. If only she could have a baby.

Jacob sipped the last of the tea and reached across Sarah to the flower pot. He picked a geranium and wove the red blossom in Sarah's hair. She smiled and tilted her head to model her hair design. "What else can we do that's nice?" she asked, as Jacob paid the bill. He thanked the waiter and said with his mischevious smile, "I know. Let's go for a swim."

"Swim? Where?"

"In the river, of course."

Sarah looked around, hugging herself. "I can't," she said.

"Stop it. Of course you can," Jacob said, "look at me." With a quick glance around he pulled off his underpants, hung them on a broken branch, and splashed naked into the water. The sun glistened on his buttocks as he jumped up and down.

They had walked upriver until they came across a clearing in the reeds that grew into the river, where a fallen tree trunk that lay in the water had made a quiet lagoon for them to lie in. Thick trees concealed them from the road, which was deserted apart from the occasional military truck trundling by. Beyond their little tranquil spot the Neckar flowed fast and strong.

"Come on, it's beautiful," Jacob called out, splashing his face and sinking to his knees. Sarah had kept on her bra and panties. She looked around again with an air of desperation. She pulled her bra around to the front to unclip it, leaned forward and shrugged herself loose, and placed the bra on Jacob's pants. She took a step into the water until Jacob, whose eyes were devouring her, said, "Not yet. All the way. There's nobody here anyway."

Sarah shook her head and rolled her eyes as if to say, boys will be boys, and not giving herself time to think, in one swift motion pulled her panties down and stepped out of them, tossing them onto the pile of clothes. She laughed as the water chilled her to the crotch. "You see," Jacob called as he waded to her and held her. They kissed on the lips and were warmed by the sun. They sank into the river until it reached their necks and Sarah felt Jacob's urgency against her. "No, no, not here," she said, and swam away to hang on to the tree trunk. "You're insatiable," she said.

"You're irresistible."

"You're a sex maniac."

"Thank you."

He waded to her again and they stood near the bank where the water reached their knees. They embraced and kissed, watching their naked reflection breaking and reforming as one body in the windblown water. Jacob brushed Sarah's wet hair from her mouth as she began to kneel when:

"Yo, give 'er one from me!"

"Move over Fritz, Alabama's here!"

"Oh, man, check those boobs!"

"Look, he's Jewish!"

"What an ass!"

"Not his, hers."

"Cap'n, throw anchor!"

"Stop the boat, I want to get off!"

And just as quickly the swift-flowing river swept the G.I.s on the rubber pontoon past the lagoon and out of sight.

Jacob and Sarah couldn't stop laughing until they sank into the quiet water and she curled her leg around his waist and drew him to her, and they grew silent and breathless and they were laughing no more as the waves lapped around them.

That evening they strolled hand in hand along Hauptstrasse, lost in the maelstrom of citizens on the evening circuit, and stopped for a drink with five hundred others in University Square. The beer was cold and pleasing and Jacob sighed in satisfaction. They seemed to have regained their place among the ranks of the townsfolk. They were home.

Jacob enjoyed pointing out who was who. The best-dressed were the Nazis who had kept their homes and jobs and wardrobes in their pristine town. The scruffiest were the foreign slave workers who sought transport to their homes in the east. And in the middle were the homeless German refugees who refused to leave town because however bad it was in Heidelberg, it was better than anywhere else.

A slim man in a long gray coat, pinstripe trousers, and a well-brushed black homburg sat next to them. In his lapel he wore a Red Cross pin. When an American officer walked by, the man stood to rigid attention and saluted. The officer didn't acknowledge him.

Jacob looked at Sarah. She had noticed too. "Times have changed," she said.

Had they ever. They held hands across the table. For days they had hardly left the room together. Now they wanted to be out and seen as much as possible. At any moment Jacob could need an alibi.

TWENTY-NINE

Heidelberg,
June 8, 1945

By curfew at nine thirty, streets were deserted, the moon's dim
light glistened on damp cobbles, and in the cozy dining room
at the Schwartzer Bock guests sipped ersatz coffee, drained
their Schwindelcognac, and signed their exorbitant bills. Business was good. From his table where he sat alone by the huge
ornate ceramic stove, adorned with azure and emerald-green
tiles, Ari watched Hans and his parents finishing their beers
at the Stammtisch and wishing each guest a loud good night.
The swing doors creaked as they passed through to the staircase leading to their bedrooms. Not wanting to draw attention to himself, Ari signed his bill and walked in the steps
of an elderly couple. He nodded good night as he passed the
Seelers but Frau Seeler beckoned him with a wave.

"You will be leaving in the morning, Herr von Schuhmacher?"

"Yes, that is right, Frau Seeler, thank you for a wonderful
stay."

"It is our pleasure. Would you like a packed lunch? What time will you be leaving? Checkout time is noon."

"Oh, I'll be gone by then, thank you. No need for a packed lunch."

"Where to next?" asked Mr. Seeler. He had a surprisingly high voice for such a big man. "Oh. Just to Mannheim." Mr. Seeler opened his mouth to say something else but Ari wouldn't let him. "Well, it's late for me, early start in the morning. Good night, everyone, and thank you again." Hans Seeler studied him without moving a muscle. It was the closest Ari had come to him and one glance told him enough. Seeler's elbows were on the table and his hands rested beneath his chin. His jacket sleeves were creased at the biceps. Thick fingers, big hands. Strong and fit. One less Nazi bastard, Ari thought.

In his room, Ari waited for the yellow band of light beneath the door to indicate Seeler had entered his room. To see it more easily, he had turned his own light off. He was ready but to be sure went through his gear once more. With light, or in the dark, it was all the same to him. Left trouser pocket. Flashlight. He turned it on and off. A strong beam. Battery's good. He replaced it with a fresh battery anyway, putting the old one in his bag. Hard to come by. Right pocket. Seven-inch dagger. Right leg strap, the backup ten-inch. He took his Enfield pistol and moved the hammer from safe chamber to loaded. Five bullets in, twelve more in the belt pouch. Just in case. His holster was on his left hip.

His overnight bag was packed. He'd paid for the room upfront on arrival. Now he just had to lie back and wait.

It was eleven fifteen when the light went out in Hans's room and Ari allowed himself to doze. He heard the scratching of mice, or rats, and the persistent sighing of wind through the window-frame. Footsteps above, the flushing of a toilet, a door quietly closing until soon the hotel was silent and dark.

Every twenty minutes he looked at his watch, and he waited for two hours to pass. He breathed lightly and easily, and with twenty minutes to go, he took out his knife. He looked out of the window. He was ready.

Outside, it was a cool night with a quarter-moon and a slight drizzle, perfect for a not uncomfortable wait in poor visibility, to see and not be seen.

Omri hid in the dark recess of the café entrance. In his pocket his right hand played with a sock stuffed with dirt, which he would stick in Seeler's mouth as soon as he opened it. In his left hand he held a wooden cosh, just in case. And if all hell broke loose, his Sten gun was strapped to his chest, beneath his German army jacket.

Farther up the street, with the hotel and the café in view, Yonni waited at the wheel of the jeep; he looked at his watch and turned the engine on.

He was thinking. That cake Ari brought was really good. Maybe they could get some more on the way out. He checked the gasoline gauge. Handled the pistol on the seat. Looked over his shoulder and back toward Omri. Even though he knew he was in the awning, he couldn't see a hint of him. That Omri: He was like a snake, he could wait all night and nobody would see him till he slithered out. And by then it was too late.

Just a few minutes to go until the killing.

Curfew. The street should be empty but . . . movement caught his eye. Leaning forward, he looked tensely into his near side mirror.

Behind him a lone figure had appeared and was running toward the jeep. He was growing bigger in the mirror. Yonni's hand closed on his gun. He felt the adrenaline racing. Thoughts chased each other: Could be nothing to do with us, a guy running away from something. He's not army or police, if he was he wouldn't be alone. Coincidence?

No such thing.

He released the safety catch. One of us? Only two people know. He depressed the handle, leaned against the door, opened it a fraction, ready to burst out if needed.

The man was waving.

Yonni left the jeep and crouched on the sidewalk, behind the open door. He held his gun in firing position, arm out, body twisted to reduce the target.

Ten meters away the man halted, bent from the waist, hands on knees, heaving.

"Yon . . . Yonni?" he panted. He could hardly breathe.

"Password," Yonni said.

"The rat." The man tried to raise himself, said it again, "The rat."

"What day is it?" Yonni said, lowering his gun.

"Hanukkah."

"Okay. So what is it?"

"Call it off. Now. Immediately." He was leaning on the jeep, every breath a gasp. "Don't do it. Word from Blue. And Red."

"Quiet, you'll wake the whole street," Yonni said, climbing back into the jeep seat. He flashed the headlights twice short, followed by one long. He did it again. Omri would know now: it's off. "Why didn't you drive here?"

"I did. Damn jeep broke down."

"See the corner café? The first door past the turning?" The man nodded. "Go there. It's Omri. Tell him. Make sure." The man threw his head back, took in a deep breath, and ran to the café.

When Ari opened the door for Omri he already had the key to suite nine in his hand. His face was covered with a black commando mask and the streetlight glinted on the blade of his dagger. He handed Omri the pillow. Omri whispered: Won't be needing that.

Even beneath his mask Omri could see Ari's jaw fall as he told him the hit was off: The cloth clung to his open lips. He nodded, crept back to his room, collected his small bag, hung the keys on their hooks, and quietly closed the hotel door behind him.

By dawn, driving south, after a quick briefing from Red, who they met for the first time, and a coded radio talk with Blue, they had the full story.

They were hunted men. The U.S. army was looking for them. They needed to get to the British zone yesterday.

The service numbers and names they had given the foot patrol in Stuttgart were now confirmed as false, the mess they had left behind needed a culprit, and they were known to be in Mannheim heading for Heidelberg. They were one step away from serious jail time for murder. So don't make things worse, call off the hit, keep calm, and get back to base.

Moreover, Red told them, the Jewish Brigade had new orders; they were to be reassigned to Holland, all five thousand men. The assassination campaign was bad enough, but much worse from the British point of view was the Bricha, the smuggling of Jews from Europe to Palestine carried out secretly and against all orders by Jewish Brigade soldiers via the Italian coast. The solution, the British had decided, was to move the entire brigade out of temptation's way, to Holland, about as far from the Mediterranean as they could be sent.

So they should report back to base as quickly as possible and be prepared for fresh orders. Needs were changing. The killing season was over. It was more urgent to beat the British blockade: to bring the Jews home.

"Told you," Yonni said at the wheel. "Killing Nazis makes you feel good but it does more good to bring the Jews to Palestine."

"Yeah, that's why the Brits won't let us," Omri said.

"They can't stop us," Ari said. "Not forever."

"So you're right this time, then, Yonni," Omri said. "But what about that evil rat bastard?"

"Fuck him," Yonni said, slapping the steering wheel. "The one that got away."

THIRTY

Heidelberg,
June 10, 1945

Midday. Lauerstrasse, a narrow cobbled street. Dark green ivy wrapping the painted houses trembles in the river breeze, wooden window shutters slowly swing and creak. At the open door of number 13, Frau Bohrmann pours water from a bucket into the pot of geraniums on her yellow windowsill, while an ancient dog with hanging teats slumps at her feet in the sun. Two boys in shorts play hopscotch, hopping from square to square. A horse and cart clatters by, piled high with branches and firewood for sale in the market. A wooden wheel lurches into a jutting stone and a long branch falls to the ground. The two boys grab it and flee. Gazing from the attic window of a sky-blue house, old Herr Glas contemplates it all, and listens to the bold tones of the great bell in the Catholic church tower, jutting above the rooftops, chiming twelve times.

A serene and balmy day. Outside.

While inside the love nest at number 9, it is stormy weather.

Jacob stomped to the table, back to the bed, got up again, and fell on a chair. Back to the bed, where he threw himself onto his back, staring at the ceiling. Back to the table.

"For God's sake, sit still," Sarah hissed.

"I promise you, so help me God, I will do it. So stop it now. It's no good."

Sarah closed her eyes and pressed her lips together and breathed in, trying to control her fury. She emphasized each word. "Jacob, please, consider it isn't just you now, it's both of us, together."

"I have, you know I have. Look, for two days, two whole days, we thought they'd do it. Okay, now they can't, I understand, it was too good to be true. But that doesn't mean it's all over. What, all of a sudden all my promises, everything I have lived for since the camp, I'm going to throw it all away . . ."

"What do you mean throw it all away? That's exactly what you're doing, throwing all this away, all we have found together, all we mean to each other, that's what you're throwing away . . ."

"That's not what I mean, you know that. I mean I can't throw away all my plans, my promise. I must . . ."

"Oh, stop it, for God's sake, what plans? Who are you fooling? You couldn't kill him any more than I could. Let him go, let it all go, it's the future that counts, our future, not the past. Don't you realize, he ruined your life and now he's ruining you again. He killed your brother, now he'll kill you. You'll get caught, and then . . ."

"No, I won't. I know what to do. I know exactly how to do it."

"No, you don't. You said so, you've got no idea."

Jacob lay on the bed, staring at the ceiling, breathing heavily. She was right. He had no idea. No idea at all, and if he was right, the Rat was leaving in four days. Four days. The only way to do it now is just to follow the bastard and club him on the head till he's dead.

"I know how to do it," he said.

"How?"

"I know how."

"How, then?"

"Trust me. I know."

"But I don't trust you!" Sarah shouted. "I don't trust you, all right? I don't want you to get caught. I don't want to lose you. I don't want any of this." She clung to him. "Oh, please, Jacob, please stop it now. You're not a murderer. It will ruin you. You'll get caught. I can't lose you, I can't." She threw herself onto the bed. "For God's sake, don't I mean anything to you?"

Jacob sank onto the bed next to her and took her hand. "Sarah. Oh, Sarah." He pressed her fingers to his lips. "Don't you think I care? Of course I do. But listen, please listen. You didn't go through what I did. Believe me, I know you went through hell, but it was a different kind of hell. I don't even really know what happened to you. But if I tell you just one percent of what this man did, and he wasn't the only one by a long way, you'd feel the way I do. I can't kill them all. But this one man, I can kill. Just one. I swore I would. It kept me alive. I'm nothing otherwise. If you had been there . . ."

"Oh, shut up already. You think I can't imagine? You think you're the only one who got hurt? But that isn't the point. I understand, okay, I get it! But that doesn't mean you have to sacrifice your future, our future, because of what happened then. Don't tell me Maxie would have wanted that. He'd want you to live, to marry me . . . to . . . " She burst into tears. She had tried not to, she didn't want to, but she did.

She had been about to say ". . . to have a baby, to start a family," but that was something she could not say. And it hurt so. Her soul could not bear the weight of her loss. She had been ruined for ever. She could never give him what he wanted, even if he agreed, even if they lived together, married . . .

Jacob looked at Sarah, crumpled on the bed, her cheeks damp with tears. He sat next to her, placed his hand on her shoulder, which rose and fell as she wept.

Was she right? No. Or yes? Was it worth it? He didn't know. He took his head in his hands. He felt nauseated. It was a choice between two evils. But then, what in life is not? Everything has its opposite. Whenever you take something, you give up something too. Every scrap of food he had begged or stolen or hidden in Bergen-Belsen was a scrap of food someone else could not have. Every breath of life he had taken was taken from someone else. If he was alive now it was because so many others had died. And now: To kill Hans was to risk it all.

What to do? He didn't know. He didn't know!

He sighed, and stared at the wall. But if he did do it, then how? Every way he looked at it, he would get caught. But he had to. He just had to do it, and he had to escape, too. He'd work it out. But when? No time.

He'd had enough. Without thinking, he said, "Sarah, stop it now. I have something to do. I'll be back soon." He hated to leave her like this, but his legs seemed to carry him out the door. He stooped to pick up his jacket and hat.

He walked toward the Schwartzer Bock, thinking of Isak Brodsky. The Russian hadn't explained why, but it was over. Strangely, he trusted him. He said it was all planned, it was about to happen, and then it had got called off. Well, that left it up to him now. It always had been.

If he asked himself what was left over from Bergen-Belsen he could only say this: nothing. They had stolen every reason to live. They had all hung on to life, not because life was worth living but because that was what one did. It is what has kept the human race alive despite the greatest of odds. Species come and go, they grow, they weaken, they die. Only we have gone from strength to strength. Why is that? Because we want something, that's why. We don't just live for the moment, to eat, sleep, procreate. We have things to do. We may not all agree on what they are, but we all have something to do.

And I, Jacob thought, I know what I have to do. Sarah will never agree. All right. But I have one thing to do, just one, and then . . . well, who knows. Then we will marry and live happily ever after.

But first he . . . wait!

There he is. Halfway down Hauptstrasse, by the two G.I.s, going into the bookshop. Brown jacket and no hat. Glancing over his shoulder and up and down the street, Jacob didn't see any of the Rat's friends. Seeler was alone. Jacob pulled his hat lower over his brow and entered. There were two long, narrow passages between four tall rows of books stretching into the depths of the shop. They ended at a big glass door open onto a small garden with chairs and tables. A little café. It occurred to Jacob it must be a nice place to sit and read. Should come back with Sarah. As Seeler browsed along the shelves, Jacob stood near the cashier in the center of the store, leafing through a book. After five minutes it dawned on him what he was looking at: *A Young Wife's Guide to a Happy Marriage.* He put it down and picked up a photo book on the 1936 Berlin Olympics.

Over the top, with his hat low, he saw Seeler strolling to the cash register. His hand trailed along the spines of the books as he glanced at their titles, he was almost stroking them, and occasionally he stopped to study the pages. His eyes didn't flicker and search as if checking for victims, he didn't have one hand on his thigh to reach down and pull out a whip from his boot, his mouth wasn't set in a sneer. Instead, surrounded by rows of books, he looked as harmless as a schoolteacher. So ordinary. Apart from that stupid mustache.

But as Seeler approached and Jacob turned his back to him, Jacob's skin crawled. The hair stood on his neck. Right now, if he wanted, if he had a knife, he could do it.

Sarah had stopped crying now, after Jacob had left. She lay exhausted on the bed. They had been fighting all morning, ever since they woke up. Going over the same ground, over and over. Jacob had said again that she didn't know how to hate. He kept saying that. And she had said, "That's right, I don't know how to hate. And I don't want to.

"But I do know how to love." It was true, and she surprised herself. Jacob had asked her and she didn't have an answer to the question: How could she go through all she had gone through, and still be so full of love? What, there were so many good Germans?

"No, of course not, even the quiet ones weren't good, they didn't care about anyone except themselves, they did anything to stay out of trouble. I know that," she had said. "But if it was the other way around, would we have been so different?"

So it had gone, for hours. Sarah said, "I don't love them. Of course not. I don't condemn them, that's all. The truth is, I just don't care about them, that's the difference between you and me. I just want to get on with the rest of my life and not have them ruin that, too. And not here, either. Somewhere else. With you."

Jacob had tried to stop her, to get her to be quiet, to agree with her. But he couldn't, just couldn't, give up on Maxie, his friends, his oath to his dying brother. Part of him wanted to, yes, that was true. But how could he, and live with himself?

Around and around they went. About how he would do it. About how he would get caught. And what they would do to him. And to that, he had no answer. All he kept saying was "I have to do it. Now. Or it will be too late."

It was hopeless. She felt like beating the poor little pillow. Whatever she said, he was as stubborn as an ass. And then the fool had wanted to make love. She had kicked him.

Lying on the bed, curled around the pillow, she knew only one thing for certain: She loved him as much as life itself and she would do anything, anything at all, to keep him.

And that is when the idea began to form. The mist was clearing. She sat up slowly, her jaw clenching, her mind racing. Yes. It's possible. It could work. It must. She nodded faintly to herself and her face set in determination.

I could do it right now, Jacob thought, moving away from the cash desk, putting down one book, picking up another. But then what? His back to the cashier, he stayed close enough to overhear, Seeler was asking about a book, Jacob didn't get the title. Something about Argentina. The salesman said he could order it. Jacob tilted his head closer to hear better.

"Can you have it here in three days?" Seeler asked.

"Yes, certainly, sir, we will have it here in two. We close at seven, if you can come just before then we will have it for you, or the next morning."

"Friday afternoon it is, then. Thank you. I'll come just before seven o'clock. You think you'll have it by then?"

"Yes, sir."

"Because I'll be leaving the next day. That's very kind. Thank you very much. Should I pay now or then?"

"Half now?"

Seeler handed over some notes, asked for a receipt, said good day, and walked out of the store.

He's leaving on Saturday?

Automatically, Jacob followed. It was easy, following those ears in the crowd. He took the usual route. Ten minutes later, Seeler reached his favorite beer hall. Jacob saw him greet some friends, all young men about the same age. Probably all Nazis, he thought. As usual they laughed and chatted up the waitress and ordered beers. Shameless. And free. He could feel himself snarl. They're getting away with it, all of them.

There must be thousands of them, tens of thousands, all over Germany.

That's when the dark cloud he carried swirled into a vortex, like a tornado leaving calm in its wake, and his confusion cleared. He knew what he had to do.

He had decided.

He almost ran to the castle road, to the vendors with their military souvenirs, and looked through their collection of knives, laid out on wooden boards. There were short paratrooper knives with wooden handles. Long stabbing knives for trench warfare, close combat daggers and combat pocketknives that folded in half. He held a ribbed-handle boot knife and weighed it in his palm as if he knew what he was doing. Tried the same kind with a ring handle. And the more he looked and held and balanced, the more he realized there was no way on earth he could take such a thing and stick it in another human being.

He couldn't bear the idea of piercing flesh and pushing up to the hilt into tissue and muscle and nerves, and he knew it wasn't as if the Rat would just stand and take it. He'd scream and struggle and hit back. He saw them falling over, and even with a dagger in his heart he could imagine the Rat fighting for his life, getting the better of him. And how would he even know where the heart was? And how would he get in front of him and close enough? And if from behind, in the dark, where to stab him?

There was no way he could do it. Sarah was right. He wasn't the kind.

He'd have to shoot him instead. But the noise. He'd have to be close or he'd miss. It would take at least two shots. Even if they were alone, people were always close by. Nowhere was private in Heidelberg, which was crawling with people. There were three or four times as many as the town normally held. He'd get caught.

Jacob walked away. There was only one thing for it. He'd have to find a metal club. And not tell Sarah another word. She'd already thrown away one knife.

THIRTY-ONE

Heidelberg,
June 11, 1945

Sarah strode the last fifty meters with pursed lips, a firm chin, and straight shoulders, her wooden heels clacking like knitting needles. She paused at the window to adjust her hair, fluffing up her shiny hazel curls that fell across her collar. Her gray woolen coat was open so that its mauve silk lining played off her mauve beret. She had chosen a new white crepe de chine blouse that was wavy and glossy and open to the second button, revealing a hint of cleavage and a string of pearls, which she now knew to be imitation but were almost as translucent and filmy as any from the ocean floor. She ran her hands down her pleated burgundy skirt, pressed her lips together, and with an index finger wiped away a tiny smudge of lipstick. With a deep breath she opened the door and entered the hotel, wafting with her the keenest aroma of eau de cologne.

She walked straight through the dining room to reception at the end of the short corridor. "Hello, I'm looking for Frau

Seeler, please?" she said to the rather dowdy woman perched
on the stool behind the desk.

"Yes, good day. I am Frau Seeler."

"Oh, good day, my name is Gertie Haas, and I've come
about the job. I understand you are looking for a waitress? I'd
like to apply for it. It is still free, I hope?"

"Yes, that's right, we are looking. But it's more than just a
waitress. We all do a bit of everything here." What a pretty,
elegant girl, Frau Seeler was thinking, and so well spoken. She
must come from a good family.

"Oh, I'd be happy to do anything at all, whatever you need.
To be honest, I really need a job."

And no airs and graces, no nose in the air. "It's hard work,
for fair pay, live in if you like with food and board, but of
course the pay wouldn't be quite so much in that case. It's a
long day but there's a break in the afternoon." She should ask
her questions but her mind had strayed. What a nice pretty girl
with such a pleasing, genuine smile and sparkling eyes. Just the
girl to stop Hans from leaving; he'd like her. Who knows? As
Sarah answered how much she would appreciate any opportunity both to work hard and to learn the hotel trade, which
surely would be a growing field in the new Germany, what with
all the Americans in town and the rebuilding in Mannheim
and everywhere, Frau Seeler had already heard all she needed
to hear: church bells. She smiled. And the cooing of babies. But
hold on, Trudi, don't get carried away.

"Well, dear, have you worked in a hotel before?"

It seemed that Gertie Haas was perfect. Although she had
never worked in a hotel she had spent years waitressing in
Berlin, she knew how to sew and darn, could cook a little and
was very happy to learn more, and was used to long, hard
hours, as she had grown up on a farm near Hanover. She even

spoke a little English. Frau Seeler couldn't wait to tell Wolfgang. It was so hard to get good help. Everyone wanted a job but nobody wanted to work, or if they did they were the wrong kind of person, foreigners or poorly spoken. She couldn't have hoped for better than this young Gertie Haas.

Just as she was thinking of how to delay the pretty young girl until Hans came home, the door opened and there he was. He swayed by the door-frame for a moment, leaned against it, collected himself, surveyed the room, and with a quizzical look made his way to the bar.

He had had a few beers and chasers but knew he could hold his drink as well as the next man. It was mid-afternoon, after all. He aimed a kiss at his mother's cheek and listed toward Gertie. "A kiss for the gracious lady," he tried to say. "Polite thing to do, you know."

After introductions, Frau Seeler said, "Hans, would you be so kind as to show Miss Haas . . ."

"Oh, please, call me Gerti." *He needs a shave.*

"Of course, thank you, and you can call me Trudi. All right, Hans? Show Gertie around the hotel and then we can have a nice glass of wine and we can talk things over. All right, my dear?"

"That would be lovely."

Over Sarah's head, Hans raised an eyebrow to his mother. She nodded back with a smile.

Sarah tried to maintain her composure as she followed the Rat. It was too strange. His ears were just as Jacob had described, but otherwise . . . it was impossible to put this man in an SS uniform with jackboots and . . . and all the rest. She had come to hate, but he looked so . . . ordinary. His words were a bit slurred, he was clearly tired and must have been drinking. He smelled of beer and cigarettes.

They were in the dining room and he was telling her about the big ceramic stove. Its carved tiles were glazed green and blue and had been in the family for two hundred years. Like most of the antiques hanging from the ceiling or on the walls—musical instruments, hunting tools, kitchen utensils, and antlers and horns—it came from an earlier family restaurant that had to close because the building was so old it could have fallen down at any moment and had to be demolished. The first restaurant there had been in 1786 and the building itself was even older. There had been a students' drinking club upstairs where they cleared the chairs, sprinkled sawdust, and fought duels. But those were the good old days. That's all forbidden now.

The stairs were added with the new floors in 1912, just before the Great War, they're narrow and they creak, be careful, and he stood aside so that she could go first.

As she mounted the stairs Sarah could feel the heat of her cheeks. She could feel his gaze through her clothes. Hating herself, she swayed upstairs and he followed four steps behind, and she knew his eyes never left her haunch. If he grabbed her bottom, what would she do?

"This is the first floor, five single rooms, I'll show you one." He knocked on the first door, and when there was no answer he turned a key in the lock and pushed the door open. "After you. Just so you can see what we have to offer." She peered in and he put his hand against her back and gave a little push. "Nothing to be afraid of. See. Quite small but cozy."

It was. A double bed with a fluffy white feather bed and two large white pillows, a carved wooden wardrobe, antique water jug in its glazed white bowl, a pretty Bavarian-style dressing table and chair. Sarah nodded. Simple and tasteful.

"It's a nice view from the window," Hans said, pointing.

"Oh, I'm sure, it's a very nice room," Sarah said, and backed out into the corridor.

"There are two shared bathrooms on this floor. Upstairs, three rooms share one bathroom and there are two suites with their own bathrooms. I'll show you one of those."

They turned at the mezzanine and again, as she climbed the stairs, she could feel Hans's eyes boring into her bottom. Ever so gently she swung her hips.

"Suite nine," he said. "This is where I'm staying for the time being. Let me show you, it's our best room. I can even offer you a schnapps, the best."

"Oh, no, thank you, I hardly drink and certainly not in the afternoon. And not just before I talk to your mother," she laughed. "I'm hoping she'll give me a job here."

"Oh, I think you don't have much to fear about that. Here, please, sit down, I'll pour a small glass."

Sarah sank into the soft sofa, and made herself smile.

He sat on the chair, poured himself a glass, said "Prost!" and drained it in one, filled it again, and half-filled a second glass, which he placed in front of Sarah. She looked around. "What a nice room," she said, "and what a nice hotel."

"You think?" Hans said, rolling his eyes. "I'll drink to that," and he drank again, banging the glass down on the table. It was closer than he thought.

He stood up and went to the window. "Good view of the street from here, not noisy at all. Very few cars." He stood over the sofa. "I'm tired."

Sarah looked up with a sweet smile. Their eyes met and hers widened just a touch. She saw his chest rise and fall, his trousers twitch.

She shot up. "Well, thank you, Hans, you're so kind, I'd better go and talk to your mother."

"No hurry, no hurry, she'll be glad that we're talking." He fell down into the sofa and patted it. "Sit back down, we have time."

"You're sweet. But really, I should be getting along. Maybe another time . . ."

Hans took her hand and pulled her down. "This is another time." He snorted and his head fell back against the high back. Sarah jumped up as if she'd had an electric shock. He lay back, his eyes were closing.

She bent down and kissed his cheek. "Hans, would you like to see me tomorrow?"

His eyes flickered wider and wider. Sarah's face was centimeters from his. Her lips so close. He strained his neck toward her. "Yes, I would, here, will you come back?"

"That wouldn't be right, would it, Hans? I mean, your mother . . . I know. Let's meet by the river, we can go for a walk."

Hans stood and took Sarah's hand. He went to kiss her but she stepped back. "Hans, no, please, I've just met you. I'm not like that. But, tomorrow. Let's meet tomorrow by the river. Would you like that?"

Hans nodded. He was breathing fast. "Yes, yes. What time?"

"Well, I will be busy during the day. How about, um, let's say eight o'clock? That will give us an hour and a half before curfew. Then you can walk me home." She looked down, shyly. "Does it get dark about then? Am I being a bit forward? I don't mean to be, but . . ."

"No, you're not, not at all. Yes, let's meet at eight o'clock by the river. Between the two bridges there's a small wharf with some benches. We can meet down there. You know it? Below the road, it's nice and . . . quiet there."

"Yes, I know it, Hans. That's where I was going to say. It's perfect for us. Eight o'clock, then. But don't be late, we won't have much time."

"I'll be early! Yes. And I'll walk you home afterwards."

"You're such a gentleman."

"My home."

Sarah threw her head back and laughed. "Hansi!"

THIRTY-TWO

Heidelberg,
June 11, 1945

Jacob paced in their small room with growing nausea. He wiped his clammy forehead and pulled off his sticky shirt to splash himself with cold water.

And then he paced again. He held the steel rod in his right hand, and thwacked it into the palm of his left. It was thirty centimeters long and three fingers thick. He'd bought it in the hardware store, it was some kind of construction tool. He balanced it in the middle on one finger to find its central point. He practiced smashing it down from above his head. Swinging it in from the side. Up sharply from below if he had to crush his balls. But with all the will in the world, and egged on by the baying spirits of six million Jews . . . Six million? No way. But that's the number on the radio . . . still he could not bring any power to the blow.

He stood above the bed and arranged the two pillows. He held the club above his head and wanted to obliterate them but brought it down like he was dusting a carpet. Harder, man, harder! He tried again, but he knew at that rate he wouldn't swat a fly.

He could not bring himself to unleash his hatred. The terrible fury in his belly only made him want to vomit. He rushed to the sink, but nothing happened.

Jacob looked at his sweaty face in the mirror and down at the club in his hand as if at a mirage, for he was sure of two things. He was not a killer. Yet when the time came, when the Rat passed by, when it was Maxie's moment, he would do what he had to do. Hell, yes. Jacob hefted the club as he paced in the room, taking himself back to that hateful place, summoning up all the demons that howled for revenge.

When the time comes, he promised them, watch me.

Just in time, he looked out the window to see Sarah approaching. She's all dolled up, he thought, as he kneeled at the bed and hid the club underneath.

"Why so smart, darling? You look gorgeous." He kissed her on the cheek and sat down. "Where have you been?"

"A job interview, it went well, I think. I have to go back tomorrow evening."

"Really? Why? You didn't tell me. Where?"

"A restaurant in Weststadt. I heard they had a vacancy and I thought, Why not? I can't depend on you forever."

"Oh yes, you can. Why would you want to work? We have plenty of money. You should stay at home."

"And look after you?"

"Exactly. And I'll look after you, too."

"Oh, I see. You go out all day and have fun while I stay at home all day and . . ."

"You can go for a short walk in the morning."

". . . ha ha . . . and clean, cook, and . . . I don't think so. My mother, I am not."

"What's the job?"

"Waitress."

"What do you know about being a waitress?"

"Nothing."

"Oh, you should get it, then."

"What's so hard about being a waitress? Anyway, I don't mind either way, it was a good excuse to put on my best clothes."

"Well, you look beautiful. Come here."

"Stop bossing me about. You come here."

Jacob was half lying on the bed, one leg hanging to the floor. Sarah was standing by the kettle, which was just beginning to whistle. Jacob patted the bed and made a leering face. Sarah turned away, shaking her head.

"You have no right to deny me my conjugal rights," Jacob said. "You only earn that right after we have been married for six months."

"Three."

"Five."

They settled on four and a half but Sarah had another idea. "Guess what. The cinema's open again. Let's go. Guess what the first film is?"

"How should I know? Anyway, we'll never get tickets. The whole town will want to go."

Sarah smiled and raised her eyebrows as in, aren't I a clever girl? She put her hand in her top pocket and came out with two bits of paper. "Two tickets for tonight's showing of *The Gold Rush*." She spoke like an announcer: "The sound version of Charlie Chaplin's 1925 hit film. And guess what?"

"You keep asking me to guess what. What is there to guess? Come here at once." He patted the bed furiously.

"*The Gold Rush* is the only silent film to be nominated for an Oscar for best sound production."

"What time?"

"Six thirty. At the Schloss Kino. We should leave here at six, we'll be in plenty of time."

"So the interview went well?"

"Yes, I think so, the owner was nice. About sixty years old. He needs help because his wife is sick. What have you been doing?"

"Nothing much. The usual."

They drank tea, chatted over a sandwich, and strolled to the cinema, where they sat in the middle of one of the back rows. When the lights went out they held hands and settled in for the film. Jacob looked at Sarah, at her expectant upturned face, and marveled. She glanced at him and smiled. "I know," she said, leaning toward him and pecking him on the nose. "We're so normal."

They shook with laughter as Charlie Chaplin stuck two forks into two bread rolls like legs and feet and danced them across the table and back, a ballet of bread, kicking their legs and twirling their feet, his eyelashes and mustache twitching in time with the music, and all the while the silent genius smiled and nodded in glee. The audience loved it with more than just a shade of desperation. Weeks could go by in most people's lives without a smile.

The audience tittered nervously when Charlie began to boil his black leather shoe in the pot for Thanksgiving dinner, and when he said, "We have something to be thankful for," a knowing murmur passed through the theater. But if there was a damping shudder of recognition among the Germans it passed into hilarity when Charlie twirled the boiled shoelace on his fork like an extralong strand of spaghetti and chewed it with a beatific face.

Sarah laughed so much, Jacob looked at her. Is she hysterical?

He looked at the screen and back to Sarah. Is it that funny? Am I missing something? When Charlie said, boiling his shoe, "Not quite done yet. Give it another two minutes," she went into such a paroxysm that Jacob tried to shush her. When Charlie delicately pulled the leather from the sole, exposing the skeleton of nails, like pulling the meat from a fish, and sucked on the nails as if on fishbones, and held a bent nail in the crook of his little finger as if wanting to pull a wishbone, Sarah seemed to be banging her head on the seat in front.

Jacob looked at her in alarm, although he was chortling himself. But as Charlie took his first tentative bite from the leather sole, and chewed cautiously, as if the shoe might bite him back, Jacob fell silent and stared at the screen. Sarah sensed his tension and stopped giggling. "What is it, Jacob?" she whispered in his ear.

His eyes still fixed on the screen, his hand began to crush hers. She struggled to pull it away, and held his arm. "Darling, what is it? It's just a film."

"Maxie and I ate a shoe once," he said. "You just have to keep chewing."

Afterward they agreed it was a hilarious film, the little American was a genius, and they hoped the Schloss Kino would stay open. They felt like staying out for a drink but they had to get home to beat the curfew. Most of the way they walked in silence, a loving and companionable quiet. But their thoughts could not have been more opposed.

When Larsen hit Big Jim over the head with a shovel, Jacob sniffed. If only it was so easy. A fight, a shovel, The End. How hard do you have to hit someone, he wondered? How many times? And where is the best place to hit them anyway? On the back of the head? The top? The front? The side? Isn't the temple the most vulnerable spot? He should have found out.

Too late now. All he needed was for the Rat to be found dead, his head caved in, he the prime suspect, and somebody to say, "Oh yes, the Jew was asking just today where is the best place to hit someone on the head."

As for Sarah, she walked with her arm around Jacob's waist. Their hips rubbed as they walked, she pulled him to her so tight that their thighs met and they could have been walking on three legs. It was a funny film, but funny sad, and although she had laughed throughout, it was the sadness that remained. It was the sadness that touched her most, for it was her own sadness that was brimming over.

Before they had left the room Jacob couldn't understand why she had insisted on taking a bath. You're so perfect, he had said, don't change a thing, you smell divine. But it was the disgusting smell she had wanted to wipe from her body. She couldn't kiss Jacob with the Rat's odor in her pores, she needed to scrub herself clean.

And now as she walked so closely with her lover, she found herself at peace with her choice. To save Jacob from himself, to save their love and their future, she would take the deed upon herself, she would find the strength, she had to, she who couldn't hurt a mouse. She would do it not from hate or lust for revenge or anything negative, but for something positive, to save themselves. She had talked about something similar with Hoppi. They had discussed the question "When can a good person do a bad thing?" That was when they had to steal food to live, and to steal it from people who already didn't have enough. But at least they had ration cards to get more. And they were Nazis who would have reported them to the Gestapo in an instant. Why should they care if the Nazis had enough food? They had agreed: We are good people and we are doing a bad thing for a good reason.

Is murder the same? she wondered as she withdrew her arm from Jacob's waist and took his hand. Jacob looked down at her and smiled. "Love you," he said.

Sarah cried that night as they made love, and so did Jacob. Their tears mingled on their hot, damp faces as they kissed and trembled in each other's arms. It was their tenderest moment: They held each other so tightly they could hardly move, joined at the belly, as if for the last time.

THIRTY-THREE

Heidelberg,
June 12, 1945

Morning light glared through the parted curtain and stung Jacob's eyes. He turned away and covered his head with the pillow, struggling for sleep after a disturbed night of uneasy racing thoughts and distant images that danced behind his eyelids. Until one sensation erupted so sharply it jolted him awake. He sat up and opened his eyes and jerked his head from the blinding light. It was the Rat. And his thought was: Today's the day. And it came to him: All night as they slept, the steel club called from beneath the bed.

Still . . . last night . . . he closed his eyes in pleasure and lightly kissed Sarah's arm.

"Good morning," she murmured. Uuuhmuhhin . . . "What time is it?" Uuuhtiiissseeet. So much to do today.

"Would you like to go for a walk this morning?" Jacob said, squirming. "The castle gardens are beautiful, everything's blooming. We can have lunch afterwards."

A knot had already formed in his stomach and he lay back

with his hand on his belly, trying to calm his guts. It would be a long day, he needed to keep busy. If only he could tell Sarah, but she would try to stop him and she'd be right, too. He knew it wasn't much of a plan but, given that the Rat was leaving within a day or two, it was the best he could do. He felt like crying. He might never see Sarah again. If the Germans arrested him, anything could happen. They could take him to the station and beat him and claim he had resisted arrest, tried to escape. Very unfortunate. Shot attacking an officer.

He shook his head. Stop it. If there was any danger of being caught he knew what to do. Run to the Americans, turn himself in. He'd be safe there. When they heard the story, they'd give him a medal.

Or turn him over to the Germans. No, they couldn't. Could they?

And also, what is the best way to hit his head, downward or from the side?

Sarah plodded to the bathroom naked. "Nice idea, but can't. Busy. For the interview this evening."

"Why this evening? Why so late?"

"Dinnertime, apparently they're very busy, they want me to help, I think. Something like that. I don't really know but I said I would come then."

"Don't forget the curfew, it's a long walk from Weststadt."

"There's a tram now."

"Oh, good."

After breakfast Sarah told him she had to see the chaplain in half an hour. They had arranged to talk about some volunteer work.

"You're in demand," Jacob muttered, feeling nauseated again. He hurried into the bathroom while Sarah finished dressing. "Back here this afternoon?"

"Yes, darling, bye."

He heard the door close and came back to the bed, wiping his brow. He leaned down, searched with his fingers beneath the bed, and found the club. The steel was cold to the touch, so he held it against his forehead.

Sarah walked along the Neckarstaden above the river until she came to the steep stone steps that led down to the concrete wharf. They hugged the wall with a sheer drop on the outside of about five meters; enough, the townfolk hoped, to prevent the periodic flooding of the Neckar from inundating the lower part of the Old City.

She paused at the top, looking over the side. To the east, upriver, the sun hung above the treeline of the forest and sparkled on the damp roofs of the town, chasing the night chill from the streets. She had to shade her eyes with her hand to see the shadow of the castle against it. She looked away. When the sun set in the west, it would be directly downriver, over the other bank. That would be at about eight o'clock. They would meet at sunset and by nine, earlier even, it should be dark.

She hoped so anyway. She couldn't bear the thought of seeing his eyes. She was about to do something that would change her forever. That she could never share with Jacob, would always keep a secret . . . or would she? When they were old and it didn't matter anymore, would she take Jacob's wrinkled, veined hand and say, Jacob, I have something to tell you? Remember the Rat? It was me. I did it. To save you. To save us. Would she do that? Could she? Should she?

Sarah sniffed and smiled tightly. Don't be melodramatic, girl. But it was true. She looked at her hands, turned them around, rubbed her palms together. Tonight, tomorrow morning, she would be a different person. Better? Worse? Did it matter? What mattered was that Jacob would not do it, for he would be caught and their lives would fall apart, again, so soon after the horror from which they had rescued each other.

No. Not again. She wouldn't let their lives be destroyed again.

What if it didn't work? What if she was caught? Sarah looked out, across the river, at the woods on the other side, at the low line of homes fitting snugly in the hillside. I'd like to live in one of those homes one day, she thought, with Jacob.

But if they catch me?

She shook her head. They can't, she thought, they mustn't. They won't.

But if they do?

Sarah thought of something Jacob had said to her when they argued. "If I die, what does it matter? How many times can a man die? I died so many times in Bergen-Belsen." She hadn't said so at the time, she didn't want to encourage him, but really, he was right, when he said, anyway, what could they do to him if he killed the Rat? They wouldn't put him to death. A survivor takes revenge on a notorious SS camp guard. A slap on the wrist. They should give him a reward.

But that wasn't what frightened Sarah the most. She wasn't too worried about Jacob getting caught. It would just be a matter of time till they were together again. No, it wasn't that that scared her. What terrified her, what had made her reach the decision that went against every fiber of her being, was that she didn't think Jacob could do it. The Rat was a beast, and if Jacob attacked the Rat, she was afraid it would be Jacob who would be killed.

Sarah sighed and sat on one of the benches. There were three, two meters apart. They might not be alone this evening. Probably every young lover in town would be there to watch the sunset. She sighed again. It would have been the perfect place to sit with Jacob.

Two kilometers away, at that moment, Jacob neared the alley. It was off Bergheimerstrasse, just past the Lutheran church, which was on the other side of the street. He walked with a purposeful step, eyes fixed ahead, and he was thinking that he didn't care anymore. You can only dither so much. Finally, you have to act.

He felt the reassuring cold of steel against his leg. He had brought it just in case, to get used to the feel and weight of it, and if he had an opportunity he would take it, but his plan was to scout out the area and return in the afternoon.

He had never seen Seeler alone in the mornings. He had always been in the company of friends or one of his parents. But later, when he went to the beer garden, apart from the first couple of days, he was usually alone and he always returned alone at night, around eight o'clock, no doubt before the hotel kitchen closed. He never seemed drunk, but after a few beers he should be slower to react.

Jacob turned into the alley and stopped, facing the street. From here to the left turn into Kirchstrasse and the hotel was about another seventy-five meters up the main street. He stretched out his arms. The alley was about two meters wide. He turned and peered along it. The usual mess and garbage and stray cats. He walked down to see where it went. The farther he walked, the sharper the stink of cat urine until it opened onto what seemed a wasteland, a neglected space among three residential blocks. Perfect. No reason for anybody to walk through. He could wait and not be bothered by anyone. He walked back to the other end and thought it through.

He would see Seeler coming from a distance. As he came opposite the alley he would grab him by the coat and pull him in and hurl him against the wall. Seeler slowed by drink, the element of surprise, the shock of his aggression, all that should give him a second or two of advantage, maybe three. Not more. In that time he had to pull him in, raise the club, and smash his head. But really smash it, a knockout blow right away, and then finish him off on the ground.

What if he missed him and he walked by? You'd have to start on the street and drag him into the alley. Or do it all on the street. A very bad idea. Jacob heard himself saying: Don't miss him!

But what if he's on the other side of the street? Let's hope not. So far he's always been on this side. But if he is, cross the road, follow him, do it there. No other choice.

Either way, whatever happens, the best place to run is back down the alley. Yes. Jacob walked up and down the street a few times, judging distances, times, wondering how busy the street would be. Most people would be home by then.

He followed his escape route down the alley to the empty space and saw three exits, one through each tall building. He walked to each and realized it was also perfect. To escape, all he had to do was run down the alley, walk quickly across the open ground, not to attract attention, pass through the middle building, and he'd come out on the other side at Alte Eppelheimerstrasse and just stroll away.

If he was lucky nobody would see him. And if they did, they wouldn't chase him down such a sinister alley. He could soon disappear into the crowd.

With a light step, Jacob walked to University Square for a beer. He almost smiled to himself. Maxie, this could work . . .

At the round Stammtisch by the bar, Adolf collected the plates after the Seelers' breakfast, while Hans sucked and searched for remnants with his tongue. His mother had laid her hand on his and his father heaved a sigh that wobbled the length of his body. Herr Seeler opened his mouth to continue but Hans indicated toward Adolf. When the clattering ended and Adolf walked carefully away, balancing plates and leftovers, Wolfgang Seeler said his piece. Trudi had tears in her eyes. "But it's so far away."

Wolfgang shook his head sadly. "I know. But the boy's right. There's an organization to help. He has to go. Somewhere faraway, at least till we know what will happen here next."

"I'll never see you again," Trudi said tearfully, stroking Hans's forehead. "My baby, my little baby."

At that Hans laughed. "Come on, Mutti, look at me, I'm not your baby anymore." He took her hand and sucked her middle finger. "Mutti, drinkie, drinkie, I'm hungry, I'm hungry."

She pushed him away with an attempt at a smile. "You know what I mean. You'll always be my baby."

Her husband snorted. He leaned over to the bar and lifted the ceramic top off a large plate and put the plate on the table. "Here, Hans, eat this instead. Something to remember us by." Lebkuchen, the Seeler gingerbread specialty, not only at Christmas but all year round. Hans took one and savored it. "Mutti, it's the tastiest ever." Frau Seeler smiled as if she had been blessed by the pope in St. Peter's.

Her smile spread further, she looked as if she would burst, when Hans told them his news. "I'm seeing that girl tonight. Gertie Haas. The one who came for the job."

"Really?" Trudi said. "She's so lovely."

"Yes, isn't she," Hans said. "And I can see exactly what you're thinking."

"Maybe you will want to stay after all," his mother said. "She's beautiful and kind and honest, she would make a perfect wife . . ."

"Aren't you getting a bit carried away?" her husband interrupted. "They haven't kissed yet." He turned to Hans. "Or have you?"

Hans shook his head with a tight grin. "Not yet, no."

"Oh, I'm so excited. Of course she's going to work here, she would do wonders for the place, laughing and talking to everyone, oh, Hans . . ." Trudi took his hand between both of hers. "It's time to marry, you're thirty-two . . ."

"Thirty-one."

"Thirty-two in six weeks. Why don't you stay here, see if you like her, please, it's such an opportunity, girls like that come by once in a lifetime . . . Hans. Don't go away. You'll be all right here. You've only been home a few weeks. Please." Her eyes were red again and the tears traced her plump cheeks. She leaned toward him as if to kiss him, pleading with her wet eyes. Wolfgang placed his hand on her arm and squeezed, as if to say, it'll be all right, my dear. It'll be all right.

Hans was burning to tell them, but he couldn't. It would endanger everything. There were at least another fifty like him doing the same thing, and many more in the pipeline. It hurt them now but the pain would wear off and later, as soon as possible, he'd be in touch and let them know where he was living and what his new name was and then, one day, when it was safe, he'd come visit.

He had to keep it to himself. They thought he was running to Argentina, that the organization would take care of him there, and that was true for the most senior SS. But for the junior ranks it was a cover story. He was going somewhere else, and not so far. In two days he would leave on what looked like a journey of ten thousand kilometers, but that would take him barely three hundred.

With genuine new papers, a new birth certificate, a new name, everything for a new identity, a new story, he would be traveling only as far as a small town in the Black Forest where a post as Hauptwachtmeister awaited him in the Steinkirchen police force. Low- to medium-rank SS servicemen with new identities were being inserted into the police across the country. They were protected. And sworn to silence. Until summoned to the cause, which would rise again when the time was right, when the so-called victors finally understood who the real enemy was: the Communists.

He could throw them a bone, though. "Yes, she is very nice," he said. "Who knows, maybe we will fall in love. But she will have to come join me over there, at least in the beginning." He raised his eyebrows at his mother. A simple woman.

Beautiful Gertie Haas, he was thinking. They fell for her. What I could do to that body. A smooth talker. His face hardened as he remembered last night. Tonight would be different. Lying bitch. She thought she was so clever, but then they all do. Lying, just to get a job. Licking his ass for the money. He could smell a Jew from the other side of the street. They're all the same. And they'll all get the same.

We'll see how smart she is back here with my belt in her mouth.

THIRTY-FOUR

Heidelberg,
June 13, 1945

The big man leaned back with his legs apart, his hands folded on his stomach, and a satisfied smile across his face. From his shaded café table on the corner of Apothekergasse his eyes flitted from pretty girl to pretty girl in the noisy crowd in the market square. Each day there seemed to be more people and more cheer in the air. More young men, too. German soldiers were drifting home, some still in uniform, some on crutches. The American occupiers moved in groups, spreading chocolate and nylon stockings, buying souvenirs and women. Even the refugees looked sharper in their donated clothes, especially the girls. But he was looking for one pretty girl in particular.

He tensed but before he could jump to his feet he realized how little the hands were that covered his eyes from behind. He pulled them free and forced the hands to his chest, bringing Sarah's body over his shoulder. He kissed her on the cheek.

"You got my message, then," she said. Her closeness woke

another image: Sarah's contorted face, torn clothes, filthy and smelly, cowering in the corner like a beaten dog, whining for help. It went as quickly as it came. Her hair was washed and shiny, and in a simple white blouse and black cotton trousers, smiling and relaxed, she looked as if she had not a care in the world.

"Well, well, Sarah Kaufman, I do believe you are the most beautiful girl in Heidelberg, and I should know because I have been sitting here for half an hour ogling most of them."

"And thinking of your wife, I hope."

"Thank you, Sarah. Yes, as a matter of fact, thinking of my wife. This damned war is over but I still won't get home for months, maybe a year, who knows. I hardly remember what she looks like. Three years it's been, more. I wonder how many children she has now."

Sarah took his hand. "She is such a lucky woman. I wonder if she knows."

"She knows I am a soldier, that's what she knows. She probably thinks I have syphilis by now."

Sarah snatched back her hand. "Do you?"

He roared with laughter. "You can't catch syphilis by holding hands."

"Do you?"

"Of course not. Have a drink?"

She drank a coffee. She added real milk, not because she liked coffee with milk but just because they had some. "When are you leaving?" she asked.

Isak sighed. "In a day or two. We've done what we came to do, some coordination work, now we're trying to delay going back to Berlin for as long as we can."

"I can imagine." Sarah let her eyes wander the market until they settled again on Isak. She gazed thoughtfully at him and slowly closed her eyes. A teardrop clung to her eyelash, and

Isak took her hand back. "I was just thinking, Isak. I owe you everything." She placed her other hand on his, until all four hands formed their own little tower of trust on the table. "How did you find me? Who sent you to me? What angel cared for me?"

Isak squeezed her hands.

"I think it was Hoppi, I really do. It was Hoppi who sent you to me." Sarah took back her hands and wiped her eyes. She had put on mascara and now the back of her hand was black and her cheeks were smudged. Isak leaned forward, spat on his hand, and wiped her cheek clean.

"Ugh," Sarah said.

"It's good luck, where I come from."

"Yes, I can see, you're so lucky."

He laughed. "Yes, yes I am, so far anyway."

"Isak, there's something else, an idea I have, something else I have to ask you . . ."

In their room that afternoon Sarah was surprised that Jacob didn't show more interest. "They're coming this evening," Sarah had told him. "I met Isak to say good-bye, he's going back to Berlin, and he knew about it. Eighteen Jews from Theresienstadt, just like you said you heard, remember? They're coming tonight." She had thought Jacob would be excited. Isak hadn't known their names or where they had come from but it stood to reason that some of them would be from Heidelberg, or why else would they come here at all? Jacob may know some of them. She grew up out of town in a farming village but Jacob had lived right here in the middle of the old Jewish quarter.

But his mind was somewhere else. He was barely listening. He was staring at nothing, his jaw twitched, and he was drumming with his fingers. His lips moved.

"Jacob, are you talking to yourself? Did you hear me at all? Why don't you go to welcome them? There may be someone you know, and think how nice it would be for them, to meet a Jew here? I'd go myself but I have to be in the restaurant." She wanted him to be at the Volkshochschule when their bus arrived, that's where Isak had said they would be taken. The freed prisoners would be given beds in the high school, food, money, and clothes. Chaplain Monahan would be there too, and a few Jewish soldiers from the Sixth Army.

"Why do you want me to be there so much?" Jacob had said.

"I already told you." She nagged and nagged until Jacob promised faithfully. "All right, all right, I'll go there," he said.

"And wait till they come. You should get there early, they could come at any time. Be there about seven o'clock."

"All right, all right."

Sarah kissed him. "And you'll wait till they come. Whenever. Promise?"

"What's so important? Promise."

She kissed him again. Anything could happen. He might need the alibi. And she might need the time.

THIRTY-FIVE

Heidelberg,
June 13, 1945

As the minute hand labored from five to six o'clock in the afternoon, Jacob sat down, rose, sat down again, rose and paced nervously in the small room, and muttered to himself. "What is it,
stop it," Sarah said again. His pacing stopped her from sleeping,
not that she could anyway. She was as wound up as he but hid it
better. He gave her one glass of water followed by another. He
boiled the kettle. "Here," he said, "have a cup of tea."

To himself he said: Sarah, go pee already!

He needed to go to the alley. He was ready. But he couldn't
get his club. It was under the bed and Sarah was on it.

After an hour of mounting anxiety it occurred to him to go
to the bathroom and leave the water running, a suggestive
background tinkle that soon had its effect. Sarah rolled to her
side and sat with her feet on the floor before heaving herself
up, saying, "Darling, you left the tap on."

"Oh, sorry."

She went to the bathroom and sat down. Jacob lunged under the bed and called from the door, "I'll go now, don't want to miss them, see you later," and closed the door behind him. At the doorstep he sucked in air and sighed in relief, tapped the steel hidden along his leg, and set off for the alley by the Lutheran church on Bergheimerstrasse.

He should have said good-bye properly, but how could he? Even though anything could happen now. Would he come home tonight? His stomach had been feeling more and more knotted, his throat constricted, and now that he was working his way fast through the aimless afternoon strollers, pulling to the side and accelerating as he overtook each shuffling couple, perspiration began to dampen his forehead. His hand gripped the steel through his pocket.

His face hardened as he walked. He felt as if he were about to cast off an unbearable burden. He was about to strike a blow for all those who never could or would. Heaven and hell demanded it. He had been thinking too much for too long, he told himself, now was the time for action. He heard Sarah: Don't do it, Jacob, revenge is wrong, it will ruin you, it will desecrate you, it is the path to moral destruction, we are not the killing kind.

Be quiet, he told her shrill voice. After all we have been through, and you still don't know how to hate.

Nearing the alley, Jacob thought, But I do.

As the sun sank across the river and the shadows lengthened in the city streets, the narrow alley darkened and dusk crept across the road. Perfect, Jacob thought, lurking in the shade, an obscure outline in the gloom.

Strange that he just slipped out, Sarah thought. He'd been distracted. She was sure he was worrying about the Rat. She was sure he was planning something that he didn't want to tell her about. Of course he was, he was running out of time. She had to act quickly, before him. As she walked along Neckarstaden to the wharf, she fiddled with her blouse and opened the third button. She glanced down to see her bare skin, and her lips set in grim purpose.

She hated what she was about to do, hated it with all her soul, and feared it too, but she saw no other way. If Jacob attacked Hans, he would be either killed himself or caught afterward. If he was caught, he would be sent to jail, and German prisoners could beat him to death in the cell. Or at best he would serve many years in prison. What else could happen? Plenty, and they all meant the same: Their life together would be over. She would lose him. Just as she had lost Hoppi and the baby, her family, her happiness. She had lost everything, more than a soul could bear, and then she had found Jacob, dear Jacob, so busy making money and organizing their life and planning their future, and yet so consumed with hatred and lust for revenge.

She hadn't stopped Hoppi from leaving, she had learned her lesson the hard way. Now she must stop Jacob.

And this was the only way. She glanced at the watch that Jacob had given her with some tale of what he had bartered with this person to get that from that person and in the end here it was, a pretty Swiss timepiece that she didn't want or need. Who had it belonged to? What suffering had they endured to make them part with this family heirloom? What had it bought them: a piece of meat to feed the children, for how many days? Two?

It was ten to eight. She looked toward the wharf and saw ahead the gap in the river wall where the steps went down. Was he waiting? Her heart, fast until now, began to pound and she breathed in short sharp bursts as her body absorbed what was about to happen. What, you just understood? she told herself. You just realized? Calm down. She gripped the wall and leaned against it with both hands, supporting herself and taking large gulps of river air.

She resumed her walk along the wall until she reached the steps. This is it. It's all or nothing now. She couldn't do any more. She took a deep breath, touched her hair, adjusted her beret, and took the steep steps carefully. She didn't want to fall, but still she felt shattered. Her heart was broken.

This is where she should have been meeting Hoppi.

"Where is the bastard?" Jacob said to himself as he paced from the corner to the alley and back again. He'd been waiting for an hour, looking at the corner where the Rat would come from if he was leaving the hotel, and the other direction, where he would first see him if he was coming home from the beer garden. Either way he'd pass him, if he was on this side of the road. He'd been getting cold in the alley, he hadn't realized that it acted as a wind tunnel, funneling a blast from the open space at one end to the main street where he was standing. He should have brought his coat but that would have got in the way. He raised his right shoulder and rolled it in its socket, stuck out his elbow and rotated his wrist, keeping his striking arm limber and loose. He brought out his steel club to feel the weight, get used to its heft in his grip. It was warm after being close to his skin. Smooth and deadly. It'll go through bone like a hammer. Maybe he should have got a hammer? Would a hammer have been better?

And all the time he was thinking of Sarah. He should have been thinking of the Rat and Maxie and the others, psyching himself up, readying himself for killing. Instead his thoughts were full of their love, her warmth, her body, the contentment he could not have dreamed possible just a month ago. He poked his head around the alley corner in case Seeler was coming.

Funny, he sniffed, her sleeping on the bed when he had to go. Even without being aware, she had done her best to stop him being here right now, and if she knew what he was up to she would go crazy. She would do anything to stop him. Lucky she doesn't know, then. She didn't understand. All he wanted to do was this one thing, and then it would all be over. Debt paid. Promise kept. They would leave, go somewhere else. Or even stay in Heidelberg. At least until he had made enough money to really start a business somewhere. He had counted his money that morning. He had more than nine hundred dollars in American, a small fortune in the circumstances. And all that in a month. A construction business. He'd worked it all out. He'd import construction material for sale, and also build homes and offices. Big buildings. Everybody needed work, everybody needed a home, the destroyed city centers would need to be rebuilt from scratch. He'd hire architects, designers, builders, tradesmen of all kinds, he'd put the deals together. He could live in Heidelberg and make the right contacts with the Americans, and work in Mannheim and maybe Frankfurt. Both towns were lucky if one in three buildings was standing after the Allied bombing. Glass, he thought. That's it. They'll all need windows. I'll start a glass business too, supply myself and everyone else.

Start quickly, he said to himself, that's the secret, get to work before anyone else.

He peered around the corner again. There weren't many people in the street, it would be easy to spot Seeler.

He'd get number 9 back, he was sure of that. The house had belonged to his family for so long there would be no problem. The Bergers wouldn't be so happy, though. Or the neighbors. They'd all stick together. They hadn't changed. But that didn't matter. They'll all do what they're told, they're good Germans, that's the trouble. What's the joke? There could never be a revolution in Germany, the police wouldn't allow it. He'd make money quickly and then they'd leave. America. Palestine. Who knows, maybe Paris? He'd always wanted to see Paris. He could run the business from there.

"Where is that bastard?"

THIRTY-SIX

Heidelberg,
June 13, 1945

While Jacob fretted in the alley, rose-streaked water washed against the wharf in the wake of a tugboat pulling a platform loaded with military crates and piles of boxes. The setting sun touched the trees and its last rays cast a cool glow on the bench where Sarah sat, taking deep breaths, focused on what she had to do. With a slight breeze it was chillier than she had expected. She did up the buttons on her blouse, thought better of it, and undid them again. If only she had a mirror.

She had arrived just in time. Two benches were occupied by young couples and since she had claimed the last one two more couples had come who now sat with their legs dangling over the wharf. They held hands and kissed and lay their heads on each other's shoulders, and again she thought she should have come here with Jacob. Or Hoppi.

Nerves made it hard to swallow, she could feel her heart beating. She looked up over her shoulder. People were leaning on the wall, gazing across the water, waiting for the sunset or just resting during their evening stroll. Their faces were lit by an orange glow. It could not have been more serene: for them. As for her, how quickly it all changed. From terror in basements and bushes, alone and starving, to hot baths with her lover in their lovely little home. In what? A month? Her eyes closed. It didn't seem possible. Was it too good to be true? She heaved a sigh of contentment, a gentle smile played on her lips. Until she started: Yes, it may be too good to be true. If it all goes wrong now.

She had almost forgot why she was here.

In the alley, Jacob's heart was racing. It's almost dark. Where is he? Don't say I missed him. His mouth was dry. He licked his lips. He should have brought a bottle of water. He should have worn a coat. He should have come earlier. He should have done a lot of things. How long to wait? Verdammt! Damn, tomorrow's Saturday, the Rat's leaving for Argentina, this is my last chance: Where is the bastard!

Jacob peered around the corner yet again and jerked his head back as if he'd been shot. It's him. It's the Rat. Now his heart slammed against his ribs. Thirty meters away. Close. From the hotel then he came. Only now it occurred to Jacob. He was coming from the right, so he'd have to pull him in with his left hand. His weaker arm. He might not have the strength. Or should he hold the club in his left hand, wait for Seeler to walk by, grab him with his right arm, then pull him inside? He didn't have the power or the coordination to hit him with the club in his left hand. He'd need to pull him in, throw him against the wall, transfer the club from his left to his right hand, then hit him. Shit. Why hadn't he thought of it before? He could hear the heavy steps now. Is the ground shaking? The Rat was wearing a coat and a hat. He could grab the coat. But with which hand? He held the club in his left hand, ready to grab Seeler with his right, his stronger arm, as he walked by. Or just club him in the street with both hands and then drag him into the alley? If he falls, people may see him. He pressed himself back against the wall, tried to push himself into the bricks, he thought his heart would explode, he smelled his own sweat, he prepared his legs to pounce. At the last moment he changed his mind and held the club in his right. He'll pull him in with the left and hit him at the same time. Or pull him in with both hands. But what about the club?

Jacob sensed him before he saw him, a premonition of him, his aura, maybe it was the evil that preceded him, and now a leg appeared in the frame of the alley walls followed by his bulk and another leg and he was past.

Jacob could hardly breathe. What happened? Had his heart stopped for an instant? He gasped for air, slumped back against the wall, hung his head forward, and heard the dull thud of the club falling by his feet. Inside, his head was screaming, howling, it was Maxie, and he turned and threw up against the wall.

Sweating, groaning, he felt a hand stroking his head, lips brushing his neck, he shivered, heard a loving whisper in his ear, and he dropped to the ground, where he sat against the wall and could barely support his head. He felt his strength drain away, all his energy fade; he could have slept for two days on the spot.

It's over, he thought. Sarah was right. There was no point waiting for Seeler to come back home.

He couldn't do it.

His body had understood before his mind, and said no. If it meant losing Sarah, he didn't want to. Between Maxie, who was dead, and Sarah, who was alive, at last he chose. His heart leaped. He felt a tear of joy.

Jacob pulled himself up and steadied himself against the wall. He swirled saliva around his mouth and spat out bile that had burned his throat. He took deep breaths and looked back down the alley, to the light at the end, the courtyard, the middle building, his escape route.

He stubbed his foot on steel and looked down. He bent but stopped halfway. He straightened and walked out of the alley, leaving the club on the ground.

He's late, Sarah thought. Maybe he won't come? Another young couple came down the steps and approached her bench. She waved them away with a gesture and a smile and they went to the edge of the wharf and sat with their legs hanging over. Where is he? Has something happened? Jacob? She felt her hands trembling, held one out to see if it was shaking. At that moment, with one arm stretched out, with the sun almost behind the hills, Hans Seeler took her other hand, making her start, and she felt the bench shake as he fell down next to her. "I didn't frighten you, did I?" Hans asked.

"I didn't hear you coming," Sarah said. "I was daydreaming. Isn't it beautiful here?"

"Oh, yes. When we were small we jumped into the water from here, the river was nothing like it is now. It was clean. There was a rope ladder to climb back up." He stood, went to the edge, and looked along the wharf. "It's gone. Everything's gone. It's all so different now." He sat next to Sarah and took her hand again, resting it on his thigh.

She looked down. Her hand was so small in his big fist. She should have been afraid but a calm settled upon her. Rarely in her life had she felt so sure of herself, so sure that she was doing the right thing, the only possible thing. She closed her eyes for a long moment, as she breathed in, telling herself, Be strong.

He had been gazing into the distance. Now he looked down, at her hand, and stroked it. "Well, well, Gertie, here we are." He smiled at her.

"Yes, Hans, here we are."

"Gertie Haus."

"Haas. Gertie Haas." She squeezed his hand.

"Oh yes, Haas. Where does that name come from?"

Sarah frowned at him. "Where does it come from?" She shrugged, as if to say, doesn't everyone know? "It's from Hase, hare. You know, the saying. 'Wo die Fuchse und die Hase einander gute Nacht sagen.' Where the foxes and the hares say good night to each other. It means in the middle of nowhere. Because my family, going way back, came from tiny villages in the north, in the middle of nowhere. Hase became Haas, I suppose." She laughed. "What about Seeler, where does that come from?"

"I have no idea."

"Well, Hans Seeler, here is a question you should be able to answer." She peered through the dusk, at the young couples gazing across the water at the big red ball; searching up and down the wharf; over his shoulder and pausing at the people standing at the top of the steps. "What did you do during the war?"

"Well, that came from nowhere," he said, turning to look at her directly. "Anyway, you ask as if the war is over."

"Isn't it?"

"Which war? Against the Americans? Yes. Against the Bolsheviks? It's just beginning. But, so tell me, you want to work in our hotel?"

"Yes, I do, I hope so, your parents are very nice."

"Oh. And I hope I meet your approval too."

She took her hand from his. "Why, who decides? I imagine if your mother needs help she would decide, no?"

"Well, jobs are hard to find these days, very hard, especially good ones. And yes, actually, I do have something to say in the matter." He raised an eyebrow and moved closer. "Isn't that why you wanted to meet me?"

Sarah looked away, across the river, toward the sun, whose reflection, as it sank, sent a shimmering column of orange across the darkening water, pointing at them. The sky was turning a delicate pink, diaphanous among the gathering night clouds. The young couples kissed and hugged. She looked over her shoulder, toward the steps. *Where are you? Please come now. Now!* A knot tightened in her stomach as she searched among the people gathered on the road above. It was hard to see faces in the fading light.

"No, it isn't," she said. "Why would you think that?" The pink glow of the sun sparkled in her dark eyes. He leaned forward and she leaned back, away from his thin lips, his stinking mustache. He stopped her with his hand behind her head, his fingers curling in her hair, and as her eyes widened, her heart pounded, he pulled her toward him and their lips met. She pinched hers and squealed with disgust. Desperate, her eyes wide, she stared over his shoulder at the group at the top of the steps, forcing herself to see through the gloom, and there, standing on the top step, a big man. He raised his hand and waved and walked down two steps.

Sarah jumped up and screamed. "How dare you! Leave me alone. Don't touch me." The young couples turned and looked as Hans sat up in surprise. He stared as Sarah hit his shoulder and slapped his face. "Help, leave me alone," she screamed, a thin, piercing cry. Hans stood up and grabbed her shoulder. "Gertie, what are you doing, be quiet." Sarah kept screaming and Hans slapped her in the face, not very hard. At this Sarah screamed louder, held on to his jacket, and pulled and wriggled, as if trying to escape his grasp.

Isak bounded down the stairs, shouting at the man to leave the woman alone, and leaped onto Hans, striking him in the face. Hans, shocked, stepped back. "Why, you Jew bitch," he yelled at Sarah, "I didn't do anything." Isak punched him again and sent him sprawling to the ground. Sarah was screaming, "Help, he attacked me, help!" Now everyone was watching, the young lovers, the strollers above, as the two men struggled on the ground. Hans had kicked out behind Isak's knee and his leg had buckled. He fell awkwardly to the ground, saving himself with one arm and fending Hans off with the other. He understood from the perfectly judged kick—Seeler knows how to fight. Finish it quickly. He roared and threw himself onto Seeler, his weight forced him to the ground, and he punched him in the head, once, twice, he seized his neck and smashed his head into the concrete. But Hans lashed out with his elbow, catching Isak in the eye, and he wriggled away and kicked Isak in the arm and rolled over to the edge of the wharf, and as he rolled his right hand went into his coat and came out with a pistol that, even as he rolled, he whipped into a straight arm as if the pistol were his hand, and he was pointing at Isak's chest.

But Isak's gun was already in his hand, and as Hans fired Isak dropped and fired too, a thunderclap and its echo. There was a scream from a woman on the wall as Isak heard the crack of a bullet missing by millimeters. She fell to the ground. But Isak didn't miss. He had thrown himself to the side and on one knee aimed the Nagant pistol. At dusk Hans formed a perfect silhouette in the red glow. He hit Hans in the chest, once, twice. The .32-caliber bullets hurled Hans back. Splashes of blood looked like smudges in the dark. He teetered over the edge and, with everyone agape, he tried to rise but sank to his knees. His good arm clawed at the brick as he toppled over the side of the wharf and splashed into the river. His arm flailed as he tried to keep himself up in the current, which pulled him out.

"He'll drown," somebody shouted.

"He's dead anyway," another voice said.

"No, he isn't, look," a woman screamed, "someone help him."

Isak watched the body go limp in the current. He glanced at Sarah. She had thrown herself to the ground. Their eyes met. Hers were wide with shock. He looked back at the floating body until there was a scream through the dark, "Hilfe, hilfe."

Isak tore his jacket off and pulled off his shoes. "I'll save him," he yelled, before anybody else could. "Call for help."

With powerful strokes the big Russian swam out and turned downriver and quickly caught up with Hans, whose head was lolling to the side, half submerged. He had been shot just above the heart. Hans croaked and gasped for breath, kicking to keep his head above water while one arm floated uselessly, and with the other he tried to fight off Isak. The current swept them out, they hit a sudden cold stretch, it was too much and Hans's head sank as his legs weakened. Isak came at him from behind, like a lifesaver, and took hold of Hans's head, cradling it with one arm as he struck for shore with the other, kicking his legs. A wake of blood trailed them, dark in the gloomy orange light.

"What are you doing?" Hans gasped, unable to understand. Was he saving him? After he shot him?

Now a crowd of people were running along the road above the river, pointing and shouting at the drifting men. They ran faster but there was no way down the high wall to the river to help until the ruins of the next bridge, half a kilometer away. They shouted encouragement to Isak as they raced.

Sarah was sobbing on the bench. It was dark now, as a

crowd of people comforted her. An elderly woman held her to her breast. "There, there, dear," she was saying, "we all saw it, him hitting you like that." Two policemen pushed through the crowd.

And in the water, as the current pulled them downstream, a dark blot on the darker waters, Isak Brodsky, kicking with his legs to stay up, put his mouth to the ear of Hans Seeler and breathed, as water washed over Hans's face and covered his terror-stricken eyes, "Can you . . . hear me?"

"Yes," Seeler gasped, coughing, spluttering. "Save me . . . please."

"Save you?" Isak said into his ear, in a calm, clear voice, as if he were standing on the road, not swimming backward in the dark Neckar, night setting upon them. "Save you? SS-TV Unterscharführer Hans Seeler . . . in the name . . . of the . . . Jewish people . . . I sentence you . . . to death."

With that he shifted his weight until he loomed above Seeler's face and pressed his chest down, and the weight of Isak's body kept the Rat's head underwater until the frantic threshing and flailing died and Seeler's body went limp and the bubbles stopped rising and it was all over.

THIRTY-SEVEN

Heidelberg,
June 13, 1945

That's strange. What's different? From the door Jacob surveyed the room: crumpled sheets on the unmade bed, clothes strewn on the chair as if she'd been trying everything on, the bedside table with a cup of water and some toilet paper rolled into a ball, the sink full of dirty dishes. That's unlike Sarah, he thought, she must have left in a hurry. He lingered on the cheap oil painting of Heidelberg Castle at dusk from across the Neckar; there must be one in every rented room in town. He closed the door behind him, took off his clothes, threw them on the bed with Sarah's, and went into the shower.

He let the water run over his body and felt the relief wash over him, felt the dust and the grime of the alley wash away. There was hot water again. He turned the tap down to leave some for Sarah, too.

He watched the water course along his arms and drip from the hairs of his chest onto his belly and to his feet. There was something different. He had put on weight since Bergen-Belsen, but not much. He had always been thin, and as he soaped himself he could feel it. In the camp his skin had hung, it was like a loose shirt, and now it was tight, he had filled out with muscle.

Soap and water. Hot water. Oh, God! Maxie smiled, those impish eyes. How old? Six? Seven? When they had stopped having baths together? He wished he could see his mother's face but he just couldn't fit together the pieces. She leaned over the bath and rubbed them with soap, first Maxie standing up and then him. Maxie would splash him and the water ran over the floor and Maxie had to mop it up himself. He would always pull the top of the mop so that Maxie couldn't clean up, and they'd chase each other naked through the house, with Mutti running after them shouting, "You're dripping, you're dripping, you're making a mess." They'd had a fight and he'd hidden Maxie's duck. Or was it a cow, a rubber cow? Maxie was always a crybaby.

Often they'd get into the same bed and Maxie would say, "Tell me a story." He made them up. About things he had done in school, with the older boys, in which he was always the hero. Maxie soon nodded off, and he'd get up and fall asleep in his own bed.

In Bergen-Belsen they had shared a wooden board all night because he didn't have another one to go to. He didn't have any stories to tell and Maxie didn't fall asleep, he babbled and the open sores made him shift and toss so that Jacob couldn't sleep either.

Maxie had been semi-delirious for weeks as the typhus took hold. The beating from the Rat had only killed him quicker. It was probably a relief.

Jacob turned off the shower and wandered into the room, drying himself. He knew now it wasn't the room that was different. It was him. He felt lighter. He was floating. If I were walking outside, he thought, there would be a spring in my step.

All the way home he had thought of Maxie. His oath hadn't been worth much, as it turned out. What did that say about him? The thought of revenge had given him a will to live, brought him home even, and then, when it came to it, he couldn't do it. In his heart he knew he didn't even want to. There was no revenge that justified throwing away his own life, and certainly not if it harmed Sarah, too. What's the proverb? If you seek revenge, dig two graves. Maxie would have wanted him to live, have a family with Sarah, that would be the true revenge. He sighed. They could adopt, there would be many Jewish orphans. And others.

Just not blond and blue-eyed.

Nine thirty came and went and Jacob stood by the door, looking up and down the deserted street. It was dark and the rooftops gleamed dark blue in the moonlight. In the houses lights were turning off one by one, as his mind began to race.

The most likely explanation was that Sarah had missed the last tram before the curfew and had to stay over in the restaurant. Probably the owners lived upstairs and they had a spare room, or she was sleeping on a sofa in their living room. There was no way to let him know. Yes, that must be it. Or could she be stuck in the street after curfew? No, it wasn't like that anymore, it wasn't a shooting curfew. At most they would arrest her. Could something have happened to her? Could she be in the hospital? An accident? The tram crashed?

Jacob paced in the small room. Just when he was looking forward to holding her, telling her how much he loved her and how right she had been, that all his talk of revenge and killing was all pointless, it was all vanity, that nothing mattered more than their life together. She would be so happy. He had so many plans. Where was she? He imagined every terrible possibility, while telling himself to calm down.

At eleven fifteen his heart stopped. There was a knock on the door. He looked at it. If it was Sarah, she would just come in. Who could it be? The police? What had happened?

Jacob got up from the bed, where he had been lying fully clothed. His pulse was running away, he tried to control his breathing. He collected himself and walked slowly to the door, staring at it, trying to see through it. With his hand on the handle he froze, and tried to swallow. He couldn't. There was no point delaying this. He stepped back and swung the door open.

An old man with shaven gray stubble for hair and a white beard stood in the door-frame. His face was deeply lined and his cheeks seemed to hang from his jaw. His eyes were sunken and dark, and bloodshot. He wore a new coat that was too big and hung from his shoulders.

A shock of disappointment ran through Jacob. He managed to say, "Hello, can I help you?"

The man stared at him and his mouth moved, his teeth showed, an attempt at a smile, before a word came out: "Jacob."

A sob came so suddenly and from so deep that Jacob had to catch his breath.

"Papa?"

"Good luck, then," a voice said, and a policeman walked away.

The two men stared at each other, mouths open. Jacob was rooted to the spot as his father brushed past him. For a moment he continued to stare into the deserted street.

"Nice," his father said. He walked to the bed and sat down, testing the springs. He looked up and smiled and shook his head in wonder.

Jacob's jaw hung open. When he could, he said, "Would you like some tea?"

"Yes, please."

Jacob could not fill the kettle. He was shaking too much.

"Let me," his father said, "you were never much good in the kitchen. Sit down." He took the kettle and filled it and lit a match and put it on to boil. Jacob couldn't take his eyes off him.

Solomon Klein found the tea and put a spoonful of sugar in a cup and looked at the kettle, waiting for it to boil. He's shrunk, Jacob thought, and he wasn't tall to begin with. As he gave the cup to Jacob, Solomon said, as if his son were late from school, "Where is Maxie?"

Jacob took the cup and felt the tears heating his eyes. His eyes met his father's. He shook his head and felt himself shiver.

Solomon looked away. "Do you know what happened?"

Jacob nodded.

"Were you with him?"

"Yes."

"Where?"

"Bergen-Belsen."

Solomon took his cup and sat heavily on the bed. He gazed slowly around the room until he noticed Sarah's shoes by the bed, and the pile of her clothes that Jacob had put on a chair. He glanced at Jacob and nodded in approval.

Jacob told his father all about Sarah.

He told him about Maxie.

He told him about Dr. Berger and Schmutzig and the house.

He showed him his money and told him about his plans for the future.

He never mentioned the Rat.

When he asked Solomon, his father talked a little about Gurs, less about Auschwitz, and nothing about the rest. Why burden the boy?

They held hands while they spoke and neither said the half

of it. At one o'clock in the morning Jacob offered his father the bed. "Sarah will probably come in the morning," he said.

"You sleep here too," Solomon said.

"Yes, we were used to two in a bed, me and Maxie."

"What? You had a bed?"

"Not exactly."

Solomon was snoring before Jacob came back from brushing his teeth. Air escaped from his nose like exhaust from a tank. Jacob pushed him onto his side until he sounded merely like a motorbike. Is that an improvement? he wondered. He lay on his back, his head on his hands, listening to his father with a smile on his face. He could hardly believe it. As for Dr. Berger, he couldn't wait to see his reaction when his father went home. He would take him there tomorrow. "We thought you were all dead," indeed. His father was a tough old cookie, he had never known it as a child. He'll have the good doctor out by the scruff of his neck in no time. His smile spread. He was thinking of Sarah, how happy she would be when she came back in the morning. His father alive, him choosing a future with her instead of that mad fantasy of revenge. The Rat would get his due eventually, he'd make sure of that. Let the Americans handle it. Or God will intervene. Maybe he'll get run over by a bus.

Jacob breathed in deep and let the air out long and slowly, an extended sigh of satisfaction, as if his heart were smiling, and felt himself settle in the homely darkness. His eyes were heavy. He turned onto his side and, dreaming of Sarah, drifted into a quiet dark place, clammy, damp, that held him tight. It was an underwater cavern. He was suspended beneath the water, hanging in the comforting gloom, there was a shaft of light and it glowed and sparkled on the brilliant orange gills of ten thousand goldfish darting in waves and swells around him. He stretched his open fingers to reach out in the water and golden specks of light shot through them and welled around him and shifted together like dunes of golden sands in the dry desert wind. He curled into a ball and felt warm and good as he floated in the womb.

Far, far away, an engine's quiet rumble, the snap of a carefully opening door. A gentle draft, cool on his ears. He moved as the womb wall closed in on him and he shifted to make room and the wall was soft and warm and nestled against him and put an arm around him. He was drifting and turned and her lips met his and as the misty veil rose he heard Sarah breathe into his ear, "Jacob? Darling? There's a man on my side of the bed."

In 1939 eleven hundred Jews were living in Heidelberg.

In July of 1945 there were eighteen.